BOOKS BY BETH BROWER

The Books of Imirillia

The Queen's Gambit
The Ruby Prince
The Wanderer's Mark

The Q

The Beast of Ten

THE
WANDERER'S MARK

Rhysdon Press

The WANDERER'S

BOOK THREE OF IMIRILLIA

MARK

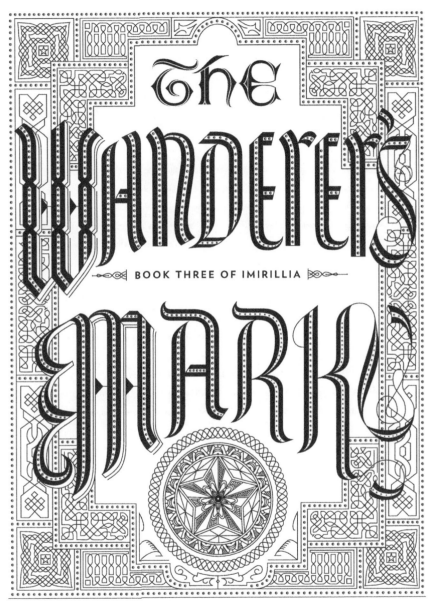

BETH BROWER

Copyright © 2016 by Beth Brower

Published by Rhysdon Press
Printed in the United States of America

Publisher's Cataloging-in-Publication data
Brower, Beth. The Wanderer's Mark : Book Three of Imirillia / Beth Brower ; p. cm.
ISBN 978-1535114080. Fantasy. 2. Adventure and Adventurers —Fiction. I. Title.

Third Edition 2017
10 9 8 7 6 5 4 3

ISBN: 978-1535114080
Text was set in Adobe Garamond

Cover by Kevin Cantrell Studio
www.kevincantrell.com

To Allysha, who was not only a patron saint of my young reading, but who has been attentive and mighty in her role as godmother to my literary children.

Your faith in them gives me courage.

&

To Kip, who has journeyed, who has set his compass for true north. Who has stood beside me in all kinds of weather, hand in mine, and kept bright my dreams.

I look at you and marvel that I was the girl to be with such a fine soul. My heart is yours.

THE NORTH
WILDS

GHYR MAER

THE
ZEAAD
DESERT

THE KOTAAH
HILLS

CAPABOLT

CAPABOLT
MAJOR

CAPABOLT
MINOR

THE
ARONEE
DESERT

DYSIGALOS

ALUTE

ALLIET

THE
STONE SEA

THIRA

ALLYON

CREETH

ERELYRE

- - - BOUNDARIES OF IMIRILLIA

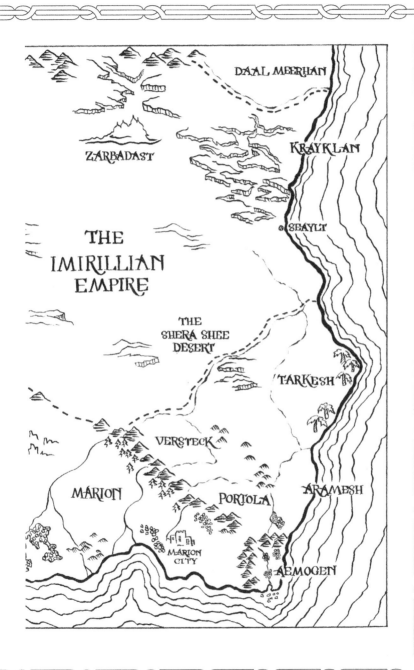

DAAL MEERHAN

ZARBADAST

KRAYKLAN

SEAYLT

THE
IMIRILLIAN
EMPIRE

THE
SHERA SHEE
DESERT

TARKESH

VERSTECK

MARION

PORTOLA

ARAMESH

MARION
CITY

AEMOGEN

*In loss the Illuminating God
declares a journey. His mortals release
their loves, just as the desert is stripped
of its beauty, and they, His children,
are hollowed and hallowed.
For loss is His sanctifier.*

—The First Scroll

Eleanor hit the earth with a jolt and fell against the wall, her cheek striking the stone. The square of light which led to Basaal and his life disappeared as Basaal put the stone back into place. Eleanor was left in complete darkness. She reached out and touched the stone wall. It was slippery, and damp.

Basaal had told her to follow the wall with her left hand. What if she had been turned around in the fall and went the opposite direction? Her instincts told her to go left, so she placed her hand on the wall and began to move, pushing away any thoughts of what could be occupying the darkness. Several minutes passed, then Eleanor came around a corner, where she could see a soft glow in the distance. Dantib.

Eleanor moved down the tunnel. When she reached the corner, she looked around it carefully. Dantib was there, hunched against the stone, waiting.

"Eleanor?" he asked. Her name sounded strange in his heavy accent.

"Yes," she said as she stepped out before the stable master.

The old man stood, slightly hunched, and motioned to her. "I will tell you more once we have left the city. For now you must follow, quick and close."

Basaal was at war, but it was a war with himself as much as it was a war with his father. The covenants of his Safeeraah were wrapped around him like the strong roots of a tree; while they held him up, they also tied him in place. Basaal now felt that they called for opposing actions.

How could he deal with Aemogen in honor—the honor the Illuminating God required of him—tied as he was by covenant to his father, when he could not condone his father's current course? And was loyalty to the empire the same as loyalty to its emperor, even as the emperor crossed every line given by the Illuminating God?

Shaamil had separated himself from the religion—he did not practice any form of prayer, he neglected any devotion save public display, and he had exiled the prophets from Zarbadast when Basaal was a boy—enough so that Basaal was still surprised his father had honored Eleanor's claim to marry Basaal. The emperor thought he could manipulate Basaal more effectively with her alive, no doubt.

"Are you ready to be purified?"

Basaal jerked his head up. "Come again?" he asked.

Ammar had just come from his apartments, meeting Basaal in the general corridor of the main palace. There were several servants passing around them, bowing wordlessly, giving space to the two princes.

"Are you ready for one more tedious ceremony?" Ammar asked.

"I've never minded ritual," Basaal answered, still distracted.

"No, you haven't." Ammar fell into step beside him. "What is Eleanor doing while you're away?" he asked. "Raiding the archivist's hall?"

"Eleanor?" Eleanor was beneath their feet now, making her way through the tunnels of Zarbadast. "She is unwell today, doubtless from all the festivities," Basaal answered.

Ammar frowned. "What are her symptoms?"

"Ah—" Basaal ran his fingers through his hair. "A general tiredness is all."

It was an extensive maze of tunnels that ran beneath the palace. And Eleanor wondered who else besides Basaal knew of them—or used them. Dantib must have memorized the route, for she could see the careful attention evident in his face each time he stopped, as if he were trying to remember the correct way through.

Though his movements were agile, he was a very old man. The torch that he held was small, but its light was bright on his gnarled, knotted hand, testifying to years over years of work.

She did not know how long they had been moving through the tunnel, but he finally stopped and motioned towards a dark square above them.

"It is unlocked," he whispered. "All that you must do is press the wooden door up, and it will give. I will help lift you. Then you must drop the rope down for me. Be quiet as you can."

He dropped the torch, smothering the embers with his foot. Eleanor blinked in the darkness, looking up. She was now able to make out lines of light around the trap door above her head. A sound from farther down the tunnel echoed towards them, and the muscles in Eleanor's body gripped her bones.

"A rat," Dantib whispered.

Her eyes were now adjusted to the dark, and Eleanor could see he had laced his hands together, motioning for Eleanor to place her foot between them. Doubting he could lift her, Eleanor did as he asked, pushing up and steadying herself against the tunnel's ceiling.

The wooden door was close, and with a bit of effort, she pushed it open as Dantib held her steady. The rich smell of spices filled Eleanor's lungs, and she grasped the edges of the stone floor above her, pulling herself up despite the tight strain in her shoulders. Catching her breath, she could feel the hard stones against her knees.

She reached forward in the dim light of what appeared to be a storeroom and found a small rope with a loop at one end. Lowering it into the tunnel below, she gripped it with all her strength as Dantib's weight pulled the rope taut. Dantib reached up—first, with a single hand, then, two—hanging onto the edge. He seemed unable to bring himself up any farther. So Eleanor dropped the rope and grabbed the old man's wrists, careful not to make any noise as she hoisted him up into the storeroom.

Once Dantib was free from the tunnel, he shut the trap door and locked it. Meanwhile, Eleanor looked around them. The room was filled with barrels and various crates, the aroma of spices thick in the air. It was kept cool, and little light trickled in.

Dantib motioned for Eleanor to help him as he rolled an old, faded rug over the door; then they shifted several barrels to cover it. When all was back in place, the entrance to the tunnel was completely concealed.

"Where are we?" she whispered, out of breath.

Dantib motioned for her to be quiet and led her up a stairway to the ground floor. They passed a small, barred window, and the stable master removed a pebble from his pocket. Standing on his toes, he lifted his hand up and dropped the pebble through the bars. The sound of soldiers could be heard in the corridor above, and Dantib froze, waiting for the footsteps to pass. Once the hallway had quieted, Dantib nodded and led Eleanor down the hall, pausing at the corner and looking around it carefully. Peering over Dantib's shoulder, Eleanor could see the front doors of a building. They were open, but two guards stood on the street, talking to each other and watching the people. She could also hear more soldiers moving in a room nearby.

Eleanor was petrified as she waited for Dantib to do something, but he just stood there watching the street, then looking down the hallway behind them. Someone laughed, and Eleanor heard footsteps approaching. The muscles in Dantib's face shifted, and his eyes returned to the front gate. Just then, a man riding a horse appeared outside on the street. It was the guard, Basaal's guard, Zanntal.

Eleanor allowed herself a slight feeling of relief as Zanntal motioned to the soldiers at the door, calling them over to him. The men stepped a few feet into the street, and Zanntal kept them occupied with a description of supplies he needed for a royal feast. So Dantib and Eleanor flew around the corner just as another soldier came into view. They slipped silently out the entrance, behind the guards, into the busy, festival-filled street. Eleanor looked back once at Zanntal, but he paid them no attention. Pulling her headscarf down over her face, she let out an anxious breath and followed Dantib. They lost themselves in the city.

The ceremonial council—and its purification rite—was to be held in a large room in the main palace. In only a matter of moments, the brothers had all assembled, speaking amongst themselves until Shaamil entered the room.

Basaal watched as his father took his seat at the head of the long table. They had not truly spoken all week, and he was uncertain if the hint of goodwill exhibited after the wedding ceremony still held. The emperor's face was unreadable, but his eyes were active, scanning the faces of his sons as they took their seats. Emir sat opposite the emperor, the remaining brothers—Ashim, Arsaalan, Ammar, Kiarash, and Basaal—flanking both sides.

When all were seated, Emir stood and began the ceremonial council.

"Who is it," he began, "that has come to swear himself to the Illuminating God, the empire, and the emperor?"

"It is I," the brothers responded simultaneously.

"And who is it," Emir continued, "that comes on this day of purification to make himself clean before the same?"

"I," Basaal said alone.

"Then, let us begin."

The smells of the street were fair and foul: spices, refuse, crowds of people, vendors calling out their wares, bright colors, and laughter. Today was the largest festival of the year, and not only did all of Zarbadast turn out but, as Basaal had said, many people had also come in from the provinces to buy, sell, and celebrate.

Eleanor's simple brown clothing did not call attention, for it was poor in comparison to what she saw around her. Dantib held her by the elbow, guiding her through the crowds, following a path that crossed the busiest streets.

"How much time do we have before they begin looking for us?" Eleanor asked in a side street that Dantib led her down.

"The prince said we would have, at the very least, one hour, at the very most, three," he said. "Almost an hour has already passed."

Eleanor pulled again at her headscarf. "What is our plan?"

"There are many travelers in and out of Zarbadast today," Dantib explained. "We must leave through the East Gate and reach the eastern rock lands before nightfall. Our horses are waiting a handful of days outside of Zarbadast. Are you prepared to travel all night?" He peered in her eyes for a moment.

"Yes," Eleanor said, her heartbeat up her throat as she looked around the jumbled marketplace they were passing through. "Just show me where to go."

Dantib grabbed Eleanor's hand, and they fled through the endless maze of stairs and streets, moving towards the east.

⸺⸙⸒⸒⸺

"Basaal?"

Basaal shot his head up like the flick of a whip's end and looked into the eyes of Emir.

"Pardon?" he asked.

"The correct answer would be, 'Yes, My Lord Emperor.'" Emir's tone was impatient. Evidently, seven days of celebrations had worn on the first son, and he had little tolerance now for this final ritual.

"Yes," Basaal said as he nodded towards his father, repeating the words with all the steadiness he could muster, "my Lord Emperor." Shaamil paused, his eyes on Basaal, then turned his attention back to the words that Emir was speaking.

The ceremony continued, and Basaal shifted from the uncomfortable emotion in his chest, the hollow pounding in his ears threatening to undermine his warlike state of mind. But the fear gnawed at him that at any moment Eleanor would be reported missing. Basaal again tried to give himself over to the words of the ceremony. But it was another failed attempt. His thoughts could not leave Eleanor for a moment, and he felt strange, as if he had defeated himself and lost his center.

"*Honor for Imirillia, Honor for Imirillia, Honor for Imirillia, and blessing upon her emperor,*" the brothers repeated together. Basaal joined late in the chant. No one seemed to have noticed.

"Basaal," Kiarash hissed.

Basaal blinked and looked up. They were all staring at him.

"It's time to make your covenant to the empire," Emir said.

"Yes, I was—I was thinking," he explained. "I was preparing myself."

Basaal stood in place, his hands clasped before him and his head bowed, and repeated the ceremonial phrases. He remembered all the words, but his mind was still with Eleanor, who should have slipped from the palace storehouse by now, into the streets of Zarbadast. As he spoke, he thought about how Dantib and Eleanor would run down into the markets, weaving amongst those there to observe the day of purification. Then Dantib would lead Eleanor to the East Gate and out onto the busy road, where merchants, travelers, pilgrims, and revelers would be pouring back and forth in a busy stream of celebration.

He finished speaking his pledge and knelt on the ground beside the table as a silver bowl was placed before him. Pushing his sleeves back, Basaal dipped his hands into the water, washing them in symbolic promise of cleansing himself to honor God, empire, and emperor. Then Emir handed him a towel, uttered a final blessing, and it was over.

Kiarash clapped Basaal on the back and helped him stand, which dissipated his dreamlike vision of following Eleanor from the city. The noises of the room flooded his ears, and Basaal finally felt present. Each brother congratulated him, and Kiarash made a comment about being the only brother still unmarried.

"Aside from Ammar," Kiarash rushed to add. "Not that he could get a girl if he tried."

Ammar did not look entertained. Shaamil rose from his chair at the head of the room and actually smiled as Ashim said something to him that Basaal could not hear. Then he walked to where Basaal stood and extended his hand. "You have taken upon yourself the covenants of cleansing necessary to fully commit to God, empire, and emperor," he said. "May you have the honor to keep them." Basaal took his father's hand and nodded. Then Shaamil continued. "Your seriousness in this thing pleases me."

He hadn't meant to jerk his head up so fast, but Basaal did, looking directly into his father's eyes. He found no sarcasm evident there, no biting edge, but rather the shadow of sincere affection. Ironic, Basaal thought, that this had been the only holy ritual he had ever undertaken in his life where his mind was not fully present.

"Do I please you, Father?" he asked.

Shaamil lifted his ringed hand and touched Basaal's neck only a moment. Then, saying nothing, and with Emir at his side, he left the room. Basaal watched him go, feeling a sense of mourning. In a matter of hours, his ever-shifting relationship with his father would turn once again, twisting like the dry root of a starved desert plant whose wood would soon split irreparably. And Basaal was sad for it.

Arsaalan grabbed Basaal's arm. "Come," he said, "and spend some time with us."

"I don't think we should invite him along," Kiarash said. "His sparrow's song is so saccharine I can hardly bear his company."

"I'll come," Basaal accepted with a forced smile. "Eleanor is much more to look upon than Kiarash, but if Ashim promises to be there, I'd be happy to make the sacrifice."

In truth, it could not have been better had he planned it that way. This would buy Eleanor and Dantib the time they needed to disappear into the rocks east of Zarbadast.

Kiarash pulled at Ashim's beard and mentioned something about bad taste.

"If you are going to be absent, would you mind if I check on Eleanor?" Ammar said from behind Basaal.

Basaal half turned. He had not realized Ammar was still in the room. "Why?" he asked.

"Jealous already?" Kiarash laughed. "That's a bad sign."

Ammar's brow knit, and he looked at Basaal strangely. "You said she was not feeling well. As her physician, it would be unsuitable for me to ignore her fatigue."

"Clearly," Basaal said, almost too readily. "Yes. It's only—I don't—I believe she was sleeping when I left. That is to say, she meant to rest," he explained, trying to hide his unease. "But please, visit. I just did not want you to wake her—that is all."

"I have a task that will take some time, and then I will go," Ammar said. "Eleanor never does sleep long, even when ill."

"Yes," Basaal said, and he shrugged so stiffly that he almost laughed at himself. "And tell her I won't be far behind you."

The soldiers passed without looking twice in their direction, but Eleanor still felt her stomach twist until they had moved farther up the street. The eastern gate stood ahead of them, a tall, arched display of beautifully carved stone. Soldiers stood near it, eyeing the many people pouring in and out.

It was late enough in the day for them to leave the city unnoticed. So, although Eleanor's entire body was beating with the drumming of her heart, she and Dantib passed through the gate, waiting patiently for the crowd to give way. She held Dantib's arm with her covered hand, being careful to keep her headscarf pulled down, and tried to imitate the tired motions of the vendors and herders around her.

Walking away from Zarbadast without looking back was a surreal task for Eleanor. It seemed strange and so unbelievable that she was free of the city. Using a staff he had purchased in the market, Dantib altered his walk to reflect his many years: a worn figure with his knapsack, old sandals on his feet. No one would have ever guessed the treason he was committing.

Soon, they were pushed to the side of the road by a small band of horsemen and blended into those on foot as they spread out towards the eastern deserts.

"Rocks," Dantib said to Eleanor not long after getting onto the road. "There are many rocks and canyons. By the end of the day, we will have dropped down into one of them and will be lost from the view of the main road."

"Will we get far enough to be untraceable?" Eleanor asked quietly, aware that her accent would set her apart if overheard.

"Be the Illuminating God willing," Dantib replied.

Then, as if it were a sign, a woman called out to them. "There, you, old man! I've sold my wares and travel east the day long, if you wish a ride."

They turned to see a woman, covered with a jangle of cheap trinkets, her skin tight and discolored from years under the desert sun. She was driving a jumble of wood barely passing for a cart, pulled by an equally disreputable donkey.

Eleanor bent her head as Dantib greeted the woman warmly. "Seraagh herself could not have made a better offer," he said. "My dear woman, I accept your ride. We have many days left in our journey and would appreciate a rest to our bones."

With Eleanor's help, Dantib lifted himself into the front of the cart. Then he began a congenial conversation with the woman while Eleanor climbed onto the back, sitting on the edge of the cart, where she could see the massive city spreading out behind her. There, to the north of the eastern gate, rising above a cacophony of buildings and structures, gleamed the white perfection of the seven palaces.

Eleanor grabbed the sides of the cart as the donkey shifted and moved forward, taking them over three rather large holes in the road. Pulling her teeth together against the resulting rattle, Eleanor watched as she moved farther from Zarbadast. Farther from Basaal, and his rituals and his honor and— Eleanor gripped the cart harder, taken off guard by the pain she felt at the thought of leaving him behind. If only he had come. If only he had come with her.

Basaal had endured almost two hours of long, stretched out anticipation, envisioning when and how the storm would break. As much as he tried to listen, Basaal could not take his eyes from the doors of Arsaalan's grand salon, speaking only an occasional observation, waiting—and waiting.

It took longer than Basaal had thought for Ammar to come into the room, white-faced and stern.

"Basaal." Ammar tilted his chin at him and stepped into the corner of the room. This was the first test, acting a part before his brothers. Basaal stood and walked to Ammar.

"Yes?" Basaal held a drink in his hand, swirling its contents. "Is Eleanor well? You did tell her I was coming?"

"She's not there," Ammar leveled.

"Isn't there?" Basaal said, drawing his eyebrows together. "Strange. She must have gone to the women's quarters."

"I searched there." Ammar led Basaal by his elbow farther away from the other brothers. "She has not been there all day."

"But—"

"Hannia has not seen her either," Ammar said.

Basaal could no longer look Ammar in the eye. He swore and stepped away, marching from the room. Kiarash called out to him, but he did not turn around. Ammar followed at Basaal's elbow.

"Certainly she's somewhere," Basaal said through gritted teeth. "Did you check the archives? The gardens?"

"I have begun asking, that is all," Ammar said. "I did not want to put the palace into an uproar unless—"

When Basaal reached his palace, he encountered a panicked Hannia, who repeated that Eleanor was not there and could not have gone anywhere else. Basaal walked from room to room, ignoring the frantic questions from the maid and ignoring the unspoken questions emanating from his brother. He walked through all of his gardens, and he checked every room. Servants and guards stepped away, wary of the murderous look Basaal conjured onto his face. By the seven stars, he hated this deception.

"The women's quarters," Basaal said, finally addressing Ammar. "You're certain they were searched in their entirety?"

"Yes."

"Hannia, have them searched again," Basaal said.

After the maid left, Ammar narrowed his eyes at Basaal. "She won't find her there."

"I know," Basaal said. "I wanted her out of the way."

"Where is Eleanor, Basaal?"

"I can think of only one other person who might know," Basaal said.

"You are really going to bring this accusation before the emperor?"

"No—perhaps," Basaal said, moving his hand across his face. "But who else could have done it?"

Ammar's mouth twitched, his response sounding thick. "Who else indeed?"

If Basaal had expected the luxury of taking the news to the emperor himself, he was not surprised when he did not receive it, for it was not long after Hannia had been sent off that the captain of Shaamil's imperial guard arrived.

"The emperor wishes to know if the rumors are true," the captain said.

"I am certain she is somewhere on the premises," Basaal answered angrily.

"He has ordered that all personnel be charged with searching the entirety of the seven palaces."

"Yes," Basaal said. "I was planning on mobilizing my own men immediately." Basaal nodded to one of his personal guard, who stood waiting near the doorway. The soldier bowed in return, then left to organize the search.

"If you have nothing further to say," Basaal said to the captain, pulling at the sleeve of his coat. "I will join my men."

"You are to return to your palace with the Vestan," the captain insisted. "They will track her movements from there."

"But the Vestan are out of the city," Basaal said. "Let my own guard—"

"The Vestan are in the emperor's palace," the captain interrupted.

Basaal's eyes narrowed. "What do you mean?" he demanded. "It's the day of purification. They should be gone from here." The captain did not answer. Rather, he turned on his heels and disappeared down the corridor. Basaal felt genuinely furious now. "The Vestan are supposed to be out of Zarbadast!"

"What sort of playacting is this?" Ammar asked as he grabbed Basaal's shoulder and shoved him back into the wall. "What have you done with her?" he demanded. "Don't pretend that you had nothing to do with it."

Before Basaal could say anything, a company of six Vestan came around the corner. Basaal shook himself free, stepping forward, ignoring Ammar.

"What do you want?" he snapped at the assassins.

"The emperor has ordered us to your apartments, Your Grace, to find the missing Aemogen queen."

Ammar followed Basaal with a glare so fierce that Basaal dared not look at him. As Basaal led the Vestan into his apartments—his palms wet, his eyes alert—he kept frantically counting the hours since Eleanor and Dantib had escaped. Would it be enough?

"She was here in this room when I left," Basaal said, pointing toward the open windowsill where they had sat together before her disappearance.

The Vestan spread out wordlessly and began to canvass the chambers, paying attention to the slightest print on the rug or movement of a drape.

"I swear it, Basaal," Ammar hissed quietly. "If you had anything to do with putting Eleanor's life in danger—"

"Do you really think me capable of that?" Basaal turned and shot these words back at his brother. "You think that after all my efforts, I would let her go? That I would be such a fool?"

Ammar did not reply, but Basaal's performance had done little to alter the expression on his face.

The next several minutes passed by in a blur, a blur composed of motions so slow he felt he was pacing at the bottom of the ocean, fighting a heavy weight against every limb. It took no more than a few minutes for the Vestan to take their search into the bedchamber. A few members of Basaal's honor guard entered the room to report the progress of the search. Among them stood Zanntal. Being careful not to look in his direction, Basaal listened intently, arms folded, staring at the floor.

"Nothing has yet been found inside the palaces," the guard said as he reported. "There is no evidence to show if it was an escape or an abduction. Should we begin to search the city?"

During the report, Basaal had looked up once towards Zanntal. The soldier had stood, serious-faced, quiet. But when he caught Basaal's eye, the side of his mouth lifted into an almost imperceptible smile.

She'd gotten out. Basaal hoped his internal relief appeared in the form of external frustration. "Search the city—" Basaal began.

Then another Vestan came into the room. "That will not be

necessary," he said. "We have found two tunnels leading from the bedchamber."

Basaal waved his guard away with a flick of his wrist as he turned to face the assassin. He knew that there were three escape routes from his bedchamber. So the question was, which did they find?

"One door opens from a back room," the Vestan said. "We are tracking it. A second was found under—"

Basaal felt a rush of anxiety and his mouth twitched.

"—a bureau in the small corridor. Are there any others?"

"Yes," Basaal said. His mouth felt dry as he answered. "There is a third passage."

The Vestan's eyes gleamed, and he bowed. "Please," he said, holding up his hand for Basaal to lead the way.

Wordlessly, Basaal stepped past the assassin. He had spread a map out on the table, scattered notes across its surface, and now walked past it with all the disinterest he could muster. "There is a third way to leave these chambers," he said, "from the garden."

Basaal stepped down into his garden and through the patterns of red blooms and grasses. "There," he said as he pointed to the back wall. "You will find a wanderer's mark carved into the stone, indicating an escape route directly over the wall," he explained. "Though, I doubt that anybody could have used it."

"Why not?" It was Ammar who asked the question.

"Because," Basaal said as he turned to look at him, "its existence is unknown to any but me, and it would be impossible to scale the wall by oneself, let alone be successful escaping on the other side. Ideally, one would use it during a rainstorm."

"A rainstorm?" the assassin inquired. This was the first time in his life that Basaal had ever heard a Vestan ask a question in sincerity rather than for intimidation.

"There is a small opening thirty feet down that leads into the aqueducts," Basaal replied. "You could make the jump if there was enough water to catch you. Without the rain," he added, "you would need to have a very long rope and no one at your back." He eyed the Vestan before continuing. "Since I've not discussed the existence of this with anybody, especially not with Eleanor, your time would be better spent searching the other gardens," he suggested. "For you know better than anybody the endless secrets of Zarbadast."

With that, he turned away, leaving the Vestan and Ammar to stare up at the high wall.

⚬⟨⟨⟨⟩⟩⟩⚬

"Thank you," Dantib said as he smiled at their benefactor before easing his stiff body down onto the road. Eleanor followed suit and came around to take his arm. It was dusk, and they were now far from the city. It lay in the distance, spread out across the waves of sand.

"We are grateful for these hours of rest," Dantib told the woman.

"May you follow your stars," the woman said, and she smiled, trying to catch a view of Eleanor's face, seeming curious about the mute girl who had kept to herself all day. Then, with a sharp, two-note whistle, she set the donkey in motion and continued down the nearly abandoned road.

Dantib did not hurry off the road, rather he scanned the sandy layers of the horizon as he slung off his water-filled pouch, and then they each took a drink. The wind had picked up, and despite her headscarf, Eleanor could still feel it whip and whistle around her ears. Dantib fished a few pieces of dried fruit from his heavy satchel, and Eleanor accepted one gratefully, turning back towards the distant city, watching as the lights began to appear in the haze of the desert evening.

"She is a beautiful city," Dantib said as Zarbadast began to illuminate herself.

"Yes," Eleanor acknowledged. "Do you think he will be all right?"

Dantib frowned and waited a long moment before answering. "I have asked myself that question many times." He shifted his packs, and Eleanor checked to see if her own bag was secure. Dantib turned and waved a gnarled hand across the graying landscape. "Now we are on the edge of the eastern rocklands. It is a forgotten terrain, full of cracks and crooks left behind by the ancient rivers long dried up."

And as Dantib spoke, Eleanor thought how he too was made up of ancient things, all cracks and crooks and wisdom. She could see why Basaal had been drawn to him.

"And we will travel through the night?" she asked, tired, but ready to walk.

"Yes," Dantib nodded. "We will not stop these four days yet if we have any hope of disappearing into the East."

Nodding, Eleanor followed Dantib into the serpentine ravine.

The Vestan were none too gentle as they threw Basaal on the ground before Shaamil's throne. Basaal's arm, still tender from the challenge weeks before, rattled with pain. He breathed in fast, sounding like a scared snake, his face hovering inches above the floor. A bead of sweat dropped from his face, and Basaal thought it strange, for he felt as cold as the rivers of Aemogen.

It had been twelve hours since Eleanor's escape, and Basaal had been confined to his palace, unable to move from his private apartments, watched constantly by the Vestan. His father had not called for him and had not wished to see him—until now.

The emperor soon ordered the Vestan to get out. Even when they were left alone, Basaal did not move to look at his father. He breathed against the white marble, waiting for Shaamil to speak.

"You miserable wretch." The words were clipped in the emperor's mouth. "Get up."

Basaal pulled himself to his feet, deliberately throwing his shoulders back as he looked into the eyes of his father.

"What have you to say to me?" Shaamil asked.

"As I have told your imperial guard, and as I have told the Vestan, I have nothing to say that you do not already know."

"Nothing?" the emperor said, his voice sounding as the wind scratching across the rock hills north of the city.

"I have nothing more to say," Basaal repeated.

"The Vestan have no word of your wife, even after hours of searching." Shaamil's mouth twisted up. "It's as if she were swept away like a single grain of sand in a windstorm. Gone. Scattered among ten million other pieces without a trace. I warn you now, if I find you had a hand in any of this, I will kill you outright."

Basaal stiffened, the corners of his mouth turning down as he spoke. "I wouldn't expect any less."

"Let us then suppose," Shaamil said, and his voice rang with accusation, "that you had *nothing* to do with the queen's disappearance. Let us suppose that you stand wronged. What is your price?"

"My price?" Basaal glowered. By the stars, he was so tired.

"The price of your retribution," Shaamil explained. "What price do you exact for such a valuable loss? Is it one life?"

"One life?" Basaal asked, confused.

"Is it one life?" Shaamil repeated. "Or is it two? The desperate impression you gave was that this woman—this girl, really—meant a great deal to you. And now she has been taken away. So her value must be beyond the cost of just one life. Is it three times as much? Is it four times?" Shaamil demanded. "What would satisfy the debt? The death of a dozen people? Of a caravan? Should a city be ransacked to pay the debt of her loss? A country, even? Answer me!"

Basaal stood petrified, terrified of what his father might do in his own name.

"What is she worth to you, Basaal?" Shaamil pressed. "How many thousands must die to atone for her loss? Answer me!"

"I—I can't. I don't deal in such terms," Basaal said. "To reckon the value of any loss with the death of the innocent is madness."

"But you must learn!" Shaamil yelled. "As a prince of Imirillia, every action you take reverberates endlessly into the lives around you. You cannot make a decision without having some act to balance it. You try—you have always tried—to tip the scales, not expecting repercussions or consequences. But that is not how this world works. That is not how this empire works, the Imirillian Empire, which you have sworn yourself to in the highest rituals of honor. So, yes, the disappearance of the Aemogen queen carries a price, and it very well may be of every man, woman, and child in her country."

"Father!"

"What? Is it too much for you? The thought of every wretch in Aemogen dead? Would you rather I find someone closer to blame? The palace guards, perhaps? Do we take the head of every guard on duty at the hour of her disappearance? Or, do we take the heads of their wives and children?"

"You deal in unbalanced scales, Your Grace," Basaal snapped.

"Do I?" Shaamil challenged.

"Yes!" Basaal cried. "As you did in Aramesh, you transfer the sins of one onto the heads of many, and that is not justice."

Shaamil lifted an eyebrow and pressed his fingers together as if thinking. "You do not condone my scales?"

"No!"

"One for one, is it?" Shaamil asked.

Basaal bent his head, pursing his lips, waiting for his father to call for his life in payment.

"One for one," Shaamil repeated. "But if that is the scale with which you wish to play, then this loss of great value demands another of equal value to you. Who should it be? One of your brothers?" Shaamil suggested. "Annan? The woman who serves your house? What is her name, Hannia? What about your sister, Laaeitha? She is of little value to Emir. Would her life compensate in payment, I wonder? What about one of the children?"

The coil of his father's words seemed to squeeze his chest, and Basaal let his rage show clearly on his face. This was not the man who had shown approval, even love, earlier that same day. This was the beast that had swallowed his father whole, consuming him with its vile power. Now, in the shadows of the deep night, this man did not even look like his father.

"You see, Basaal," the emperor continued, "you cannot insulate yourself from consequences any more than you can insulate every-thing you love…from me."

Basaal shook off the hiss of his father's words. "I will do my duty," Basaal said, "but do not—I beg you—do not bring any other into your quarrel with me, Father."

"Every life you love is entirely in your own hands, Basaal. If you step straight, they will be well. Now, go," Shaamil said as he waved his hand. "You have five days to prepare your company for the journey south, and then we leave."

"We?" Basaal asked.

"Oh, yes," Shaamil articulated with force. "I am accompanying you south with six thousand of my own men in case you need *help* in subjugating Aemogen."

CHAPTER

TWO

The gold and silver patterns of the afta dar began to disappear beneath the rough cloth as Eleanor rubbed it over her already tender skin. It had been more difficult than she'd anticipated to wash the afta dar away despite Hannia's promise it would be an easy affair. But she knew they did not have much time, exposed as they were beside the silt-filled desert pond.

Dantib stood, leaning against his staff, appearing to be a patiently waiting herdsman, but Eleanor could read the tension in his face. She scrubbed harder. They had now traveled through the rocky passageways of the eastern desert for three consecutive nights, settling into rock-covered crevices for a few hours during the day before setting out again in the hot sun.

"In two more days' time," Dantib said as he watched behind them, scanning the sand and stones in their rocky upheaval along the horizon line, "we will come to a small village where I have our horses. We will dye your hair there as well, for I dare not stop longer. The Vestan move quickly, and I have no way of knowing what they know."

Eleanor pulled off her uncomfortable boots—her heels were covered in blisters—and began to scrub the afta dar from her feet and ankles. It came off easier than it had from her hands.

"What are the chances," Eleanor asked as she worked, "that they could have found our trail among so many? As we left Zarbadast, there were streams of travelers, coming and going in every direction."

"Yes," Dantib said, but he did not speak further.

Eleanor wished she could leave her feet sitting in the mud puddle, but, as soon as the last remnants of the bridal paint had been washed away, she pulled her boots back on and stood, adjusting her rough garments and ensuring her headscarf was in place.

She rolled her sleeves down until they covered most of her hands, but not before Eleanor looked again at Basaal's mark on her arm, a reminder that her time in Zarbadast had not been a dream. Eleanor did not quite believe it. These three days in the desert had taken her mind back to crossing the Zeaad and the Aronee. Eleanor's many days resting in the luxury of the seven palaces seemed too soft for the grittiness of the world to which she had returned.

"Come," Dantib said, and they set out again.

Step after difficult step, they traveled farther east.

Neither the quietude of the space nor the firmness of the answer could allay the intense trepidation Basaal felt in his bones. He could not believe what he had just heard.

He had prayed, seeking guidance, counsel of the Illuminating God. But he had not expected it to come so fast. Nor had he expected it to be so clear—and so confusing. Basaal prayed again for a different answer, but none came. He begged, offering a plea as desperate as any he'd ever uttered, but he petitioned in vain.

After a long hour of silence, he finally took himself away from the garden and tried to forget the resounding answer he had received from the Illuminating God. Too upset for anything else, Basaal called his personal guard to his training yard and spent the remainder of the morning fighting, aggressive and angry. Once he had exhausted himself, he fled to his rooms, falling into a chair beside the window of his sitting room, trying to quiet the turmoil inside.

Without really thinking about it—more from a habit born of the last three days—Basaal took the thin gold bracelet of Eleanor's from his pocket. He moved his fingers across the three pendants now attached to it: the ruby from their wedding day, the wanderer's mark he gave her after their wedding, and the golden circle with the rising bird he had given her in Aemogen. After the interrogation by his father, Basaal had strung these three pieces of jewelry onto her bracelet. It felt like a talisman of sorts, a token.

"Apparently, Father may actually be convinced you had nothing to do with all this."

Basaal looked up to see Ammar standing in the doorway.

"And what of it?" Basaal growled.

"I am not so easily, shall we say, *convinced.* As you know."

"What do you want, Ammar?"

"A conversation," he said. "An admission. An honest answer."

"I can honestly tell you that I did not see Eleanor out of Zarbadast."

"Semantics," Ammar said as he offered himself a seat near Basaal.

"What?" Basaal asked, looking over at his brother's face.

"The words you chose to use," Ammar explained. "Semantics.

They don't mean you did not help orchestrate the escape."

"Go to the devil," Basaal snapped, closing his fist around the pendants and tucking them back into his jacket.

"So, you will not say more than that?"

"My own honor," Basaal said as he folded his arms and gave Ammar a hard smile, "requires that I neither confirm nor deny it."

"If you confirm, it is to your death," Ammar said, providing the reason. "If you deny having anything to do with it, you will look a fool who could not control even one wife. Stupid indeed," Ammar observed. "No one should expect you to utter a word."

Basaal did not respond.

"Well played," Ammar said. "Every idiot in Zarbadast understands that point of pride." The physician stood. "I must be going, for I have my own preparations to make. Yes," Ammar nodded as he saw Basaal's face. "I too have been ordered to accompany you to Aemogen. If I weren't so curious to see the place," he added, "I would blame you for the massive inconvenience of it all."

As Ammar turned to go, Basaal sighed ruefully.

"I just didn't expect it, that's all," Basaal said to himself as much as to his brother.

Ammar only partially turned, not looking at Basaal's face. "Expect what?" he asked.

"To feel so miserable."

<hr />

Eleanor's legs were shaking as they descended a ravine trail towards a small desert town. It was as insignificant a place as Eleanor had ever seen. She pressed her dry hands against the stone to support herself, forcing the leather pouch Basaal had given her to rest against her back so that it would not swing in front of her as they made their way.

"Soldiers," Dantib had been saying. "Soldiers would have been sent out if the Vestan failed, companies in all directions. If the emperor was so inclined, there would be a reward on your head, and so we must trust no one we meet. If he does not make your disappearance publicly known, we will have a better chance of surviving our journey to the coast."

"Why would he not make it known?" Eleanor asked despite being short of breath. "I would think Shaamil would want me punished at any cost."

"Were it to become common knowledge that you had run away, Basaal's great shame would also become public," Dantib explained. "He would be ridiculed, becoming *a laugh of the street*, as we would say."

"His great shame?" Eleanor stopped, and Dantib looked back at her.

"Oh, yes." He ran the back of his wrist across his brow. "For a wife to run from her husband is a grave insult on a master's reputation. It could ruin the reputation of a man even in Basaal's station. This was a severe choice he has made to spare your life."

Eleanor wanted to curse Basaal. So absorbed in his own ways, yet so utterly selfless. Each night since they had left Zarbadast, before Eleanor was asleep, she had thought of him, wanting to see him again. But even in her dreams he did not appear.

They descended into the town, and Dantib led Eleanor through the few dusty streets to a small house on the far edge of a tired road, near a stable. Dantib looked around the street and then knocked on the crooked door before pushing it open.

"Father!" a middle-aged man said as he rushed towards them, a child at his heels. Dantib embraced the man, and Eleanor closed the door behind them. His much taller son swallowed the stable master up in his embrace, and Eleanor ventured a timid smile at this reunion. Basaal had never mentioned Dantib had family.

"This is Eleanor, Queen of Aemogen," Dantib said, sounding proud of his charge. Eleanor nodded her head to the man. "Eleanor, this is my son." The man nodded in return, but his eyes were hard.

"And your name?" Eleanor asked politely despite the grime of the journey.

"No, no names," Dantib said and shook his head gently as he smiled at the young boy now wrapping himself about Dantib's legs. Eleanor assumed he was a grandson.

"Oh," Eleanor verbalized her surprise.

"You see, no one in Zarbadast knows I've a son."

"Not even Basaal?" Eleanor asked. The son snorted, but Dantib ignored him.

"Especially not Basaal, I'm afraid," Dantib said. "While he serves his father, I cannot trust even him with this information. It is better this way."

Dantib's son muttered something that Eleanor could not hear. She did not feel particularly welcome but was too tired to care.

"I will call you Ali," Eleanor said, determined to be polite. "It is a common enough name."

"We best get the two of you away," Ali answered as he looked towards the door. "Although, helping the prince is against my principles."

"Do not tell me he is boring you with his principles!" a middle-aged woman said as she swept into the room, smiling. "Papa!" She kissed Dantib on the cheek and gave her husband a look, demanding his cooperation, before she turned towards Eleanor with her arms open. "You must be the Aemogen queen," she said as she embraced Eleanor and then put a hand on Eleanor's face. "This prince is a good man to have let you go back to your people," she added.

Ali snorted. His wife ignored him.

"Papa enlisted our help only after the strictest confidence was secured," she explained. "We will keep your secret."

"If it doesn't kill us all first," Ali grumbled as the young boy pulled at his fingers.

"You may call me Kaaie, as we are not using our real names," she said and winked at the game. "Follow me." Kaaie led Eleanor into a small back room, where she had prepared a rag and a basin of water. "You can wash, and we will take care of that hair."

Kaaie did not leave the room, but rather stayed to help Eleanor, speaking about nothing in particular as she prattled away pleasantly. As she listened, Eleanor washed her face and arms, around her neck, and then her feet, wondering how long they would stay with Dantib's family. Wondering if it was safe. When she removed her headscarf, Kaaie gasped.

"Your hair!" she exclaimed. "They said it was the color of flame, but I did not believe them, no." She stood and ran her fingers through Eleanor's tangled locks. "And I am supposed to help you turn it brown." She clucked in a way that reminded Eleanor of Hannia. "What a shame."

Kaaie helped Eleanor lift her rough, brown dress over her head, speaking casually about the dust, the heat, and the desert as she settled Eleanor into a chair before a rough-hewn table that held another shallow basin. "Just lean your head back," she said. "Yes, just so." Then Kaaie lifted a jug and poured its contents over Eleanor's hair. "You must be still awhile before I can wash the hair dye out again."

"How do you know how this is done, changing the color of my hair?" Eleanor asked, careful not to move in case it would interfere with Kaaie's work.

"My husband, Na—" she began to say but stopped herself. "I mean, *Ali* is well known for his work with horses. He takes after his father," she said, smiling as she moved the dye through Eleanor's hair thoroughly. "In Imirillia, color can be everything, and so, if a man owns a horse that he wishes to be black or red, well, my husband will see it done."

"And Basaal knows nothing of this? Knows nothing of you?"

"Papa decided years ago it would be best," was all Kaaie would say.

Hours later, after Kaaie had run water over Eleanor's hair and braided it down Eleanor's back, and after they had rested and eaten a simple meal, Ali took Eleanor and Dantib out to the stables under the blanket of night.

"Your horses are prepared and ready for the journey," he said as he held a light up in the stall. Dantib joyfully greeted a simple, gray horse that Eleanor guessed was his own.

Ali looked at Eleanor briefly, then tilted his head towards the neighboring stall. "Your mount is here," he said as he tilted his head and held the lantern up. Inside, a dark brown horse moved towards them, nickering and seeking Eleanor's attention.

Eleanor narrowed her eyes and stared before blurting out, "Hegleh?"

The horse tilted her head and whinnied.

"You're all brown!" Eleanor said as she moved her hands down the horse's cheek and kissed Hegleh between the eyes.

"So are you," Ali said with little patience.

"Hush!" Dantib quietly chided his son. "Now we must go. The ride east will require great speed, and we dare not endanger you anymore."

"You must promise me you will be careful, Father."

Dantib rested one of his knotted hands on his son's shoulder. "I go with the Illuminating God."

"But," Ali argued, "you go for the devil." Ali's face collapsed on itself, and he embraced his father. "I am afraid for you."

Kaaie had come into the stable, and she put her arm around Eleanor. "It is right you should go back to your people," she whispered into Eleanor's ear. "My husband is hurt and angry; do not let him plague your mind. Papa loves his prince and goes with you willingly."

"And your son?" Eleanor asked as she looked at Kaaie and smiled, hoping to distract herself from the guilt she felt anyway. "He is asleep, then?"

"Thank the seven stars, yes," Kaaie nodded. "Here is your saddlebag, full of food for your journey east." She placed it over Eleanor's shoulder. "I wish you all that is good." She kissed Eleanor's forehead and tucked a piece of loose, deep brown hair away from Eleanor's face and back under her headscarf.

And with no more ceremony than Dantib embracing Kaaie once again, they checked their supplies, mounted their horses, and rode out into the darkness.

Dantib did not look back.

The moon was slender, but the night did not feel very dark. They rode hours and hours before Dantib finally pulled them to a stop in the early morning. Giving the horses a drink, he drew a map in the sand to show Eleanor how they would ride to the closest river. They dared not rest long, for the cool of night was lifting from the sand as the sun rose on the eastern desert.

Soon, the day grew very hot. Eleanor found this more difficult than her journey through the Aronee and Zeaad because the rocks jutting up in the sand caused Hegleh to question her footing. Riding so long with little rest brought about a stiff response from her muscles and blisters every time the horse hesitated. Eleanor gritted her teeth and kept going. She would soon be on the ocean and then home, Eleanor reminded herself when her hands ached beneath the reins, or when the muscles in her legs murmured against the steady pace. Dantib continued much as he had the entire journey, without complaint.

They spoke little the first days after leaving Dantib's family. But a few mornings afterward, they came across a hollow in a rock near the river, and Dantib agreed it was safe to stop and rest. Then he began to speak to Eleanor just as she was settling her sore, dusty body onto the ground.

"You should not mind him." Dantib was caring for his horse, and he did not look at Eleanor. "My son," he clarified. "You should not mind my son. He has seen much sorrow, and it is through his pain that he speaks."

"He did not approve of your work in the palace?" Eleanor asked, leaning her head against the rock behind her, too tired to eat the dried fruit they had rationed from Dantib's pack.

"No," Dantib said as he rubbed a cream into the legs of his gray horse. "But he did not always feel so vehemently as he does now. You see," he said, grunting as he reached his fingers down the fetlock of his horse, "they had a child, a son who married young." Dantib stood up straight, arching his back before walking over towards Eleanor and settling himself beside her.

He brushed the sweat away from his forehead. "Imirillia prospers to the west," he continued. "The caravans go abundantly between Zarbadast and the cities and countries found there. But here, in the East, where I am from, we live scattered through rock and desert, poor and hungry, and it is hard for a man to provide. The port in Krayklan has a northern road that runs to Zarbadast. But, farther south, we do not benefit. When my grandson's wife died in childbirth," Dantib said as he shook his head, "my grandson was distraught and felt there was no life for him in the East. He resorted to migrating to the more prosperous country of Aramesh, to the south. That was three years ago."

"Just before the Desolation," Eleanor said, her face falling to the sympathy she felt. "He was in Aramesh?"

"He had left the child with my son and daughter-in-law, and, when word came of Shaamil's revenge, we waited. My grandson never returned. We suppose he must have died beneath the hand of Imirillia's own army."

Eleanor sat still, somber, and the image of Blaike's body, gashed and empty, crossed her mind. She shook her head at the waste. "I am sorry," she whispered. "I am sorry for it all."

"You know that Basaal has his own sorrows from Aramesh." Dantib looked kindly on Eleanor. "My son does not know the prince spared so many. He does not know who Basaal is, so he does not understand my devotion."

"And why have you not told him?" Eleanor questioned the stable master.

Dantib's lips played with a soft smile, and his eyes lifted gently to Eleanor's face. "My dear, there are journeys to be had, and we must not dilute the struggle, or we do those we love a disservice. Now, sleep," Dantib urged. "We have been riding hard. I feel at peace, as our way has been blessed. We will begin again soon enough. You can rest."

※

The horses continued to struggle across the eastern sands, and the physical demands of the journey did not lessen. The jolt of Hegleh's pace screamed against the blisters on Eleanor's hand and legs, but her thoughts were bent on Aemogen, and she would not relent. Every part of Eleanor's body was tight, and anxiety was eating from her heart into her bones. She felt like she was on fire with worry every time they passed another party or saw riders in the distance.

Dantib held a harmony with the horses that Eleanor could not fathom. Sometimes, as if he were privy to their thoughts, he drove them hard, beyond what Eleanor supposed was their strength. Other times, he gave them rest when Eleanor could not see a reason for a slower pace. She fought against the temptation of impatience, watching over her shoulder for any sign of the Vestan, wishing to push on. Despite her nervousness, Dantib would not push the beasts.

For several days, Eleanor and Dantib progressed steadily towards the East, dropping south at certain markers that Dantib had memorized. They encountered few travelers: none with hostility or much curiosity.

"The people of the East," Dantib explained, "value their independence and mind their own business."

Despite the arduous nature of desert travel, the first weeks passed safely. They were hidden in the barren rock deserts of the East with no whisper of the Vestan. As their confidence increased, they began to spend hours speaking and telling stories. He told her of his childhood in the desert, of how he secured his first palace job, and of meeting the child Basaal. She, in turn, spoke of Edythe, her father, and her people.

Listening intently, Dantib would occasionally share his observations on life. Eleanor's mind was greedy for the wisdom he held, and she saw how Dantib warranted Basaal's high esteem. There was a sweetness in the old man's company that led Eleanor to forget her blisters and sores, the dirt, and the wind. As the days passed, her feelings for Dantib grew tender, her blisters began to fade, and although they subsisted on little, there was always enough. Soon, Eleanor would remind herself, she would be sailing to Aemogen, and all would be well. For the first time in months, Eleanor's dreams were only of home.

CHAPTER

THREE

"I had forgotten what it meant to travel with Father," Basaal said as he reclined in the comfort of the emperor's personal tent, a small map rolled out across the floor.

"Yes," Ammar said, not looking up from where he was writing at the table, replying with thick sarcasm. "An extended wing of Zarbadast; all the comforts of home."

Basaal sat up and laughed. "You need to get out more," he said. "I daresay no one in the world travels as we do now. I certainly never do—unless with Father."

"It's hot," Ammar replied as if that mere fact alone discounted every comfort.

"It's spring," Basaal chided, "and almost as temperate as the Zeaad ever gets. Thank the seven stars it isn't any worse. You do realize," he added, "that Father has several companies of soldiers whose sole occupation is to procure and deliver fresh fruit?"

"The grapes have too many seeds," Ammar replied.

Basaal grinned, then picked the map up from the floor, his eyes wandering towards the eastern roads, where Eleanor and Dantib should be, following a path to the coast.

If the Illuminating God would only grant it.

"Trying to see if you can find your wife among the landmarks?" Ammar asked. Basaal looked up. Ammar was studying him.

"Leave off it, Ammar. I know nothing of her whereabouts."

"And neither do the Vestan," the emperor's voice came from across the pavilion. Basaal and Ammar looked at each other before acknowledging their father as he came through the door of the tent with two of his generals. "Strange," he said, "that she should be so capable of disappearing with no leads or trace." Shaamil walked across the soft carpet of rugs and sat down at the table near Ammar. "I did, however, receive a singularly interesting missive." The emperor moved his eyes to Basaal's, a slight smile on his face.

Basaal cleared his throat. He and the emperor had hardly exchanged a civil word over the last few weeks of their travel. "Yes?"

"The stable master, whom you dismissed with such"—Shaamil paused—"*exhibition*, has turned up missing. And so has the horse you gave Eleanor."

"Really?" Basaal had no need to conjure up any emotions, for his panic sounded like interest—it sounded like anger. "Any further news?"

"The old man was from the East," Shaamil answered. "Several companies have been sent to scour the desert and ask questions in any manner that will produce answers. If the queen is trying to reach the eastern coast, she will not get far. We will intercept her before she could hope to find a port."

Basaal licked his lips and rolled up the map slowly in his hands, his pulse racing. "And, when they catch her?"

The emperor looked at Basaal. "She has sealed her own death."

"I'm sure that they did not see us," Eleanor said aloud, more to allay her own fears than to calm Dantib. In the early afternoon, a line, a shoddy caravan of sorts, had appeared on the horizon. The small band was moving south until a group of riders broke away towards the southeast, the direction Eleanor and Dantib were traveling. At first, they had dismissed it out of hand, but Dantib grew increasingly nervous and eventually turned their horses towards one of the rocky crevices nearby. They wound down through a small canyon, and as night fell, Dantib found a place, tucked away from sight, where they would wait a few hours before striking out again.

"The caravan will be resting, and we can distance ourselves," he told Eleanor as he gave the exhausted horses almost the last of their water. "The next river is less than a days' journey to the east."

"Is this river like the last one?" she asked, remembering how they'd had to sift the last stream through Eleanor's headscarf to drink any of it.

"I believe so." Dantib set a saddlebag on the ground.

"That is not quite the style of living I had accustomed myself to in Zarbadast," Eleanor laughed.

Screaming startled Eleanor to her feet as three armed men came rushing into their makeshift cave. With their scimitars raised, they pushed Dantib to the ground away from the horses. Eleanor tried to run, but a man with only one eye grabbed her arm and wrenched it behind her back, forcing her to the ground.

"Please!" Dantib spoke from on his knees. "We are humble travelers. Take what you might, but leave us in peace."

A rather tall man stepped forward and laughed, calling to his companions in the cave. Eleanor tried to look up, but the one-eyed man brought his hand down across her temple, causing a flash of pain. A stone bit into Eleanor's knee, but she dared not shift again as the men spoke.

"The gray horse is as much dog meat as anything," the tall man said. "But the brown mare will fetch a fair price."

"Take the horses," Dantib said, sounding feeble and old.

The tall man looked at Dantib, and then his eyes wandered towards Eleanor. She watched as best she could without catching the ire of her one-eyed captor.

"Bring her to me," the tall man said. Eleanor was forced to her feet.

The man standing over Dantib said something she could not understand, and the three men laughed. Dantib must have understood the dialect, for a protective flash crossed his eyes and his chin quivered angrily.

Eleanor was forced to stand before the tall man. He reached a hand towards her, and she tried to slap him away. But her captor grabbed her wrists and held them tight behind her back. The tall man touched her face and turned her head, pulling off her headscarf. He said something to the other men in their own private dialect, and then he moved his hand down her neck to her shoulder. Eleanor flinched, and he laughed, stepping forward and trapping her between himself and the one-eyed man. He sheathed his scimitar and brought his hands to her waist.

"Don't touch me!" Eleanor spat in the man's face. He smiled in reply. Eleanor lifted her chin and threw her shoulders back. He caught the full force of her disdain and hesitated, glaring back before roughly pressing his thumbs into her lower abdomen.

"She's not with child," he said in Imirillian, giving her a jaunty smile. Then he touched her chin softly and stepped away. "Bind them, and bring the horses. We must return to the column before daybreak."

The third man, who stood over Dantib, procured some rough rope from his tunic. Soon Eleanor and Dantib were tied together, walking beside the tall man, with the other man leading the horses behind them.

"Are they marauders?" Eleanor whispered to Dantib when she found a chance to speak.

"Worse," Dantib whispered back. "They are slavers. We are being taken into the Shera Shee."

The night sky spread over the desert in its entire splendor, a perfect companion to the endless grains of sand beneath Basaal's feet. He had taken himself away from camp to wonder at the stars, to pray. He was sore from the evening's entertainments, where his father had made him perform in combat exercises for the amusement of the men. It was really, Basaal suspected, a way for Shaamil to reinforce his own power. Basaal's shoulder was sore where he had taken a blow, and he moved it stiffly around as he studied the endless display of lights above him.

It was not long before Zanntal found him.

"My Prince?" Zanntal said as he approached Basaal.

"Zanntal," Basaal said, nodding. "How is life at the rear of the column?" he asked, for they had spoken little in the last handful of weeks.

"As I prefer to be at a distance from the emperor and his men, being attached to your small company suits me well."

"Distance can be a glorious thing," Basaal agreed. His gaze moved across the still desert, and he closed his eyes briefly, as if there were a physical pain he could not quench. "I am in desperate need of it, and so I came out here to think, to be away, and, most of all, to pray. It comes—"

The prince hesitated before continuing. "Sometimes, things become too much to bear and I must open my mouth and pray as if the Illuminating God were drawing the devotion out of me, and I will burn in His all-consuming fire if I cannot utter the words on my tongue. Tonight, I felt such a need."

Zanntal remained quiet.

"It has been weeks, you know." Basaal looked down and kicked the sand with his boot. "I've refused to pray since we left Zarbadast. I have never gone so long without paying my devotions."

The soldier watched him, seeming unsure if Basaal was waiting for a response.

"Why so long?" Zanntal finally asked.

Basaal laughed. "Because the Illuminating God told me to do something I don't think I can do, and because I don't understand why he asks it of me."

"But tonight, the desert called you back?"

"The Illuminating God called me back, and I must obey." Basaal linked his fingers behind his head and gazed above him. "Everything in me desires to be aligned with his will. But I doubt what he has asked of me, and I cannot reconcile myself to it."

"What, then, did you pray for just now?" Zanntal asked curiously.

Basaal shrugged and looked back up to the spangle of lights, twisting above the desert. "Myself. My devotion. The Aemogen queen."

Back in Zarbadast, when Basaal had sworn Zanntal to secrecy and asked him to play part in Eleanor's escape, Emaad's friend had simply nodded, sworn a covenant, and done his duty. But Basaal struggled to keep his thoughts of Eleanor always to himself.

"I once told Eleanor that she was not my guiding star," he confessed abruptly.

Zanntal waited. But when Basaal did not continue, he spoke. "And were you right or wrong?"

Sighing, Basaal dropped his hands, set his shoulders straight, and clasped his hands together behind his back as he looked into Zanntal's eyes. "Both."

The guards walked with torches around the perimeter of the misery-filled camp. When Eleanor asked Dantib about it, he did not hesitate before responding.

"The dogs," he whispered as if it were prophecy. "The guards carry torches to frighten wild dogs who follow caravans, especially slave columns, in hopes of food."

"What food is there to be found in this place?" Eleanor sighed miserably into the sand.

"Us," Dantib said. "The weak, the sick, the dead. It is for human flesh they wait."

Bile rose in Eleanor's mouth at the thought, and she swallowed hard. Whatever hell fate could call up, Eleanor had not been expecting this. They had come so close to the sea. A tear escaped from her eye and pressed steadily down her cheek, leaving a wet line that caught the cold air of the desert night. She did not know their final fate, but Eleanor knew they had failed.

There were a few dozen miserable souls chained in the slave column. Eleanor and Dantib were linked together, forced to march at the rear. Shackles had been secured around their waists and wrists, and they had been walking for three days with little water and only a bite of bread for food.

Two of the slavers had taken the horses away, heading west in hopes of selling them to a caravan for a fair price. Dantib had lifted his manacled hands towards hers for comfort as Eleanor watched Hegleh disappear into the setting sun. Eleanor's boots, itchy as they were, had been taken to vend along with Dantib's overtunic and Eleanor's leather bag. All were to be sold to the West, except them. They would go farther into the Shera Shee.

Now, a day later, her feet were raw and tired, bleeding from a misstep earlier in the day. The manacles would strip her wrists of their skin before long, and Eleanor could not move past the numbness of her shock. She remembered a time when she was young; Edythe had tripped Eleanor as they'd run towards the coast near the fortress of Anoir. It had been an accident, but Eleanor came down hard, the wind sucked from her lungs as she hit the dirt. It had felt like forever before she could get her body to take in air, to breathe. She had rolled to her knees and gasped at nothing, feeling frightened.

This was how Eleanor now felt—gasping, her fingers clutching the ground, but no air would come. Clarity felt impossible, and she could barely see the image of Ainsley's towers as she faded into sleep.

———◦◦◦◦◦◦———

"The Kotaah Hills are up ahead, and then we drop down through the Aronee," Basaal said as he pointed to the distant haze.

"I can read a map," Ammar remarked lightly to his brother.

"Can you?" Basaal raised his eyebrows. "I am all surprise. I did not know you could read anything. Now," he added, "stop being so bitterly sarcastic, and enjoy the news that we are well into our journey."

"Only to make the same journey home on some nameless day," Ammar replied.

"Hopeless." Basaal patted Refigh good-naturedly as he scanned the desert before them. The fall winds, which had perturbed him on his journey north to Zarbadast, were not to be found now in spring, and they rode without headscarves.

They were weeks out of Zarbadast, and the pulse in Basaal's blood quickened in anticipation as they headed south. Ammar often rode beside Basaal, who was attached to the body of the emperor's honorary company. They sought asylum in the back, riding just before the soldiers, wishing to spend no time with the pleasantries born of royal expectation.

The sound of a rider caused Basaal to turn his head. It was a messenger bearing his own colors. Basaal nodded to Ammar and turned out of place to meet the soldier.

"Yes?" Basaal asked the messenger once the man had pulled up his reins and caught his breath. The messenger lowered his eyes to show respect, then looked at Basaal's face.

"A request from your honor guard," he began, "one called Zanntal. He seeks your counsel with all immediacy and desires Your Grace to come straightway."

Basaal nodded. "I'll come now. To the rear column?" he guessed.

"I was sent to tell you that he waits half a league east of the column," the man explained. "It would be my pleasure to show Your Grace where you may find him."

Hearing this, the hairs on the back of Basaal's neck lifted. "Lead on, then, soldier."

They rode down the line, passing thousands of soldiers, supply lines, and pack animals: an endless array of might. Basaal received glances from the men as he rode past, but he did not meet any of their eyes. When they reached the rear companies, consisting of his own men, the messenger pointed to a small knot of figures out across the desert, waiting.

"He asked you come alone," the messenger said, appearing worried to send Basaal without a guard.

"Then, alone I will go," Basaal replied. "Zanntal must have reason for it." Leaving his officers, Basaal continued towards what increasingly appeared to be a pathetic merchant's caravan. Zanntal pulled his horse around, intercepting Basaal twenty feet out.

"My prince, these men approached the rear column, eager to sell their horses and a few humble goods."

"Yes?" Basaal ran his eyes over the filthy men.

Zanntal paused. "I—I recognized the horse, the brown mare. Is that not Hegleh, the horse you gifted to Queen Eleanor?"

Basaal narrowed his eyes and cursed. Then he spurred Refigh forward, and Zanntal spun his mount quickly to follow him. As Basaal came upon the two men, he saw instantly they were slavers. They had half a dozen horses, Hegleh and Dantib's gray mare among them.

"Your Grace," one of the slavers said, grinning a dirty grin. Then he bowed. "Your servant thought our beautiful mare would please you. Indeed, she is fine enough, even for a prince."

Basaal dismounted and grabbed the man by his throat. "Where did you get such a horse?" he demanded.

The slaver's eyes widened, and he shook his head. "I found them. Found—"

"Liar!" Basaal threw the slaver to the ground and dropped down, closing his hand around the man's neck. "I asked you where you found that horse," Basaal hissed. "Which of the filthy slave holes did it come from?"

The man struggled in Basaal's grip before he said, "It was—" He gasped for breath, and his companion, standing nearby, spoke out.

"The edges of the East Desert, Your Grace!"

Basaal released the man's throat and looked up at the filthy slaver who had spoken.

"And the people?" Basaal asked, his voice all fury.

"There were none—" the second slaver began. But Basaal jumped to his feet and drew his sword. "Katerah!" the man yelled as he stepped back, away from him. Basaal was too quick and caught the slaver by the arm, shaking him.

"Where?" Basaal demanded.

"They were going through Katerah for market," the slaver said, stumbling over his words.

Basaal threw the second man to the ground. "You know better than to operate the slave trade in Imirillia. I should kill you outright. I'll not reimburse you for the stolen horses." The slavers did not protest but, from their knees, looked towards each other with wide eyes.

At Basaal's signal, Zanntal dismounted and secured the stolen mounts.

"Do you carry any other goods from these travelers?" Basaal asked, standing over the men, his sword tip hovering above the sand near their faces.

"The saddlebag of the brown horse," the second slaver said. "Just some clothing and a leather traveler's purse."

Basaal's breath was constricted by the anger he was trying to control, and he kicked sand at the men's faces before turning away in disgust.

"If I see you heading back in the direction of the Shera Shee, I will send my men after you. Go!"

The slavers rose from the ground and gathered their four remaining horses. Then, mounting two of them, they rode as fast as they could away from the anger of their emperor's seventh son.

Basaal cursed under his breath as he paced in the sand, trying to think if he'd ever heard of a place called Katerah.

"Zanntal." His voice was hoarse when he finally spoke. "I need you to do something for me."

"What would you have me do?" Zanntal asked, still holding the reins of the stolen horses. Hegleh seemed relieved to see Basaal and was docile and quiet. Dantib's horse was so old he paid no more mind to Basaal than he had to the slavers. Each had been beaten with whips and bore the scabs of the abuse.

Basaal covered his eyes, trying to maintain control. "I need you, Zanntal, to take these horses into the Shera Shee and find the place called Katerah. You must—" His voice broke with a harsh sound. "You must find her, Zanntal. You must find them both. And then, you must see them down into Aemogen. Can I trust you to this?"

Basaal looked at the soldier. And when Zanntal nodded, he took a deep breath. "I will see you have money," Basaal continued. "Let me send an officer to supply you for the journey. I dare not bring Hegleh back to the column lest she be recognized. You must wait here," he added, "until my officer returns with what you need. I will give you money enough to buy back Eleanor at any price, but you must not reveal you do it in my name." Basaal stared at Zanntal, frightened by his own intensity. "Do you understand me?"

"I will see it done," Zanntal promised in a whisper. It seemed a strange sound in comparison to the near shouts from Basaal. "I can maneuver the dangers of the desert. The Aemogen queen will be traced."

Basaal reached for Hegleh and laid his forehead against her cheek in desperation. She nudged at him, so he moved his hand affectionately around her ears before moving to the saddlebags. Some of her clothes, as well as Dantib's, the footwear he'd given Eleanor, and her bag. He withdrew it and, somewhat hesitantly, opened it. It carried nothing of value: a piece of stale bread and a rag, smeared with dirt and blood. He was about to close it, when he saw the pouch of seeds he had gifted Eleanor tucked into the bottom. Heartsick, Basaal secured the latch on the saddlebag and turned away.

He was terrified.

The Imirillian company pushed on, past the Kotaah Hills, into the Aronee. Emperor Shaamil usually maintained his silence, except to speak with his generals and, occasionally, his two sons. Whatever comments he did direct at Basaal were acidic in nature. Basaal brushed aside the sting of his father's words and performed mechanically, if not admirably, when the officers met with the emperor. He would maintain his authority as leader of the conquest, and his mannerisms manifested that. The emperor began to praise his son in public, only to make a cutting remark about Basaal's performance once they were alone or in the company of Ammar.

Basaal threw his mind into the game of negotiating the emperor's moods, while his heart was sick for worry. Zanntal had left weeks ago, and Basaal had no way of knowing how much time Eleanor and Dantib had been in captivity. Even a few weeks of crossing the desert in a slave train could be enough to kill a person, let alone an old man. Little water. Little food. Basaal doubted that Zanntal would find the stable master alive.

And Eleanor. He could not recall her face without feeling a wave of absolute panic coursing through him. He knew that a young woman in a slave train could be misused in the cruelest of ways, if not by the slave masters, then by those willing to purchase her. Only Basaal's stiffest determination could keep his emotions in check as they crossed the Aronee, passed through the city of Alliet, and dropped down into the hills of the stone sea above Marion.

One night, while they were still in Alliet, Ammar came across Basaal as he was sitting in the very same room where Eleanor had resealed his Safeeraah. The physician looked at Basaal's swollen eyes and wet face and said nothing. Rather, he uncharacteristically sat beside Basaal and placed his arm around his shoulders. Neither spoke, and Basaal did not explain. But Ammar stayed with him, in silence, far into the night.

Eleanor cried out as her wrists were yanked and the shackles dug into the raw skin beneath them. Dantib had stumbled again, and he was trying to get back up, but Eleanor could see the trembling of his lips. Spittle clung to Dantib's face. She turned and looked about, panicked that the one-eyed slaver might have seen them fall. Then she knelt down, giving Dantib her bound hands so that he might grab onto them and lift himself up.

A slaver at the rear of the column rode towards them. At the same time, the one-eyed slaver cast a gaze in their direction. He yelled something, the anger in his words seeming to singe the already hot desert air. The slaver from behind dismounted and yelled something at Dantib. As the stable master was trying to regain his footing, the slaver kicked the old man in the stomach. Dantib fell with a groan and turned, dry heaving into the sand.

"Stop!" Eleanor cried out, trying to scramble towards Dantib as best she could despite her chains. "Leave him be!"

But the slaver kicked Dantib again and yelled something at the one-eyed man, who'd come up behind them.

They argued back and forth in their unintelligible dialect as Eleanor reached her hand out to touch Dantib's elbow. He understood the words of the slavers. And as Eleanor watched his expression, she saw a look of resignation. Before she could speak, the one-eyed slaver pulled Dantib toward him and stuck a key into the lock of his shackle. As he pulled the iron bindings away, Dantib's arms fell, and he collapsed to the sand. Then the tall slaver, who guarded the rear, pulled the chain from the shackle around Dantib's waist as the one-eyed man unlocked that shackle as well.

Dantib was now free of all his chains. Eleanor tried to wipe the sweat from her eyes, but she was yanked to her feet by the tall guard. Then he pulled her back in the direction of the large column.

"No!" Eleanor screamed as she yanked her hands away. But the chain, now detached from Dantib's shackles, flew like a giant snake, whipping around and catching on the ankle of the one-eyed slaver. He screamed out in pain as Eleanor scrambled across the sand, stumbling beside Dantib.

"They can't leave you!" she cried, but she was jerked again to her feet.

"Go!" Dantib pleaded with her. "There is still a way for you to live. Go!"

"No!" Eleanor said as she fought the arms of the one-eyed slaver now yanking her back mercilessly as the taller man kicked Dantib once more.

A flash of lightning came across Eleanor's back and wrapped around her neck, flicking up her chin and stinging her lip. There was blood. She cried out as the one-eyed slaver brought his whip down on her back again—and again. He yelled at her in Imirillian, calling her a fool, useless, as the lash continued to come again and again and again.

Eleanor dug her fingers into the sand, but nothing fought back against them, and it was no relief from the pain. *Flash.* The agony was blinding, and as she screamed, her lip tore all the more. In one last burst of anguish, Eleanor raised her hands above her head and begged for mercy.

The one-eyed slaver called out, but it was no longer a scream of anger, rather the surprise of fear. He stepped back, away from her, and looked at the other slaver. Eleanor's sleeve had fallen down to her elbow, revealing the mark of the house of Basaal, seventh son.

The slaver cursed under his breath and threw his whip to the ground. Then he looked nervously at the tall slaver, who, in turn, looked back towards Dantib.

Eleanor could not tell if she was breathing or sobbing, but a horrible sound came from her throat as she sank her face into the sand. There was no hope for them now. Dantib would die, and she would not last out the day.

Kale, the head slaver, came back to see to the commotion. The one-eyed slaver pulled at Eleanor's wrist, causing her to scream against the pain of moving, and pointed to the mark on Eleanor's forearm.

"Interesting," Kale said in Imirillian instead of in the Shera

Shee dialect. The one-eyed slaver blurted something out, and Kale shrugged. "Bad luck?" he said. "Perhaps. The old man we will leave for the dogs, but put the girl back on the chain line. We will dispose of her as soon as we can, preferably for a good price."

The one-eyed slave pulled Eleanor up from the sand, eyeing her suspiciously. Numb fire raged through Eleanor's back, the tatters of her worn clothing becoming soaked in blood. She whimpered as she was forced to her feet and braved the scorching pain to turn her head back towards Dantib. He had lifted himself to his knees, crying. Eleanor knew they were not for himself—these tears, the last his withered body had to give—but for her.

They had not gone far before Eleanor could hear the howls and snarls of dogs fighting as they tore into Dantib's frail body. Eleanor dared not watch, but she wept openly, stumbling along on her torn feet with the slave train.

She did not know what gave her the courage to move, but Eleanor continued forward. They had linked her into the main line behind a woman who seemed to resent Eleanor's struggle. Once, Eleanor lost consciousness, waking in searing pain with an aggressive pull from the one-eyed slaver. Her lip had split again, and blood ran down her chin. Seeing this, the woman in front of Eleanor sneered.

It was long past dark before they stopped. So delirious was she in her agony that she gave no thought to food, although someone offered her water. It tasted of blood, but she drank what she could, then set her head on the ground. The sand beneath Eleanor's side, as she lay in dumb pain, was the softest thing she could recall to memory. She was too tired to feel much of anything save despair.

After the company had settled, Eleanor watched the slavers

walk the perimeter with their torches, a hole as big as the sky eating her from the center of her body outward. Dantib was dead, torn apart by dogs and left to the mercy of the sands for his burial. Basaal's dearest friend, sacrificed. She cringed at his memory.

⁕

Nothing had been left inside Eleanor but pain. Whatever native strength she had drawn on—from the moment she had put herself into the hands of the Imirillian army—had dissipated, had fled. And now, being empty, the loss of Dantib, the whipping, and the heat had broken her. She knew she would never see Aemogen again.

Sleep was not kind, neither were the long, wakeful hours of silence and starlight. Eleanor's open wounds screamed against the harsh fabric of clothing, so she lay perfectly still, the edges of her torn flesh pulsing feverishly. She knew she could not go another day. Her fate would no longer move her towards home. So Eleanor thought of nothing. Nothingness was a refuge from the pain of being separated from all that she loved. Nothing. Nothing. She repeated this thought. And the night wore on.

Eleanor must have dozed, giving in to some thin form of sleep, for the image of Basaal, leaving his garden after prayer, appeared before her eyes just as she opened her lids against the heavy weight pounding in her head. The night was still dark, and the image faded. Eleanor bit her lip, then gave a quick intake of breath, her eyes watering at the painful reminder that her lip and chin had been split open by the whip's tongue. But she clung to the image of Basaal from her dreams. Basaal and his rituals. Basaal and his prayers. Basaal and his Illuminating God.

"Oh, God," Eleanor groaned, an expression of futility more

56

than a plea for comfort. "Oh, Basaal's God." She pressed her cheek into the sand and spoke aloud in her native tongue. "For whatever comes from uttering your name, I ask for it."

And, finally, Eleanor slept.

———

When she woke, a dim light was in bloom above the horizon, and the filthy camp was beginning to stir. She knew that they would soon eat a dried crust of bread and then continue farther south into the Shera Shee. But the despair she had known just hours before was…gone.

Spare as you are spared.

These words spread out in Eleanor's mind. She moved her impossibly stiff neck. Her eyes felt swollen as she blinked, and she knew that the pain in her back would be hellish as soon as the slavers lifted her to her feet.

Eleanor again looked towards the lightening sky. *Spare as you are spared.* It was not a line she remembered from her studies.

"Up. Up!" came the call as the slavers walked among their inventory. "Up!"

Chains began to scrape and clink, and Eleanor tried to lift herself but could not. She almost felt patient as she waited for the one-eyed slaver to yank her into the pain of the day ahead. As she moved her feet, a soft resistance responded, and Eleanor, with great struggle, propped herself onto her elbow, gritting her teeth as the chains moved against her swollen wrists, her curiosity outweighing her pain. The girl. A little girl who had been watching Eleanor for days with hungry eyes was curled up like a kitten, her head resting against Eleanor's ankles.

"Up! Up!" the slavers demanded.

Eleanor was forced to her feet and given dry bread. She grimaced but did not call out. But the child, yanked up onto her knees, seemed dazed and dropped the bread they'd given her to crawl towards Eleanor's skirts, where she whimpered.

Too tired to speak, Eleanor moved her chained hands down towards the girl's head, brushing the hair back from the child's eyes as best she could.

"Shh," she managed to say.

Eleanor bent down and retrieved the child's bread from the sand, brushing it off and offering it to her. As the girl took the bread and opened her mouth to eat, Eleanor saw that her mouth was an infected, bloody mess, for the child had no tongue. It had been cut out.

"Of all—" Eleanor began and closed her eyes, for her misery-laden back now felt like a gift in comparison.

"Here," she said as she took the girl's bread and placed it between her own lips to soften it, helping the girl eat what little she could.

"Better?" Eleanor asked.

The child, who could have been no older than five—maybe six—stared at her blankly. She was a thin, small little thing with wide eyes. Eleanor helped her eat what she would. Then the one-eyed slaver walked by and chained them together. He showed no remorse for Eleanor's pain but was human enough to secure the child to Eleanor with a strong, rough rope rather than with a heavy shackle.

"Stay close to me," Eleanor said in Imirillian, hoping the girl could understand.

The call of the slavers went up, and they moved on into another unrelenting day.

Following her astonished surprise of finding herself yet alive, Eleanor made a decision. She was in captivity and had no control over her days, let alone over the wretched outcome of this filthy venture. What she did have, Eleanor repeated to herself, was her mind. She was a scholar. She was a thinker. For years, she had cultivated her ability to reason, to question, and to press and pull on thoughts. And so, Eleanor began to use her mind.

She decided she would count steps, she would study any break in the blank, sand-filled landscape. When, in the heat, hunger was beat out only by her tremendous thirst, Eleanor would retrieve any thought or quote she could call to mind, repeating the words over and over and over. When the child faltered, Eleanor would carry her, for a quick reminder of Dantib's fate was enough to keep Eleanor clinging to the girl so that they would not catch the ire of the one-eyed slaver or of Kale, the leader, who, since the day she'd been whipped, had marked her with his eyes as he rode alongside the column.

One morning, to Eleanor's surprise, the child wrote out a name in the sand in large, off-balanced characters.

"Sharin?" Eleanor read, looking up for confirmation. The girl grinned and wrapped her hands around Eleanor's fingers. "Can you write anything else?" Eleanor asked.

Sharin shook her head. No, she could not.

Her back did not feel like it was healing. Rather, she woke each morning in terrible pain as the filthy garment, torn in several places, ripped away from the infected skin that had seeped into it while she slept. At night, especially, she could feel the pulsing heat of fever. And so, in an effort to defeat the madness of the pain,

Eleanor would begin again—counting, quoting, and mapping the stars.

Finally, the caravan stopped in a dust-filled crack that the locals called Katerah, the Imirillian word for *memory*. This town wound through a narrow crack between the cliffs, a forgotten pit of the earth filled with the poor of the Shera Shee. Several buildings had been constructed in precarious layers going up the steep cliff faces. The dust-covered locals looked at her and the other captive humans with mild disinterest. Children even ran through the caravan, calling out and laughing, while the slave traders tried to kick them out of the way.

Stumbling over the hardened dirt of the road, Eleanor was relieved for the shade the gap provided, hoping that they would rest the night here. A dozen or so long days had come and gone since Eleanor had lost Dantib, but the infection from her whipping had stayed in her back. It still throbbed, but did not move into the rest of her body. She wondered if this was a grace from Basaal's Illuminating God and had tried to think of him each night when darkness again claimed the day.

Her wrists, still swollen and numb, bothered her no more than the whipping did, for having caught the eye of Kale, the head slaver, and the way that he watched her—laughing with the other men, passing his eyes over her with interest—distracted her from the physical pain.

Pressing against her mind was the thought that he might want to use her for his own pleasures before they sold her to another master. The dye in Eleanor's hair was now fading, and in the sun, the copper of her natural hair had begun to shine through. The one-eyed slaver, who still watched her with suspicion, had called Kale over to see the copper hair near her scalp. She was certain the slavers now knew she was from the South.

Eleanor pushed these thoughts from her mind and looked at the forsaken town around her. Hearing a whimper from Sharin, Eleanor offered a dim smile of encouragement before getting jerked ahead, nearly losing her balance.

The caravan halted, and a man stepped into the narrow street. Well-dressed and hawk-eyed, he spoke to the slavers and pointed farther down the gap. After a brief argument, the few animals still in the train were ushered down the road, disappearing around the stark stone bend. Eleanor kept her head bent, trying to avoid any attention from the wealthy man who eyed the chain of slaves with discernment as he bickered with Kale. The line of slaves waited, downtrodden, and filthy, until, finally, a price to satisfy both men had been reached.

Then Kale, along with the other slavers, herded their captives into what, at the onset, appeared to be a stable, but that revealed itself to be a deep cave. Metal rings were attached to the base of the walls, and the slavers set about unchaining every slave from the column and securing their shackles to the walls. Kale attended to Eleanor himself, placing her in a separate cove from the others. He locked her in and placed his fingers roughly around her chin, speaking words she did not understand.

Sharin had remained with her to this point. But when Kale began to lead the girl away, Eleanor cried out.

"Please!" Eleanor did not know if calling attention to Sharin was best, but she could not bear the thought of her being chained among strangers. "Let me see to the child's needs," she pleaded. "I will care for her."

Kale thought for a moment but then shook his head and took Sharin away. Eleanor breathed out in frustration, tears that long since should have dried up coming to her eyes. Leaning her head back against the cold stone, she tried to steady her breathing and defeat the desire to cry.

People were beasts. They were cruel and petty, self-serving. No wonder Basaal had been so incredulous when he'd first come to Aemogen. Eleanor lay down, wondering if Aemogen had ever been as good as she had truly believed it was. Far into the night, as Eleanor waited in fear for whatever Kale might do, she told herself Aemogen had been as she had remembered, and that people were what she had always believed them to be.

He never came. Eleanor woke cold yet so grateful that she forced herself to her knees and uttered a prayer to Basaal's god. The slavers, tired themselves from the desert trek, slept late and made no hurry to feed their captives. When they finally did, the meal was seasoned rice with a small portion of meat.

Eleanor ate hungrily and almost laughed aloud. She had never, in all the feasts of Zarbadast, tasted anything so good. Her outlook improved when a woman entered, bearing a pitcher of water and some rags. They were to be cleaned, made presentable. Eleanor washed her calloused feet first, then her face, and she laughed at the order of it. She asked the woman humbly if her hair could be braided. And after saying no three times, the woman acquiesced.

Later, Sharin began crying somewhere in the cave. Exacerbated, the one-eyed slaver brought her to Eleanor and instructed that the child should be kept quiet or else they would both be thrown into a snake pit. Wrapping her arms around Sharin, Eleanor vouched for her good behavior. She held the girl close, braiding her hair and singing Aemogen lullabies to her in a whisper.

Basaal heard his father's voice outside their tent. Then the large curtains were held open, and Emperor Shaamil, dismissing his generals with a wave, entered alone. Basaal stood, bowing his head in respect, then returned to his seat, studying a map while his father served himself from the refreshments table.

"The terrain is pretty enough," Shaamil said as he seated himself at the table.

Basaal looked up, then leaned back in his chair, bemused. "What, no lecture?" Basaal said, unable to stop himself. "No scathing comment? Just a pleasantry about the landscape?"

Shaamil took a sip of his drink. "Save your sarcasm. I can be civil." Basaal looked for the edge in his father's eyes, but it had softened.

"It is beautiful country," Basaal replied, surprised he felt almost hungry for his father's sincere conversation. "The farther south, the more beautiful it becomes, especially Aemogen."

"Your mother certainly thought so."

"Did she?" It was the first time Shaamil had referred to his mother since her death. As a youth, Basaal had supposed this was because his father had been indifferent to her.

"Yes—" Shaamil looked as if he would say more, so Basaal waited, watching closely. The emperor's hand carried a slight tremor—what any of his warriors would have called *the death mark*, a symbol of having lost complete control of your physical faculties. Basaal frowned and studied his father's face.

Why had he not seen it? Why had he not marveled before at his father's age? But there it was, his father had grown tired and worn, his mouth curving downward, forming deep furrows that lined his face. Shaamil's dark hair suddenly seemed grayer, and his eyes, though bright and sharp, clearly carried the weight of all his years. Shaamil had aged; he had aged since Aramesh.

"Father." Basaal steeled himself with the courage of too much time already passed. "I have always considered you aware, conscious, respectful of the Seven Scrolls and of our Imirillian religion. Yet, I have never considered you devout, held by all the strictures of religious law."

Shaamil looked towards him, taking a moment for the words to sink in past some memory he appeared to be recalling. Then he gave a quick nod but did not speak.

"Why, then," Basaal continued, "did you honor the request of the Aemogen queen, that she had claim on my hand? That was a very strict observation of old law: that she be given to me, for the sake of the Safeeraah, rather than to Arsaalan for wife?" *Was it only to manipulate me*? he wanted to add.

Shaamil cleared his throat. Yet, instead of acting provoked, the corners of his mouth moved upward in a slight smile. "I saw how you looked at her."

Basaal felt a flush rise up his neck. "What do you mean?"

"Do you know what I have always considered your greatest weakness?" Shaamil responded.

Basaal waited.

"For all your talk of honor," Shaamil continued, "you have never known your own heart." Basaal shifted his weight, feeling, for the first time, how warm the air was inside the tent.

"What is it you are saying to me?" Basaal asked.

"You looked at that girl the same way your mother used to look at me," the emperor said simply. "But that is over, and you've clearly sustained no more damage than your lost pride. I had supposed your feelings for her to be less shallow than they are. She won't live now, anyway." He took another sip of his drink.

It was late in the day that Kale came for her. Pushing Sharin aside, Kale grabbed Eleanor behind the neck, forcing her close to him as he whispered threats. "If you make any sort of noise or called any attention to yourself," he muttered, but then he unlocked her from the wall. He gave her a headscarf and told her to pull it over her face. Then, with her wrists and waist still shackled, he forced her from the cave.

She blinked in the purple light. Standing in a line were some of the women of their train, younger women, mostly, lined up and waiting, their heads bent. Kale approached a merchant who was standing with another man of means, speaking casually. The stranger's hand held the reins of a horse.

She could not hear their words, but, from their gestures, Eleanor guessed he was here to purchase a young woman. Panic rose in her chest, and Eleanor, for the first time since her capture, cleared her mind to make a decision. If she did as Kale had ordered and stayed quiet, avoiding this man's attention, she would soon be back in the cave and at Kale's mercy. But if she were taken away to an unknown fate, although she would be free of Kale, Sharin would be left here alone.

She knew that there would come a time when they would separate her from the child. But for Sharin's sake, Eleanor could not choose it to be sooner rather than later. She looked down, away from the buyer, who had begun looking at the women farther down the line, and she tried to make herself disappear.

He moved closer, occasionally asking a question about one of the thirteen girls and women standing there. Kale answered his questions in the voice of a man selling rugs or spices: eager to part with his wares for a good price.

Eleanor studied her feet as the man worked his way ever closer to where she stood. When he finally came to her, he paused, looked a moment, then moved on. Eleanor breathed a silent sigh and dared not shift. The man began to move past her neighbor to the last woman on the line, but then he took a step again towards Eleanor.

"I want to see her face," he said casually in an accent she did not recognize.

The one-eyed slaver stepped forward and none too gently pushed Eleanor's chin up. She swallowed and looked right into the man's eyes—it was Zanntal, Basaal's honor guard.

Eleanor gave a surprised noise that may have sounded like fear, but that she knew to be complete relief. His eyes searched hers for the briefest of seconds before he looked at the worn, blistered skin of her face, the whip mark on her lip and chin, and the shackles on her wrists. Then he moved on.

Eleanor panicked. Had he recognized her? Should she call

out? She looked down again at her feet, waiting. She would wait. Eleanor told herself it was logical to wait.

When Zanntal reached the end of the line, he spoke for some time with Kale and the merchant, asking questions, pointing to different women, and sounding disinterested and calm. Then a cry could be heard, a child's cry. And Eleanor was rattled by the sound of Sharin's voice coming from the cave, for she sounded inconsolable.

Like a stone hitting her stomach, Eleanor felt the cost of her freedom, which had become a possibility only moments before. If Zanntal were here to rescue her, then her choice was no longer between Sharin and being free of Kale. It was between Sharin and Aemogen.

"I'll take that one," Zanntal said, his voice cutting across her thoughts. Eleanor looked up. He was pointing at her.

Kale's eyes narrowed. "She does not come at such an easy price."

"We've already settled," Zanntal insisted. "The price was pre-determined, and that is the girl I choose."

"And I am telling you now that she is triple the price you offered—with acceptable coin in hand tonight," Kale insisted.

Zanntal looked angry. His pride had been challenged in this bargain, and he would not lose to a slaver.

"Triple the price?" he demanded, his cheeks lifting in impatience and scorn. "Give me an additional slave," he said, "and then I'll pay your price."

Kale laughed, but the wealthy cave owner said something sharp to Kale and then spoke to Zanntal himself.

"Man or woman?" the merchant asked.

Eleanor shook her head ever so slightly, but Zanntal seemed not to notice.

"What men do you have?" he asked curiously.

"A dozen or more of all ages," the merchant said. "We could bring them out. Or, you could come in."

Zanntal looked towards Eleanor, and she shook her head again.

"Let me take the girl through with me," Zanntal said, "and I'll see what you have in your cave."

The merchant ordered Kale to unlock Eleanor. The slaver was not happy, and he jerked impatiently at the manacles around Eleanor's wrists as he released her. After unlocking the ring about her waist and drawing out the chain, he grabbed her by the arm and led her, looking regretful, to Zanntal.

Zanntal guided Eleanor gently by her elbow as Kale led the way with a torch, shining it at the slaves chained against the walls. Eleanor looked desperately for Sharin.

"The child," she whispered. "The child!"

"Quiet!" Kale could not have understood Eleanor's words. He gave Zanntal an apologetic look as they passed from slave to slave.

"I do not see anything of interest among the men or the older women here," Zanntal said, sounding bored. "So, unless you have a child," he added, "I feel the original price for this girl must stand."

"There is one child," Kale replied impatiently. The one-eyed slaver had followed them in and motioned towards the back, his eyes glinting at Kale.

Zanntal sniffed the air in disgust. "Bring the child out to me," he insisted. "I am tired of this wretched hole." He led Eleanor back out of the cave and approached the waiting slave merchant. Eleanor stood quiet, staring at the dust, hearing the beat of her heart loudly in her head.

It seemed the slavers were forever in the cave. And Zanntal

was beginning to show signs of impatience. When they finally emerged, Sharin's cheeks were tearstained. Although she was bound, she tried to run to Eleanor. Zanntal stepped forward and looked at the girl. He opened her mouth, disregarding what he saw there, and studied her face before nodding.

"I will take the woman and the child for triple the price we agreed on," Zanntal said. He withdrew a bag of coins from his tunic and counted the money out into the merchant slaver's eager hand. "If there were any other decent slavers near here," he added, "I would have turned on you the moment you changed your price."

Zanntal handed Sharin's rope to Eleanor and nodded to the merchant, Kale, and the one-eyed slaver. Then he pulled his cloak evenly over his shoulders and motioned Eleanor towards his horse.

"Up with you," he said crisply, lifting her onto the horse. "And nothing untoward or back you'll go." He lifted Sharin up into Eleanor's arms, then mounted behind Eleanor. A click from his mouth sent the horse flying from the gap that was Katerah.

Outside of Katerah, Zanntal had taken a gamble. He had promised a hermit farmer, who lived in a dismal stretch of the desert, that if he would watch Hegleh and Dantib's gray mare while Zanntal rode into Katerah, he would be paid enough gold to leave his desperate existence for a life of luxury. This was explained to Eleanor, and they retrieved the horses with haste.

Eleanor, exhausted from relief, could barely keep herself astride her horse, let alone hold Sharin. So Zanntal tied the horses into a line and brought both Eleanor and Sharin back onto his own mount, cradling Eleanor in his arms as she, in turn, clung to

Sharin. After an hour, he stopped and readied camp, setting a tent and building a small fire in the bottom of a gorge.

When Sharin had fallen asleep, Eleanor wrapped Zanntal's cloak around the small girl. Then she left the tent, joining Zanntal near the fire. He sat crouched, mixing several spices and powders together that he had retrieved earlier from his knapsack. He looked up briefly at Eleanor before returning his attention to the fire. His scimitar hung about his waist, and Zanntal was ever watching and listening to the noises around them.

Eleanor sat down, pulling her knee up under her chin, feeling the stiff pull of the scars forming on her back. "Will you tell me now how you came to find us?" she asked.

Zanntal did not answer immediately. He pulled a small kettle, filled with steaming water, away from the fire. Moving his hands in deliberate motions, Zanntal put his spice and powder mixture into the water, stirring it with a small spoon. He tasted it and appeared satisfied, for he poured a cup for himself and one for Eleanor. She took his offering gratefully, testing the tea against her lips before deciding to let it cool.

"The slavers who took your horses," he answered, "made the mistake of trying to sell Hegleh to the emperor's column."

"The emperor's column?" Eleanor frowned. "Does Emperor Shaamil ride with Basaal?"

"Yes," Zanntal said candidly. "After your disappearance, the emperor mobilized six thousand of his own men to join with Basaal's seven thousand waiting in Marion. After I intercepted the slavers," Zanntal explained, returning to his narrative of Eleanor's discovery, "the prince—" Zanntal paused. "He pressed them for information about where you were being taken, then sent me to find you straightaway."

"Is he well?" Eleanor stared into the small cup in her hands before looking up at the man.

"He was very angry when I last saw him. I do not now know how he fares now, but I believe they must have passed through the Aronee and into Marion by this time."

"And you were sent to what end?" Eleanor ran her tongue over the forming scar on her bottom lip.

"To see you to Aemogen," Zanntal replied.

She swallowed, her eyes heavy, and looked down at the sores on her wrist. "Did the prince have anything else to say, aside from charging you see me to Aemogen?" she asked after several silent moments.

With a slight sound, Zanntal cleared his throat and nodded. "He wanted me to ascertain if you had been harmed in any way."

Eleanor set her cup near the fire and stretched her fingers towards her sore back, pulling her arms closer. It could have been worse, much worse. She heard Sharin stir inside the tent and breathed a sigh of relief.

"Nothing that cannot heal," Eleanor said, trying not to falter.

They spoke no more that evening. Eventually, Zanntal put the fire out and stood watch, his scimitar drawn. Eleanor retired to the tent, placing her arms around Sharin, and slept soundly. She dreamed that she was almost home, and hope was no longer an impossible shadow.

When Basaal slept that night he saw the fall of the Imirillian Empire. The tall turrets of Zarbadast began to crumble into themselves, as if smoke had come from stone. The ornate craft of centuries past, adorning the tall towers and arches, disappeared into the white cloud of the seven palaces' destruction. He heard thunder, born of marble and brass slowly crashing, turning weightless as it tumbled upon all that lay below, turning the city to chalk and ash. A purple haze loomed ominously over Zarbadast, and the dying yellow sun, low and tired, still touched the walls of the remaining buildings, the sanctuaries, the monuments, until they were overcome in the spreading cloud that came down from the fallen palaces.

The city responded with the deep, penetrating rumble as sand-colored facades descended into dust. There were no people, Zarbadast was empty. Yet, the memory of every soul who had ever graced the desert streets now cried in a pitiful wail as all was covered in the dust of the decimated relics that were once Imirillia.

When all had fallen, a great silence hung over the desert city until night alighted itself on the barren ruins, calling forth a holy wind. It was not gentle but mighty and full. It did not gust and sway but moved as one continuous stream, a show of awesome force and power. The wind continued all night long. The moon did not show her face, and all was darkness and sound and terror.

Finally, come morning, when the sun again lifted itself above the desert sands, all was as if man had never been—all was forgotten.

Basaal opened his eyes.

"We have come far south," Zanntal explained as he drew a map for Eleanor in the sand. "As I see it, the fastest way to your country is by passing through the edge of Aramesh and then dropping into Partolla, then crossing the Arimel Mountains to the north of Aemogen."

Sharin was playing in the dirt around their feet, remaining close to Eleanor, still not trusting Zanntal. "The mountains cannot be crossed," Eleanor said as she rested her hand on the girls shoulder and shook her head, "especially in spring, when the glaciers would be impenetrable. That is why," she added, "except for the pass and the port, Aemogen is so secure."

Zanntal considered her words as he stared at his makeshift map. "The emperor's army has assuredly by now crossed into Marion." He traced the path of the army. "We can reach the Arimel Mountains in five or six days' time," he said, looking back up at Eleanor. "Yes," Zanntal insisted, upon seeing her astonishment. "That is how far south the slavers brought you. Now, I lived in the northwest mountains as a boy, in the peaks above the Deeatnaah monastery," he explained. "Our livelihood came from our skill of negotiating this difficult terrain. There are some towns in Partolla, near Aramesh, where we can find supplies and ropes."

He moved his fingers in the sand and looked calmly at Eleanor. "Prince Basaal once spoke of your unwarranted trust in me. If this is indeed the case, then trust me to help you across those mountains. We can drop into your country without negotiating the armies at the pass," he assured her. "Seven to ten days after we reach the mountains, and no more."

"Basaal spoke to you about my trusting you?" Eleanor asked openly.

"Yes." Zanntal nodded. "When he asked me to play a part in your escape from the palace."

"And why did you agree to help?" she asked.

Zanntal did not look away, and Eleanor could not mistake his sincerity. "Because when I saw you in Zarbadast, I felt I had known you all my days."

Eleanor smiled. "Yes."

"I will see you to your country," Zanntal insisted. "By whatever power that determined we should meet, I will see you across those mountains."

Eleanor pointed her finger at the map. "Are you telling me that I can be home in fewer than twenty days?"

"Yes," Zanntal said firmly.

Eleanor clucked in reply and grinned.

———◦❊◦———

Two more days south, and they left the Shera Shee behind. Eleanor could not help smiling as the majestic, blue Arimel Mountains rose in the distance. For the first time in weeks and weeks, the ground felt *real*. Zanntal had produced Eleanor's herdsman boots, Dantib's tunic, and her leather satchel, which still held the seeds Basaal had gifted her. She threw the satchel over her shoulder and thanked the Illuminating God for it.

Dantib's tunic was repurposed for Sharin's needs, and Eleanor took Zanntal's headscarf to cover her own hair: by now, a motley brown with two inches of copper at the scalp. Her face felt raw—sunburned and windburned.

"I'm quite certain I look ridiculous," Eleanor said as she was securing the tunic around Sharin's waist with a rope. "My friends will hardly recognize me."

The soldier said nothing.

Zanntal had taken to the little girl, and he was quick to help Eleanor in her care. Sharin gave him smiles as she clung to Eleanor's skirts, shyly eating the food Zanntal gave her with deliberate determination. Eleanor asked her questions about her family, but Sharin just stared, neither nodding nor shaking her head.

As they traveled, Eleanor began to talk to Sharin about

Aemogen, of spring and summer, the harvests and the flowers. She described the sea and the green. And although the girl did not understand what all of Eleanor's words meant, Zanntal, she noticed, would listen intently. Sometimes he asked questions. As the Arimel Mountains grew before them, they spoke of their childhoods, experiences, the political challenges facing Aemogen, and the cultural challenges facing Zanntal's kin, whom he had left several years ago.

When they reached the Partolla towns, the people there took them for what they presented themselves to be: a family traveling south. Eleanor's physical appearance was not such an anomaly here in the South, and Sharin clung to her so tightly that no one questioned their story.

Zanntal had money enough for food and a little clothing, and, in each town, he would casually accumulate more rope. Soon, Dantib's gray mare became their stock horse. He bore the supplies patiently, paying little attention beyond trudging along their path and seeing to his own personal needs.

Zanntal scanned the snow-glossed peaks ahead of them. "This is not beyond what I have seen in the mountains of the high north," he said. "Granted, they were never this tall," he added, his face creased. But it was with confidence that he scanned the crevices and crags. "What is the Aemogen word for mountain?" he asked.

Eleanor told him. "Why do you ask?"

"If I am to spend any time in your country, I will need to know the language," he explained, "unless you plan on sending me back to Imirillia."

"Of course not." Eleanor smiled, and then her face fell. "You are not—how is it said—sworn until death to Prince Basaal?"

Zanntal shook his head. "I swore to Emaad, and he is dead. My allegiance is now my own to give for how long I wish it. Prince Basaal understands this."

They took to the foothills. Nights were cold, now that they had traveled so far south. And when they woke in the morning, there was frost on their blankets. The horses did well on the first few days of travel, up through the rising foothills. But on the third, they began to encounter passes that would require their small company to climb with their supplies tied to their backs.

"We are going to have to go on without the horses," Zanntal told Eleanor early that afternoon.

"I know," she admitted, trying to give Sharin comfort, for the girl had been crying off and on since morning. Eleanor's hands were shaking, and she felt light-headed. But the mountains smelled like home, and Eleanor was determined to see Aemogen before many more days passed.

Hegleh had patiently climbed the uneven hills, nickering only in light complaint. Now, as Eleanor and Zanntal secured their supplies to their backs with ropes, it was time for her to say good-bye to Basaal's horse. Eleanor moved her hands along Hegleh's neck, whispering her thanks to the beautiful beast, removing the bridle, and then kissing her between the eyes.

Dantib's gray horse, who had held no great affection for anyone save his master, was already wandering down the slope, following the lines of bright, spring grass. But Hegleh paid the gray horse no mind, following Eleanor, Sharin, and Zanntal instead as they continued up through the ravine.

"Go," Eleanor said, and she waved the horse away as it struggled up an outcropping of stone. "Go away. You can't follow us here." Hegleh whinnied and blew out her nostrils, upset that Eleanor did not wait for her. Sharin began fussing again, and Eleanor held the girl's hand as they continued to climb.

When they reached a crag where Hegleh could not follow, it tore at Eleanor's heart. But, mouth pressed into a line as she fought her tears, she continued. Hegleh's whinnying could be heard long after they had lost sight of the mare.

———◦—◦◆◦◦◆◦◦—◦———

While Emperor Shaamil and Ammar ate, Basaal stood, studying the map of Aemogen carefully. Ranjen, one of Basaal's officers who'd remained at the Marion encampment, now sent reports daily: Basaal's troops were pressing their way up the pass with little to moderate progress as they cleared away stone and rubble. The Aemogen archers kept them at bay, and it was slow work.

Running his fingers over the map, Basaal tapped a finger on Ainsley. He'd had no word from Zanntal in well over a month and had no way of knowing if the soldier had even found Eleanor and Dantib, let alone helped them back to Aemogen. Basaal leaned against the table. This whole business with Aemogen had long since gone sour, and Basaal worried he would not manage to do what the Illuminating God had asked of him. It was going to take all his courage to even try.

"When the road passes near Marion City," Shaamil said, his words interrupting Basaal's thoughts, "we will stay as guests of King Staven's hospitality for several days. The army can continue towards the encampment."

"Now there's sense," Ammar said more to himself than to his father.

Basaal looked up at his father, displeasure evident on his face, and he sighed audibly. Ignoring the black look he received from Shaamil, Basaal left the map table and paced along the luxurious carpets, now far more dusty than they had been months ago.

"What is it you object to?" Shaamil asked as he continued to eat his dinner, giving sharp, sidelong glances as he chewed deliberately.

"Nothing," Basaal answered as he ran his fingers through his hair. If anything, he should be grateful for these few extra days before having to make a decision. "I care as much for my uncle as I care for—" Basaal waved at the air. "I can't actually think of anyone that I like so little as him."

Ammar laughed, but the emperor swallowed and took a drink before delivering the acerbic words, "Not even me?"

CHAPTER

FIVE

There were times when Eleanor knew her confidence in Zanntal's plan was fixed. After working their way up and over a difficult pass or at the end of a long day of struggle and ropes and cold, she would look back at their progress and feel sure. But there were other days that made it hard for her to keep any hope.

Eleanor yelled as she slipped, burning her hand as she tried to grab her rope. The rope left several agonizing slivers in her already swollen and blistered fingers. She yelled again as she waved her fingers in the cold air before thrusting them into a patch of iced over snow. This particular moment was one of many that had convinced her their small group was mad and would end up dead before they ever found their way through one of the treacherous gaps and down into Aemogen.

"Are you all right?" Zanntal called back to her. Sharin was strapped to his back, and her face had crinkled in pain when he yelled. The infection in Sharin's mouth seemed better, but a fever had set in, and Eleanor had stayed awake most of the night, trying to comfort the shivering girl.

The routine Eleanor had adopted since they'd begun their ascent was feeling immense guilt for not having left Sharin with some family along the borders of Partolla, followed by a counter argument that they could not trust Sharin's fate if she had just been left in a village alone. Eleanor could ensure a good future for Sharin in Aemogen *if*—she added with mounting stress—they could find a way to survive the Imirillian invasion.

Eleanor slipped again, and this time, she could not stand the pain of the rope and let go, falling to a ledge, banging her knee against an outcropping of rock. Zanntal said something, but Eleanor lifted her hand and stared at the shredded flesh. There was blood on her fingers.

"Eleanor, are you all right?" Zanntal repeated from above.

"No!" Eleanor said, feeling the word fly out of her mouth to match her frustrations.

"You're exhausted, I know," Zanntal said as he looked down over the edge, watching her struggle. "Have you injured your knee?"

"It smashed against the rock," Eleanor said with a cringe.

"Should we stop?"

"We can't afford to stop while there is still daylight," Eleanor said, gritting her teeth as she stood, wiping a drip of blood from her cheek with her tattered sleeve.

On they went, the sun disappearing behind the peaks to the west. It grew cold. Sharin seemed worse now, yet Eleanor could do nothing for her until they stopped for the night. It took a long time to maneuver the crevices before them, and Eleanor's fingers were still struggling to grip the ropes.

When the terrain grew even more challenging, Zanntal tied Sharin to Eleanor's back while he slowly negotiated the climbs, securing what ropes he could to pull Eleanor and Sharin up to safety. When it was finally time to stop, to sleep, and to rest, Eleanor held Sharin in her arms. She tried to tempt her with whatever small amount of water and bread she could, for the girl refused but very little.

"Do you think she will die on this mountain?" Eleanor asked Zanntal as she moved her thumb over Sharin's cheek, lulling the girl to sleep.

"No," Zanntal said, and he was confident. "Tomorrow, or the next day, I am hopeful we will find our way through to the south side. We will go down into your country before many more days."

Despite the cold air against her face and arms and the almost unbearable burning of her hands, Eleanor smiled and kissed Sharin's now sleeping face.

"You cannot know what this means to me, returning to Aemogen," Eleanor said.

Zanntal's expression seemed serious, but his eyes were certain. "You can thank me after I start a small fire and make an herb poultice for your hands," he said. "We are fortunate to still have enough supplies to not make us desperate."

Eleanor had secured the bundle to her back, and asked Zanntal to tighten the knots, as her hands were too stiff to be effective. The soldier said he would. But in the course of preparing to leave their makeshift camp, he had forgotten. So had Eleanor. Only later that morning, when Eleanor was facing the task of pulling herself up ten feet of a steep cliff, did she remember it had not been secured as tightly as Zanntal had always insisted.

"I can't help you with it now," he called down. "Climb up, and we'll secure it."

"My arms!" Eleanor called back up. "They're too tired. Can I tie myself to your rope?"

"Yes," Zanntal shouted. "Hurry. Sharin is crying, and I can't give her any food until you can get up here."

The muscles in Eleanor's forearms were tight and strained. She wrapped the climbing rope around her waist and maneuvered it to make the knot Zanntal had taught her days earlier.

"I'm ready."

"Yes," Zanntal answered.

Eleanor had spent a portion of every day wondering why she had not thought to find herself some men's trousers. After granting herself a moment to again curse her thoughtlessness, she began to pull herself up the face of the small cliff, her purple fingers clinging to whatever edges she could find.

Though not as harsh as it had been during the night, the wind left the rock face cold, and Eleanor shivered despite herself. When she reached her hand up to grab a small shelf, the rock beneath her left foot gave way.

Eleanor cried out as she fell, and the rope jerked around her stomach with such force that she felt as if her back would break in half. The ill-tied supplies slipped from their place and tumbled down the cliff face, bouncing and then falling into a steep fissure. Eleanor's arms flailed, and she could hear Zanntal yelling something. Rock and dirt came spilling down from above her head, and Eleanor struggled to right herself and grab the cliff face.

"I'm trying!" she shouted against the steady stream of words she could not understand. Finally, her hand struck the rock, and Eleanor managed to slide her fingers into a small crevice.

"Ah!" she yelled, pulling with all of her strength until she could find a steady place to put her feet. Once she had, she could feel the rope slacken as Zanntal regained his lost breath.

He came over to the edge and looked down.

"And that was nearly all the food?" he called down, scanning the remnants of what could be seen below them.

"Yes," Eleanor yelled, clinging to the cliff, her pulse beating against the unmovable stone. "Should I go down?" she asked. "Can I salvage anything?"

Zanntal cursed—something Eleanor had not heard him do before—then shook his head. "No. It's all fallen beyond reach. Any effort would be futile, a waste of strength. Let me untie Sharin and set her down, and I will help lift you up."

It took several minutes of negotiating the cliff face, but Eleanor was finally pulled up over the edge. Zanntal gathered her into his arms and uttered a phrase of relief, although concern still marked his face.

"I have some bread and very little dried fruit," he said. "Water we have but little."

"What about the snow?" she asked, breathing hard against Zanntal's chest.

"Yes." Zanntal nodded. "But it must be melted first, or we would seal our deaths."

He helped Eleanor to her feet, and she walked to where Sharin lay, huddled halfway under a stone. Zanntal brought out a bite of bread. While he fed the girl, Eleanor stood and studied the pass ahead. It looked more navigable than anything else they had seen the entire day, and Eleanor breathed out in relief. After Sharin was fed, they continued.

Late in the day, just as the sun had turned the sky gold and pink and the wind began spinning past their ears, Eleanor lifted herself to the top of an outcropping.

"Zanntal!" she cried over her shoulder. "Aemogen! It's Aemogen!"

Stretched out beneath a smattering of white clouds, the woods and fields of Aemogen rested serenely far below them. Zanntal came up behind Eleanor, Sharin asleep on his back. He did not speak as his eyes wandered across what could be seen of the green country.

"No view was ever more beautiful!" She laughed, gripping on Zanntal's arm.

"Let us be careful," Zanntal warned. "It looks as if the glaciers on this side are larger than anything we have yet encountered."

Eleanor felt too happy to care, and they soon began their descent.

King Staven looked no happier to receive the emperor and his sons than Prince Basaal had felt to be received. Basaal's obvious displeasure and Ammar's taciturn silence left Shaamil to be the most pleasant of the party. This amused Ammar, at the very least.

Once the two brothers had withdrawn to Basaal's private quarters, Basaal ranted to Ammar about having to spend time in Marion City. Their father had been seen to a far more elegant suite, but the physician had chosen the hospitality of his brother, who claimed his mother's rooms without so much of a "Hello, Uncle. How are you?"

"I would warn you against the baths," Basaal mentioned cryptically to his brother.

"Why is that?"

"Oh, you may get stuck conversing with one or more of my

relatives," he explained. "And the bath never struck me as an ideal place for a gathering of lost kin."

A frown of agreement came from Ammar. Then he half disappeared into a room that a maidservant had just finished arranging. "I would like to wash and change," Ammar said, "and go an entire day without seeing your charming face, dearest brother. Good night." Ammar closed the door behind him, leaving Basaal to wonder how he would explain Ammar's absence at dinner.

"I'll just see about having your trunks sent up," Basaal shouted after his brother, "since serving Your Ornery Grace is certainly not below my dignity."

"I would rather think not," came the reply, and Basaal, despite himself, laughed aloud. Then he sent a servant to bring up Ammar's things.

After several death threats, Ammar did come to dinner in the end. As Basaal sat down to sup with King Staven and his court, he caught the eye of his elderly cousin, Telford, Thayne's brother. Telford winked. Basaal's expression, in return, was almost murderous. He had no idea what he could say to his cousin about Eleanor's whereabouts, and the guilt of it made Telford's watchful glances unbearable.

After a stiff and quiet meal—the emperor sitting beside Staven, playing games of subtle word manipulation in between compliments about the food and drink—Basaal found out that they were to be treated by a concert of musicians. Upon this announcement, Basaal groaned aloud, which caught the attention of Staven, who, in return, glared at Basaal.

It was another hour before Basaal could escape.

"Ah! I hoped I'd run into you," a voice said.

Basaal jerked his head up, immediately chastising himself for seeking solitude in one of the formal gardens. Of course, Telford was having him watched, just waiting for his chance to pounce.

"The last thing I would think this to be is an accidental run-in, Cousin," Basaal stated hotly once Telford had come close enough to fall into step with him.

"Still wearing black, I see," Telford said, grinning good-naturedly as he straightened his hair. It had come askew in his rush to catch up with his cousin. Basaal hoped such silly fashion ideas were not hereditary.

"What do you want from me?" Basaal asked.

"Last time we met, there was an untimely interruption," Telford said as he looked across the garden. "Let's go down this corridor of crab apples to that stone gazebo," he suggested, pointing to an alley of trees in full spring bloom. "There's someone just up ahead," Telford explained, "whom we should avoid."

Basaal obliged with a grumble.

"As I was saying," Telford continued, "we were interrupted before I could fulfill my part of the bargain." He withdrew an old, faded letter, its seal long since broken. "A letter, from your mother. She mentions you. Needless to say, I don't think she dressed you in black at the time, expecting you to be scowling at the world. But mothers rarely see foul markers in their own children, so it wouldn't have made a difference," he added, chuckling at his own joke as they arrived at the stone gazebo. He handed the letter to Basaal. "I do believe the words *thank you* are often said in such circumstances."

"Go to the devil," Basaal replied as he slid the worn letter into his stiff jacket.

"Touchy."

In a rush of anger, Basaal grabbed his cousin by the lapels and forced him against one of the pillars. "I do not need any smart comments from the likes of you. I know you're here to ask about Eleanor, and I have nothing to tell you," Basaal hissed as he shook his cousin. "Nothing."

"My dear boy, calm yourself down," Telford said, his tone turning businesslike. "I do want to ask you about the whereabouts of the queen. But you mustn't take it so personally—you will give yourself stomach problems, and at my age, there is almost nothing worse."

In frustration, Basaal released Telford and took himself to the other side of the stone structure, sinking onto a bench and covering his face with his hands.

"I could be killed," he explained, "for what I am about to tell you."

"You're in luck," Telford said. Basaal could hear Telford settling himself down on a bench opposite him. "I don't blabber."

Basaal looked through his parted fingers at the older man. "I lost her," he said.

Telford shifted his mouth. "How does one *lose* somebody exactly?"

"I arranged for her escape to the eastern coast, as my letter informed you," Basaal said, "but on my way down to Marion, I found out she had been taken by the slavers of the Shera Shee."

No reply came from his cousin.

"I sent one of my best men to a place, a slave market of sorts, where we know they were taken, to search her out, unbeknownst to my father." Basaal sat up and placed both of his hands on his knees, forcing whatever composure he still had to take the lead.

"I suppose your connections have not heard anything yet of her return to Aemogen?"

"No." Telford looked wholly serious for the first time. "But, if you've got a man on it, I shouldn't lose heart completely."

While making a sound of desperation, Basaal raised his eyebrows and made a gesture with one of his hands.

"Oh dear," Telford said.

"What?" Basaal asked, his voice thick with the emotion he had been trying to control for the last several weeks.

"Nothing, my boy." The courtier was all sympathetic sincerity. "Nothing."

Eleanor's feet could not move fast enough for her as they left the foothills. After two long and careful days, they had found themselves on easier footing, for the snow had long since retreated in the crags they had come down through. After another day and a half of traveling, they reached one of the roads north of High Field fen. She felt so hungry to be home that the pain of forcing her body to hurry seemed a small price to pay for reaching Ainsley sooner. Zanntal, carrying Sharin, had followed her pace tirelessly. It was on this lonely road that she saw a rider, a fen rider. One of her own men.

"You there!" Eleanor called out to the fen rider. He looked towards them with a wary expression on his face, and she did not blame him. The three of them were a spectacle, to be sure, having run out of food two days previous and with little to live on the days before that. Eleanor was sure her own hollowness was accentuated. Even Zanntal's cheekbones were more pronounced.

The rider pulled his horse around. "May I help you?" he said, anxious to continue on his way.

The moment caught Eleanor's tongue in her throat. What a tremendous difference must have taken place for her own fen rider not to recognize her face. Eleanor straightened her shoulders and tilted her head sideways, stifling her exhaustion.

"I—" she began.

"Your Majesty!" The rider's face went terribly blank as he dismounted his horse and fell to the ground, kneeling. "Forgive me. I was not—I did not expect—"

"Thaniel," she said as she motioned him to stand.

The rider nodded, his mouth hanging open as he rose to his feet. "I offer you my horse," he said, "my—my—anything, My Queen." His eyes searched Eleanor's face, resting on her marked lower lip and chin. Eleanor cleared her throat, and he looked away.

"What I need, Thaniel," Eleanor said firmly despite her light-headedness, "is for you to ride for help. My companions and I are in need of food and rest and conveyance to Ainsley as soon as possible. Can you secure horses and food from the nearest fen—High Field, is it not?"

"Yes." Thaniel bought his chin down sharply. "I will find horses and food—and help," he said. "An honor, My Queen." He mounted, spinning his horse around so fast that Eleanor was afraid it would fall on him. "Stay on the road, and we will find you!" he yelled back. And his horse was racing through the trees before Eleanor had a chance to say anything else.

"One of my fen riders," Eleanor breathed out to Zanntal in complete happiness as if that were all the explanation that he would need.

"Annan!" Basaal yelled at the approaching rider as he rose up in his stirrups. Before his father could call Basaal back, he spurred Refigh forward. He dismounted with haste, practically throwing himself into a run, as Annan did the same, and then they embraced. Basaal laughed, so relieved to see his friend—so relieved to finally be away from Staven's court.

"We are yet five days out from camp," Basaal said, "only having left Marion City yesterday." Basaal hit his friend on the shoulder. "What brings you out?"

Annan motioned behind Basaal, and they grabbed their reins, leading their mounts from the road. They bowed respectfully as the emperor and his retinue passed, and then Annan turned to answer Basaal's question.

"When word came you had entered Marion, I decided to meet you," Annan answered. Mounting their horses, they fell back to the rear of the company, beyond where anyone could overhear their conversation. "I came across the emperor's men on my way. Six thousand?"

"Yes," Basaal said, and he blew the air in his lungs out deliberately. "Add that to my seven thousand, waiting near the pass, and we will be thirteen thousand strong."

"This conquest does not require those numbers," Annan said, creasing his eyebrows.

"No," Basaal agreed. "Nor such personal attention from the emperor. But this has turned from a conquest into a political statement. No doubt King Staven is meant to take note of it as well as the Aemogen council."

Annan eyed Basaal. "There are rumors—" he began, pausing before continuing, "that have come down with the messengers. Many are about you, your father, and your marriage to the

Aemogen queen."

Basaal adjusted his weaponry and gave Annan an exaggerated grimace. "You tell me the progress we are making at the pass," he replied, "and I will answer what I can about said rumors." The concern in Annan's face did not dissipate with Basaal's words—it increased.

Weariness did not stop Eleanor from moving her small company forward, her eyes straining in hopes of seeing the rider returning on the road. Sharin was asleep on her shoulder, having cried herself to sleep from hunger. They walked slowly, finally stopping for a long while at a stream that came near the road.

Sharin whimpered, still shivering from the cold, and Eleanor now felt strange comforting a child. She was home. She was Queen. She would command her armies in war. And now there was a child in her arms that she had taken full responsibility for by bringing her home to Aemogen. Whatever maternal strengths the journey had required of her felt ill fitting now, like a garment sized for another person. But Eleanor did her best to comfort Sharin, helping her drink the fresh water, watching the road eagerly for whatever help Thaniel might have found.

When no one came, they continued, despite the late-afternoon sun growing yellow and low on the horizon.

"There," Zanntal finally said, pointing not down the roadway but across a wide field, green with spring grass. A band of horses was barreling towards them. With relief, Eleanor slipped Sharin to Zanntal and left the road, walking—running almost—waving her arms.

"Thaniel must have found soldiers," Eleanor called back. "They are no farmers." She thought she spoke loudly, but Zanntal did not seem to hear her words, neither did Sharin stir. Too tired to speak again, Eleanor turned back towards the riders, her eyes finding any kind of focusing difficult.

They were now almost upon Eleanor, calling out to her. And then the lead rider swung down from his horse and ran to her. In a single motion—a grace Eleanor had not thought she would see again—Aedon gathered her into his arms, lifting her tired body from the ground.

She was home.

CHAPTER
SIX

Eleanor slept for three days. It was a deep sleep—endlessly falling into the layers of her mind—and she felt, if she chose, she could be lost to it forever. Part of Eleanor would not have cared; she was so weary. Her dreams were the texture of the desert, the gold and heat, and sometimes, she could almost feel the touch of her Imirillian prince.

When Eleanor woke, Aedon was sitting at her bedside, reading a dispatch. The indescribable comfort of this private room—in whatever farmhouse Aedon had found—caused her to lie quiet. She watched him without speaking, noting his familiar expression, and the customary mannerisms of Aedon in concentration.

Eleanor smiled. And as if Aedon could hear the sound of it, he looked up and met her eyes.

"You're awake."

"Yes," Eleanor said. She cleared her throat and began to cough. Aedon waited patiently and offered her some water, which she took gladly. Try as he might, Aedon could not ease the worry from his eyes. "I am so relieved to see you." These words came from

Eleanor as a deep, overdue breath.

"When you failed to return," Aedon said, stretching back into his mind to find the words, "I had supposed this prince had broken his promise. Day after day—the months that passed and all of Aemogen pulling together—" He paused, leaning forward so that his elbows rested on her bed, and took her hands in his, being careful with her raw fingers.

Several moments passed before Aedon could again speak, his face caught in a grief she did not understand. Eleanor, too tired for words, creased her eyebrows and narrowed her eyes to ask him what he was thinking.

"The farmwife bathed you," he said, his voice coming slow and measured, and Aedon looked down at the quilted blanket as he spoke. "Before she dressed you, she asked me to come into the room, for she was disturbed by the scars on your back, your wrists, and feet, and by the mark on your arm." He looked up, directly into Eleanor's eyes. "I asked for discretion—that she not tell anyone what she saw—for I could not bear the thought of you becoming the subject of any speculation." Aedon bit at these last words and took his hands away from hers, rubbing his eyes with his fingers. "Oh, Eleanor, you have been so long away."

"I can't recall how long—"

His answer came quick. "Two hundred and twenty-seven days."

"In truth?" The weight of all those months now felt heavy on Eleanor's chest. "I suppose that it must have been."

Aedon's mouth quivered, and he wiped his eye, reclaiming her blistered hands in his. "What happened to you?" he asked gently.

Eleanor tried to answer, but she was so tired that the words would not come.

"Sleep," he said, seeing her expression. "We'll talk afterward."

The afternoon light from a small, thick-paned window accentuated the lines in Aedon's face, revealing where a tear had run down his cheek. "And I will be here when you wake up."

There was something she knew she wanted to speak of, that had consumed her mind, but now it had fled. So Eleanor nodded, and closed her eyes, her hands still in his as she turned towards him, pressing her cheek against the pillow. It would come, she thought. Tomorrow, it would come.

"Oh, yes," Eleanor said, finding these words just before she lost consciousness. She had wanted to ask him about the fighting at the pass.

⟡

"We are at war," Eleanor said the next morning when Aedon entered her room. If he was surprised to see her up, dressed, and sitting at the small table, he hid it well. Shoes had been left for her in the room, and Eleanor had braided her hair up, hoping it would not look as strange, but the braids made it worse. She had procured a quill, ink, and scraps of paper and was scribbling numbers and dates as best as her hands would allow.

"You knew?" Aedon asked.

"Yes." Eleanor motioned for him to take the other chair. "Only a few days before I escaped from Zarbadast—"

"So he did take you to Zarbadast?" Aedon interrupted.

Eleanor brushed past Aedon's question. "Prince Basaal received a missive saying that fighting had broken out at the pass. It was a mild winter, then?"

Aedon knit his eyebrows and sat down. "Shouldn't you be resting one more day?"

"The war calls me to Ainsley immediately. You know this,"

Eleanor said, looking Aedon in the eyes.

"Yes," Aedon replied with the tone he always used in council meetings. Eleanor almost smiled, the familiarity of it being such a complete feeling of home. "You also look half dead," he continued. "You've no weight on you—your bones show through your skin—and you have dozens of unaccounted for scars on your body. It is important that I see you back to Ainsley, yes," he added. "But, it is more important that the queen, leader, and figurehead of our government gets there alive."

"I am not ill," Eleanor insisted. She raised her hand to quiet Aedon as he moved to speak. "Assuming we are near High Field fen, it is a two day ride to Ainsley Rise. I will agree to take it in three if we can leave today."

"Four days," Aedon countered.

"Three," Eleanor insisted stubbornly. "I need to know if the emperor has arrived in Marion."

"The emperor?"

"Yes," Eleanor stated. "As a warning to Prince Basaal, he has come to supervise the conquest personally—with six thousand of his own troops."

Aedon's mouth twitched. "Six thousand? Combined with those already in Marion, we now face thirteen thousand men?"

"Yes," Eleanor responded.

"Well, that will change Crispin's plans," Aedon said, and he sat back in his chair and ran his fingers across his chin. "We should send a fen rider immediately."

"How did you come to be here?" Eleanor asked, frowning, a question she had forgotten to ask Aedon yesterday. "Why were you at High Field fen?"

Aedon looked down at the table. "There was a casualty at the pass, a friend of mine, who was from High Field," he explained. "I came with the company delivering his body to pay my respects personally to his family."

"Doughlas is from High Field," Eleanor said as she leaned her elbows across the table and rested her face in her hands, still looking at Aedon. "Did he know the man?" As Aedon looked away, Eleanor froze. "Aedon?" she said, using his name with the full weight of a question behind it. "Aedon, was it Doughlas you brought back to the fen?"

"Yes."

Eleanor stood up, causing the chair behind her to clatter against the floor. Not Doughlas. Aedon watched her, his expression torn. She could hear movement outside the door—worried voices.

"We go now," Eleanor stated before Aedon could protest. "Prepare the company to ride for Ainsley Rise."

Then Eleanor turned and marched from the room.

Zanntal did not wish to be left behind. Eleanor was preparing to mount the horse Aedon had found for her while trying to appease her friend. Aedon, Thaniel, and the rest of the company were waiting.

"I would ride with you," Zanntal stated plainly in Imirillian, no other option a consideration in his mind.

"And I would have you," Eleanor said, equally as frank. "But I must ride in haste, and you told me yourself Sharin has come down with a deep fever and should not be moved."

The soldier looked at Eleanor with obvious consternation. "My place is with you. There is a family here to tend the girl."

"Zanntal." Eleanor took a long breath and laid her hand on

his forearm. "She is tired and scared. We are the only people she knows. I ask you, please, to patiently wait until Sharin is well. Then both of you will ride for Ainsley."

"And if the fighting breaks out before then?"

"I will send for you if we go to open war sooner than expected. I promise you that."

Zanntal surrendered. "May the Illuminating God bless your way," he said. "I will come when I can and stand beside you in the fight."

He helped her mount and then stepped back, watching, as Eleanor and her company rode on to Ainsley.

For the first time since she'd left Aemogen, it was a complete relief to be back up on a horse.

"I *can* ride," Eleanor had said shortly to Aedon earlier, when he had questioned her conveyance. "If I can grit my way through the Shera Shee, I can ride a horse to Ainsley Rise."

"Fine," Aedon had said as he set his face and shrugged.

For the first several hours, Eleanor peppered Aedon with questions regarding the state of affairs. Aedon answered comprehensively.

After she had ridden out to stop the Imirillian army, Aedon stayed at Colun Tir with a small company until a spy confirmed the news that the Imirillian prince had ridden towards Marion City with Eleanor. Edythe, upon hearing the news, had been distraught, frozen in grief and immobilized only for one day, before taking her place as regent, and fully occupying the role.

"She has grown up," he remarked with no further information. He also explained that the explosions had left the pass completely damned up, and it would have remained so until late spring, but the winter was unusually mild.

"Even the mountains seemed to catch little snow," Aedon said as he motioned towards the northern range at their right. "Were it a normal year, we would be working frantically to prepare ourselves against the inevitable drought. As it is, I've a small committee of fen lords seeing to that problem while the rest are involved directly in the war. They are all at Ainsley now, save Danth, who insisted that every man was needed at Common Field," he added.

"It was not too long into the winter," Aedon continued, "that the guard at the pass reported Imirillian troops were investigating. Despite the cold, there was little snow to keep them away. So, they began to send men every day to begin the task of clearing a way through. But Crispin deployed several companies of archers, who worked on keeping them at bay. The Imirillians, in turn, sent their own archers to protect the men clearing away the rubble. And, not long after that, small skirmishes began.

"And so," Aedon said, "it has continued the last several months. A few weeks of snow slowed any hope of Imirillian progress, but there was enough of a thaw that they have again begun their work. We always have five hundred men stationed to guard the pass, while the others spend their time at home: working in their trades, preparing for spring, and training for combat. Now that spring has come upon us, it is only a matter of time before the Imirillians come again in force. Word from our Marion sources confirms what we've long since suspected: the Imirillians will only go so far until their prince returns to begin the conquest in earnest or until he sends a message authorizing a steady attack." Aedon gazed across the greening fields. "So, while we have been at war, we have been spared far more than we otherwise might have."

"How many casualties?" Eleanor asked. She had hoped Aedon would supply the number himself, but he had not.

"Just shy of two hundred men," Aedon said, clearly considering this a small number. "We've done well, considering it has been nearly five months of struggle."

"Two hundred men?" Eleanor said, looking at Aedon in disbelief.

"We've come off extremely light. Crispin has been miserly with those fighting in the pass. Cautious almost to a fault."

"Yes," Eleanor grimaced. "I applaud you for the caution. But two hundred men? That's the size of a small fen, gone. Two hundred families—" she faltered.

"Yes. Two hundred mothers and widows," Aedon said practically. "And we will be lucky if we do not lose ten times that amount."

"We should have surrendered," Eleanor said, struggling with the guilt of the lives lost.

"No," Aedon disagreed.

"Bringing down the mountain has made Emperor Shaamil so angry, he's declared openly that the people of Aemogen will not be spared."

"We met with the fen lords," Aedon said. "The decision was to fight. We all decided to fight, and we are a long way yet from defeat."

"But can you see a way to victory?" she asked.

"Crispin and Thistle Black have been working on that," Aedon replied.

"And what does Gaulter Alden think of their ideas?"

Aedon's expression dropped. "I forgot I haven't told you yet," he said, chastising himself. "Gaulter Alden is dead."

"What?" Eleanor reined her horse up sharp, forcing Aedon to do the same. "When? How? At the pass?" The ground was spinning, and Eleanor lifted a hand to her eyes to steady herself.

"No," Aedon said, regretful. "He passed away no more than a month after you'd left. He was old, Eleanor. A fever took him, and he was glad of it. His wife had been gone long enough, and seeing you rushing out like that—" Aedon paused and held up his hand. "Stop, Eleanor. I see that look on your face. He would have died had you been there or not. The man was old and past his time."

Eleanor closed her eyes, feeling dizzy. "I need to get down, Aedon. Help me get down."

Aedon dismounted and signaled to the other riders to move ahead and set up camp. Then he helped Eleanor dismount. She dropped the reins of her horse, walking off the road into a field, her face in her hands.

"Do you need water?" Aedon asked as he followed her, offering Eleanor a drink from his water pouch.

"No." Eleanor sat. "I'm dizzy. Can we just sit awhile?" she asked. "Rest—space to think—that is what I need."

Aedon brought Eleanor's horse over and staked it with his own, then he came and set himself on the grass beside her.

"You're tired," he said after some time. "And I keep forgetting—" he trailed off and made Eleanor take a drink anyway. "If you insist on pushing yourself," he added, "then I insist you give yourself a fighting chance at it." They both were silent for a few moments.

"Who else has died that I should know about?" she asked after a time.

Aedon listed the names that were familiar. A few were distant cousins of Eleanor's.

"Most of the casualties were men you would have recognized, but they were farmers and thatchers, and you would not have known them by name. We've a record of the dead back at Ainsley

Rise. And every few days, Crispin sends a message from the pass."

"I will acquaint myself with it as soon as we return home," she said as she lay down on her back in the grass, staring up at the late-afternoon sky. Aedon, too, lay on his back, a blade of grass between his teeth, thoughtful.

"I'll never forgive you for that," Aedon said after a time.

Eleanor looked over at him. "For what?" she asked. But he would not meet her eyes.

"Riding out like that before the Imirillian army," he finally answered.

"You've already forgiven me," Eleanor answered back, her voice subdued. "I can see it in your face."

"Then you misinterpret," Aedon spoke sharply. "I believe you took ten years off my life."

The ground rumbled under the thunder of thirteen thousand soldiers marching in place. Basaal could feel the vibration buzzing in his hands through Refigh's reins. Then came the sound of trumpets. Then there were banners, soldier's livery, all marked with the symbols of Emperor Shaamil and of Basaal, seventh son.

As the royal company came over the rise, just above the swollen war encampment, Shaamil raised his fist, and all the men, standing in perfect lines, began an endless roar that rang in Basaal's ears. He shifted in his saddle and then raised his own arm. The noise became deafening. If Shaamil had noticed that the soldiers gave out a louder sound in response to Basaal, he showed no sign of it.

Ammar rode beside Basaal, frowning at the companies of Basaal's men, which were adorned in red and black. They had spent the winter, waiting patiently, and now their time would be coming. The soldiers of Shaamil's forces wore a shade of purple so dark only the bright sunlight could catch any color out of it. Standing at perfect attention, both armies turned their shouts into the war chants of Zarbadast. The men's hunger for a fight, Basaal knew, would be insatiable.

As he rode towards the line of tents waiting for the emperor and his sons, Basaal heard again in his mind the words he had heard that morning in prayer before he had left Zarbadast. He felt a shiver as he stared at the men before him. He watched the nape of his father's neck, knowing clearly what the Illuminating God had asked of him. The words came crowding into his mind now, louder than all the chants and cheers of men ready for war.

"*You shall not lead your army into Aemogen.*"

Again, even in the warmth of the mid-spring afternoon, Basaal shivered.

CHAPTER
SEVEN

Ainsley was at war. As they rode in from the north, Eleanor could see several encampments of soldiers out beyond the western gates.

"The men of the northern fens gather here at Aemogen for training as they prepare to serve three week's time at the pass," Aedon yelled over Eleanor's near gallop. "There is also the southern camp, as I told you, near Rye Field fen. They are ready to mobilize as soon as we call for their aid."

The towers of Ainsley Castle held steady against the sky, and Eleanor could feel the beat of her heart, the emotion stinging her eyes as they came nearer. Up through the northern gate they rode, sweeping towards the western side of Ainsley Rise. A horn blew from above, and the men of the encampment let out a cheer as Eleanor's small company entered the gates of the courtyard.

Then Edythe came running out, followed by a stream of people. Eleanor dropped from the horse into Edythe's arms. They were laughing, and Edythe was crying and rushing through words Eleanor could not hear. Aedon stepped behind Eleanor, his hand on her back, leading her through those gathered.

Then a commotion caused the crowd to split as Hastian, Queen's Own, came sprinting, holding the sheath of his sword in his hand to keep it from swinging as he ran towards Eleanor.

Despite knowing better, Eleanor and Edythe, with warm mugs of tea, sat up late into the night talking on Eleanor's bed. Edythe spoke of Gaulter Alden, Doughlas, their preparations, the long winter, and how she had stepped into role of regent.

"I'm sure Aedon mentioned how Crispin and Thistle Black are testing a new idea of weaponry involving the powder," Edythe said.

"Yes." Eleanor nodded. "But not many details beyond that."

"Tomorrow, Crispin is expected to arrive," Edythe explained. "He has a plan that, until I heard another six thousand men were to arrive, I was sure would work. Now, I am not so certain."

Eleanor's head was hurting, and she wished for just one night to push the threat of war away. "Tomorrow, we will discuss it all in detail. But tonight let's forget about the war and just talk about anything else."

"Would it be too hard if I asked you to tell me of Imirillia?" Edythe inquired as she leaned against the pillows, burrowing farther beneath the warm blankets. It felt to Eleanor like an overwhelming request.

"I hardly know where to begin," Eleanor admitted, the words soft on her tongue. "It makes me want to smile and cry simultaneously. Each memory of beauty is accompanied by another of shadows." She leaned her head against the headboard and closed her eyes. "I can hardly believe I'm home," she said. "It still feels strange, as if I'm wearing a garment that doesn't quite fit me anymore."

Edythe reached her hand up and touched Eleanor's chin.

"Did he hurt you?" The question had been asked lightly, but Eleanor could see that Edythe feared the answer.

"No." Eleanor squeezed her sister's fingers. "No. We became partners of sorts, actually."

"Then, how come the scars and sores on your back? Your wrists? Your hands?" Edythe asked.

"The journey home." Eleanor pulled her hand back and covered her wrist instinctively. "I was caught by slavers, but one of Basaal's soldiers rescued me, helping me home at Basaal's request."

"What is he like?" Edythe asked as she set aside her mug and moved closer to Eleanor. "Wil, as Prince Basaal, I mean."

Pausing, Eleanor leaned her head farther back into her pillow. "He has made more of his character than I would have thought possible of anyone in his place. I respect him immensely."

Edythe frowned as if catching a hint in Eleanor's face. "What happened between you?"

"He did not order the raid on Common Field," Eleanor said, forcing the words she had wanted to tell Edythe into the open. "I know you do not want to hear this, but I think you should be aware that the attack was carried out without his orders, and he was furious. His aim in spending time in Aemogen was to negotiate a peaceful surrender so that no lives would be lost. He still carries Blaike's death on his shoulders."

The blood drained from Edythe's face, and she began to absently pick at Eleanor's coverlet, remaining silent while Eleanor watched her movements.

"Do you still mourn Blaike?" Eleanor felt out the words, trying to find a way to discuss his death.

"It has not yet been a year, Eleanor."

"No," Eleanor agreed. "Almost, but not quite."

"There has not been time for grief," Edythe said quietly. "But I do not really wish to discuss it, if you can understand."

"I do," Eleanor confirmed in an instant, "better than you suppose."

Edythe looked to Eleanor's face. "And what about the mark on your left arm?" she asked.

Eleanor had no answer. There were stories she was not ready to tell.

<hr />

Crispin arrived late the next morning.

Eleanor sat at her desk, reading several months of back reports. She had left Edythe to conduct the morning audience, so when she received news of Crispin's arrival, Eleanor directed he should come straight to her private audience chamber. As the door opened and Hastian showed Crispin in, Eleanor almost laughed, moving to greet him. He surprised her by dropping to his knees and bowing his head.

"My Queen."

"Get up and greet me properly," Eleanor exclaimed with a laugh. He stood as he was told, but his air remained stiff and formal, a subject to his queen. As they studied one another, Eleanor realized the quick smile and boyishnness she'd once known in him was now gone, replaced by the heavy new responsibility she could not help but notice weighing down his shoulders. She also noticed that he wore the insignia Gaulter Alden had always worn.

She wondered what he saw in return. Crispin looked as if he would speak but was waiting for her to address him first.

"You have done well," Eleanor complimented him, motioning towards the stacks of hastily written reports on her desk. "I've spent the morning reviewing your reports from the pass. And I am favorably impressed by your leadership and command there."

"Had I not received the encouragement of the council and of Edythe," he explained, "you must believe I would have never assumed this position for myself. Please consider the other worthy men for this post," he added, "which was never mine to take."

The impatient smile that flickered across Eleanor's face felt like a stolen expression of Basaal's. "On old Ainsley, Crispin, you know very well you're the man for the job," she said. "And I couldn't be more pleased. I ask, as your sovereign and your friend, that you remain at your post."

Crispin bowed his head, relieved. "As it pleases you, Eleanor."

Baffled by such a foreign formality in Crispin, Eleanor now soaked in the sound of him speaking her own name. She threw her arms around him and kissed him on the cheek, and he responded like his old self, lifting her to her toes and saying something about needing to feed her more.

Before she dismissed Crispin to wash and change, Eleanor said, "The war council and the fen lords will meet as soon as you are ready. I understand you and Thistle Black have come onto an idea that will benefit us in this fight. I ask that you come prepared to share with me the particulars."

"I will," Crispin said as he bowed. Then Hastian opened the door, and the young war leader passed into the corridor.

"Hastian, how long has Crispin been like this?"

"Your Majesty?" Hastian asked. The Queen's Own furrowed his brow in an exaggerated manner.

"His mood, his bearing," Eleanor said, motioning her hand

towards the door Crispin had just exited through. "This new seriousness."

Hastian cleared his throat. "It's hard to say."

It took time for Eleanor to gather the courage to walk into the library, where her council and all the fen lords were waiting. She was just so…. Well, Eleanor admitted to herself, she didn't know what. But she felt broken into too many pieces and worn thin and uncertain of how to pick her life back up again. After claiming as much self-decided hope as she was able, she entered the room.

Edythe had joined them, her chair at the opposite end of the table from Eleanor's. As Eleanor sat, the rest of the council followed suit. Then she said the first thing that came to mind: "I hope that, this time, someone bothered to search the library."

Aedon and Sean smiled. The fen lords not privy to the joke looked at each other in confusion. Then Crispin stood, his face flushed as he pushed back his chair and walked past Eleanor to search the rows and rows of books.

"We are quite alone, Your Majesty," he said as he bowed upon his return before sitting down in his chair.

"Then, let us begin," Eleanor said as she looked around the table, making eye contact with Thistle Black, who sat at the far end near Edythe. Having not noticed the querulous fen lord before then, Eleanor gave him a private smile, which he returned.

"I'm—it's good to be here, in Aemogen, with all of you. My memories of you kept me filled with courage. Now," she said as she cleared her throat and looked at the table, "to business. I'm sure you have all heard by now that Emperor Shaamil has decided to accompany Prince Basaal to ensure the success of this conquest.

He brings with him only a fraction of his army: six thousand men. Added with the army of Prince Basaal, we now face thirteen thousand.

"Now, I also understand," she continued, "that Crispin and Thistle Black, of the South Mountain fen, have been working on a stratagem involving a new weapon of sorts. Although many of you might already be familiar with the idea, I would like a full report. Crispin?"

Eleanor felt a simultaneous twinge of sadness and pride as Crispin stood, looking older and strained, shuffling the few papers in his hand before looking up.

"After Your Majesty stalled the army at the pass," he began, "Thistle Black and I were investigating the damage done by the lines of powder. The damage was—as you will come to see—immense. So, we began to wonder if the powder could be manipulated in any other ways to aid in our defense," Crispin said, and to Eleanor's relief, he looked up and grinned quite like his old self. "Don't believe Thistle Black when he says this was his idea. I thought of it first."

Thistle Black harrumphed in response.

"I wondered what would happen," Crispin continued, "if the powder were to be placed inside a restricted environment: a metal sphere that one could hold in a hand or a box full of Bryant's blacksmithing scraps. With much care, we began to experiment along the eastern coast."

"And?" Eleanor asked as she raised her eyebrow.

"Devastating," Crispin replied, his grin turning into a steely smile. "Though, you'll probably not forgive me for some of the damage the eastern coast has sustained," he admitted. "The smithies throughout Aemogen have begun the construction of two or three types of this powder weaponry, mainly hollowed spheres that can be filled with powder and lit by a long fuse at a great distance. In the meantime, Lord Thayne has been spending time in Marion, recruiting a small company of mercenaries sympathetic to our cause. We consulted the treasury before offering a price if they agree to help us with our endeavor."

"And what do you plan to do with these powder devices?" Eleanor asked.

"The only thing I believe we can do," Crispin replied, looking around the table before looking back at Eleanor and lifting his chin. "We plan to attack the Imirillian encampment."

Eleanor stood over the map of the Imirillian camp, watching with interest while Crispin laid out his plan before her. The war council also listened without interrupting.

"The Marion Company will—at an appointed time—set the devices here, here, and here," Crispin explained, pointing to each location on the map. "One of them is also a food supplier, bringing in barrels of who knows what almost on a daily basis. We will make quick use of that. Our own team will be prepared to set up a line here," Crispin said, his fingers moving across the map. "And here. And there among the horses, which is where we hope to strike first. Our men will come through the tunnel to Colun Tir, then fan out into the woods to form a solid line. They will later leave the trees under cover of darkness and wait for the explosions to pass before bearing down for the attack. We've already practiced wrapping the reins and such in woolen cloth to mute the noise of the cavalry waiting in the darkness."

"And what if some of the devices go off late?" Eleanor tapped her finger against the map.

"A circumstance we hope to avoid, a chance we take."

"I know from the mining reports that handling powder in any form can be quite dangerous," Eleanor challenged. "Are you certain we can put all of our devices in place without putting the soldiers, the tunnel, or the absolutely necessary element of surprise at risk?"

"Thistle Black and I have some ideas that I have prepared here," Crispin said as he held up a stack of worn papers. "And we will only use teams of experienced miners to set the lines on the night of the invasion."

"Which is?" Eleanor asked.

"Our original plan," Crispin told Eleanor, "was to attack twenty-seven days from now, in the middle of the night. It is the next new moon," he explained. "The valley would be in impenetrable darkness."

"No moon means that Seraagh is on some mission," Eleanor said, then drew a long breath. "That sounds appropriate." Aedon looked curious about her comment, but Eleanor pressed on. "Let's start at the beginning of your plan and walk through each move, in detail, to see if this is even a possibility."

The council met through the rest of the day, working out questions, scenarios, and timing. Placing stones on the map, representing divisions of the Aemogen army, they discussed how best to use their small force. Crispin told Eleanor of the number of powder weapons they had built.

"We are working on a handheld variety," he explained. "But, as you can imagine, it's proven quite dangerous." Pausing, his face turned sober. "We've lost two men over its invention."

"The original plan was brilliant—when we were only going against seven thousand," Eleanor said at length. "Against thirteen, we will have to build in more assurances." She ran her eyes across the scenario they'd envisioned on the map. "If we can," she added.

"Surprise and disruption," Thistle Black said, repeating the opinion he had been sharing all afternoon. "Our success will entirely depend on that. If an army of thirteen thousand breaks through the pass, we've no hope. Either we do this, or we die trying."

"Aedon has told me about your training rotations," Eleanor said, looking towards the bank of windows. Daylight was disappearing fast. "Let us bring all the men into full training at Ainsley. The southern troops must be called up now if we are to be ready in twenty-seven days."

"But what of the crops?" Aedon asked. "It's just as urgent this year as it was last year to put seeds in the ground on time."

"The situation has changed," Eleanor stated. "Women and children must finish the work."

"Can they plant enough food to sustain us through this coming year? With all the struggles the inevitable drought will bring—"

"They must," Eleanor said, cutting Aedon short. "If we want to preserve Aemogen, it is time for all of us to do more than is possible. The seed bringers and their assistants must take responsibility for aiding the women and children to plant the fields."

Aedon's mouth worked silently, but his face looked resigned, and he nodded. "You are right," he said. "I only wish that you weren't."

"We've heard some of the miners saying they won't close down their mines to come," Thistle Black growled. "Not many, but a few up and down the line."

Eleanor looked at Thistle Black without blinking. "I will send a fen rider with a message to all mining fens that the mines will be shut down—effective immediately—save the closest mines which may provide raw materials to our blacksmiths. If the other mines fail to follow suit, I will charge whatever man that refuses with high treason, and he will hang from the west tower."

Eleanor knew the men were taken aback with her abruptness.

"Is there anything else that we have left undone for this afternoon?" she asked. Eleanor looked at each man on the council. They avoided her eyes but did not move. "What is it?"

Crispin looked at Aedon, then back at Eleanor before he spoke. "We all want to know what happened to you, Eleanor."

Silence filled the room.

Eleanor looked at the men before her, friends, councillors, pillars that had held her up through the first years of her reign. Her eyes met Edythe's. Considering what she should tell them, Eleanor lifted her hand to the back of her neck, moving her fingers over the scars there. She breathed out and leaned back.

"All right," she said.

Eleanor began her tale. She told them of waiting for Basaal, having him hand her Aedon's note, and starting their journey to Marion City. "I could not accept Staven's offer," Eleanor said and then paused. "Every instinct in me felt it to be a false direction for the people of Aemogen."

Then she spoke of their journey north, describing the stone sea, the Aronee desert, the long nights in the desert, and Annan's kindnesses to her.

"Despite the fever, I will never forget my first view of Zarbadast." Eleanor paused, remembering the vision of its pulsing, burning coals, spread across the golden sands and of Basaal helping her to stand, placing his arm about her waist.

Next, she spoke of the people, the city, and the seven palaces of Zarbadast. Eleanor told them of the emperor's challenge in great detail. Both Crispin and Aedon listened more intently as she described Basaal's fight and her mind games with Emperor Shaamil.

Eleanor pressed on to her escape, describing Dantib and their trek through the desert. The men's faces were attentive as Eleanor spoke of being captured by the Shera Shee slavers, enduring Dantib's death, finding Sharin, and suffering injuries from the chains and the whips.

Eleanor spoke of Zanntal with great warmth, explaining how Basaal had sent him, and describing how Zanntal had paid off the slavers and helped her and Sharin through the desert then over the Arimel Mountains.

It was dark when Eleanor finished. Every detail shared. Every moment recorded except two, the morning that Eleanor sealed Prince Basaal's Safeeraah and the fact that the wedding did happen before Eleanor's escape. Of these she said not a word.

Sean was the first to speak. "It sounds like Wil, Prince Basaal, I mean, acted honorably."

"Honorable?" Crispin said, choking on the word. "He's the enemy who seeks our destruction. He's our foe and the reason Eleanor has experienced such an ordeal. There are no thanks or praise owed in his direction. Did he aid our queen? Yes. But his campaign still continues on the other side of those mountains," Crispin said as he pointed towards the western windows. "His army still waits to subjugate our people and steal our sovereignty."

Eleanor flushed. She had spoken little of Basaal, for she did not want to listen to the opinions of others about him. It was difficult enough to sort out her own knotted thoughts. Eleanor sat to one side of her chair and raised her hand to her forehead.

"I think," Aedon said slowly, "that Sean was addressing the

basic idea that Prince Basaal not only did all he could to ensure Eleanor's safety and protection but also refused to act in a way that would remove himself from the leadership of this conquest, thereby preventing his father or brothers from repeating what has happened too many times before to other countries."

Aedon took a quick breath, then continued. "He has sought to preserve Aemogen as best he could while honoring the obligations of his birth," he argued. "He even spent six months trying to convince us to surrender so that it might be a bloodless conquest. And, when we would not listen," Aedon added, "he trained our men to fight. He is not without honor—"

Crispin balked, but Aedon lifted his hand, his voice quavering in anger. "I do not excuse him for any wrongs and deceptions or for the *pain*—" Aedon said, the word flickering like a flame in his voice, "that the queen endured as a result of his treachery. I only say the man is not without honor."

Aedon stood, as if he could not handle sitting any longer. No servants had yet entered to light the lanterns or candles, and his face was difficult to outline against the dark windows.

"There is nothing else for us to do this evening," Eleanor said as she also stood, her fingers pressing softly against the mark in her skin, hidden beneath her sleeve.

"At least the view is tolerable," Ammar said before he dropped the curtain of the tent back across the doorway and returned inside. Basaal followed, none too fondly, after receiving a faceful of tassels.

Shaamil sat in conversation with his Vestan, occasionally looking towards Basaal and Ammar, each having claimed an elegant couch. Ammar sat reading a scroll. But Basaal draped himself comfortably across the couch with one of his legs hanging over the armrest while the other tapped the beat to an Imirillian folk tune on the rug. Basaal hoped his nonchalance would cover the questions he was turning over in his mind. If he was not to lead his army into Aemogen, then surely the Illuminating God must have some plan, an alternative that would present itself in Basaal's thoughts.

Once Basaal had decided he would do what was asked of him, he had pleaded in prayer for direction—for understanding. Nothing. Nothing had come. And so, Basaal began to run through the options in his own mind. He could run, leave Marion, leave Imirillia, and disappear. If he did this, the emperor would commandeer his troops and his assets, directing or dispersing them as he pleased. Also, he could never return to Zarbadast, and there would be no way to ensure that his men would be taken care of. Not a promising option.

If he led a rebellion, ordering his troops to not fight, the emperor would have Basaal killed. Or, if Basaal's army remained loyal to him, then the Imirillian forces would kill each other in a desperate civil war. He would be executed or would have to seek exile far from the reach of the Imirillian Empire which was "impossible."

The word was unintentionally spoken aloud by Basaal to the silence of the tent.

"What was that?" Ammar asked.

"Nothing," Basaal said, returning his thoughts to his problem. Earlier, he had called a meeting with his own officers, the emperor and his generals, and to Basaal's distaste, the Vestan. But Basaal had been left unsatisfied with the reports of their progress at the pass. They were to meet again that afternoon, but he wished he could go himself to see—

Basaal swung his leg down from across the armrest and stood, pulling at his fingers. Shaamil dismissed the Vestan, and his eyes followed Basaal.

"Father," Basaal said. "I am going to postpone the meeting planned for this afternoon."

"And, why is that?" Shaamil asked.

Basaal walked to the refreshments table and poured himself a drink. "The reports are insufficient for my taste," he explained. "And I'm not the military leader to sit and wait, as it is. I wish to assess the progress for myself. I will ride out to the pass and view what progress has been made, which I will then report upon my return. You can see the mountain across the valley—it's close enough. I'll ride out this afternoon, inspect the operations, and spend a night or two in our encampment there, for morale, and all of that. When I return, in two days' time, we will continue our war council."

Shaamil's eyes narrowed, as if he was guessing something Basaal could not get at.

"You do not approve?" Basaal drained his glass and faced his father.

"I do not disapprove."

"It's settled then," Basaal stated. "I will come and say good-bye once I have gathered my things."

Basaal left the tent in search of Annan to ask if his friend would ride out with him part of the way. In case Basaal decided the only way to obey the word of the Illuminating God was to run, to disappear entirely from this place, he wanted to feel prepared. And that meant saying good-bye.

Later, wearing his full assortment of weaponry, Basaal mounted his horse and set off across the valley with Annan at his side. For the first time in Basaal's life, he saw no clear options before him, and his only recourse against the overwhelming impossibility was a wave after wave of adrenaline rushing through his veins. He almost felt giddy, the vaporous result of throwing himself into a plan he had no idea how to calculate getting into his head.

He pushed Refigh hard, challenging Annan to a race, playfully hurling insult after insult back on the wind toward his friend in challenge. When Basaal finally pulled Refigh up short, and Annan had caught up to him, Basaal was grinning at the freshnness of the day, his cheeks red from the cold edge on the spring wind.

"It's still a bit brisk out here," Basaal said. "I can hardly imagine what a winter must be like."

"Cold," Annan said, then he changed the subject. "What, exactly, has made you so…*exuberant* today?"

Basaal laughed and decided to speak honestly with this friend. "I have never felt quite so desperate, so split and trapped. And suddenly, everything strikes me as absurd or meaningless. But," he added, "despite the futility of all this struggle, you'll have to admit it is a beautiful day."

Annan's face creased, but he did not speak. They settled into a steady pace, with Basaal occasionally remarking on the mountains, Marion, and the conquest. Annan did not answer often, but Basaal could see that his friend continued to worry.

"You can turn back here," Basaal told Annan. "You've come just over halfway, and I will feel better, knowing you are back at camp, keeping an eye on things."

"And you are certain you do not need me to come to the pass?"

"Yes." Basaal nodded. "A few days, and I will be back, ready to face the emperor with a clear head and, hopefully, a better idea of how to do what is asked of me."

Annan looked at Basaal quizzically, but he turned his mount.

Basaal paused now, the wind ripping across his face, and reached his hand out, clasping Annan's forearm. Annan wrapped his fingers around Basaal's.

"Life unto death, as one soul, fealty forever," Basaal said, repeating their oath. Then he leaned closer to his friend and, hands still clasped, reached his other arm around Annan, embracing him as much as he could. "Until we meet again."

As they pulled away from each other, Annan again looked at Basaal strangely. "Go with the Illuminating God."

Basaal felt a smile of trepidation on his face. The giddiness had passed, and he could again feel the weight of what lay ahead. "I endeavor to do so," Basaal assured him.

Then they parted: Annan, towards the camp on the plain, and Basaal, to the mountains.

Snow still hung along the higher peaks. And as Basaal rode through the foothills, he encountered cold patches of ice and stiff snow. When he was close enough to see the pass, it was vastly different than what it had been. Yet, as he stared at the crumbled stones settled into its place, Basaal could not quite remember how it had looked the first time he had ridden through it.

A soldier at the entrance hailed the prince. "Your Grace,"

Basaal nodded down at the man. "I've come to see for myself the progress made. Where will I find your officers?"

"Your Grace will come upon the Imirillian encampment around this bend. It is a safe distance from where we are working, and the Aemogen archers cannot reach it."

Evening was setting early in the canyon, and Basaal pulled his cloak around himself as he urged Refigh up the road. A second guard hailed him, bowing before Basaal and pointing him on towards the camp.

"How many guards patrol this part of the mountain?" Basaal asked the second guard.

"A dozen guards maintain posts en route while a company rides through every hour," the guard informed him. "Any curious Marions, including a company of King Staven's guards, have been turned away directly," he added. "Most have gone without a fight."

"And how many soldiers work on clearing a way through the rubble?" Basaal asked. "I believe that Annan reported a few hundred."

"Just a small number," the guard answered. "Three hundred, as there is very little space to work in."

Basaal acknowledged the answer and then continued up the road. Camp lit up before him as he came around a slight bend to the right. Then a trumpet sounded, and the men stood at attention. A cold evening colored blue the remaining light, and the mountains smelled fresh and crisp. Basaal rode to the center of camp, dismounted, and greeted the two senior officers, who had come out to meet him upon hearing the trumpet.

Basaal ate with the officers, asking them questions, taking hold of the important details, and exchanging stories. These were all his men, and he knew them well, for they had ridden with him for almost five years now. After eating, the talk turned towards speculation and conversation determined by mood and interest rather than strategic planning.

Basaal should have been more comfortable as he sat in the tent with his officers. But he wasn't. His weaponry strangled his thoughts, his clothing felt uncomfortable, and Basaal could not settle himself in mind or body.

"Is our young prince restless?" the eldest officer asked with deference.

"Yes," Basaal admitted. "Quite restless, I am afraid."

"He's missing the young wife," another officer joked, something he would have never uttered save at a war camp around a fire, where those rules of decorum loosened with the flames.

Basaal raised his eyebrows and shrugged, muttering something comic as he played along with the joke. Annan had mentioned that rumors of Eleanor's disappearance had spread among the men, but many seemed reluctant to believe it, and so Basaal would give no confirmation.

"I may go out for another ride," Basaal said as he yawned and stretched. "My horse will not forgive me, but I cannot settle. No need to wait up," he added, "as I can find my own way to a bed."

This statement elicited another comment from one of the officers about Basaal's marriage bed, and the officers gave a laugh as Basaal stood and called for Refigh to be saddled. All the men stood as well.

"Ride safe, young prince," the older officer said as they saluted Basaal. "We will wait for your return."

CHAPTER

EIGHT

Basaal pulled Refigh to a quick stop, breathing hard, his heart pounding. The Safeeraah stuck to the sweat of his forearms as he pulled off his quiver and bow and then removed his cloak, wrapping it around itself and putting it in his saddlebag. He placed his weaponry again over his shoulders and drew another long, cold breath. Spring was well upon them, and yet, the mountain air still carried the crisp taste of frost. What a feeling. He almost wished he could spend a winter in this part of the world.

A myriad of stars surrounded the slivered moon, the depth of the night ennobling them in their brightness. Basaal patted Refigh's neck, thanking the horse for his run and, now, for his patience. In the quiet serenity of the blue night, Basaal had finally achieved peace. He looked back at the moon, set among the stars, and thought of the night when Eleanor had found him during the Battle Run and he had told her of Seraagh.

Eleanor.

Basaal walked Refigh through the darkness of the plain and looked down the mountain range to his left, towards the tower he had come across last summer, where he had sworn to Aedon that Eleanor would return in safety. Was anybody there? he wondered. There was no light to be had, and Basaal tried to judge where on the mountain the forgotten fortress would be.

It wasn't too far, surely. Enough distance that no Imirillian patrol would have found it, yet close enough that he could reach it in an hour's time. It primed Basaal's curiosity, his knowledge of this fortress and the fact that there was another way through the mountain into Aemogen.

Basaal cleared his throat and leaned forward in his saddle. Perhaps whatever Aemogen guard was stationed at the tower would have news of whether Eleanor had made it home to Aemogen. His heart played a sharp tattoo, and against all good judgment, Basaal began to entertain the idea of reconnoiter. He knew full well that the last time he had tried to investigate the tower, it had only served him to be captured. Basaal turned Refigh back towards the encampment in the pass, looking a bit wistfully at the dark mountain and towards the tower.

He could know tonight. Basaal could know if Eleanor had returned—tonight.

Basaal's knowledge of the terrain and of the layout of the tower was speculative at best. What a fool's errand, he thought as he smiled at himself. It was dark, though, and he could take his time. In a few hours, he could know. And then, if he decided to follow through with his half-mad thought, Basaal could get on with the business of disappearing from this place.

"Or die at my father's hand when I refuse to mobilize my men," he muttered at the darkness. "Which would be much more honorable."

Basaal pulled his jaw to the side and looked from the pass to the heavily wooded mountains on his left. Then he pulled at Refigh's reins and headed towards the hidden Aemogen tower.

Judging the distance as best he could after entering the wood, Basaal found a quiet, secluded thicket and tied Refigh in place.

"I won't be long," he whispered, securing his quiver and bow to Refigh's saddlebag. His sword and knives he kept on his person.

The faint moonlight held no sway over the forest floor as Basaal picked his way along, careful, quiet, knowing that this fool's errand could take half the night and still not offer up the results he desired. Soon enough, Basaal came across an old, half grown-over road, leading up the hillside. He stayed in the trees above the road, trusting it to lead him near the fortress tower.

Spent leaves from the previous year gathered in thickets and patches. Basaal took more care, frustrated. Sand made no such bother. Pausing often, he could hear nothing save for what he hoped was the odd woodland creature. Above these random scuttlings, the woods hung with silence. He began to feel cold.

After what felt like hours, a dark, silent shape rose up through the bramble of trees. The tower. Basaal paused mid-movement, all his efforts focusing on quieting his breathing. There appeared to be no life, no guard, and no evidence that anyone had set foot there for years. But Basaal knew this was not the case, so he waited.

An hour passed. Nothing.

Basaal's feet burned from holding still for so long, and he finally shifted forward, feeling along the solid rocks and quiet avenues of ground with his boots. He had come up to the rear of the fortress, where an old stable lay, heaving under the weight of the many years it had been served neglect. Basaal dropped down and pressed himself against the stones of the stable.

Again he waited. Nothing.

Silently calling down every Imirillian blessing he knew, Basaal touched the Safeeraah on his arm and then, ghostlike, crossed the deserted courtyard. Pausing by the open mouth of the tower's back entrance, he hesitated only a moment before disappearing inside.

———◦⟨◦⟨◦⟨◦⟩◦⟩◦⟩◦———

Eleanor woke with a start. She breathed out in the darkness and waited for her eyes to adjust before shifting in her bed. The moonlight shone very little through her windows, and almost all was black. She had thought she had seen a figure, a black figure, moving throughout the palace. Eleanor turned on her side and stared at the arched windows, a frown on her tired face, wrinkled with sleep. No, he had not been in the palace, she realized, though the corridor had been familiar. It was a strange dream, and Eleanor closed her eyes to will herself back to sleep.

And then she remembered. The man had been walking through the halls of Colun Tir. Eleanor froze with fear. Their entire plan rested on the secrecy of that tower. A bolt surged through her. Throwing her blankets off, she sat up, swinging her legs over the edge of the bed, breathing heavily.

"It was a dream," Eleanor whispered as she wiped the cold sweat from her forehead. "It was a dream."

———◦⟨◦⟨◦⟨◦⟩◦⟩◦⟩◦———

Empty. Basaal moved through each narrow hallway and searched every room, finding no trace of habitation. Several storerooms were filled with barrels, old or new he could not tell. But Basaal found no passage. Breathing out, he drummed his fingers against a cold stone. Somehow the Aemogens could get through the mountain. If the tunnel did not connect to the tower, then where was it? The stables? Somewhere out in the woods?

Walking soundlessly back through the corridors and down the stairs, Basaal snaked his way through the courtyard towards the stable. Then a branch snapped in the darkness.

Basaal froze and crouched down, moving the remaining distance in two low strides. He slumped against the wall beside a worn, misshapen woodpile. All was quiet. His eyes traveled through the darkness but could see no one. Cursing himself silently, Basaal knew it was time to find his way back down the mountain. He would have to leave, Eleanor's unknown fate a stinging burden.

As he was about to leave, another sound came from the woods nearby. Pausing, Basaal watched the trees. Then it happened: a light appeared, a brief flicker of flame. Then it was gone. Basaal felt his pulse racing up his neck. He should go. All common sense told him that he should return to the camp in the pass. But he was compelled—by something utterly irrational—to follow.

The light flickered again in the distance. And Basaal pursued it in silence through a small glade and over a stream, bubbling up from the ground, the only part of the dark wood able to catch and toss back the moonlight. He pressed the toes of his boots into the soft earth, careful to avoid the detritus of leaves and twigs left after winter. His eyes grabbed at every visual anchor available, until they settled on a crag beyond the trees.

After waiting for a good while, hearing nothing and seeing no flicker of light, Basaal moved stealthily towards the rough outcropping, looking for any passage or trail. There was none. Cold to the touch, the stone of the crag felt solid beneath his fingers, unyielding, with no hint of a passage.

He moved himself along the rock face until, so subtle and set back that he almost passed it by, he saw a crevice large enough for a man, perhaps even large enough for a horse. He slipped through it and paused, his ears straining for any hint he was not alone. Nothing came. Basaal went farther in.

And there, to the left of the crevice, out of sight to any curious eye unwilling to explore, appeared the shape of a large door, set back into the rock. Ignoring the shivers now settling in his spine like a cool frost, Basaal reached his hand out. Solid wood, hidden hinges, strong—and the door, Basaal discovered, was open.

A two-inch slash of deep black revealed that it had not been closed properly. Was it an accident? Had the person sneaking through the woods hurried in, forgetting he had not secured it? Or was it a trap? Basaal pulled his fingers away from the opening as if they'd been burned.

Impossible, Basaal thought. No one could have heard him, or seen him. He waited, torn between his instinct to run and his desire to see what he might find out. No noise came from the other side of the door. It was as silent as any tomb Basaal had known. Minutes passed, each second ticking in time with the pulse in his throat. He pressed his fingers against the door, applying just enough pressure to feel an almost unnoticeable shift. There was no sound. The hinges, Basaal guessed, had been oiled.

Basaal wrapped his fingers around the thick door and pushed it open just wide enough for him to slip into the darkness beyond. It was blacker than pitch inside. He slid himself over to the back of the open door, hiding in its shadow. The air inside the mountain passage had a thin smell, laced with minerals and time. Basaal could hear the sound of water dripping, echoing sharply in the distance.

Blinking rapidly several times, he waited for his eyes to catch hold of anything. But the darkness would not give, and he dare not move forward without a light. A drop of sweat moved down Basaal's face, and he cursed this slip of judgment. What was he doing here? It was time to return to the Imirillian camp.

With a decided step, he moved back outside into the dim moonlight. It appeared almost bright after the deep black of the mountain passage. Basaal wanted to run, forcing himself to move through the woods as cautiously as he dared until he again approached the tower. Going around the back of the stables, he worked his way back down the mountain towards Refigh.

After what felt like a long descent, Basaal paused to gather his breath and his thoughts, to stop the pounding in his heart, and to take stock of where he was. There, through the trees, he could see the road that would lead back down to his horse. Blowing his spent breath from his lungs, Basaal almost smiled.

What a fool. What a lucky fool. He uttered a prayer of thanks and then stepped forward towards the road.

Someone grabbed his arm and pulled him back, hard.

With a trained response to his panic, Basaal brought his free elbow down on his assailant's arm, and there was a crack and a pained grunt. He was free for only a moment before what felt like a thousand hands tore him from the moonlight and ripped him into the darkness of a nearby bramble. Basaal struggled against what felt like an entire company of soundless aggressors, blind in the darkness.

After solidly connecting with the faces of three more men, Basaal was thrown onto his back, slamming his spine against a tree root. Then, in a rush of sound, he was pinned by half a dozen men. His hands were bound before him. Then someone else punched him hard once—then again.

Basaal spit blood, swearing, and breathed out in the Aemogen language, "I'm bound, you idiot! I'll not give you any more trouble."

After one more solid smack, a gag was forced over his mouth. It tasted like mildew, and he tried, fruitlessly, to spit it out. They pulled him away from the tree, someone holding a knife at his back as they stripped him of all his weapons. It was a thorough search: not a knife was left in place.

Then he heard a hiss and saw a small flicker of light appear before his eyes. After spending half of his night in the dark woods, this single flame was painfully bright, and Basaal shut his eyes as they watered against its brilliance.

"I don't believe it," a voice said.

Then another man murmured something about a traitor.

Basaal's head hurt, and he scowled as he continued to blink the tears from his eyes. The effect, he was certain, made it seem as if he was crying. He tried to laugh and ended up choking on the dryness from the gag. He coughed. What a pathetic sight he must be.

The flame went out.

"What do we do with him?"

"We take him back as a prisoner," came the answer. "Quick, let's get away from here before any other damn Imirillians find their way up the mountain."

They forced him to stand, marching him back up to the tower more quietly than Basaal had been, as they were accustomed to the mountains. Basaal watched for any opportunity, any chance of escape, but he had half a dozen men around him, who did not leave him unattended for one moment from the time they captured him until the time when they brought him to the stone face of the mountain and forced him back through the open door in the crevice. Basaal stared at the deep blackness, listening to the sounds of those familiar with the space moving through it. Then the door was locked, and he was forced to the ground against the wall.

"You move, and you die," came a warning from a voice that sounded familiar.

The quick rush of a flame filled the air as a torch light flared into being. Basaal lifted his bound hands to cover his eyes, and when they had adjusted, he looked around him. He was in a carved mountain room, leading off into the darkness in two directions, and half a dozen soldiers stared at him in shock.

A man that Basaal recognized from the castle guard stepped forward just as a sound came from outside the door—a whistle, then a sequence of knocks. The torch was extinguished, and no one moved. After a bottomless minute, the same sequence was repeated with a slight variety.

"It's him," someone said, and the locks were opened. As the soldiers pulled the door open, a shadow entered. They latched it shut immediately.

The man muttered something—a password, perhaps—and the torch was again lit. Whispers rattled above Basaal's head. He heard the name Wil being said. And when he looked up, the shadow stood gawking at him.

"On the grave of Ainorra Breagha, it is you," the man said.

These words came from a hunched over, grotesque looking man with teeth askew and a crooked nose: dirty and stringy, a vagabond seller of sorts. But his voice did not match his bent and filthy exterior. It carried the fine tenor of a well-bred gentleman.

"You don't recognize me, do you?" the man asked. "Well,

turnabout is fair play, or so they say."

The man removed his teeth, and Basaal started as the grotesque figure began to melt away. He detached his nose and removed two large patches of sunburned skin from his face. Then the stranger grimaced as he stripped off the thick eyebrows from his own brow. Finally, he stripped his coat away, having been stuffed and filled. Free of this restrictive garment, the stranger stood up straighter. And with the sweep of his hand, he stripped off his grimy wig to reveal beautiful hair of silver.

The man breathed deeply. Thayne. It was Thayne of Allarstam, Telford's younger brother and, therefore, Basaal's own cousin. Thayne rubbed his hand across the stubble on his chin and turned to the soldier behind him.

"Successful in every way, Ansell," Thayne said to a soldier beside him. "I am supposed to report to Ainsley, and you well know I am eager to get back." Thayne waved towards Basaal. "How did this come about?"

Hushed and hurriedly, Ansell related how they'd taken the prince. To Basaal's chagrin, they had been aware of him since he first approached the towers. Basaal leaned his head back against the stone and made the sound of a sigh. Thayne glanced at him sharply, then back as the captain finished.

"And what does he have to say for himself?" Thayne asked, looking at the gag in Basaal's mouth.

"It just all happened. We've had no time to do anything save let you into the tunnel."

"Yes, well." Thayne folded his arms. "I am going to take him back into a storeroom while your men prepare us dinner. The prisoner eats, too," Thayne added, seeing the soldier's expression. "Get to it. I'll find out if he came alone."

Two soldiers lifted Basaal to his feet. He was pushed behind Thayne through the twists and turns of the cavern. Storerooms, indeed, they were, but Basaal could not see what was concealed in the packages and crates or what was piled in the corners. In a small room with a table, a handful of chairs, and a few candles, Thayne lifted a candle to the torch, and after it lit, sent the guards on their way.

"I shan't need you," he assured them as he lit several more candles, melted onto the table with their own wax. Then Thayne offered Basaal a seat, and he removed the gag. "I trust there will be no shouting and carrying on," he asked as if he already knew the answer.

"Thank you," Basaal said as he wiped his face on his sleeve. Thayne did not unbind his hands. Sitting down across the table from Basaal, Thayne set his face in an amused frown.

"And so, my ghost returns," Thayne said. "Are you flesh and blood this time or merely an apparition?"

Basaal knew Thayne expected no answer, and he gave none.

"Telford was right," Thayne said. "I was a blind fool to have not known you as Edith's son. A few times, the thought pressed on my mind, but I was in too much disbelief. How could it be? So, I gave up the thought. But my, you carry her eyes and her face. Those cheekbones," he added, "handsomest trait of the family, I'm afraid."

"How about if we skip the formalities and cut through the questioning as well?" Basaal said briskly, leaning back in his chair, staring at the dirty but elegant figure of his older cousin. "I am alone. No one knows I am here. I've never revealed—neither to any member of my military staff nor to my family nor to any friend that I know—the existence of this passage or of the towers.

And my horse is tethered farther down the abandoned road in the woods. Did I answer all of your questions?"

"Not quite," Thayne said as he folded his arms and looked with disapproval at Basaal. "I see you have no desire to discuss our common connection or your mother, so we will move on to far less agreeable topics."

Basaal raised his eyebrows to disagree with Thayne but then altered his face to an impassive expression.

Thayne's eyes narrowed, but it was in pain not anger. "Why am I to believe you?"

"I'm not without honor," Basaal said as he lifted his sleeve again to his face. His nose was running. The moment struck him as a odd, a bit funny. He fought back a desperate smile. Thayne's eyes missed the smile, for he was surveying the Safeeraah along Basaal's forearms.

"Hotheaded, brash, self-serving," Thayne said, ticking off a list of negative attributes. "All of these I grant your character readily. But foolish ness? Carelessness? No. So, why are you here?"

"I was curious," Basaal said as he shifted.

"Son, if we are going to be straight, let us be straight. Curiosity never bound an Imirillian royal to do anything without good purpose behind it. Why did you come up?"

Basaal leaned his head back and lifted his bound hands to cover his eyes. Curiosity may not have ever bound an Imirillian royal, but pride had. And his own pride was insisting he not reveal his heart to this man.

The sound of footsteps came down the tunnel into the hewn-out room, and their food was delivered: dried apples and pears, dried meat, bread, and a little cheese. Thayne nodded to the soldier as he set the food before them. Basaal watched from behind his hands, searching desperately for any plan of escape that might come into his mind. Before the soldier could leave, Thayne made a motion and spoke. "Tell your captain that the prince has a horse in the woods, away down the tower road. Bring the beast back, and erase any trail that you can. We must act soon if the tower is to appear abandoned before daybreak. The trees must also be put back in place. We've four hours yet before morning."

"Yes, sir." The soldier nodded. "We will see it all taken care of."

The trees needed to be put back in place? Basaal wanted to ask about this odd allusion to camouflage, but he did not.

"Let us not waste time," Thayne said. He looked at his food but did not touch it. "What brought you on this fool's errand?"

"I swear," Basaal shot back in frustration. "Is this a family trait?" Basaal lowered his hands from his face. "Between you and that brother of yours, I've been asked more stupid questions—" He trailed off, almost expecting Thayne to laugh, to respond with something clever, and to ask the question again, as Telford would have done. Instead, Thayne's face froze, and he matched Basaal's glare with one of his own.

"Get on with the facts," he warned, "if you wish to be spared the uncomfortable realities of being a prisoner of war in Aemogen." Thayne's voice was as cold as his Marion eyes were blue.

"I, quite foolishly, wanted to know if I could find out any information regarding the return of the queen to Aemogen," Basaal replied. "Don't believe me, by any means, but it is the truth of the matter," he said flatly.

"Eleanor?" Thayne pressed. "Returned?"

"That is what I came here to find out. The original plan we had arranged—for her to sail down the eastern coast—fell apart. And, by chance or by the grace of the Illuminating God, I came to know that she had been taken into a rather dangerous part of the empire. So, I sent one of my best soldiers to find her."

"Taken?" Thayne's jaw tightened.

"By slavers," Basaal admitted, sounding much more calm about that prospect than he had ever felt.

Thayne leaned forward, resting his elbows on the table, his eyes relentlessly boring into Basaal's own. "So," he said, "you are telling me that you, Prince Basaal, came up here in search of news of Eleanor's fate with what—less than a month's time before battle? Thirteen thousand men are waiting to decimate Aemogen, and you chose to go on a self-indulgent field trip to see if your enemies' monarch was safe in her bed?"

Basaal looked at Thayne and did not answer. He was already cursing his own stupidity, so Thayne's mocking disbelief wasn't necessary.

"Eat," Thayne ordered as he began to pick slowly at his own food. Basaal lifted his bound wrists expectantly. After chewing on a piece of bread and swallowing, Thayne nodded towards the prince.

"Your arms still work, I presume."

Grumbling in Imirillian, Basaal began the uncomfortable process of looking like a complete fool.

"Have you heard back from your soldier, the one you sent to find Eleanor?" Thayne asked while playing with a piece of dried fruit.

"No," Basaal answered sharply, giving up on his food and dropping it back down on the table. He settled back against his chair with a flourish to indicate he was not interested in looking like a captive monkey while eating.

"You say you had planned a route to the East?" Thayne pressed.

"I promised Aedon I would see her escape," Basaal replied. "Zarbadast was the first opportunity with any likelihood that she—or I, for that matter—would stay alive. She left the city with my most trustworthy friend and confidant well over two months ago now. I can't—" he faltered. The memory of Eleanor interrupted Basaal's thoughts, and he looked down towards the floor, remembering the moment when he had opened his hands and watched her fall into the darkness below.

"On Old Ainsley, Telford was right." Thayne's voice sounded uncomfortable—thoughtful.

"About what?" Basaal asked.

"You're still in love with her."

With a string of Imirillian curses coming from his mouth, Basaal kicked the table in front of him, sending his plate rattling across the wood. Several candles toppled, leaving only one flame standing. He looked away from Thayne, angry. Invaded.

Thayne's frown deepened. "Dear me."

Time passed, and neither man touched his food. Thayne appeared to be thinking through a bevy of internal details with no intention of speaking to Basaal. Basaal, in turn, should have been planning his escape but found nothing but blankness. The only thought rattling around his mind was how impertinent Thayne's assumptions were. The bastard.

After some time, Thayne picked up the toppled candles, relit them, and set them upright back on the table.

"I'm not really a man of war, you know," Thayne said. "So I make this possible breach of secrecy for humanity's sake and because I know for certain that we are not going to let you go."

Basaal continued to stare anywhere else but at Thayne.

"Yesterday morning we received notice that Eleanor has indeed returned to Aemogen."

A bolt, a crack—something sharp split Basaal's chest, and he closed his eyes, leaning forward, covering his face as best he could.

"By now," Thayne continued, "she should have reached Ainsley Rise. I am leaving, come morning, for the castle."

These words fell on the table between them, for Basaal scarcely heard anything Thayne had said. Basaal took several deep breaths, muttering the words of a ritual prayer to steady himself. Eleanor. Eleanor was safe. Calmness began to smooth out every sharp edge of anxiety he had carried with him. His promise was fulfilled, and there was only one thing now for Basaal to do: figure his own destiny, be it escape or death. His honor had now answered for everything else. A smile born of relief crossed his face, and he sat up straight.

"What do you plan to do with me?"

"Take you as prisoner to Ainsley."

"To my death?"

"I won't deny it's a possibility," Thayne replied.

Basaal shrugged. "Then, let's get to it."

CHAPTER
NINE

A few days passed before Eleanor relieved Edythe of the morning audience.

"I don't know why I should feel nervous," she confided to her sister the first morning she'd decided to return. Edythe gave Eleanor a stabilizing smile.

"There will not be many matters to address," Edythe assured her. "Preparations for war have taken the space of so many things, and requesting an audience is made up of the everyday. I shouldn't wonder if you've only one or two people to see at all."

But word must have spilled down the Ainsley stair and into the city that Eleanor was to attend morning audience, for the throne room was full of people, waiting for a glimpse of their returned queen. Eleanor wore a bright blue gown that Miya had taken in at the waist, according to the fashions of her gowns from Calafort. Eleanor hoped the results would give the illusion that she'd not lost so much weight. That it did not do.

"Don't take too much time with alterations, Miya," Edythe had said, shaking her head. "We hope to be letting those darts out within the month."

There were very few requests—and nothing extraordinary—until the acting captain of the guard came forward. He was a young man recommended by Crispin, whom Eleanor was deciding upon.

"There has been a serious altercation in the streets of Ainsley," he reported. "Both men have been brought to the castle for trial."

"Bring them in," Eleanor said with a wave, certain that altercations happened all the time in Zarbadast, and Shaamil never bothered. The thought was amusing.

The first man Eleanor did not recognize; the second, she knew all too well.

"Thistle Black," Eleanor said as she set her elbows on her armrests and leaned slightly forward. "You have been fighting in the streets of Ainsley? Who is this poor man to have aroused such ire?"

Aedon, who sat along the western wall with the rest of the council, almost laughed at Thistle Black's ready humility.

"I've no desire to be a friend of this rogue," Thistle Black explained. "And I do not even know his name."

"Sir?" Eleanor said. "Yes, you with the swollen eye. What is your name?"

"Rols, Your Majesty," the man replied as he bowed farther his already bent head.

"And what caused you to catch the anger of Thistle Black?" she inquired. The man, Rols, kept staring hard at the floor, his cheeks burning. "Thistle Black, what happened?" Eleanor insisted, her face dropping its humor.

"This man was speaking lies in the streets, Your Majesty," Thistle Black said. "And I wanted to show my, ah, disagreement with the tales."

"And what were these lies?" Eleanor asked, her voice turned steely.

"That—" Thistle Black faltered. He looked towards Aedon for a moment, then stubbornly back at the queen. "I'd rather not say."

Eleanor wrapped her fingers around the edge of her armrests. "Speak."

"This man claimed that your virtue had been taken by the men of Zarbadast," Thistle Black explained. "That they'd...well, I would rather not say. But I felt it my right"—he paused for emphasis—"my *duty*, to defend the honor of your name, Majesty."

Whispers filled the throne room like the sound of a rushing river.

Eleanor's expression flickered, and she turned an iron gaze on Rols. The man was visibly sweating and trembling, the redness on his pock marked cheekbones turning a deeper shade of scarlet. Eleanor glanced at Aedon, who looked like he would kill the man if he'd been given the chance.

"Look at me, Rols," Eleanor ordered. The man had closed his eyes, but to his credit, he moved his chin up and opened his eyes obediently at his queen. She did not give him a smile. "Have you been to Zarbadast, Rols?"

"No, Your Majesty."

"Then you make a bold claim as to knowing what happened while I was there."

"Yes. I—please," he said, his lip beginning to tremble. "I'd heard—*stories*, just stories, about the city and didn't know."

"No, you did not know," Eleanor said, tilting her head to the side. "And would anything that may or may not have happened cause you to remove your fidelity?"

Rols pressed his lips together, his eyes wide and glass-like. When he spoke, his voice was shaky with emotion. "No, My Queen."

"Well then, I would rather not be discussed in the streets," she said, her voice cold. "But you have not been brought in for slander, rather for fighting." Eleanor moved her eyes to Thistle Black's face. "Neither, I repeat, *neither* of you should have engaged in public brawling. I assume it must have been disruptive or caused property damage for the guard to feel it necessary that I should see you."

"Only the post of a butcher's shop sustained injury," Thistle Black admitted gruffly.

"Well, I'll require a fine to cover the costs of repairs," she said. "And then, I propose that the guard let you cool your heads in my dungeon for a day. Old Ainsley! If grown men cannot control themselves in Aemogen, I've little hope for our chances against the Imirillians." Eleanor pressed her lips together, then looked again towards Rols. "Have you been preparing with the men of Ainsley for battle?"

"Yes, Your Majesty."

"And is there any other reason why I should question your loyalty to myself and to the crown I wear?"

"No, My Queen," he said, and he fell to his knees. "I am as loyal as the day," he said emphatically.

"Remember that," she said, "the next time you are tempted to drag my name through the filth of the street, speaking what is not known, least of all understood." Eleanor could not bear the weight of the room. so she turned towards Thistle Black with a lighter smile, lifting her intonations towards humor. "Thistle Black, next time you feel the need to defend my honor, use that edged tongue of yours rather than those clenched fists. The butchers of Ainsley must not be so put upon. Dismissed."

A soft wave of laughter followed as Eleanor told the guards to take both Rols and Thistle Black to the dungeons. She was glad of the lightened mood and tried to push past the event as soon as she could. What a spectacle.

The final petition was simple, but Eleanor did not give the small farmer much hope. "Were it not a time of war, I could make an immediate decision," she explained. "As we are preparing ourselves to go against the Imirillians, I must first speak with your fen lord, and then we will see if your needs can be met in a timely manner without sacrificing the higher needs of the nation."

As she finished, the doors to the throne room burst open.

"We have him!" a soldier announced. "We caught him at the pass!"

"Who?" Eleanor demanded of the breathless soldier.

"The Imirillian prince!"

Eleanor shot up from her throne just as a company of several men entered. Crispin, hand clenched around Basaal's arm, brought him roughly before Eleanor. Basaal was bound and gagged, and when saw her face, his legs almost gave way, he faltered. Eleanor recognized his stunned expression as relief. Impatiently, Crispin forced Basaal onto his knees before her, and the prince stared ahead blankly, making eye contact with no one.

"My Queen," Crispin said, though he was out of breath. "The men have captured the Imirillian prince near Colun Tir. He claims he was alone and that he is no spy. Aside from his weaponry, this was all he carried on his person." Crispin opened his hand to reveal a small bracelet of gold with three pendants attached to it. Then he threw it to the ground before Basaal.

"Away with you," Eleanor said forcefully, keeping her voice as clear as she was able. "Away with all of you. Crispin, you and your men clear the room and wait outside. Only Hastian needs remain—and Aedon."

Crispin moved to speak, to question her orders, but he checked himself and bowed, clearing the throne room of curious observers before closing the large doors with a sound that echoed inside Eleanor.

Her heart jumped short of its beat as she again looked down at Basaal. Tussled, worn, bruised on his face, his eyes cloaked in a state of no emotion as he knelt before her. He wore his presence well despite all this, that indefinable pride which filled the space around him, reminding her of the might of Zarbadast. Reminding her what it was like to be with him.

Tracing his bent figure with her eyes, Eleanor stepped down from the dais. She knelt before him, her skirts a puddle around her, her knees touching his through the fabric. Eleanor reached her hand hesitantly towards him before she pulled it back. Basaal moved his head up and looked into her face.

With the steadiness of his long breaths as the only sound, Eleanor lifted her hands and moved them around his neck to the knot that held his gag in place, untying it with practiced fingers. Basaal watched her, his eyes wandering from her eyes to her chin. When the gag gave way, her lips quivered as her wrists pressed lightly against the curves of his neck and shoulders.

The line of Basaal's mouth was emphasized by the way his eyebrows were knit together. He appeared resigned, separate, studying her face from some strange distance. As she drew her hands away, briefly touching the skin beneath his jaw, Basaal blinked, and the corners of his mouth turned down.

Pushing the fabric of her full skirt aside, Eleanor found the pendants—so casually tossed to the floor—strung together by the delicate bracelet Basaal had gifted her. She reached down, her fingertips feeling the worn, stone floor before surrounding the ruby and gold tokens. Eleanor lifted them, turning her hand over to look at them: the rising bird, the ruby she'd worn for the wedding ceremony, and the wanderer's mark. They felt heavy in her palm, almost like she was holding a living thing, beating and alive. She felt that it was his heart—or her own.

Her hand was shaking, and she could smell a trace of cinnamon coming from his dirty cloak. Bringing her eyelids down, Eleanor wrapped her fingers around the jewelry in her palm and then lifted her eyes back to his.

"Did they hurt you?" Eleanor asked as she lifted her free hand to the edge of his face, her fingers touching his skin, nervously, like a butterfly.

Basaal hissed in a breath at her touch, flinching, but he did not answer her. Eleanor paled, pulling her hand back, remembering Basaal knelt before her as a prisoner of war, and she was Queen of Aemogen. And she must get away from him, before something in her split apart forever.

She stood, hastily pulling herself to her feet, pressing the pendants into the palm of her hand and shaking her head back and forth. "See that he is settled in the dungeon," she said for either Hastian or Aedon to hear. "In the king's cell."

With the feeling of a fabric ripping between them, Eleanor stepped away, turned, and walked past the dais, disappearing through the door behind the tapestries.

Eleanor went straight to her chambers. Edythe, who was sitting with her embroidery, laid it aside when she saw her sister's face. "Eleanor?" she asked. "What's happened?"

"He was right!" Eleanor choked in near rage. "Oh, Edythe, why didn't I listen?" Her anger came strong and clear. Her teeth clenched, she had tears in her eyes, and her chest burned.

"Who was right?"

"I have been broken, Edythe. I have no strength left." Eleanor fell to the ground, kneeling, a sob catching in her throat. "They have captured Basaal. They brought him before me. I looked at his face, knowing full well the destruction he has brought down on all of us. Yet, knowing that his fate is in my hands rips at me!" Eleanor said fiercely and clenched her hand into a fist, hitting it against her chest. "And all I wanted was to reach out to him. I tried, but I can't! Don't you see?"

Edythe came to Eleanor's side, kneeling and pulling her sister against her shoulder.

"I cannot love him," Eleanor sobbed, "because he has been sent to destroy my people. And yet—" Eleanor pressed her face against Edythe's shoulder. "He could hardly stand my presence, so what does it matter? I cannot speak to him of anything—not of Zarbadast or the Shera Shee or the fate of Dantib. I can't abide the pain, and I feel so far away from here, from all of it—the stone, the gardens, the people—I am hopelessly far away. My journey has changed me, and I feel so empty, and I can't—"

Eleanor clung to her sister, the feelings of sorrow wrenched from her core as she sobbed. Edythe held her, whispering softly, stroking Eleanor's hair, and crying soundlessly alongside her. It was a long time before Eleanor's sobs turned into slow, unsteady whimpers.

"You are not empty," Edythe said through a clenched jaw, and she spoke from her own determination. "You are grieving. Yes, you have changed. There is no way around our own life experiences.

We must live through them, and we do." Edythe pulled away and met Eleanor's eyes. "You have not been depleted. You have been added upon. Gift this to your people. Draw strength from who you have always been, and draw wisdom from what you have now seen."

The abysmal weight of it all pulled at the corners of Eleanor's eyes, but she nodded, pressing her forehead against Edythe's shoulder, wondering if she could trust herself to her sister's words.

"I am sorry, Eleanor, that you and the prince are on opposite sides of this war. I am sorry that it is confusing and uncertain and cruel. It's no small thing to love someone despite how they have hurt you. It is no small sacrifice you offer."

They sat in silence for a long time. Eleanor's head hurt, her neck was stiff; her heart carried the weight of a thousand scrolls.

"What am I to do with him?" Eleanor finally asked.

"You must sleep awhile first," Edythe answered.

"Yes." Eleanor sniffed, but she did not move. She stayed there, kneeling against Edythe, trying desperately not to think of the prisoner in her dungeon.

<hr/>

The afternoon sun seemed determined in its brilliance, flooding Eleanor's receiving chamber with light. She sat at her desk and waited. Then the door opened. It was Aedon.

Eleanor did not look at his face. Rather, she glanced towards the near-blinding light pouring in through the window. Aedon settled in the chair opposite hers, his place during countless discussions before.

"You've been crying," he stated simply, not needing an explanation. Eleanor wiped her eyes with the back of her fingers and sniffed before looking at him.

"How familiar are you, Aedon, with Aemogen law?"

"Very." The inflection in his voice made Eleanor think he thought it an odd question. "As you well know."

"Five centuries ago, there was a small set of amendments that have little practical use in our time," she explained. "And consequently, they have been largely unknown. One amendment is in regard to alien citizens on Aemogen soil."

Aedon waited.

"A foreigner living on Aemogen soil claims no protection from the law until they have been here one year." Eleanor exhaled. "But, if they have spent half a year in the country, then they become subject to the discipline of the law as would any citizen."

She placed her elbow on the arm of the chair and leaned her head against the parted fingers of her hand. "The prince spent one hundred and eighty-three days in Aemogen: three days beyond a half year."

Aedon's eyes narrowed, and he frowned.

"He will not be tried under the law of war," Eleanor continued, "for espionage from an opposing country, which, in Aemogen—unique from other countries—means lifelong imprisonment. It's a tricky bit of law, but when you come to the end of it, there it is. Rather, he will come before me to be tried as any citizen...for treason."

She pulled at the inside of her cheeks to steady herself before continuing. "And because of the nature of such treason—and its direct relation to the crown during a time of war—he will be charged for high treason, punishable by death if he is found guilty. And we both know," she faltered, "that he will be found guilty."

"And so you must put the one that you love to death," Aedon

stated, his voice soft.

Eleanor looked at him sharply, all pretense draining from her face. She had not told Aedon; she had not told anyone before confessing to Edythe.

"I can't deny what I saw between you this morning," Aedon said, seeming to feel that he should offer an explanation. "Had you not cleared the throne room, all of Ainsley would know it as well."

Eleanor sat back in her chair and moved her middle finger against the wood grains of her desk. *Does Basaal know it?* she almost asked. She knew it didn't matter if he did. He would go to his death either way. And her worry of what he must think of her could not overshadow the decisions her own conscience must make. And yet, the integrity she'd cultivated as a monarch insisted he did not deserve to die. To say nothing of her heart.

Aedon visibly swallowed. "You are the queen," he said. "And this is a time of war. You have the power to overturn any of this." He waved his hand. "Declare what you will, and be ready to lead your army in three week's time."

Eleanor shook her head, bringing her fist down on the table so gently there was no sound. "You know that I reign over this people with the integral understanding that I will not put myself above the law. This is essential to the power and might of the Aemogen sovereign. Otherwise, I would become no better than Shaamil—a law unto myself." Eleanor paused before continuing, "The people must see this go through the proper channels, for it is their right, and I will not desecrate that sacred trust."

"What would you have me do?"

Her answer came quickly. "When it is asked if anyone will stand and speak on behalf of the prince, I will do so. That means I forfeit my right to run the trial," she said. "Because he will be tried as a citizen, you, as head councillor, are eligible for this position. Because it is a time of war, Crispin becomes eligible as well. This means one of you will be given the last vote and the other will be given voice to run the trial."

Aedon nodded. He knew all of this.

"I appoint you to be that voice," Eleanor said.

"Because you hope I might sway the council to spare his life?"

"No," Eleanor sniffed, her emotion refusing to lie dormant. "Because you will hear the arguments for and against Basaal, and I trust that your judgment will be less clouded than Crispin's. Basaal will receive a more just trail."

"That leaves Crispin with the deciding vote."

"Yes, if it comes to that," Eleanor acknowledged.

"And you trust him with that place?"

"I trust you to argue against me in a just manner," she stated, "which automatically leaves Crispin with the last vote. That cannot be changed."

Aedon's face wrinkled with worry. "I will need time to prepare, to study precedents."

"There is no time," Eleanor said, shaking her head apologetically. "I know that you would like there to be, but we cannot have this trial disturb our preparations for the attack. We have one chance to beat Imirillia, and our preparations there are paramount. The trial will be in the morning. His fate must be decided," she added, "and I must live with it."

"I had suspected you would offer him as ransom to bargain for peace," Aedon admitted. "I've considered his capture a godsend."

Eleanor said and shook her head. "The emperor will suspect Basaal has conspired with me. I am sure his suspicions do not fall far from that possibility now. And even if he didn't suspect anything, his pride would not let him settle through a hostage negotiation, not even to save the life of his favorite son."

Eleanor sniffed again and shook her head. "It would kindle his anger, and he would not rest until he saw all of us destroyed. A ransom would do us no favors and only extend the time it takes to learn our own fate in this game, perhaps even throwing our plans to the wind. No, the trial will go forward. And I must balance my integrity between my duty to the people and my duty to my own conscience."

Aedon looked out the window as the sun began to disappear behind the distant mountains. "Fine then," he said. "I will lead the trial."

"There is one more thing," she added. The lines around Eleanor's eyes moved from pain. "Something that I—I cannot do, so I ask it of you."

Basaal had stretched himself across a stone bench that was built into the far wall of his cell. It was a quiet space, and he assumed it had been put to little use over the last several years. He had tried to pay attention to where it sat below the castle, but he gave up and focused on keeping thoughts of Eleanor from his mind. His preferred thought was to berate himself again and again for his capture.

In frustration, Basaal closed his eyes and leaned his head against the stone. What a weight he had carried with him since he had sent Eleanor and Dantib into the desert—so terrified, yet so determined to be honorable. And Dantib had followed willingly, never mentioning the countless worries he must have had. Dantib. The guards had told Basaal nothing when he had asked about Dantib, nor had they given any information regarding Zanntal. Yet, he knew they had arrived in Aemogen.

But her face. He could not think of it without feeling sick. She was gaunt, and tired, her braided hair discolored as the dye faded. Despite all this, she was the most beautiful woman he had ever known. The scar that wrapped around her neck and across her chin, leaving a fine, white line in her bottom lip, had obviously come from a whip. And guessing who might have caused it was an excruciating exercise.

A sound in the hallway brought Basaal's mind back to his cell, and he sat up. Had Eleanor sent for him? Was she preparing a reunion between him and the stable master? Would she see him hang? It would be foolish to ransom him to the emperor; Shaamil would not take the bargain.

Adrenaline shot through Basaal's body as the sound of keys rattled in the door. Then it was pushed open. Aedon walked in. Basaal sat up and leaned forward, waiting for Aedon to speak.

"So," Aedon said, "they found you at Colun Tir?" Aedon stood with his arms crossed over his chest.

"Yes."

"Were you sent there? Whom else have you told of that place?"

"No one," Basaal said, leaning back against the wall, impatient with the questions. "Thayne has heard the confession already," he added. "I had gone down to see the work at the pass and let my foolish curiosity take me to the tower, following the delusionary hope that I might somehow overhear if Eleanor had returned home in safety."

"That is twice that you have been caught there. I've never known you to be careless."

Basaal attempted a cocky grin. He wasn't sure it came off well.

Aedon sighed as if he would rather Basaal had not been caught at all. "I've come to say you will come to trial in the morning for high treason against the crown. There will be no attempt at ransom."

"No. It would do no good. My father is not the kind of man to keep his word in such things." Basaal felt a strange relief. So it was to be death, then.

"Eleanor has told me some of what transpired," Aedon said, then paused, trying to speak graciously. "I thank you for keeping your word."

Basaal did not reply.

"She returned over a week ago." Aedon looked as if he did not know why he had supplied that information. "She is tired."

Reaching his hand down, Basaal picked at his boot, uncomfortable with being watched by Aedon as he processed this information. "The last I knew," Basaal said, "was that she and Dantib had been taken by slavers. I sent a member of my personal guard to search them out."

"Zanntal? He found her," Aedon said. "Eleanor wanted you to know he is staying at High Field fen with a sick slave girl they'd rescued and will travel up to Ainsley when able."

"And Dantib?" Basaal asked, finally looking up. "Is there any mercy to grant me time with him before my trial?"

Aedon looked about him uncomfortably, and then back at Basaal. "He died in the desert. The queen asked me to come tell you this."

Basaal's mouth opened. He tried to get up, to stand, to act, but his legs shook. He fell back onto the stone bench, taking a breath as if he had come up for air from a deep ocean. His lungs were collapsing inside of themselves, his breathing becoming quick and panicked. Air could not be had, and the walls were closing in around him. He tried to stand again, but he could not lift himself. Everything had fallen; the world had fallen—and it had taken Basaal with it.

When Basaal was finally able to look up, Aedon was gone, and Basaal was left alone with his own misery.

❦

Each time Basaal woke, it was still night. And death. Death was before him. Basaal did not think on the trial, but rather on the hanging that would follow. And it would be the end, a blissful end to the struggles of his life. He would find rest and bring the fate he had placed on Dantib onto himself. His death would help him accomplish what the Illuminating God had asked of him. The relief of the thought caused a twisted smile in the darkness. He could live through to the end. If only the end would come tomorrow.

CHAPTER

TEN

"Not black," Edythe said. "You would look a widow."

"I'm suited for it." Eleanor threw these words at her sister.

When Edythe did not answer, Eleanor turned again to the pile of gowns on her bed.

"What then?" her sister tried again, patient with Eleanor's turmoil that had nothing to do with gowns. "You've refused to wear anything I have put before you."

Eleanor had banished Miya and everyone else so that she might prepare herself. The trial was set to begin shortly, and she felt awful. "What color does one wear to sentence someone to die, I wonder," Eleanor said fiercely.

"You do not know that the council will decide on death," Edythe said. "You will argue, and they may find mercy." Edythe held up a deep red gown of simple velvet. "What about this?"

"I can't wear red," Eleanor said without explaining its tie to Basaal. "Or blue or green or any other color that makes one feel happy about anything." She slammed the door of her wardrobe, and it bounced back open against the force. "How can I do what

I must?" Eleanor brought her hands up to her face in desperation, as Edythe patiently combed through Eleanor's dresses.

"This then," Edythe said as she held up Eleanor's simple gray dress, accented in places with silver beads that looked like stars. "It's elegant, but no one could say anything cheerful about it."

Eleanor kicked the thick black gown away from her feet and turned to look at Edythe. "I'll look half dead and half queen." She snatched the gown from her sister's fingers. "An authentic state-ment," she added bitterly. "I must not look too young when I send him to die."

Edythe forced Eleanor to slide the gown over her chemise.

"Are you sure you do not wish to wear white? For courage?" Edythe asked, attempting to persuade Eleanor one last time.

"White is for battle," Eleanor spat.

"Exactly."

"The gray will suit."

Edythe moved behind Eleanor to secure the back and then hesitated. "I—" Edythe faltered.

"What is it?"

"I had forgotten the back of this dress drops down as it does." Edythe sounded apologetic.

Eleanor thought for a moment of her tortured skin, laced and branded with knots and twists of discolored scaring. She moved her tongue along the thin line in her lip.

"Such it is," Eleanor said at length, her voice full of desperate venom. "It will give them something besides my virtue to discuss in the streets of Ainsley." The gray gown was secured with a lace down the lower back, so Edythe was able to pull it tight enough to fit Eleanor's diminished frame.

"And now," Edythe murmured, "we must secure the crown."

"The crown?" Eleanor inquired, moving her fingers absent-mindedly along the scars on the back of her neck.

"This is a trial during wartime," Edythe said matter-of-factly. "You, therefore, are required to wear the battle crown into the throne room, even if this goes forward as a civilian trial. I asked Hayden about the protocol."

"I suppose I ought not to have worried whether I looked too young," Eleanor said as she stared at herself in the mirror. "Between this gown, that crown, and my face, I will look one hundred years old." The corners of Eleanor's mouth creased down. "No matter. I feel it."

⁓⊰⊱⊰⊱⊰⊱⁓

When Eleanor entered the throne room, all were present. Her councillors sat stiffly, Aedon especially, and the many who had come to observe were deathly quiet. Crispin sat in his place on the council while six of his guards stood in the center of the room, Basaal between them. His wrists were bound before him. His clothing was, as ever, black as night. Eleanor looked anywhere but into his eyes. She sat for a full minute to gather herself before rising again. All in attendance followed, and then the trial began.

"Under Aemogen law," Eleanor began, "this man, Prince Basaal of the Imirillian Empire, is to be tried for high treason against the crown of Aemogen." Eleanor's voice was clear. "As some of you might be unfamiliar with the proceedings of a treason court, I will explain. Fifteen sit in judgment to hear any arguments presented for or against the accused. In most cases, the ruling monarch governs the trial and casts the final vote in the proceedings. I have abdicated this position for this trial in favor of Aedon, the chief councillor of all fens. He will direct the trial. And as we are in a time of war, Crispin, the war leader of Aemogen, will cast the fifteenth vote." Eleanor felt the next words on her tongue before she spoke them. "I will argue on behalf of Prince Basaal."

Murmurs followed as Eleanor stepped down the steps of the dais and waved a hand, dismissing the guards that stood around Basaal, and taking her place a half step in front of him. A general sound of shock filled the room as the audience saw, very clearly, Eleanor's exposed back. She thought she also heard Basaal's intake of breath but could not be certain. She could feel Basaal's eyes, though, wandering over the angry, thatched scars.

His chains clanked against themselves, and a shiver ran down Eleanor's spine. Aedon rose. The fifteen men—both fen councillors and members of her war council—sat in a line behind him on the west side of the throne room.

"Prince Basaal of the Imirillian Empire," Aedon began, "because of the amount of time spent in Aemogen, you are to be tried for high treason, equal a citizen of this country. If you are found guilty, you will be sentenced to death and will be hanged."

"The council," Aedon stated, "does have the power, by majority vote, to amend the sentence if sufficient cause is found. Let us then begin."

Aedon's bearing was stiff, but he controlled his expression so that it simply appeared as if he were speaking to the fens on fair methods of trade. "Prince Basaal led an army with the express purposes of either subjugating or deposing our queen and of taking the resources of our country—our own sovereign country—for the Imirillian Empire. Is this so?" Aedon asked as he looked at Eleanor.

"It is so," she replied.

"Using information gathered during his time here, he prepared his army for its invasion of Aemogen, which would have been successful had not our queen stalled his army as our miners worked to set the powder to bring down the pass," Aedon explained. "When both efforts on our part were successful, the prince took Queen Eleanor captive. Is this not so?"

"The events of your narration, Councillor, are true. But saying that Prince Basaal used the information he had gathered here for the purposes of his invasion is false," Eleanor argued. "The prince became aware of our plan to bring down the mountain. And, as his purpose in coming to Aemogen was to urge us toward surrender—to avoid bloodshed—he did not share news of what we intended to do with his officers or his soldiers," she explained. "Had Prince Basaal not kept the information about our plans to himself, he could have marched his army up the pass days earlier, and Aemogen would have ceased to remain an independent nation."

"Do you suggest that he had divided motives that should be taken into consideration?" Aedon offered Eleanor fairly.

"The prince himself told me, on more than one occasion, that because of his mother, Edith of Marion, who was a friend to the Aemogen crown, it was not his will that Aemogen should be taken into the Imirillian Empire."

"Then why lead the conquest?" Aedon asked directly.

"For fear that if he refused this appointment, Emperor Shaamil would have then appointed another leader, who would not be as kind," she replied. "Prince Basaal was the architect of the agreement to give the sixth months Aemogen was granted to decide and prepare." Eleanor looked evenly at the eyes of each councillor. "And anyone who observed his efforts on the battle run saw that he gave the best military training Aemogen could have received."

Sean whispered something to Briant, who nodded. But Eleanor could not read their faces, and her mouth felt dry as she waited for Aedon's next question.

"All this may be true," Aedon stated, "but his good motives pale in comparison to the deaths of Common Field. One hundred and eighty-four men, women, and children were slaughtered by his men, tech nically under his orders. Was this not so?"

The room filled with whispers.

"Yes, it is so," she responded, despite her reluctance. First and foremost, Eleanor was the Queen of Aemogen. She would not have her people see her otherwise.

"Then," Aedon said, "even if the accusation of treason were to fall—an unlikely scenario because one's motive cannot outweigh one's action—he has the blood of one hundred and eighty-four Aemogen citizens on his hands, and that is not even mentioning the guards slaughtered when the Imirillian warning came, or the over two hundred men who have died defending the pass against his army. Can anything be said to that?" Aedon demanded.

"The prince told me once that the men who had committed the crimes on the innocents of Common Field had acted without the blessing and orders of their superiors. He did not authorize or condone the attacks."

"He told you once?" Aedon asked.

"Yes," Eleanor confirmed. "As his purpose was to avoid all bloodshed, this event distressed him greatly."

"And there is no one else to corroborate his story?" Aedon inquired. "In all your time in the company of the prince and his men, you never once confirmed with anyone else that this was indeed true?"

Eleanor's initial reaction was to snap back at Aedon that she was not the one on trial. But the truth of the matter caused her to pause. She had not corroborated the tale with Annan or anyone else. But Basaal had not proven himself to be so untrustworthy that she could not take his own word.

"No one has corroborated his story," Eleanor admitted. "But his own character is a testament to its truth. I would not make any judgment that would harm Aemogen or its people, but I also would not bear the responsibility of defending a man if I did not deem him worthy to receive life over death." As she said this, she caught Crispin's eye. He sat with his face hard, his eyes traveling from Eleanor to Basaal and back again.

On they went, Aedon asking questions, discussing Basaal's deceptions, and questioning his continued loyalty to the Imirillian Empire, and Eleanor answering as best she could on Basaal's behalf.

"And after you were taken captive," Aedon pressed, "did the prince keep his word to see you safely back to Aemogen?"

"Yes," Eleanor replied. "Beyond the requirements of any man's honor, he arranged for me to be led from Zarbadast back to Aemogen, an act that would cost his life if Emperor Shaamil ever knew of it. A man called Dantib, Prince Basaal's close friend and mentor, died in the process of helping me home to Aemogen."

"Despite whatever nobility that caused him to be so sympathetic," Aedon said as he held out his hands, "the irrevocable damage has been done; the Imirillian Empire now wants Aemogen more than ever before, and the lives lost at Common Field must to be accounted for. This man is not on trial for his character. He is on trial for the act of high treason and, consequently, for the deaths caused by it."

"I think it is clearly established that, by the understanding we have of Aemogen law, he is guilty of the charges brought against him," Eleanor admitted. There was a burst of conversation in the courtroom, and Aedon held up his hand to quiet the observers. Eleanor continued.

"I am asking for pardon because of all I have laid before this council. The law would be blind if nothing else could be taken into consideration in deciding his fate."

Aedon folded his arms. "And if we pardon this man," he said, "if we let him live in whatever form—be it as prisoner, servant, or freeman—what does that tell other warring countries?"

"That we are soft and do not take our rules of war seriously," Crispin said, speaking for the first time. Everyone turned to look at him. "He should be hanged tomorrow."

"Would you sacrifice true justice only to gain the point of proving your own strength?" Eleanor questioned in return.

Crispin would have answered, but Aedon spoke again. "Your reasoning, Your Majesty, though strong, may not be enough to overturn the verdict of the council," he admitted. "Unless you have something else," he added, "we will now take our vote."

It was not enough. Eleanor's heart stopped and then beat doubly quick. Looking at the faces of the councillors, she knew her arguments were not enough to save him. She hazarded a glance back at Basaal's face. He stood silent—graceful as always—calmly staring into the space before him. And though he might never forgive her, Eleanor knew there was one thing left that she could say that might possibly sway the council to grant him his life.

"I do have another reason to be taken into consideration." Eleanor pulled back the gray sleeve of her dress from her left forearm, lifting her arm into the air. "This is the mark of his house. Prince Basaal took me into his house as an act of protection."

"Which means…?" Aedon asked.

"That this man is my husband," Eleanor said with all the strength she could muster.

Silence sliced the throne room. Crispin stared at the mark, his face going pale. Then he looked down, placing a hand across his eyes. Aedon also appeared baffled, his mouth opening and closing, and no sound coming out. Edythe leaned forward, her eyes on Eleanor.

"After the Imirillian soldiers took me to Zarbadast," Eleanor said to the unsteady rhythm of her pulse, "I was ordered to be put to death. But in an effort to save my life, Prince Basaal convinced his father that he had kept me alive to become his wife, arguing that, with me as Queen, their ability to rule over Aemogen would be easier. Upon the emperor's acceptance," she continued, "the ceremony took place. On the seventh day of celebration, my escape was executed. If it had not been for Basaal risking his own life, I would be dead now," she insisted.

"He did not hold me to the marriage," she continued. "This decision is my own, and it is what I choose. The law states that the royal head of state, the senior monarch, may validate any marriage. And as there may be those who would argue the Imirillian ceremony is null," Eleanor said, taking a stubborn breath, "I validate it."

Noise erupted. Aedon's mouth moved again, but still he did not speak. Rather, he stood stunned and silent. Crispin's head was still bent. The rest of the council appeared to be balancing between reaction and reason, payment and pardon. Eleanor's body began to shake, and she looked to Edythe for encouragement. Her sister was clutching the arms of her chair, but she met Eleanor's eyes, her worry evident.

Finally, Aedon turned and then half shifted back towards Eleanor. "Penalty for Prince Basaal's actions is death," he said. "In your role as officer on his behalf, you must present the terms of pardon that we are to consider, if the council feels to offer mercy."

"The terms I would set forth are these: Prince Basaal would be accepted as my husband, in all considerations save the title and power of king. After the war has ended, he will spend several months traveling among and serving the people of this nation, asking their forgiveness and paying his debts. He will be called Prince Basaal," she added. "The people of Common Field will have the greatest claim on his penance. He will provide this service under the direction of one chosen to enforce his parole. If he does this, and the council of fen lords accepts his debt as paid, he will become a full member of the royal household, attain the title of His Majesty the King, and receive all powers and privileges of being so."

"I would offer myself to supervise his parole," Thayne said as he stood in his place among the fen lords who sat watching the trial. "This young prince is my kin, and I take deep interest in his welfare."

Eleanor nodded, and so did Aedon, albeit slowly.

"The argument and terms have been laid out," Aedon said, turning towards the council members behind him. "I ask for your votes and your reasons. Take what time you need."

Once, perhaps twice, Eleanor looked in Basaal's direction, but he gave no hint, no sign of emotion. He stood impassive, statuesque, waiting for the votes to be cast, giving no indication as to his opinion of Eleanor's defense.

Eleanor knew that, despite what anyone else thought, she had answered for her own integrity. Would Basaal see it that way? Would a life in Aemogen not be better than death? She pressed her fingers against the mark on her forearm.

The murmurs of the councillors were the only sounds in the throne room. At length, all the votes had been written down, and then the men of the council waited as Aedon invited them to stand, one by one, and read their decisions.

Catton stood first. "Penalty of death," he said, "for invasion without provocation and for deception equaling treason."

Sean followed him. "Acceptance of pardon," Sean said, "for service to crown and country of Aemogen while trying to keep a foreign power at bay."

Then Briant cleared his throat. "Acceptance of pardon," Briant said, "for reasons just stated and for the honor of his intent."

The fen councilor of Quickly stood next. 'Penalty of death," he said, and then sat back down with no further explanation. Ten more votes were cast: five for death, five for pardon. So they stood even—seven and seven. Crispin was the last to stand. He looked down at his paper, visibly angry.

"The defendant has broken the law of Aemogen," Crispin said. "He also has sought to protect a nation not his own. He is responsible for Aemogen blood that was shed, but his actions have also spared the people of Aemogen from the full outcome of the intended war, at least for now," Crispin added.

"He has committed the equivalent of treason and deceit against the reigning monarch of Aemogen," Crispin continued. "He has also gone to great lengths to spare the queen's life and restore her to her throne and people. He is the queen's husband," he said, and then paused, looking up at Eleanor, then at the council. "It is no simple case," Crispin added. "May God have mercy on us all if I have chosen wrong: acceptance of pardon." With that, Crispin crumpled his judgment and let it fall to the table. Then he turned and exited the throne room without looking back.

Eleanor tried to speak, but her astonishment caught the words in her throat. She half turned, looking back at Basaal's face. His expression was frozen, obscure. Everyone was silent, unmoving. Fen lords, observers, even some of Eleanor's own council walked a fine line between amazement and a sticky disapproval.

Aedon cleared his throat and stood again. "The judgment falls as such: seven votes for death, eight for pardon," he said. "I declare Prince Basaal pardoned by the Aemogen High Court, and upon completion of his penance, offered full standing as a citizen and as a monarch of Aemogen." Aedon turned towards Basaal. "Now, you must kneel and swear your fidelity to the queen."

Eleanor blanched. She had forgotten that Basaal, once accepted as an Aemogen subject, would need swear his fidelity to her crown. Now there was a visible response on his face: shock, blind shock—and betrayal. Basaal cut a glance towards her, his eyes sweeping over her person disbelievingly.

"You must kneel and swear your fidelity," Aedon repeated more quietly.

When Basaal dropped to his knees, his eyes unblinking and bare, he was visibly defeated, stripped, and Eleanor could hardly watch. Looking as if the Illuminating God had abandoned him with this divisive trick, his chin fell to his chest and his shoulders slouched. Basaal looked utterly alone. Pressing his lips together, Basaal stared at the chains around his wrists before lifting his eyes to Eleanor's face. He seemed stricken as he fumbled for the words. "I swear it—" he began.

"Please," Eleanor held up a hand, unable to watch him kneel before her any longer. "That is sufficient." She turned away from him, returning to her throne as endless noises filled the hall.

Aedon ordered the palace guard to give him the key to Basaal's chains, and then, with it in his hands, he stepped forward, treating the prince with visible respect, lifting the stunned Basaal to his feet. When he inserted the key and twisted it in the lock, the shackles fell in a series of cold sounds as they crashed onto the gray stone.

Sean brought a hastily written declaration before Eleanor, which she signed, her cheeks burning. Then the council put their names beneath Eleanor's signature. Aedon had been speaking quietly to Basaal.

"My Prince," he said loud enough for her to hear, "allow me to escort you to some chambers where you might rest." Basaal nodded, rubbing his wrist, looking dazed. And he would not look at her. He followed Aedon away from the astonished din of the throne room.

Once they were gone, Eleanor stood, and without looking at a single person, left the residue of the trial behind.

CHAPTER
ELEVEN

He was standing before the window, arms folded, shoulders hunched as if protecting himself from a wind that was not there. In the chamber of the red suite, large windows stretched along the entire western wall. Only Basaal's shadow, framed in one tall arch, broke the pattern of sunlight melting onto the rich furnishings. These rooms had belonged to her parents. Eleanor took a few hesitant steps towards him and then stopped. Hearing the rustling of her gown, Basaal twisted his face toward Eleanor. His eyes were rimmed red, his expression, dark.

"What have you done to me?" he said, but the fierceness of Basaal's voice caught on itself. He wiped his eyes with his sleeve and turned back towards the window. Eleanor took a half step back. Basaal's anger was palpable, his sorrow, unbearable. "What fate is this?" he demanded. "Is the Illuminating God so angry, so displeased, that he would damn me to this prison?" His words were weighed in anger.

Eleanor blinked back the emotion, her own breath catching on the unruly pain beside her heart. She swallowed. When she responded, her tone was both challenge and sympathy. "What would you have had me do?"

Basaal unfolded his arms and turned towards her. His stance was intimidating, and his face full of pain.

"Condemn me!" Basaal yelled, lifting his hands before him like a beggar. "Declare my guilt and hang me! Give me rest, an end to the misery of this existence!" Eleanor flinched, and he continued. "Or, if your good conscience *must* see me spared, let the condemnation fall, and then help me escape before the sentence is carried out so that I might disappear completely. I could leave, be gone, far from all of this, far from my father!" Basaal was breathing hard, his eyes set, his jaw tight. He covered his face with his hands. They were shaking. "This is not my life, Eleanor. This is *not* my life."

Eleanor ran her fingers along the scars on her wrist, fighting her wounded anger. "There is a standard that I hold myself to as queen, Basaal. If I make a decision, it cannot be in the night, deceiving my own people, sneaking you away to safety against the justice of my country. Your life could either have been forfeit or have been saved—if I interceded with an argument strong enough."

She looked down at the floor. "There was no other argument strong enough, and my conscience demanded that I spare you." Eleanor took a breath and raised her eyebrows as she again countered his angry stare. "I am sorry you feel marriage to me and life in Aemogen to be such a damnation. But I would rather face that lonely existence than walk the rest of my days with your blood on my hands, knowing that I should have done otherwise." Eleanor narrowed her eyes and shook her head, letting accusation fill her voice. "Can you not remember Zarbadast, Basaal? Do you hold me to a standard you struggled to hold yourself? As if I"—she raised her voice—"should have less compunction sending you to your death than you did sending me?" Eleanor let the question hang before saying, "*Spare as you are spared.* Those are the words of your Illuminating God, and I have done so to good conscience."

Basaal's angry expression creased in confusion, but she paid his wordless question no mind.

"But I tell you this," Eleanor continued as her chest rose and fell, her heart beating a hollow drum, "I *will* hold you honor bound to remain in Aemogen until this conflict is resolved so that my people may know that you did not use this pardon to fight against them. I will hold you to that, and by your seven stars, it will be done. But after we have won this war, you are free." Eleanor cut her hand through the air venomously as a warm tear slid around her cheekbone, growing cold as it eased under her jaw and rested on her neck.

"Disappear," she added, lifting her chin. "Go far, *far* away. I can bear the shame, the embarrassment, Basaal. So bide your time until then, and then leave me to my work."

———◦◦◦◦◦———

Every emotion inside Basaal came to a head as he watched the tear run down Eleanor's face. The words she spoke had hit him hard, reverberating into the folds of raw pain within his chest. A voice inside him, some decent plea, told him to tell Eleanor how he had kept the thought of her closer than any other, told him to lay down his wrath and cross the space between them. It whispered he should tell her of his regard—of his love. But Basaal shook his head in response and did none of these things. She had already stolen his fidelity, and he felt the victim for it.

"Some courage you have," he spat back bitterly instead. "Arranged what you must behind my back, and I hear of it only after you've changed my life, only after you've made a quick theft of my allegiance." His eyes turned harder, colder. "You had not even taken thought that I might need to hear of Dantib's death from your own lips! You sent a messenger. What cowardice is that?" he practically roared. "You owed me better than that!"

"What did you want me to say?" Her fire-filled words flayed the space between them.

"I want to know how he died!" Basaal said as he threw up his arms. "You *knew* what he meant to me. Do you have the courage to tell me? Do you have the courage to speak the words?"

Color rose in Eleanor's cheeks. She pulled her head back like he had struck her face. He watched her almost falter, until, narrowing her eyes, she tossed the words at him as if he were begging for scraps, her lips quivering. "He was *torn apart* by wild dogs." Emotion threatened to tangle up her speech, and her face shifted in pain. Basaal swore. He shook his head, disbelieving. But as he opened his mouth, she lifted a shaking hand to silence him. "Don't you dare make me relive that day! Don't you dare blame me for being unable to tell you about the abominations of that place! I cannot sleep for the memory of it in my head."

Stunned, angry, Basaal took a step back. Her hurt expression gave him no mercy, no comfort, and he felt too raw to offer her any. He turned back towards the window and stretched his arms between the pillars on either side, staring into the blinding afternoon sunlight, trying to block the image of Dantib's death from his mind.

Basaal could hardly believe Eleanor's cruelty. He would not even think about his own.

He did not look back when he heard her leave.

A hasty feast was organized to celebrate the queen's marriage the following evening. The council thought it best they celebrate as a show of good faith. For the people—and the councillors—who were confused and, in part, disapproving. Eleanor sanctioned the event with a wave of her hand, but she spent the day as she had the entire evening before, locked in her rooms, admitting no one.

Aedon had come through, once. But he appeared so taken aback by the fire behind Eleanor's eyes that he treaded carefully.

"Was the prince comfortable in the red suite last night?" she snapped.

Aedon watched her with a frown. "From what I hear, he took himself back down to the dungeon, making it clear that he knew his place and would be quite comfortable in it."

Eleanor flushed but tried to respond lightly. "I see that marriage has brought out the worst in both of us. Though I am not surprised."

Aedon dropped his eyebrows, questioning her brash tone.

"I said some truly awful things," Eleanor said, looking away from Aedon's steady gaze. "So he publicly humiliates me—and deservedly so."

"No," Aedon said calmly, yet with force, "not deservedly so. Yet—" he hesitated.

"Speak." Eleanor shot the word at her dearest friend. "I can always see when you're waiting to say something."

"Speak freely?"

"You always have before."

"Not regarding matters of your marriage, Your Majesty," Aedon said, using his formal tone to make a statement. "Not on matters that are meant to be worked out privately."

"And?"

"And you better do it soon for the sake of the country you are about to lead into the most dangerous battle of its history. Tonight is your chance to win your people to this alliance. Many of the most influential men and women in your country will be present to celebrate this union, which is a good deal from them. Consider the implications if the two of you are seen warring." Aedon tilted his head to the side and scowled. "This is not you, Eleanor. This is not you. Obviously, you've sustained a great deal of hurt and pain. I am sorry for that. Now, center yourself, and act as you know you should. The sooner you find your compassion, the sooner he will find his."

Eleanor closed her eyes but a moment. Aedon's words set off an emotional tug-of-war, and she was so weary of the internal fray. The hardness that had formed inside her chest wasn't her. It had stripped her of what she had considered two of her greatest strengths as a monarch: her empathy, and compassion. But the stone anchors of pride and hurt felt immovable inside her stomach. And Eleanor was so tired.

"What word today from Thistle Black?" Eleanor asked, trying to pass over Aedon's advice. "I assume he has gone back to work after cooling his head in the Aemogen dungeon for a day."

Aedon cleared his throat. "With the additional materials from the south, he feels that we will be ready for the attack come time to leave. In tomorrow's council meeting, there will be more specifics. Crispin, as you know, has the men in continual training, and the final companies of soldiers from the south will be at camp within the next five days."

"Thank you, Aedon," Eleanor said before bending her head over her work again.

Eleanor dismissed everyone save Edythe as she finished her preparations for the dinner. Upon Edythe's quiet insistence, Eleanor agreed to wear her mother's gown, the wedding gown. White, delicate, with an elegant gold trim and design, falling gracefully around her body—it was the most flawless thing their mother had ever owned. Eleanor felt immeasurably sad as she put it on. But if she did not wear it to celebrate her wedding, people would wonder, so, to add credence to her decision, she wore the gown.

If Edythe had heard any rumors of disapproval regarding Eleanor's choice to defend Basaal, she showed no sign as she prepared Eleanor for the banquet. She even obliged when Eleanor requested no braids. So her hair was drawn up into carefully placed curls, accentuated with small, crisp, white spring flowers. Around her neck hung a beautiful necklace of gold in the form of the sweet vine, which had belonged to her mother.

After Edythe left, Eleanor sat alone, staring into the large mirror at her miserable reflection, only a few candles illuminating the darkened room with their own impatient light. The deceptions of Zarbadast felt heavier as they repeated themselves in Aemogen.

The prince stepped out of the shadows. Eleanor started but did not turn. Instead, she rearranged a curl of hair that had fallen out of place.

"I see that they were able to oblige your usual taste in clothing," she remarked. This comment was meant to be an effort toward conversation. But it had sounded, even to her own ears, like an accusation.

Basaal stood stiff, his hands behind his back, wearing black. His tunic was trimmed and decorated in gold, a pattern reminiscent to that of Eleanor's, and on his upper sleeve, in gold, was the emblem of Eleanor's house. His eyes followed hers, and his jaw tightened. "A reminder of who I now serve," he said.

Eleanor's fingers instinctively moved across her arm, left bare by the sleeve of the wedding gown. His eyes followed, and he shifted, discomfited. Eleanor choked back the words of apology that had been waiting in her mouth all afternoon and stood, turning towards him.

"My people have lost a measure of faith in me."

"Perhaps they feel you have betrayed them."

Eleanor took a world-weary breath, and said, more to the space between them than to Basaal, "Is it not faith we speak of? What of that?"

Basaal stared, but said nothing.

Eleanor lifted her chin. "I expect you to help repair this damage. Tonight you will act, as I have so often seen you do, the agreeable prince of Imirillia. I cannot wait a day to win them back, and you are part of that."

To Eleanor's pained awareness, Basaal transformed. Raising his eyebrows, his mouth shifted into a smile, both charming and disconcerting. He offered his arm. "May I?"

She stepped towards him, the ethereal fabrics of her gown rippling behind her steps as if it were from the wardrobe of a ghost. "Thank you."

They left her apartments and walked down the torch-lit hall, Hastian moving silently behind them. Edythe was waiting for them in a blue and gold dress similar to what Eleanor wore. She was beautiful.

"Prince." Edythe stepped forward and offered her hand to Basaal. "I have not yet had the opportunity of greeting you as brother. May I do so now?"

"Certainly." He was warm and sincere as he took Edythe's hand. "You must believe me when I say I am honored to be greeted as such by you and would beg you allow me to prove myself a brother to you despite—" He took a breath. "Despite it all."

"Do prove yourself a brother, Prince Basaal, as I've always felt you should be," Edythe said, and she kissed him on the cheek. After he smiled at her, Edythe hazarded a glance at Eleanor before stepping behind them.

As they approached the hall, they were greeted with music, and noise, more decoration than Eleanor could remember seeing in many years. As they entered, people stood, and then the royal pair walked the line of fen lords and councillors, greeting them on their way towards the high table. As if to prove that he could care for their beloved queen, Basaal showed Eleanor respect, dignity, and affection. He smiled, paid compliments as different heads of state were reacquainted with him, balancing humility and assurance, all the while maintaining an aloof separation. All his training in Zarbadast was coming to good use.

Eleanor said very little. She was miserable, and the weight of his touch burned.

The evening progressed well, for all its intents and purposes. Basaal performed skillfully, playing the role of charming penitent, devoted to the queen and to the cause of Aemogen freedom. Despite his aura of separateness, he praised the courage and determination of the people and expressed what Eleanor knew to be sincere feelings in regard to the independence of smaller countries.

After the remnants of the meal had been carried away and a satisfied spirit had seemed to ease the worried minds of those in attendance, Edythe bravely stood to toast Eleanor and Basaal.

"My Lords and Ladies," she began. "I am pleased to celebrate the wedding of my dear sister, our queen, to this honorable prince." Eleanor felt sick as Basaal's hand, which rested near hers on the table, pulled away. "And as my first gift to the happy couple," Edythe continued generously, "when peace has been established again, I will order the royal suite—where my parents were so happy—to be remodeled for the bride and her groom."

There were polite cheers, and Eleanor forced a smile for Edythe's sake.

"Until then," Edythe continued, "the happy couple will simply have to make do with Eleanor's current set of rooms. I do hope the prince enjoys living with manuscripts, books, and scrolls." There was friendly laughter at Eleanor's expense. She wondered how many of them knew he'd spent his night back down in the dungeon. After a few more toasts, the guests turned back to the special dishes prepared for dessert.

"I've a wedding gift for you," Basaal said to Eleanor in a quiet voice as he leaned back in his chair, his head tilted towards hers, swirling his drink around in his almost empty cup. His voice held neither affection nor contempt but a blandness that stung Eleanor all the more. "I was not going to lead my armies into Aemogen."

"What?" she asked on the heel of his confession.

"I was told very—" he paused, "*quite* clearly that I was not to lead my army into Aemogen. The Illuminating God forbade the act."

"But—" Eleanor said, leaning towards him. "What would you have done? What of your father's men? And what if he had stripped you of your army?"

"I hadn't figured that out yet," Basaal said, shrugging lightly.

He turned his eyes on her, his gaze wandering from the flowers in her hair down to the scar on her chin. "But it's too late for those questions. Now," he said and cleared his throat, "do you have a gift for me? I believe, by my tally, that you've been the ungenerous partner in both marriages now."

Scowling at his impertinent tone and choosing to ignore his subtle humor, Eleanor repeated the words from so many days past, "Considering the duplicitous nature of our marriage, I think it best we forgo the bride's gift."

The prince looked at her blankly for a moment before throwing his head back and laughing so loud the entire room paused to watch. He finished his drink off with a cheeky grin and set it firmly on the table.

"Well played, my love. Well played."

<hr/>

At the end of the wedding celebration, Thayne had a few moments with Eleanor alone. "Prince Basaal does not seem to be holding himself together well at all," he said.

"Really?" Eleanor replied, her eyes watching Basaal as he sat, speaking soberly with Edythe. "You surprise me. Everyone else seems to be taking his theatrics in stride."

"It's his eyes," Thayne measured. "Haunted as any pair I've ever seen."

"He has lost someone very dear to him, and I've done nothing to assuage the pain of that death." Eleanor raised an eyebrow. "I've raped him of country, culture, family, and home, in the single act of forcing him into matrimony with me. I'm the very devil in his eyes."

Thayne grimaced at her harsh language and rested his hand

on hers in a fatherly way. "Your actions on his behalf have been nothing less than noble and self-sacrificing. It is an ugly thing, now, to pretend they weren't." He squeezed her hand. "But you've a decision to make, my dearest."

"What is that?"

"The game is set, and now you must choose between your pride and your love for him. Only a fool could not see you carry them both."

Eleanor looked down and bit her lip, wondering when her own confusion came into fair play. But she knew it wasn't the difficulties of her own journey keeping her separate from him. "Even if I could set aside the pride, and fight the weary misery inside of me, I wouldn't know what to do with him, Thayne," Eleanor admitted, with no hardness in her voice. "Even in the pressures of Zarbadast, he never appeared as fragmented as he does now."

Thayne watched his young cousin a long moment before speaking again to Eleanor. "From what I understand, he has balanced stresses and contradictions for most of his life. Is it any wonder he might have come to a breaking point?"

"Then what do I do?" Eleanor said, watching Basaal, who was now smiling ironically, his eyes far away.

"You let him break. You let him crumble."

Eleanor didn't understand. "But why?"

"Because you are the only person in his life with whom he feels safe enough *to* break. And that, my dear, means a great deal."

Eleanor remained silent the rest of the evening.

After the ordeal was finished, Basaal had casually insisted on returning to the dungeon.

"Then you will use the entrance through my personal chambers," Eleanor said. "No need to make us look ridiculous before the entire country."

"A secret stairway to the dungeon from your own chambers?" Basaal replied, quirking an eyebrow. "The intrigue. Have you many secret rendezvous with your prisoners? Oh," Basaal said as he looked up, clapping his hands together in a way that reminded Eleanor of Kiarash. "I forgot. I'm your first one."

"There is a blanket in that room there," Eleanor said as she pointed towards the corner bedroom adjacent to her own, ignoring his laced humor. "Tomorrow we can see you more properly settled."

"Much obliged," Basaal responded dryly.

After he had retrieved the blanket, Eleanor met him with a key. "For the door at the bottom," she said. "Leave it unlocked." Then she pulled at a design in the wall paneling, revealing the opening to the staircase.

He nodded as he passed her, ducking his head as he entered the narrow doorway.

"Do you need a light?" Eleanor called down.

"I can manage without any," he said, his words echoing up the stairs.

Later, with Thayne's words crowding into her mind, sleep would not come. Eleanor spent hours trying to think of what she might say to Basaal. But there were no words, only the knowledge of the acute pain they had both suffered. She rose, pulling a white shawl over her nightdress, and opened the door that would lead her down, down the endless stairs, into the black dungeon.

Eleanor lit no candle for herself as she placed her hand against the stone and took the first step. Down and down she went, her concern giving her the courage to move forward. She reached the bottom and pushed open the door into the endless hallways of seed rooms and cells. It was loud. Had Basaal heard? Did it wake him?

She approached the cell where she'd instructed he be placed, pushed her hands against its door, now unlocked, and it gave way.

The cell was dark as pitch. Eleanor stretched her hand out before her, moving slowly. She could hear him breathing in the blackness, fast and quick, as a child would breathe on the edge of a fever. It was as if he were suffocating despite the chill of the air. Her eyes settled into the darkness, and she could see him before her on the ground. Basaal was lying on his back. Eleanor knelt down beside him, the stones unyielding against her knees.

In vulnerable trepidation, she reached her hand towards him, brushing his hair back and resting her hand on his brow. It was warm. His breathing stopped, and the turn of his head was ever so slight. Eleanor's heart pounded mercilessly, rising and falling, but she kept her hand in place, stroking his hair back, moving her thumb across his skin, willing her fingers to draw the anxiety out from his mind.

His breathing began to quiet as if his lungs understood help had come. Seeing how his left hand was clutching at his night-shirt, Eleanor kept her right hand on his forehead while lifting her other hand to his chest, coaxing his grip away, easing the tension in his fingers. Finally, he let go, and Eleanor placed her hand in his, holding it steady. And although his face was turned towards hers, Eleanor could not tell whether his eyes were open.

It seemed a long time that she sat with his hand in hers. Finally, Basaal's breathing became deep and even, and he was still. Leaning down, Eleanor kissed his forehead, lingering with her cheek against his brow, smelling the edge of his cinnamon scent, before sliding her hand away from his and disappearing from the cold cell.

CHAPTER

TWELVE

When Eleanor stepped out of the western gate into the camp, the men cried out in unison, and Eleanor shivered at the sound. Thousands of voices, her soldiers' voices. She was followed by a loose entourage of councillors, fen lords, and, as always, Hastian. The southern troops had arrived. As the men stood at attention, a ripple of voices brought about Crispin's swift appearance.

"Your Majesty!" he said, welcoming Eleanor with a smile.

"Good morning, Crispin," she greeted him back, with surprisingly more cheer than she believed she felt. She motioned him to her side, and they walked the camp, the trail of councillors and fen lords walking a distance behind them.

"I am glad to see you are feeling better," she said when they had walked far enough ahead of her entourage to allow private conversation. "I understand that the last few days have been a trial for you."

He sighed. "I trusted him so completely, you know. I'd feel a fool, especially with my new responsibilities, if I did so again."

Eleanor looked up at Crispin's determined expression, studying his handsome face. There were more lines now about his eyes, and he seemed older.

"Trust him again," she said with a force that surprised even herself. "Of that, he is worthy. If he is willing, use him in any capacity you need."

Crispin hunched his shoulders, catching his hands behind his back. He frowned at the ground as they walked on. "I will think on it. Now," he brightened, "let me take you away to the smithies and show you our progress on Black's devilish devices. The powder is not kept in there, so no worries as to its safety."

"I thought you said they were your idea?"

"They were," Crispin said. "Black has just improved upon their maliciousness. I could never have thought of filling the spheres with nails and scraps of metal."

Eleanor winced. "Don't tell me any more. I've no desire to know the workings of such a thing."

With the arrival of the southern troops, camp teemed with over three thousand men. The days were full of noise and training, every smithy in the country sending a continual stream of weapons to Ainsley. Crispin was all energy as he accounted for every detail of the planned ambush in their morning meetings.

Eleanor's council met twice a day, nailing down the logistics. She also rode out among the troops as often as she could, when she was not bent over numbers, scanning the reports of their increasing stockpiles with her calculating eyes. Reports still came from the pass, listing their casualties and the slow progress of the Imirillians.

Basaal did little to make himself available during the day. From what Eleanor knew, he spent much time in his dungeon retreat, which—with the addition of a bed, a table, a chair, and several books and scrolls—had become quite comfortable.

He would always appear in her chambers to eat breakfast in a polite silence, would take his midday meal below, and would arrive to escort Eleanor to the evening meal, where he sat at the opposite end of the long table—as was appropriate for Eleanor's spouse—and was a polite dinner companion to those who sat near him. Eleanor would occasionally flick her eyes down the table to watch, sometimes seeing that Basaal had fallen into a deep conversation with Aedon.

She and Basaal spoke very little with each other. Eleanor was frightened for him, who could appear so well to the others and so on the edge of an abyss to Eleanor. How, exactly, did you let someone break and know anything about what to do with the pieces? So she said little.

Yet, each night, at some unearthly hour when she could not sleep, Eleanor would slip down the stairs to see if his breath was calm and steady. Sometimes he seemed to be waiting as Eleanor pulled the chair to his bedside and reached her hand out for his. She did not stay long, but Eleanor never left before she knew he had fallen asleep again.

Basaal sat stiff among the members of the war council. Aedon had come earlier with a message: Crispin requested the prince to be present at the meeting, "if it so pleased him."

Basaal went.

He had become close comrades with these men during the battle run. None of them, except Aedon, seemed to know what to say whenever they saw Basaal, so they didn't say anything. He pulled at his high collar and looked up towards the ceiling.

A moment later, Eleanor entered the room. She sat in between Basaal and Crispin, looking only towards her war leader, and began the meeting by giving Crispin the floor.

"Some of you may be wondering why I have asked the prince away from his extremely demanding schedule," the war leader began, and someone snickered. Eleanor scorched the man with one glare, and everyone in the room sat up straighter.

"Proceed, Crispin," she said.

"Yes, well, I thought it would be wise—considering Prince Basaal's military expertise—to lay our plans before him and to let him detect any obvious flaws to be considered. That is, if Prince Basaal is amenable to the idea?" There was no warmth in Crispin's words, and he clearly had asked Basaal because of their great need, nothing more.

Basaal cocked an eyebrow and nodded, faltering only a quick instant before leaning forward in his chair. "By all means," he said, sounding tired.

Snapping his fingers, Crispin motioned for a young soldier to bring a map to the table. Crispin laid it out, asking for weights, and then pointed to the Maragaide Valley.

"In two weeks' time, almost our entire force of three thousand men will march to this point," Crispin said. "It will take three days. We will also maintain a force of three hundred men to remain fighting at the pass."

Basaal's thoughts went to his own men, who were also fighting at the pass; his own men, who had waited for him to come back. "And the purpose for moving your forces into the Maragaide Valley is what?" Basaal asked to distract himself.

"Because on May first eve, we will attack the encampment of the Imirillian army," Crispin replied coolly.

Basaal started, half scowling as he looked from the map to Crispin. He stood, twisted the map beneath his fingers, and stared at it. It could be brilliant. "Do you all have a suicide wish?" he asked. "Three thousand against thirteen thousand?"

"It was going to be three against seven until your father decided to join the party," Crispin said as he held up his hand. "Hear us out before you decide if it's impossible. This is what we aim to do."

As Crispin spoke about their new powder weapons and how they were to be used, Basaal began to see the nature of the Aemogen attack, and his heart began to beat double quick. Keeping his face impassive, he began to carry out the attack in his head, noting what it would mean for the Imirillian camp. His father's tent was set higher up the hill and would likely be left unscathed. But the men, both his and his father's, would be in danger of the powder weapons. And that meant many who were close to Basaal. That meant Annan.

Later that day, Thayne walked into Basaal's dungeon room.

"May I come in?" Thayne asked.

Basaal, who had been reading at the table, looked up at his cousin. "Is barging into private spaces a family tradition?"

"Yes." Thayne entered the room and eyed its thrown-together contents. He invited himself to sit on the stone bench in the wall, pushing aside a neglected pile of clothing and scrolls. "Telford mentioned the two of you bathed together. I assume that is what you are referring to."

Basaal rolled his eyes. "Have you come to invite me for a dip in the river?"

"No." The older man settled his blue Marion eyes on his cousin. "I've come to propose we leave Ainsley Rise for a few days."

After turning a page in his book, Basaal shook his head. "No, thank you."

"I think you should."

"To what purpose?" Basaal asked as he closed his book and tossed it onto the table with a thud. "Where would we go?"

"Common Field."

Basaal's face paled, but he laughed and ran his fingers through his hair. "In that case," he said, "certainly not. They would hang me within a minute of my arrival."

"I do not think so," Thayne prodded. "I thought you should leave your self-imposed prison and work for a couple days."

"Work in the fields?" Basaal asked incredulously.

"All the fens have more labor than manpower this spring, and no fen needs more assistance than Common Field," Thayne said. "You could make yourself useful."

Basaal laughed again, but it carried an uncertain sound.

"I heard you've not been out to train," Thayne said, apropos of nothing.

"Who would spar with the enemy without wanting to run him through?" Basaal asked.

"The melodrama must come from your father's side," Thayne answered.

For the first time, Basaal's laughter was sincere. He smiled in acknowledgment. "You are quite right, my lord." Basaal looked at Thayne with a new consideration in his eyes. "Why do I get the feeling," Basaal asked, folding his arms behind his head and looking upward, "that you mean to get me on the road so that we can chat?"

Thayne stood. "Because intelligence runs in your mother's family," he answered. "Meet me at the stables in an hour." Then the fen lord excused himself without another word.

The casualties list was delivered to Eleanor's desk before the end of the day. She set her face and opened the missive. There had been an aggressive move by the Imirillians. They had gained more ground, and nineteen Aemogen soldiers were dead.

The dead now numbered over three hundred. She read the names, their family names, and their fens. One was a cousin.

A knock came at the door, and Hastian sent in a messenger boy. The boy bowed, handed Eleanor a small folded slip of paper, and withdrew. Eleanor moved her finger over the note as she again read the names of the dead. Then she opened the paper with her finger and thumb.

She recognized the writing as Basaal's.

Lord Thayne has taken it upon himself to reform my moral compass. We are to be several days in Common Field. As far as your preparations to attack the encampment, I have thought the plan over, per Crispin's request, and have found it to be as good a chance as any you have.

Eleanor already knew what Thayne had in mind. He'd asked her what she thought of his idea, and she'd informed him she had no time to think of much else than of preparing for war and that he should do as he saw fit. Now, as she looked at Basaal's words again, Eleanor felt a sense of relief and a wash of regret.

Their first night on the road, as Thayne and Basaal lay upon their bedrolls, taking in the stars, Thayne opened their conversation with something Basaal felt was none of Thayne's business.

"So," Thayne said, "you and Eleanor are having a difficult time seeing eye to eye? What exactly did she demand from you that is so arduous? She did, after all, spare your life."

"I've no desire to discuss my prison terms with you," Basaal replied.

Thayne laughed. "Life in Aemogen is not a prison. And neither is marriage to one you love."

Basaal stared at the night sky above him. "Do you not understand that I live my life through covenants and obligations, many of which are to the Imirillian Empire in which I was born? And yes," Basaal admitted, "to be perfectly honest with the world, the thought that I might someday have to leave Imirillia behind to keep my fidelity to the Illuminating God had come time and again. But if I actually would was still a mystery. And now I am as you see me, forced away from my covenants and my kin, in an imposed exile."

"I see before my eyes a young man trying to live by the honor he has held himself to. By my measure, that is not honor lost," Thayne assured Basaal. "But tell me this: does your Illuminating God demand your life be lived in Zarbadast? Is *that* a tenet of your religion?"

"No," Basaal said impatiently. "Of course not."

"Edith, your mother, once wrote me a letter, saying that she thought her journey to Zarbadast had been predetermined—fate or blessing, whatever you subscribe to." Thayne paused.

Basaal shook his head in the darkness. "So?"

"So, if your mother felt her path lay in Zarbadast, why is it so impossible for you to ask if your Illuminating God desired to place you in Aemogen?"

Basaal scowled, considering Thayne to be a mad man.

"Do not look at me like that," Thayne said. "I can feel your accusatory glare in the dark." His voice was full of amusement. "I can see you have never even considered the idea that your fate might be here."

"Impossible," Basaal stated.

"But why?" Thayne asked. "I ask again, is there anything in your covenants that requires you to live in Zarbadast? Or in Imirillia, for that matter?"

"Yes," Basaal said hastily and then corrected himself. "Well, not in those exact terms. But I am covenanted to my ancestors and my posterity: to honor the place I have been given and to serve along with my brothers for the benefit of Imirillia."

"You are caught on a problem I do not see," Thayne said. "For honoring Imirillia could come in many forms." Thayne sighed. "Remember this, the same stars grace every land."

The words cut into Basaal, and he sat up straight. "Why do you speak those words?" he asked. "What did Eleanor tell you?"

"Eleanor has told me nothing." Thayne pushed himself up on his elbow. "Your mother was very dear to me, young man. I have loved her better than I have loved almost any soul of this world." Thayne's voice bore the truth of the statement. "We wrote often, especially in the early days after her departure. That line was a bit of a letter I sent when she was content but regretting her distance from home and kinsman."

Basaal moved his fingers across the gold and diamond Safeeraah his mother had given him. "What is the point of this conversation, again?" he said tartly.

"That perhaps you can choose!" Thayne said, his voice rising with impatience. "Is stubbornness your inheritance, boy? There are choices you can make without dishonoring the covenants you have made to your god and perhaps even to Imirillia. Quit damning yourself, and spend some time deciding if this is a path you may *want* to take. It is set before you. Be willing to ask the question. Did you not say that your father had ceased to consider the true welfare of the empire in his new bloodletting crusade?"

"I thought you said my coming here was fate?" Basaal replied, ignoring Thayne's question. "And now you say that I have a choice in the matter?"

"Fate and choice." Thayne sighed. "It's time you learned, Basaal, that just because a pathway has opened up to you, that even if it is the exact course your life is meant to take, you still have to choose it. As the sun follows the course of his day, you must choose the way you will follow—be it ordained by a God or otherwise."

"And has your experience been identical to mine, cousin?" Basaal asked, emphasizing this last word.

"No," Thayne said. "It has not."

"Then let me decide what my own course requires," Basaal said. "I'll thank you if we can get some sleep now."

"Had you time to consider Aemogen's plan to attack the Imirillian encampment?" Thayne asked, ignoring Basaal's irritated request.

Basaal stared at the stars above him and rolled his head to the side. "Yes."

He had considered Aemogen's plan.

"And?"

"It's terrifying."

Danth, now the youngest fen lord in Aemogen, showed no real emotion when he asked Basaal for help planting the final field before dark.

"It won't be long," Danth said. "And as the men and women here have been working at it a lot longer than you, I figured I'd ask you to give it a go."

Basaal nodded, grabbing an edge of hard bread and pulling himself up to the wagon Danth was driving.

"I see they've given you the heel," Danth said after some time.

Basaal chewed the difficult bread and swallowed. "Yes," he said. "With almost every meal, they give me the small, hard end of the loaf, even when there are other pieces to be had. I'm beginning to take the hint."

Danth was slow in responding, but when he did, it was with quiet words, and none of the brashnness he'd shown in their first meeting almost a year ago, when they'd fought before the fen. "In Common Field," he said, "the end of the bread is for luck."

Basaal was taken aback. "Luck?"

"Tradition holds that it signifies you've a hard road and may there be luck in it. Or something of the sort."

"And here I've been, grumbling about it for the last four days," Basaal said, his face flushing.

"Don't feel the badger," Danth replied, and he actually smiled. "I've made more mistakes as fen lord than there ever was on the earth, and they still go chancing on me."

"How has it been?" Basaal approached carefully.

"Whoa," Danth said slowly to the horse as it took a misstep and jerked away. "At first, I kept feeling angry and sayin' to myself, 'This isn't how it's supposed to go, is it?'" Danth pulled up to the freshly plowed field, spoke a word to the horses, and then dropped the reins. Basaal waited for him to continue. "But it took me about as long as it took to say the words for me to realize that saying them did me no good. There was a new place for me in this world, and if I was going to take it right, I had to let it be what it was and try to find some peace about it."

"Do you mean you forgave?" Basaal asked.

Danth looked towards Basaal a long moment. "It means I forgave you."

Basaal did not know what to say. Danth seemed no more comfortable with the words than the prince, and so he motioned to the bags of seed in the wagon. "If we're to get any work done before dark, we'd best get started."

⸺⟨◦⟩⸺

Even with Basaal gone, Eleanor's nights of wakefulness did not disappear. More and more, she lay awake, thinking, wondering. But in her loss of sleep she found solitude. Her days were not restful—they had too much to accomplish before the attack—but at night, despite the exhaustion, she felt a hint of clarity through the fog, like the moonlight that invaded and illuminated the dark castle corridors.

It was in the throne room where Eleanor found herself sitting for hours at a time. Though dark and deep, the shadows did not bother Eleanor. Here, she could spread each mental thread out—like ribbons across the floor—and sit and stare and think. If Hastian was aware of her wanderings, he did not interfere, and he did not follow. Still, she did not feel alone. The memory of the dead accompanied these wakeful hours.

One night she saw Doughlas, or thought she did. A movement or a feeling had caught her attention, and Eleanor had looked up to see her fen rider walking from one side of the throne room to the other, as if he were on some pressing business. She lifted her hand and was about to call out his name but said nothing. He turned and looked right to where Eleanor sat. His puckish grin spread quickly across his face, and he acknowledged the queen with a nod, though his manner was not as a subject to his queen but as an equal.

Then he was gone.

———⟨⟨⟨✦⟩⟩⟩———

It must have been Hastian who told Basaal, upon the prince's return to Ainsley Rise, how Eleanor was spending the long hours of the night.

"So, this is why you are losing color and form, dropping weight, your cheeks wan and eyes tired," Basaal exaggerated as he walked toward Eleanor across the late hour of the night. It was the first time he had entered the throne room since the day of his trial. "Had I returned from Common Field sooner, I should have pestered Hastian more quickly," he added, "forced him to give up your secret."

Basaal let himself down, leaning against the leg of her throne to the left of Eleanor's feet, while his own feet fell down the steps. What she could see of him looked tussled and tired. He wore no shoes. "It's the only thing he has ever given up, you know, about you," Basaal said. "But I think Hastian was relieved to have someone else know."

"I do manage a few hours of sleep," Eleanor said, finding herself actually pleased to see he had returned. "The fighting at the pass keeps me up, the names of the dead, the preparations, the ghosts."

"You and your ghosts," Basaal said and then yawned, sounding more himself. "I'm never quite sure what to make of them all."

Eleanor shifted her head in agreement.

"You are what, ten, eleven days from marching out? On the seven stars—" He blew the air from his lungs. "Crispin says you will ride before the army and watch the battle from Colun Tir?"

"Yes," she said, leaning back, her fingers playing with loose locks of her own hair.

They sat in the silence, Basaal adjusting himself occasionally. Finally, he spoke again. "Eleanor, you need to sleep. Come." He stood and offered her his hand, which she took because she would have been too tired to stand up on her own.

They walked together, through the corridors and stairwells, back to Eleanor's apartments. Eleanor noticed that Hastian followed silently. Her Queen's Own took up his position by the door as Basaal walked Eleanor, his arm around her waist, to her bedchamber. He helped her lay down, adjusting her covers about her—just as he had those nights in Zarbadast, when they had been more honest, more brave with one another.

Afterward, instead of going down the long spiral staircase to his dungeon cell, Basaal lay down before the fire in Eleanor's audience chamber and fell asleep.

He woke early to the sound of someone moving about the room. Basaal turned his head to see Miya rushing silently past him. When he yawned and sat up, she turned, her face showing a fierce blush.

"Begging your pardon, Prince," Miya said. "I did not see you there at first, but I'm going now."

"No," Basaal said. He stood and rubbed his eyes before running his fingers through his hair. "I should be up. Go about your business, and pay me no mind."

"Yes, Your Majesty," she said, and then curtsied and left anyway.

Basaal half laughed, then walked towards Eleanor's partially open door. He knocked softly and, when there came no answer, peeked his head in. Sleeping deeply, Eleanor appeared to have not moved from the moment he had lain her down onto her bed. At the familiarity of the scene, Basaal felt one side of his mouth playing with a smile. He shut the door carefully before taking the stairs down into the dungeon to find his boots and cloak. He was going out this morning.

The sun had not yet broken into the day as Basaal walked down to the river north of the Ainsley Rise. There was a small spit of sand with a clump of cattails growing to one side. It was here he began the motions of ritual prayer, moving into a kneeling position before prostrating himself on the ground as he repeated the words of honor to the Illuminating God.

The sand felt cold against his knees, but Basaal didn't mind. It had been hard to pray in Aemogen; his anger had created a wall between him and his meditations. Thayne had been right when he had taken Basaal to work in Common Field. He'd needed the exertion. He had needed, Basaal was forced to admit, to think of others before himself. Now, as his body moved in the patterns of worship, a balance was beginning to return, and his heart felt almost calm.

Finishing the rituals, Basaal reached down into the cold sand and moved it through his fingers, feeling the grains—gritty, smooth, perfect. Now came the time for him to call upon the Illuminating God with his own words, perhaps pour out the heartache of turning his back on his own people. He placed his hands over his heart and began to offer whatever was before his mind. More than he asked for help, he asked for understanding and guidance. The sun broke out across the east, and Basaal could feel its warmth catching in his cloak and on his back. He continued to pray.

"Thy way through sand and stone," he repeated aloud several times. "Thy way through sand and—" But before Basaal could end his oblations, a feeling surged across his shoulders, a feeling of recognition, of familiarity. Then the feeling gave way to the briefest glimpse of an image: Basaal, standing with Aedon and Crispin, his sword in hand. He blinked and opened his eyes. He shook his head and stared towards the river. His own mind, surely, had conjured up the image. The picture was gone now, but it had felt so real that Basaal looked down at his hand to make sure he was not actually gripping his sword.

⁃⸪⸫⸙⸫⸪⁃

It did not take long for the clatter and clamor of training to slow to a stop when Basaal stepped onto the field. He felt like a stone thrown into a thick, muddy pond, its repercussion an ungraceful intrusion. Perhaps he should not have come.

"Prince Basaal," Crispin said as he came through the crowd, his cheeks red from training. As he approached, the war leader bowed his head in an articulate nod but did not bend at the waist. "How can I be of service to you?" Crispin seemed too tired to be calculably dismissive, but there was no warmth in his words.

A furtive glance at the men told Basaal their conflicting feelings about him were still bright.

"I had written my thoughts regarding your plans," Basaal said, "before I left for Common Field."

"I received them," Crispin replied.

"Good." Basaal looked about at the faces of the men, who were watching the exchange. "I think you may have a solid chance at it."

The war leader did not respond until Basaal's silence forced him to. "Was there anything else, Prince?"

"I'm too idle," Basaal said and then paused, his fingers pressed against the hilt of his sword. "And it would please me to keep my training fresh. Might I join in with you for this morning's exercises?"

Crispin rubbed his chin and stepped closer. "I believe you *might* do anything you would wish, Prince. Although, I cannot say if it is really *best* for the men—or yourself."

"I can cover my own back, as you well know," Basaal said as he stared Crispin in the eye. Then, lowering his voice so that only the young war leader could hear his words, Basaal added, "Unless it makes you nervous to have me here, witnessing your training, worried that I'll run back to the emperor with all your secrets." Basaal looked down at his left forearm as he checked to see if his Safeeraah was secure. "Well, rest your fears. My honor now binds me here, and I will not leave Aemogen before the battle is complete."

"Before?" Crispin replied sternly. "And after?"

Like a warhorse under the threat of demotion, Basaal pulled his chin up sharply and narrowed his eyes at the young war leader.

"You step beyond your mark," Basaal hissed. "What goes on between the queen and myself does not concern you. Don't let it happen again."

They glared at one another, all of Crispin's discipline working hard to keep him from spitting in Basaal's face. He forced himself to chew on the inside of his lip instead and did not speak. Basaal raised his eyebrows, his mouth hinting at a smile. Basaal realized he had sounded like his father, and he relished the ease of using a tone that would silence almost anybody; he hated himself for using it on someone he would still wish to consider a friend.

"Do you have a man willing to fight?" Basaal continued, trying to sound patient, although he was not—he did not need to stand here, begging for a partner.

Crispin breathed out slowly and tilted his head while allowing his boyish grin to cover his anger. "I'll see if I can find you a worthy partner."

Five minutes later, Basaal stood with his sword drawn, looking down at a trembling fourteen-year-old boy, holding a pathetic excuse for a weapon. A crowd had gathered, but Basaal's black mood held them off, and they watched from a distance.

"So, you are my worthy opponent," Basaal said matter-of-factly.

The boy's eyes went wide, and he stuttered out an attempt to explain that he was no kind of expert. The amusement of watching the boy's terror held Basaal from speaking for only a moment before he chided himself for his meanness and gave the boy a reassuring appraisal.

"No need to explain yourself," Basaal said. "We can run through some exercises and see where you are." Basaal hesitated before continuing. "From what fen do you come?" he asked. "I believe I must have seen you last year, during the battle run."

"Rye Field fen, Your Majesty," the young man said, stumbling over the address with uncertainty. "I am called Tarit."

"Tarit?" Basaal rolled the name over his memory. "You're not the potter, are you?"

Obvious pleasure spread a shy smile across the young man's face. "I showed you about my potter's shed."

"Yes, I remember. I owe you some glazes, don't I?" Basaal said as he remembered his promise. "After all this, I shall see it done.

Now, I am in desperate need of training. Will you oblige?"

Tarit's timidity was chased away by Basaal's crisp instructions as the pair began to work through the same sword exercises he had taught the young man the summer before. After this disciplined practice of technnique, he began an open spar, and Tarit threw his whole heart into the exercise. The young man had improved, and Basaal asked if he had been training.

"My mother made me work at it every day," Tarit explained, "because she wants me to come back alive."

Later that afternoon, Aedon found Basaal still on the training grounds, working with a small but willing group of men. It felt much like the battle run had, save that Crispin and his top officers stayed apart from the impromptu training for most of the day. There were also many men acting offish and grumbling, willing to serve accusatory glares in his direction rather than join in his instruction. But his small and eager group satisfied Basaal nonetheless. When the prince saw Aedon, he pulled himself away from a scrimmage and greeted the councillor.

"Aedon," Basaal said as he extended his hand.

"Prince," Aedon replied, bowing first before shaking Basaal's hand. Aedon motioned for Basaal to walk with him, so Basaal gave training instructions to the men before falling into step beside Aedon.

"I am glad to see that you've come out today," Aedon admitted.

"Adding one to the small number who are pleased with the idea," Basaal answered as he pulled at his collar in the heat of the day. "I'll not deny that I've enjoyed the drills and the interactions with the few men willing to associate with me. I have yet to be run through, at the very least."

"Yes." Aedon laughed. "Aside from Crispin's frigid temperatures and the general suspicion of the soldiers—whom you yourself trained very effectively, I might add—do you find yourself feeling more accustomed to life at Ainsley Rise?"

Basaal shrugged but did not answer. They were at the edge of camp now, standing before a spring meadow of green grasses.

"What is it you would like to speak to me about?" Basaal asked as he stopped and turned, his hand resting on his sword more from habit than from thought.

Aedon scanned Basaal's face.

"If this is about myself and Eleanor—" Basaal broke off, trying to fight the faint bristle he'd heard in his own words.

"No," Aedon responded immediately. "Only a fool would walk a second time into that burning barn. And of the many things I am, I do not believe a fool to be one of them."

Basaal's face relaxed, and he crossed his arms. "Burning barn?"

"It's an expression, not a prediction," Aedon replied immediately. "I have come for something that I had hoped you would have volunteered by now."

"Speak."

"Your leadership," Aedon said.

The words stuck to Basaal's skin uncomfortably.

"Go on," he said. "Be blunt about it."

"I can abbreviate it for you," Aedon replied evenly. "You, Prince Basaal, live by honor. From our many conversations, both last year and since your return, I know you do not believe in the aggressive tactics of your father to conquer this and other lands. You hate war and its results, although you do love fighting, and I have yet to reconcile that—" Aedon added plainly before continuing. "So, here you are, bound to Aemogen and to Eleanor by this honor. Is it really your intention to sit at Ainsley Rise as we march out to fight? If this is your plan, I would ask you to reconsider for the sake of said honor. Join with us to defend our sovereignty."

"I am only one man," Basaal replied.

"You are one thousand men in the eyes of those you have trained. Whether they can forgive you for it or not, they cannot leave the image of who you are aside. You are more than one soldier, you are practically..." Aedon lost his words, looking frustrated.

"Immortal. A demigod," Basaal answered ironically.

Aedon's face looked blank for a moment before a humorous expression crossed it. "I suppose that is one way to say it. Yes. Quite accurate." He laughed. "Although—"

"Although, you would never have said it that way," Basaal guessed.

"No."

"Neither would Eleanor." Basaal sighed. "And what of her leadership?"

"It is there, unbroken," Aedon answered immediately. "But her work for your pardon has created a distance, an unsettling feeling among some of the people. If the two of you were to unite for Aemogen, not only would it create the kind of power I believe we need to have any hope in this battle, but also the people would forgive her, praise her even, for sparing your life. You would become a king who could stand with our queen."

"You would have me go into battle against my own army? You would ask me to cut down the men whom I have been responsible for? What of them and the lives of their families?"

"I am asking you to consider it, yes," Aedon confirmed bluntly.

"This is hell." Basaal moved his hands to his hips and looked at the ground, spitting into the grass as he weighed Aedon's words. "I will admit to you," he finally said, "I've already been wrestling with this question since I returned from Common Field. I will also admit that Eleanor has promised me my freedom, if I so choose, once the battle has been decided. I have made no promises to her that I will stay and become King." He caught Aedon's eyes as he spoke truthfully. "Did she tell you that?"

"No," Aedon said, and his face creased. "Yet, I don't feel surprised by the revelation."

"The burning barn," Basaal said, kicking the dirt as these words came slowly from his mouth.

"It's an expression, Basaal, nothing more."

"I only wonder." Basaal took a deep breath. "Was it the moon or the sun that set it ablaze? Something to think about."

Basaal turned away from Aedon, returning to Tarit and the others, who were sitting and standing now in a circle. Settling himself down beside the boy, Basaal joined the casual round of conversation while the image he had seen of himself—standing between Aedon and Crispin, his sword drawn—worked circles around his mind.

CHAPTER

THIRTEEN

That night, when Eleanor again found herself wandering into the throne room, a figure was already draped across her throne. When she did not say anything, Basaal spoke.

"Your throne is more comfortable than mine."

"Is that a symbolic observation?" Eleanor asked.

Basaal replied with a low laugh, and then he straightened himself. "I can move if you would like, but I believe there is room for us both."

Eleanor almost thought to turn back around and return to bed, but he had sounded like he had in Zarbadast. And after watching the shadows on his face, she sighed and stepped onto the dais. Basaal lifted his left arm to give her room, placing it around her shoulders as she settled in next to him. It felt like coming home, the pressure of his body against hers.

"I just lost a wager with myself," he admitted. "I assumed you would return to your rooms."

"It was tempting," Eleanor admitted, yawning, half wondering if Hannia would come rushing into the throne room to send them off to sleep. "I should return and force myself asleep." The air in his lungs shifted, and Eleanor felt the pressure of his chest against her shoulder as he prepared himself to speak.

"Stay awhile with me."

The words webbed out across every dark corner of the throne room before returning to her in a single, soft entreaty. Eleanor took them in with no effort to shield herself from the emotion of it. Stay with *me*, she wished to reply.

Eleanor lifted her hand to rest on his chest, and in response, Basaal pulled her tighter against him as if they had finally given themselves permission to care for each other again.

"As I left the training fields today," Basaal said, "I passed a man whom I'd met last year. He lives with his wife here in Ainsley, a shoemaker by trade. I went to shake hands, and he refused me."

"Hmm," Eleanor said sleepily, turning her face in closer to Basaal. "Did he say why?"

"Oh, I am sure you can guess the reasons. Betrayal leaves an acidic residue, does it not?" He rested his chin on the top of her head and breathed out slowly. "He is also bitter because, during his last tour serving at the pass, he was caught by an Imirillian arrow, straight through his hand."

Wincing, Eleanor looked at her own hand, resting just below Basaal's collarbone. "No bones were broken, apparently," Basaal continued. "But the head of the arrow had been dipped in poison, so he'd had to get an amputation to spare his life."

"And so he would not greet you?" Eleanor repeated.

"No, he would not," Basaal said. "'Are we not friends?' I asked him. But Haide—that is his name—just laughed. 'Hang me if you want, Prince, but I'll not bow down to the likes of you.' And then he was off, carrying his sword with his useless left hand."

"Does this man now have any way to support his family?" Eleanor asked.

"I couldn't say."

The darkness hung about them, and Eleanor kept trying to say that when they returned from the war—if they returned—she would see the shoemaker taken care of. But sleep weighed in her bones, and Basaal's presence was so peaceful. And she needed him to stay.

"There is something I wanted to speak with you about," he said, his voice sounding far away. She thought she moved, acknowledged what he had said, but Eleanor was too close to sleep to know for certain. "Remember," he said softly, "there is something I must speak with you about."

In the early morning, Eleanor woke to find herself in her own bed. Basaal must have carried her. A sliver of the memory played at the edges of her consciousness. He may have even kissed her, but she was not certain. Not wanting to leave the warmth of her bed, yet knowing that sleep was gone, Eleanor decided to retrieve the reports from her desk and bring them back into the bedroom.

As she entered the gray-lit audience chamber, she saw that Basaal was fast asleep on the sofa near the fire. "Basaal," Eleanor whispered, and he stirred. "Basaal." The prince did not open his eyes but turned to face Eleanor, folding his arms tightly against his chest for the chill of the spring morning.

"I must fight," he answered, still half asleep. "I was told I must fight for Aemogen. And I promised I would." The words tumbled painfully from his tired lips, and he sank back into sleep.

The news burst upon them like a whirlwind or a gale out from the sea. And when Eleanor thought about it later, she was glad that days of endless rain had accompanied the tidings. The fen rider who had brought the news was wet and chilled through, but the fire in his own eyes had been warmth sufficient. His news was that Emperor Shaamil had sent a small envoy to negotiate with the queen.

"Crispin was worried if he waited for Your Majesty's approval, it would be too late to both receive the envoy and to make for the Maragaide Valley by the appointed day," the fen rider explained. "But if we received the envoy immediately, they could come and be gone before we were set to march out. And this would only increase our chances that the emperor would have no notion of the attack, seeing as how we could send back false information. Hoping to speak in your name, Crispin agreed that they might send six men, blindfolded the entire three-day ride, to Ainsley Rise. So, they set out yesterday morning and will be here tomorrow."

"Why would Shaamil be sending an envoy into Aemogen?" Eleanor asked aloud. She did not look at her council but at Basaal, who sat silent nearby.

"Did he specifically say it was to negotiate?" Basaal asked the fen rider.

"That was the implication," the fen rider answered, "but never in so many words. Crispin believes it is an intimidation tactic that we can turn for our own benefit."

"They will come under the banner of negotiation, but their terms will all be used for intimidation and the advantage of Zarbadast," Basaal said, crossing his arms and feeling caught. "If you are too subservient, your behavior will be suspect. Better to appear brash and defiant. Then the message they take back to Emperor

Shaamil will be one of ignorance and pride."

"How are we to bring a delegation of six men into Ainsley, the heart of our military encampment?" Sean asked, worried. "We cannot hide three thousand soldiers."

"I assume this is why Crispin demanded that they be blindfolded," Eleanor replied.

"And we can suspend all training on the day the delegation is in Ainsley, keeping the delegation within windowless rooms, under constant guard. It can be done," Aedon confirmed confidently.

"Let them come," Eleanor consented. "We will plan what we want Emperor Shaamil to think of us."

Eleanor had assumed Basaal would be willing to sit on a throne beside her when the Imirillian delegates were given an audience. But he said he would not.

"There is nothing for me to consider," Basaal argued. "You are asking me to openly declare myself as your ally before my father's delegation. No. I will not do that. I refuse to even be in the room."

Eleanor pressed her palms against her desk and tried again. "I am asking you to stand beside me."

"You are asking me to cause confusion, questions, and intimidation by being present."

"Those would be secondary benefits," Eleanor stated honestly. "But I want you beside me, first and foremost, for your support, your strength, your help to read the situation. You know what to watch for."

Basaal shifted in his chair, his arms crossed stubbornly, then dismissed himself from the queen's rooms without so much as another word.

"I am only asking him to consider the idea," Eleanor said impatiently when she spoke with Aedon later, reiterating the reasonableness of the request she'd made to Basaal. Thunder sounded off the windows, but the constant rainstorms that had been washing over Ainsley for the last two days were now letting up to become dismal drizzles.

"You are not asking him to consider it," Aedon countered as she shuffled through the reports from the pass. "You are telling him to do as you wish."

"That's untrue." Eleanor threw herself against the back of her chair, staring at the window. "I wish he would reconsider," Eleanor finally said, staring back at the papers on her desk, drumming her fingers.

"Is it really that important?" Aedon asked fairly. "As a matter of state?"

"No." It was not, she admitted to herself. Eleanor could face the delegation with her own mastery of the Imirillian language. Eleanor knew her craft, and she did not need Basaal to sit beside her. But she wanted him to.

"I know," Aedon said, although she had not spoken her desires. "I wish he would."

Later, she found Basaal in the dark gray of late afternoon, walking the western battlements, inconsiderate of the wind and the threat of returning rain. Once he saw that Eleanor had stepped out onto the wall, Basaal leaned against the stone battlement, waiting for her to come to him. He pulled his cloak tighter, against the chill. She stopped beside him, looking towards the west, where no hint of evening light broke the gray sky.

"Will you not stand beside me?" Eleanor asked again, as the fierce wind swept her skirts.

"Consider it a free lesson in Imirillian statecraft," Basaal said, and he pulled back from the battlement as he continued to watch the heavy gray clouds spin across the western downs. "You are always alone when choice and consequence come up against each other. It matters not who stands beside you in your life or how much they can give. There always comes a point where you are alone against the challenges you face."

A split of lightning was followed by the drum-deep sound of thunder, rolling out over the green field.

"You confuse me," Eleanor said, her voice unwavering, her expression as tempestuous as the sky. "You place peculiar limits that I don't understand." The clouds spilled open, and rain began to fall hard over Ainsley. Eleanor did not look away from Basaal's face despite the downpour. "Having a relationship with someone, friendship or love, means standing by them, standing present, even if those you stand with must face certain realities alone."

The wind spit the rain in their faces, and, finally, Basaal turned with a conflicted expression towards Eleanor. "You are asking me to come and stand before a delegation from my father and appear as if I have chosen Aemogen willingly." Squinting against the heavy rain, he brushed the water away from his face. Basaal flinched as Eleanor threw her arms up in frustration.

"You said, just three days ago, that the Imirillian invasion was unjust!" she shouted above the sound of the rain. "That, to satisfy the Illuminating God, you would stand and give yourself to Aemogen's defense!"

"And by the seven stars, I will!" Basaal cursed, shouting back. "You know I will!"

"But you will not stand with me now," Eleanor cried. "I do not think I can face this war on my own, Basaal."

He took a step closer to Eleanor and pointed towards the castle. "You have all the others! You have Aedon and Crispin and Edythe—the entire country is standing with you!" Basaal spread his hands out before him. "What difference could I possibly make?"

"Is there nothing I can say to persuade you?" Eleanor gulped back her emotions before continuing. "The strength you give me—"

She brought her hands down on the wet stone of the battlement before her and looked away from him, towards the north. The high mountains of the Arimel could not be seen, cloaked in the deepening gray of the afternoon. Eleanor was wet through, and she began to shiver as the wind increased. She knew it was unfair to ask so much of him and that, perhaps, the only strength he had left he needed for himself.

"I'm sorry." The wind carried Basaal's words off his lips, but Eleanor heard them clear enough. "I cannot stand with you."

Eleanor turned and watched as Basaal tucked his shoulders against the rain and moved south along the battlements towards the travelers' house. The muscles in Eleanor's face tightened beneath her eyes, and then she, making a defeated sound, went north.

The next morning, Basaal took himself to the river. Running low and calm, it was nothing like the river of the year before. What had then been tumbling and fervent was now quiet, an omen for little water for the year ahead. He paced along the bank, tracing his own footsteps up and down the entire morning.

The birds of the day seemed quite unaware of his mood and

continued their pleasantries as he paced in the long grass and thought of Eleanor. He wanted to stand with her, as he had done in Zarbadast, but he could not commit himself to the declaration this would make. As unfair as his forced exile was in comparison with Eleanor's futile attempts to save her small country. His heart felt still and hard and, as much as he hated to admit it to himself, sad.

And he knew his sadness would dictate the distance again growing between them.

Emaad found him sitting morosely near the riverbank.

"You missed evening meal last night."

"So it would seem," Basaal said as he flicked the blade of grass he wove between his fingers into the river.

"You were always ridiculous when sulking," Emaad challenged, glaring at Basaal with stubborn affection in his eyes. "Stand up."

"Why?" But Basaal stood when Emaad did not respond to his question.

"You refuse to close any path," Emaad said. "It is a weakness. It will always keep you between the places you should be."

"Pardon?" Basaal looked towards his brother, confused.

"Your whole life, your summer here in Aemogen, Eleanor's escape from Zarbadast… Does it surprise you that here you are, living the consequence of your balancing game between honor and what you have always known? For a freeman, you have imprisoned yourself by refusing to declare where you will stand."

"I've never been a freeman," Basaal said, his laugh a clip of anger.

Emaad shook his head and then did what he thought best, he hit Basaal as hard as he knew how. The younger brother reeled backward. Basaal didn't cry out in pain but found himself smiling as he recovered himself, dabbing the blood away from his split lip. He could feel the numb swelling against his gums.

"You want to have a go at it then?" Basaal challenged good-naturedly.

"You've spent your entire life balancing, balancing between Father, our religion, your conscience, the rights of others. Well, there comes a time when you have to choose a side. But you waited." Emaad paused, looking calm. "You waited, trying to do what was honorable—I know—but sooner or later a decision would have to be made. You refused to make it, and so, life had to do it for you," he said. "Now, here you are. You have drawn the line and find yourself on the opposite side of the emperor." Emaad laughed and fingered the line on his neck. "Is that really a surprise? The reason you've played this game your whole life is because you could never stomach the idea of becoming the man he is!"

Basaal was getting agitated. He pressed his fingers against his lip and took them away. On his fingers, the blood formed patterns in bright red: the symbol of Basaal's house, surrounded with a thousand representations of the wanderer's mark. He smeared the blood and looked back at his brother. "Why must everyone have an opinion about what I must do with my life?"

"You want my opinion?" Emaad asked. "You can't stay in Zarbadast. You know that. I see it in your face. Where would you go, otherwise, but here? Wander around the Continent, living a shiftless life? You would be racked with guilt. Your honor would haunt you every night. So, you have now what you would have chosen anyway. Give yourself," Emaad urged. "Give yourself to Aemogen. You no longer need to hold anything back. You have chosen your side, and whether you recognize it or not, it is what you would have eventually wished you had chosen. Stop moping."

"I'm not moping," Basaal said in anguish. "I'm mourning."

He opened his eyes to find blackness. It was night, and the fire in Eleanor's audience chamber had gone out. Yes, Basaal remembered, he had come back from the travelers' house after Eleanor was already asleep.

He sat up, breathing hard, his heart racing. A dream. He sat against the couch and leaned his head back in relief. He yawned, but it was at a cost, for his mouth stung. Basaal lifted a finger to his lip. When he brought it away and moved his fingers towards the moonlight, he could see blood. A chill ran through his spine. He smeared the blood between his fingers, and tried to go back to sleep. Sleep did not come.

Eleanor was seated in the throne room, wearing the black velvet gown she had commissioned in Calafort, her hair bound up with the Battle Crown in place. There was no smile on her lips. Her council sat in their places, and several companies of soldiers stood in silent attention, each soldier holding a spear in his hand, the ends of which rested on the stone, pointing to the sky. Edythe met Eleanor's eye and smiled just as the sound of footsteps caused Eleanor to look back. Prince Basaal, dressed in the most formal clothing he'd acquired in Aemogen, wearing his elegant weaponry of black and pearl. He was clean-shaven, crisp, and someone had split his lip again.

"Pardon my tardiness," Basaal said once he came before her and bowed. "You know how I suffer for my vanity."

As he was about to move aside toward his throne, Eleanor reached for his hand. He looked her in the eye, and she swallowed, grateful.

"This is a difficult thing for me." The words were spoken so lightly that they hardly pushed against the air between them.

"I know," Eleanor said, almost losing her composure. "Perhaps I was unfair to wish it. But I thank you."

Nodding, Basaal took a deep breath. "Are you ready to sound brash and impetuous?"

Eleanor's mouth broke into a smile. "With your experience, I don't doubt our success." He scanned her face, his resignation showing through the thin mask he wore.

Crispin entered the throne room as Basaal took his seat beside the queen, nodding to Eleanor. The sound of many footsteps clattered in from the corridor. As they waited, Basaal transformed, now appearing casual, almost disinterested. Eleanor met his eyes, and a strained smile was shared between them.

"Reminds me of home." He spoke in Imirillian so only she could understand. "False confidence, word manipulation—I wouldn't miss it for anything."

Two dozen soldiers entered, escorting six men, still blindfolded from their journey. One of the Imirillians was particularly tall, dressed in—what were by now—dusty white robes. Eleanor almost laughed out loud. Ammar. The emperor had sent Ammar.

Six soldiers stepped forward to remove the blindfolds, and Eleanor smiled at the physician once he found her face. The corners of his mouth turned up, and he raised his eyebrows in greeting. Then, as his face wandered from Eleanor to the throne beside her, he froze, and Eleanor saw an expression she didn't even know the physician possessed: shock.

Drakta, the man whom Eleanor had encountered in Basaal's tent all those months ago, was the leader of the delegation. Once he saw the prince, he took a step forward, intense hatred for Basaal in his eyes.

Eleanor held out a hand. "You are quite welcome to remain where you are," she spoke in Imirillian.

Shaamil's war leader glared. "Hospitable journey this has been."

"It was not meant to be so," Eleanor said, sitting up straighter in her throne. "I assume we will conduct our business in Imirillian for the sake of your envoy?"

"We don't speak your foul language," Drakta growled back.

"And what is it the emperor desires you to say? Have you come to announce your surrender?"

Five of the six men in the emissary, the officers and soldiers of Shaamil, laughed. The sixth stood with his hands behind his back, surveying the architecture of the throne room, seeming uninterested in the politics of the moment.

"His Grace, Emperor Shaamil, wishes us to tell you that your defense at the pass is charming, but he is ready to begin the conflict in earnest. With much equanimity, he again offers Aemogen the opportunity to reconsider its position."

"Under what terms?" Eleanor sounded uninterested.

"The lives of your people, all of the people, would be spared. Yours, of course, would be forfeit as well as the princeling's, I'd imagine." Drakta looked at Basaal. "Although, when the emperor hears the tale that his beloved son has gone to join the Aemogen peasants, he may want to take the boy back to Zarbadast for his death."

"Go to the devil," Basaal interjected with a challenge in his eyes. "Crawl back to your kennel and remain the emperor's yapping dog."

Drakta took a step forward, and every soldier in the room took a step towards Drakta, their spears pointing at the man.

"If you will please refrain from moving," Eleanor said calmly.

All the emotions he must have controlled for years now showed in Drakta's face as he stared down Basaal.

"Is that truly all you have come to say, Drakta?" Eleanor said. "It seems a pity to have ridden in such discomfort for days to be so utterly predictable."

He turned his burning eyes on her. "I come with a warning: If you refuse the emperor now, he will send a force up the pass, swarming like desert dogs into your country. The pass will soon fall, and all of this," he said, looking up and around the throne room in disgust, "will be gone."

Eleanor rose, and Basaal followed suit. She took a step down the dais and stood before the war leader. "Well, then, let them come," she stated slowly. "And you will find that what awaits you in this land is more hellish than you could possibly imagine."

"Desert dog, indeed," Basaal sneered as he looked Drakta up and down.

"Uuaahh!" Drakta spun his hand towards the prince. Crispin and his men rushed forward but not before a spray of white was flung into Basaal's face. Basaal screamed as it hit his eyes. He turned away, cursing.

Guards surrounded Shaamil's envoy, three of them grabbing Drakta and holding him in place, Aedon was calling for water, and Eleanor rounded on Crispin. "Did you not search them for weapons?"

"We did!" Crispin insisted, before he ordered the envoy be taken to the dungeons.

Basaal was pulling away from any attempt at assistance, swearing whenever touched, his fingers clutching at his eyes. Aedon grabbed Basaal's arms.

"Take him to my rooms," Eleanor ordered. Then she sent Crispin with a message, requesting the presence of Ammar in her chambers.

In the moment after Drakta's hand shot out, Basaal had fallen back, raising his hands to his face. He tried to open his eyes but could not. A million suns had exploded, and then darkness and pain. He cursed. Voices rang out. Someone called for water, and then there was a scuffle and shouting. The pain increased in sharp bursts, causing Basaal to breathe in suddenly, which he followed with another string of curses. Basaal could not tell who was around him or whose hands steadied his arms. Water was brought, and they began placing cool rags over his eyes as they brought him quickly to Eleanor's chambers.

It was Aedon, Basaal believed, who forced him into a chair and brought a wet rag again to his face.

"Open your eyes," he commanded.

"I can't, you bastard," Basaal retaliated.

"Basaal, hold still!" Edythe said. "That includes your tongue."

"The physician!" someone said.

"He's here," Aedon said, breathing a sigh of relief. Basaal was still in great agony from the pain.

"Your physician is useless," Basaal snarled as he fought against any assistance. "He used Arillian salts!"

"Quiet!" Eleanor said, her voice cutting through the noise, and the clamor stopped. "On Old Ainsley, Basaal, let my man attend to you until Ammar is brought up. Proceed, doctor."

"I've never seen this," Eleanor's court physician said, flustered. "But I suppose I need to wash it out as best I can."

"I would think so," Eleanor said urgently, stepping forward, and nodding to Aedon. "Help me, Aedon. Hastian?" Aedon and Hastian pulled Basaal's hands away from his eyes, and Eleanor forced Basaal's eyelid open as water was poured directly over his eye.

"Eleanor!" he shouted at her. "By the seven stars, I will never forgive you—"

She ignored him, and when the physician nodded, they forced open the other eye and repeated the process. Basaal tried to shout, but the water poured into his mouth, and he began to choke.

"So, this is how Imirillian princes are treated in Aemogen," Ammar said from the doorway, where he stood, bound, with Crispin at his elbow. "I suppose turnabout is fair play," he added. Eleanor straightened, and Aedon and Hastian both released Basaal. The prince shot forward, sputtering.

The scene that Ammar must have witnessed struck Eleanor as incredibly funny, and she began to laugh.

⋯⊷⊷⊱⊰⊰⊶⊶⋯

When Basaal woke, it was deep into the night. His eyes throbbed, swollen and burned as they were. Bandages were still in place. As he moved, a groan came from his lips.

Someone touched his cheek softly.

"Sh. Go back to sleep."

It was Eleanor.

"I am so tired," Basaal murmured.

"You should be," Ammar said from nearby. "We gave you something to help you sleep."

Clearing his throat, Basaal braved the words. "And my eyes?"

"I have done all that I know how to with the materials at hand," Ammar said practically. "The Aemogen physician had never seen Arillian salts before, but he did well to wash it out as soon as they could force you to let him. The salve I applied should remain in place for a day, so we will remove the bandages tomorrow. You should sleep through until then—I've a theory it helps with the healing," Ammar added.

"Are you feeling any pain just now?" Eleanor asked quietly.

"Yes." Basaal moved his fingers to find hers.

"I am not in any way saying you deserved this, Basaal," Eleanor said, "but you seem to have an extraordinary gift in aggravating people to violence against you."

Ammar's laugh could be heard from across the room, where he was preparing a draught for the pain.

"I thought that was the plan." Basaal coughed. "You two don't seem to be taking my impending blindness very seriously at all," Basaal said with a short breath. Every movement caused his eyes to burn all the more.

"I do not think it will cause you to go blind," Ammar said. Basaal could hear his brother's footsteps walking towards him. "Drink this," Ammar said.

Eleanor urged Basaal to sit up if he could. It was unbearable. He hissed from the pain. Eleanor put one hand to his back as Ammar brought the sleeping draught to Basaal's lips. The taste was not a pleasant one, but Basaal forced himself to swallow.

"You are a desperate sadist," he said to Ammar and then coughed again, "come all the way to Aemogen just so you can ply your poisons down my throat." The thought caught in Basaal's mind, and he shifted his head in the direction of his brother.

Ammar laughed. "I'm not here to poison you, Basaal. Do not worry your pretty head about that. I have even attended to your freshly split lip. You never could avoid a fight, could you?"

Eleanor helped Basaal lie back down. "Who did you cross fists with this time?" she asked patiently.

"Emaad," Basaal said sleepily. "It was Emaad."

"The sedative must be taking affect." Basaal could hear Ammar's voice, though it was faint now as sleep was claiming his attention. "He is confused."

Basaal slept soundly until the following afternoon, when Ammar decided to remove the bandages and assess the injury. Eleanor sat beside him on the bed, her hand on his forehead, knowing the coming pain would wake him. Ammar began unwrapping the bandages from Basaal's swollen eyes.

"I did not realize the great physician of Zarbadast made house calls," Eleanor said in Imirillian as Ammar worked. Basaal began to stir.

"I didn't realize you two could not live without me," Ammar replied. "Literally." A frown appeared on Ammar's face as he placed his fingers gently near Basaal's eyes. The burns on the skin near his left eye were raw and bright, but there was little or no damage near the right. Basaal sucked in between his teeth and spoke as he roused himself from sleep.

"You've come to kill me at last."

Eleanor's lungs tightened as he spoke. She cleared his hair away from his forehead and smiled, forgetting he could not see it.

"I am going to try and open each eye to see the damage done," Ammar said. "It will be very painful."

Basaal set his face, the same determined expression Eleanor had seen before. She reached down, her fingers wrapping around his, tight and still. Edythe entered, Miya following, carrying water, clean linens, and several springs of dried lavender.

"Ready?" Ammar asked Basaal. The younger prince nodded. Ammar pressed his fingers against Basaal's left eyelid and eased it open. Basaal flinched and breathed in tightly but held still. Ammar frowned again, then slowly pulled away his fingers and inspected Basaal's right eye.

Basaal dug his fingers into Eleanor's palm. "And?" Basaal said, struggling to speak even after Ammar had closed his eyelid.

Ammar's expression was tired. "Vision in the right eye will clarify after only a few days. The left is a more difficult guess. If there is not a full recovery, I would guess you will not loose much sight, but your vision might be blurry."

The physician held up a small vial of amber liquid. "This can be applied directly to the eye," he explained. "It was brought down from Zarbadast, and one of its purposes is to treat Arillian salts. It will burn, but it can help heal what damage you have sustained. It should be applied every hour for the next two days and then three times a day after that."

"Show me how," Eleanor said.

Ammar looked from Eleanor to Basaal. "It is simple, really," he said as he uncorked the vial and leaned it towards Basaal's eye. "Can you open your eye, Basaal?"

He did not respond verbally, but Basaal forced his right eye open, and Ammar dripped the liquid into it.

"Oh!" Basaal opened his mouth from the shock of it, as if he had fallen into a freezing river. Eleanor grimaced as he gripped her hand tighter. She glanced at Edythe, who watched the process with a troubled frown. When Basaal opened his left eye, it looked cloudy.

"Does any light come in?" Ammar asked. Basaal shook his head and clenched his jaw for the pain. Ammar placed the drops in Basaal's left eye with, from what Eleanor could see, the same searing results. He then returned the vial to the table near the window.

Eleanor placed her hand on Basaal's face, careful to avoid touching the burned skin around Basaal's eyes. There would be scars. The sound of clinking glass brought Eleanor's attention back to Ammar, who was busy mixing powders into a cup of water.

"This is what helped you sleep so deeply before," Ammar said. "Your body will have a much needed rest, and I will be here to attend to you when you wake."

Basaal nodded and breathed slowly out of his open mouth.

Eleanor moved her hand behind his neck and helped Basaal into a position where he could drink the physician's concoction. He tried to say something to her, but she could not understand.

"What is it, Basaal?" she asked. But his long slow breathing betrayed him to be falling asleep. His grip on her hand loosened, and Eleanor laid Basaal's head back against the pillow.

After Miya and Edythe had removed themselves from the room, Eleanor left Basaal alone on the bed, coming to sit in a chair beside Ammar. She covered a yawn.

"I must return to the business of state," she said, watching Basaal as she spoke.

"How came you by these scars?" Ammar asked as he reached across, lifting Eleanor's wrist and moving his fingers over the ridges.

"The slavers of the Shera Shee," Eleanor said.

Ammar lifted his cheeks in sympathy. "Are there others?"

"They cover my ankles and cross my back, like an endless line of rope," Eleanor stated. "And you can see my chin well enough for yourself." She moved her finger across the line that wrapped across her neck and up through her lip.

Ammar looked at Eleanor with an honest concern. "There is a cream, which I left back at the pass with most of my supplies, that should help. It will not take away the marks, but it would make them look less angry."

Eleanor nodded, and moved her fingers along the lines on her wrist before she stood. "Will you care for him, Ammar, while I am gone?"

"Yes."

"I will have a messenger outside the door at your disposal," she said. "You are guarded and not free to wander at will, as you are technnically a prisoner of war, but send for me for whatever you need."

Ammar gave a dark half laugh. "Would that I could be more amused by this turn of fate."

A tired smile came to Eleanor's lips. "You will find no assassins here to trouble your sleep."

"What I have found here," Ammar replied, his eyes wandering to Basaal's sleeping form, "is far more troubling, I assure you."

"He's muttering in a language I can't understand," Sean said as he walked along, almost trailing behind Eleanor. "But the farmer with him said he's a friend of yours and that so is the girl."

Ignoring all discipline, Eleanor ran into the stable yard, her hair flying out behind her. Zanntal was looking around, trying to direct the stable boy in Imirillian, tired and frustrated, holding a wide-eyed Sharin. When his eyes found Eleanor, his expression left behind its worry. Eleanor threw her arms around him. Sharin then reached for Eleanor, sliding into her arms. Holding Sharin close, Eleanor whispered comforts into her ear.

"Getting that herdsman's wife to let us leave for Ainsley was a near impossibility," Zanntal said, obviously tired and hungry. "I could not understand a thing they were trying to say, and Sharin cried the entire journey."

Miya came rushing out. "Sean said there was a child?"

"Yes," Eleanor said as she pulled Sharin's hair back from her face and kissed her cheek. "This is Sharin. She came over the mountains with me. Please take her to be washed and fed, then let me know how she fares." After Miya had left with Sharin, Eleanor took Zanntal's arm and walked with him to the travelers' house. "You may bathe and change, if you wish, before the evening meal."

"The woman we stayed with stole my robes while I slept and scrubbed them so hard I am surprised I was able to put them back on," Zanntal said. "But she did mend the rends from the mountains." Zanntal had never looked so serious. "I hope I will not disgrace you before your nobility."

Eleanor laughed as they climbed the stairs of the travelers' house. "We are not quite so formal here in Aemogen," she assured him. "What have you picked up of the language?"

"No, I need nothing," he said, stuttering over the words.

Eleanor laughed again. "It's such a relief to have you here. Tomorrow I can take you to see Basaal."

Zanntal grabbed Eleanor's arm in response. "My prince is in your country?"

"Yes," Eleanor said, turning serious. "I will tell you a little now and more after you have been settled. For Aemogen rides for war in only a handful of days."

Basaal slept the entire day, not waking once when Ammar had applied the amber liquid to his eyes. He finally stirred after the windows had turned dark and Ammar's dinner was long since eaten. Eleanor had not yet returned, and Ammar wondered if she would sleep elsewhere tonight.

Basaal yawned and lifted himself up against the pillows. He moved to rub his eyes before Ammar could warn him, and Basaal hissed at the result, leaning his head back against the wall. Ammar watched his youngest brother with curiosity.

"Did you always plan to come to her?" Ammar asked in Imirillian.

"Pardon?" Basaal replied, sleep heavy in his voice.

"Did you always plan to come to her?"

"No," Basaal said as he rolled his head back against the wall, his face pointing towards the ceiling. The movement brought lines of pain to his face. "Yet, here I am despite—"

"Despite?"

"Despite knowing that even if I were still in camp, I could never send my army against the people of this country." Basaal sighed, and set his mouth in a rueful line. "I was doubting the invasion, in whatever form, long before the Illuminating God forbade me from marching my army into Aemogen."

"Hmmm."

Knowing that his brother was skeptical of his religion, the younger prince expected no more of an answer than what Ammar gave. Basaal shifted towards his brother and tried to open his eyes. His right eye appeared to have cleared, and he could see a vague shadow where his brother was. But it stung too much to open his left. He gave up and swung his legs off the side of the bed, sitting up, feeling the warmth from the nearby fire. "You and I have had many private conversations, questioning Father's motives, especially during these last several years of his aggression. I came to respect this people and could not bear the thought of being responsible for destroying them. But that does not mean I ever thought to join them."

"If you did not come to them, how is it you are here?"

Basaal cleared his throat and felt embarrassed. "I'd developed an irrational desire to know if Eleanor had arrived home. And so, the night I rode out to the pass, I foolishly decided to investigate an old fortress in the mountains, known and used only by the Aemogen army. I was captured and brought here for public trial."

"The charge?"

"High treason," Basaal replied. "The time I'd spent in Aemogen qualified them to try me as a citizen."

"The penalty?"

"Death."

Ammar cocked an eyebrow. "The tale gets better and better."

"I've told you before of the Aemogen legal system," Basaal said as he tried again to open his eyes. "I stood before them, hearing all their accusations against me, not able to utter one word in my defense. My sentence would have been death, and they would have voted for it, every single one of the council, but someone did step forward and argue for pardon on my behalf. Eleanor."

Ammar's face was partly hid in the shadow of the melting candle, yet his eyes still watched Basaal intently. "And?"

"Eleanor argued they should spare me," Basaal said as he raised a hand to his swollen eyelids and touched the tight skin around his left eye. "She reasoned for my life by arguing I had spared her life and sought to protect Aemogen from the emperor, therefore showing character and true intent. She also spoke of all the pains I had taken to prevent another Aramesh. I do not think any of her arguments were swaying the council until, at the end, when she revealed to them and to the court that we had been married, and I was her husband." Basaal frowned. "She asked for claim on my life and volunteered the terms of pardon. In the end, they voted to spare my life."

"And let me guess the rest of the tale," Ammar said smoothly. "You, who should have been grateful to Eleanor for risking her reputation and possibly the respect of her people to save your life, instead refused to show any gratitude for the gift of it."

"She took away my choice in the matter," Basaal whispered.

"It sounds like she preserved your life." Ammar shifted on his chair and leaned forward.

"I was forced," Basaal insisted. "I could not choose to return to the service of the Imirillian Empire; I could not choose to disappear; I could not choose to stay and earn her trust. It was decided what I would do."

"Did you say as much?" Ammar asked.

"I said awful things—so did she," Basaal said and then laughed. "You know, she even told me that, after the war ends, I would be free to go, free to disappear and never see her again." He paused, speaking quieter. "That sounds just as unbearable, but—"

"Will you go?"

"I am not sure if I will even survive the war," Basaal stated blankly, "since I have promised to fight for Aemogen. And now—" Basaal groaned, lifting his hand to his eyes. "What kind of devilry were you up to? How came you to join Drakta's emissary?"

"I had convinced Father to try one last effort at diplomacy. He sent me as punishment, I am certain. Blindfolded, riding an uncomfortable horse, hearing jeers I thankfully did not understand. Drakta acted on his own accord when he attacked you, but Eleanor is right, you are provoking. It's a wonder that she loves you as she does."

Basaal opened his eye and stared at the shadow that was his brother. "I don't know what to do with love, mine or hers. I still can't grasp that I am now separated from Imirillia forever. And she, fairly or unfairly, has become the symbol of that. I've been trying, Ammar. I really have. And once or twice it's been as if we were back in Zarbadast, contented with each other's company. But then"—he made a motion with his hand—"it's gone. A word, a misplaced expression, and all is replaced by pride or circumstance. To make it easier, I tell myself she doesn't care for me in a significant way."

Shrugging, the physician sounded as if he had lost interest in the topic. "She appears to."

"What?"

"Care," Ammar said, "despite more pressing responsibilities."

"Well," Basaal said as he shook off his serious thoughts with a black grin, then grimaced at the pain of it, "how could she resist?"

Ammar guffawed. "Very easily, I assure you."

CHAPTER

FOURTEEN

"It's settled then," Eleanor said, drumming the table with her fingers. "We will send the Imirillians, save Drakta, back to Shaamil with a stalling response, as our forces move into the Maragaide Valley."

Crispin had said earlier that the Imirillians were close to clearing the pass but had no hope of making enough headway to break through Aemogen's fortifications within the week. This was a relief to Eleanor. They reviewed again the progress of the smithies, then heard a report Thayne had received from Marion. Several of the explosives were en route to Marion, and Thayne would leave three days early to be in position with his Marion troop the day before Crispin would lead the attack.

Edythe then reported she was preparing a group of women to come through the mountain to see to the wounded after the fight. They were gathering blankets, preparing basins and rags, and searching for herbs and teas.

"And will there be a celebration, per Aemogen tradition, the night before the armies depart?" Thayne asked.

The thought surprised Eleanor. She glanced at Aedon and then at Thayne, rubbing her finger along the wood grain of the table. "I don't see how we can hold with the tradition, Thayne," she finally said. "The entire nation is heading to war. It is not always a time to dance."

"Begging your pardon, Eleanor, but this is exactly the time," Edythe affirmed quietly. "All of your men are marching to battle. Their wives and sweethearts deserve to dance with them one last time. We should come together, regardless of the situation, as we Aemogens always do."

Aedon leaned back in his chair and looked toward Eleanor.

Eleanor's thoughts glanced on Blaike as she met Edythe's eyes honestly. "Then let us dance."

Hours later, Eleanor cornered Edythe in the records room and asked her to bring Zanntal with her to dinner.

"Please," Eleanor begged. "I know it is a strange request, but I cannot tell you how much I care for him and want him to be comfortable in Ainsley. I am meeting with Aedon up until we eat, and I don't want to send a soldier to fetch him into the castle. He speaks nothing of our language."

"You always give me these assignments, Eleanor. I wish I could finish some of my work."

"And I wish I did not have to review fen planting reports with Aedon for two hours before dinner," Eleanor said. "If you would like to trade, I will happily host Zanntal."

Edythe was annoyed. "I could swear we've had this same argument time and time again."

"Over what? Me bossing you through your day?" Eleanor snapped, feeling sensitive.

"You always having a list for me," Edythe said as she stood and lifted a pile of records to return them to their shelf. When a book tumbled to the floor, Eleanor picked it up and followed her sister. "Have I been unfair about it?" Eleanor asked. "Were you not grateful, when I was in Imirillia, that I had prepared you as a regent?"

Edythe turned to face her. "This is a silly argument. I will host your friend if you promise me this is not your way to introduce me to this man."

"Heavens, no." Eleanor's mouth dropped open. "I—the thought had not even crossed my mind."

"If that be the case, I will be happy to make your friend feel welcome."

———※◈◈◈◈◈※———

As Eleanor prepared for her meeting with Aedon, Ammar sat at her table, reading an Imirillian scroll she'd had in her chambers.

"Eleanor," Ammar said, looking up from his reading. "You said the Imirillian delegation is to leave tomorrow for the pass?"

"Yes," Eleanor replied as she sorted through the papers on her desk. "I have a message for your father, if you could be so good to see it delivered." When Eleanor looked up, the physician was actually smiling.

"If it does not cost me my head," Ammar said, "I would be happy to oblige."

"Happy even?" Eleanor said, raising an eyebrow. "The Aemogen air has made a positive impact on you already." She smiled and set her report aside. "I am so grateful you cared for Basaal while you were here, but I must ask you if there is anything you may have overheard of Aemogen's defenses that you are planning on carrying back to your father."

"I have nothing to say to the emperor upon my return to that *delightful* camp," Ammar drawled.

"Thank you," she said. Eleanor ran her fingers over her pile of reports and, without looking up, asked, "How is Basaal today?"

"He's out in the training yard."

"What?" Her eyes shot to Ammar's face in question.

"His right eye has all but cleared, his vision quite good. And, as he informed me forcefully this morning, if he is going to fight, he has no more use for sleeping draughts and vapors."

Eleanor's mouth curled in an unsurprised smile. "And his left eye?" she asked. "Will he regain his full sight?"

"It remains clouded—blurs and shadows," Ammar said. "Time will tell if it's to improve."

"Blurs and shadows," Eleanor repeated. "It feels like that is all any of us can see these days."

Basaal was greeted warmly when he arrived for the evening meal. Even Crispin expressed his relief that the prince did not come off worse than he had. Eleanor realized she'd not told him of Zanntal's arrival. Before she could, Edythe entered with the Imirillian soldier.

The expression on Basaal's face held more joy than Eleanor could remember having seen since Zarbadast. The prince jumped up from his place and embraced the soldier, laughing and taking a step back, his hands still gripping the young man's shoulders.

"When did you get in?" Basaal asked.

"This afternoon," Zanntal said, looking at Basaal's left eye with concern. "Arillian salts?" he guessed.

"Yes," Basaal said. "I'll tell you more later." Feeling self-conscious of the entire Aemogen court watching the reunion, Basaal led Zanntal towards the table. "I am certain Eleanor has a seat for you next to her," Basaal said. "We'll converse afterward."

After evening meal, Basaal and Zanntal spoke late into the night. The prince, needing treatment for his eyes, took Zanntal back to Eleanor's private rooms, where Ammar was waiting. Eleanor, Edythe, and Ammar were sitting before the fire, talking, when they arrived.

After Ammar had treated Basaal, they returned to where Zanntal sat with Eleanor and Edythe. It was an odd thing for Eleanor, sitting before the fire with Basaal, Zanntal, and Ammar, laughing and exchanging stories and jokes. Edythe had picked up her embroidery, not seeming to mind the conversation carried on in flowing Imirillian.

Basaal slipped in next to Eleanor, sitting close to her as he bantered with Zanntal and argued with Ammar about Imirillian politics. Eleanor spoke only occasionally, tired, content to just listen.

This time spent with Ammar and Zanntal clearly pleased Basaal. It had connected him to his lost country. And when it hit her—the understanding that Eleanor could not bear the thought of losing these men from her life—she realized that no matter how the campaign ended, it would end in sorrow.

⸻◈◈◈◈◈⸻

Before Emperor Shaamil's delegation left the next morning—blindfolded and heavily guarded, to be taken out of Ainsley Rise before dawn—Basaal arranged to meet with Ammar. But taking leave of his brother was more of a struggle than Basaal had antic-ipated.

"What will you say to Father about my being here?" Basaal asked him as they sat in the predawn light of Eleanor's audience chamber.

"I will say it as it is, in fewer words," Ammar said. "I will men-tion your capture and your decision to stand with Aemogen."

Basaal nodded and rested his hand on Ammar's shoulder. "I hope to the Illuminating God this is not a final goodbye."

After an embrace, Basaal accompanied Ammar to the waiting company in the courtyard then ascended the spiral stairs behind the travelers' house, watching from the battlements as a company of Eleanor's soldiers escorted the blindfolded Imirillians back toward the pass.

"I am sorry to see him go."

Basaal turned at hearing Eleanor's voice. She stood behind him, quiet, her arms wrapped around herself in the chill of the morning.

"Yes," Basaal agreed.

"Will you spend the day training with Crispin's men?" she asked.

"Your men," Basaal corrected. "And yes. I have been accepted back in some form or another."

"How is your sight this morning?" Eleanor replied, the concern evident in her voice.

"Better," Basaal said as he leaned against the battlement and crossed his arms. She was looking more rested than she had when he'd first returned from Common Field. Basaal had not even thought to wonder if she still wandered the halls of Ainsley Castle at night. He had been—well, he had been drugged. "Though, I do not think I will regain perfect vision in my left eye."

"Does that alter your fighting?" she asked.

"Yes." Basaal watched the meandering breeze lift a lock of hair from Eleanor's cheek. The brown dye had now faded, leaving an accidental auburn on the end of each strand. "I intend to spend what time I can training, in the hope of making the necessary adjustments come time for battle."

Eleanor gave a single nod and looked out over Ainsley. "And how is your dancing?"

"Dancing?" Basaal questioned. "Is there to be dancing?"

"Tonight, down on the large Ainsley square, since we ride out for the Maragaide Valley come morning," Eleanor explained. "You will be expected, at the very least, to make an appearance. And I would like to have you there." If Basaal had had any intention of saying no, the moment she tilted her head slightly to the side swept away any opposition.

"You do remember"—he ribbed her with a straight smile— "that the last time we danced in Ainsley, I was using it to announce my betrayal to you?"

Eleanor clucked her tongue just like Hannia would have, and Basaal found it as endearing as her expression was distracting. "Not likely I would forget that."

"I know I never will," he said, the words off his tongue before he could realize they were being said aloud. Eleanor blushed, and he could feel his own color rising before he forced a loose smile. "I will attend and dance awhile," he said casually, "if you are not above being embarrassed by my mistakes."

"It has not stopped me thus far," Eleanor rejoined as they naturally fell into step together, walking back towards the northern tower.

"No, I suppose it hasn't," Basaal said as he shrugged. "What that says about your judgment—"

"Are you trying to talk me out of dancing with you?" she asked.

"No, no," Basaal replied readily. "A fair warning is all." Eleanor's lips were pink in the morning cold, and he traced the lines of her face with his eyes.

"What?" she asked, after noticing he was watching her.

"I am memorizing the lines of your face," he admitted.

Eleanor stopped and considered him. "I am still before you."

"Yes." Basaal had no other words to counter the weight he felt in his lungs. They had reached the north tower where Hastian stood waiting. Basaal opened the door and leaned against it. "Thank you," he finally added.

"For what?" Eleanor asked him earnestly.

"You've been with me more than you had time for in the last few days," Basaal answered. "I thank you for it."

Eleanor did not reply. She did, however, step close to him, lift herself up onto her toes, and kiss the corner of his mouth, as light as the morning.

His skin still felt cool from Eleanor's kiss even after she disappeared through the tower door.

———⊰◈◈◈⊱———

"It's all in ready," Crispin said, waving his hand across the camp. "Everything in place, all supplies and weapons accounted for. Thistle Black has already taken most of the powder weapons on ahead so they can be brought through the tunnel before the men have to go through it."

Eleanor knew this, but she nodded anyway, her fingers gripping Thrift's reins for whatever comfort she might find there.

Crispin continued. "Wil—Prince Basaal, I mean—has been

invaluable in sharing knowledge about moving a large army. I am glad to have had his help, though I still retain my opinion he's a tricky devil."

"I've never said he wasn't. But it's the steadiness underneath that is to be relied upon," Eleanor said. "Have you seen him fight since the attack?"

"You've no need to concern yourself on that score." Crispin leaned forward in his saddle and looked at Eleanor. "He fights with more rage than he ever did before; the man is a dragon. If anyone can make it out of this alive, he can. Whether the rest of the men—the farmers, the craftsmen, the miners—can make it through? I've found I just can't think on it or else my courage fails me."

Eleanor spent the rest of the afternoon at her desk, staring at reports and paying them no mind. Her thoughts were on her civilian army and on the Aemogen plan of attack. They were also on Basaal. They then moved to her parents, memories she had avoided so meticulously in her mind because she could not stand how lonely they made her feel. Did they, Eleanor wondered, think she had done well? Was there any help from the dead of Aemogen?

Drums and calls were coming from the western downs, and Eleanor felt her blood respond to the sound of so many men preparing for war. She took herself to the window, flinging it wide and taking in whatever air her lungs could house. Edythe was right, they needed the dancing. But it was not for farewells. Eleanor closed her eyes. It was for sanity.

"Of course you'll join in," Basaal said, leaning against the open doorframe of Zanntal's room in the travelers' house.

Zanntal sat on his bed, back against the wall, polishing his scimitar. "I make a far superior nursemaid than a dancer." Zanntal paused and looked up at his prince. "And I am no nursemaid."

Grinning, Basaal ran his fingers through his hair. It was getting long; it needed cutting. "There are many simple dances, and even standing by, drink in hand, watching the merriment, is an evening well spent before a man rides to war."

Zanntal did not look convinced. "I'll dance with no one. As surely as no one would dance with me."

"I'm sure Eleanor will. She'd slight me for you, as clear as day. And what about Edythe?" Basaal asked with a half shrug. "You could ask her for a dance."

A disbelieving smile broke across Zanntal's face. "Edythe would no sooner dance with me than with the emperor. She humors me for the sake of her sister."

A movement in the hall caught Basaal's attention, and he looked to see Crispin just leaving his room.

"Crispin! Come help me convince Zanntal to dance."

"What? You're trying to get him to dance with you now?"

"Of course not." Basaal rolled his eyes. "Just come here."

The war leader did not come with quite the boyish enjoyment Basaal had been used to seeing from the days of the battle run, but he did come, stepping past Basaal into the room.

"Zanntal," Crispin said as he nodded.

Zanntal nodded in return.

"You might as well come," Crispin said as he put both hands on his hips. "Your battle dread will ease. We'll all end up smiling, girls will abound, and hopefully, for my sake, the drinks will flow. Come," he said, kicking lightly at Zanntal's shoe. "Don't waste your last chance at a dance, and don't throw away a night with an easy mind."

Basaal translated all Crispin had said.

When Zanntal made no verbal response, Crispin shrugged and clasped Basaal on the shoulder as he prepared to leave. Basaal was startled by the show of camaraderie, and it must have shown on his face, for Crispin actually broke into a grin.

"Oh, don't look at me like that," Crispin said. "You've thrown your lot in with ours. And I don't think many of us are getting out of this war alive, so I might as well forgive you for being such an ass."

Basaal's head went back, and he laughed. He brought his hand up to Crispin's arm, gripping it with a sense of brotherhood. "I wouldn't know how to navigate the terror of an Aemogen dance without you."

"No fear of that," Crispin said. "I'll help you through." Crispin turned back to Zanntal. "Don't go all grandfather on us now—get a move on it."

Crispin winked at Basaal and slid past the prince. Basaal looked over his shoulder just as Crispin paused and half turned to face him. "You know, I might as well say this before I get into the evening and forget I've ever owned the thought. I am almost wishing now I would have settled before this, perhaps even married. I don't know." Crispin shrugged. "I always supposed I had all the time in the world." The young war leader knocked his fist against the wall gently, pulled by a thought beyond what he had shared. "Well, I'll see you at the square."

Basaal reached absentmindedly for the hilt of his sword as he watched Crispin disappear down the hallway of the travelers' house.

The violin was eager. The violin was hungry. As Basaal descended the Ainsley stair with Eleanor's hand in his, he could hear the strains of the music already swirling around the feet of the dancers. Edythe, Aedon, and others of the royal company surrounded him and Eleanor, talking anxiously, finding it impossible to fight the music's energy that was anything but what they had experienced during the last month.

It was not as grand as the spring festival had been the year prior—there were no games or booths—but the people were gathered around the dance floor, and they were intent on each other's company. They weighed one another's words with more earnestness. They laughed, and the laughter was really a way to say good-bye. They would dance tonight, and then they would leave for war. And every pair of sweethearts refused to part for even a moment.

Eleanor's company settled on a temporary dais, where chairs had been set, and the musicians stopped their playing as Eleanor welcomed the crowd.

"We do not know the outcome of what is ahead," Eleanor said after a brief welcome, pausing as she brushed the wooden arm of her chair with the tips of her fingers in uncertainty. Basaal, sitting at her side, reached his hand up and took her fingers in his. "But, we stand together and for Aemogen. May the blessing of all those who have gone before us work in our favor. And may we return to our homes in peace come the end."

The crowd roared, and the musicians took up a lively tune that transformed the entire square into the dance. As Eleanor sat, Basaal took her hand in both of his and leaned towards her. "Well done. Shall we dance?"

"I don't think I can." Eleanor felt weighed down into her chair.

"I've spent all afternoon thinking about the next several days and I—"

"All the more reason," Basaal interrupted. "Come on." He stood and grabbed both of her hands, ignoring her protests as he led her to the center of the floor. Couples parted to make way, and Eleanor stopped her protests to smile and put on a face. When Basaal spun her around to face him, her expression was a careful mix of gratitude and peevishnness. Basaal laughed. "You might have to take the lead if I fail," he shouted over the noise.

They danced. Several melodies were familiar to Basaal, and what was not Eleanor helped him through. After an hour of music and dancing, the torchlight filling the entire square, Basaal brought his face close to Eleanor's with a question: "Where's Edythe?"

"I don't know," Eleanor said, turning in concern to scan the chairs, but could not see her sister there.

"Is she dancing?" Basaal asked.

"I haven't seen her on the floor," Eleanor said. "But I had assumed she would not join in."

Crispin had pushed through the press of the crowd to join them and asked Eleanor for a dance.

She nodded, and then looked toward Basaal.

"I'll go and see if I can find Edythe," Basaal said. "I've a hunch of where she will be." He did not waste time by searching the dance floor. He knew she would not be there. Taking the Ainsley stairs two at a time, he hurried up past the gates and into the quiet of the rise.

With the music floating around the dark, Basaal walked to the records hall, knocked on the door, and pushed in. He had been right. There she was, sitting at a table with a small candle lit, shuffling through an assortment of papers and a pile of damaged scrolls.

"You left without dancing." His words echoed in the quiet hall.

Edythe smiled and looked back towards her work as Basaal approached her table, sitting in the chair across from her. Misery was evident on Edythe's usually composed face, and she held herself together by focusing on the task before her. The papers rustled and slid as she sorted, her only answer to his statement.

Basaal waited just outside the circle of candlelight, trying to read whatever he could from her movements.

"Just too many memories?" Basaal ventured.

"No," Edythe said, her eyebrows knit in a way that reminded Basaal of Eleanor. "The memories are there, for certain, but—"

"But?"

She set the paper in her hand on the table with the others and rested her hands on them as if they might fly away. "It's been almost a year now."

Basaal shifted in the chair, leaning against one arm, his fingers spread against his cheek.

"The fear of forgetting his likeness," Edythe said, "of reshaping his voice in my head, is so frightening."

"So, you worry about betraying his memory?"

"Yes," Edythe said emphatically.

Basaal opened his mouth and then grimaced before speaking. "Has Eleanor ever told you of how my brother died?"

Edythe shook her head.

So Basaal spoke of Emaad—comprehensively and without holding back a single breeze of memory—so that the story was formed into an intricate design of what Emaad had meant to Basaal and of how, in the end, Emaad had died for him.

"I took his body away from that place," Basaal explained, "to a quiet copse of trees that had escaped our army's brutality. There was a stream there, a freshet of sorts, where I washed and prepared his body. I cried myself through all the appropriate rites, trying to remember what was to be set in place for the journey of the dead. And when I'd filled the grave, I—" Basaal shrugged and leaned against the back of the chair, folding both his arms across his chest. "I felt as if I were buried along with him."

Shaking her head repeatedly, Edythe lifted her hand to her mouth.

"After not much time, numbness sets in, and you are thankful, for it separates you from the pain," Basaal said philosophically. "But it also comes with fear, the fear of knowing that someday you will wake up and all your senses will no longer be stripped bare, the dullness of survival stolen, and you will feel the pain of it."

The wick of the candle had burned down, tilting sideways into the clear wax that had begun to spill onto the table.

"What takes away the pain?" Edythe whispered.

Basaal frowned. "It doesn't leave. But it changes, coming in waves rather than in relentless sharp misery. I suppose—" He caught an ironic laugh in his throat, and ended up just breathing out fast, his chest rising and falling. "I suppose it began to ease at some point during the battle run. It was Eleanor…it was all of you."

"Do you forget to think of him?" she asked.

Basaal lifted his fingers to his lower lip. "Never supposing that this would happen, some days pass where I realize I have given him no thought. I used to think this should trouble me, make me feel guilty for it. But I don't do it carelessly, Edythe, and Emaad would be pleased. No one is meant to love only one soul in their life. We have friends and lovers and whatever family the Illuminating God has given. That being said, any loss is irrevocable. No one steps into the place they once were. But the act of loving someone would not be so beautiful if their place could ever be filled. We need loss, I suppose. Perhaps there is something even holy in it."

Sputtering in the wax, the flame of the candle disappeared, and the smell of smoke rose between them. The music from the square reminded Basaal of what he had come for in the first place. "Come down to the square and dance."

⸱⸱⸱⸱⸱⸱⸱

Eleanor was standing with Aedon in the crowd when the musician's announced the final song.

"Have you seen Basaal?" she asked him, looking around the crowded square.

"There," Aedon said, pointing towards the base of the steps, where Basaal and Edythe had just finished a dance. As Eleanor looked over, she caught Basaal's eye. He waved and took his leave of Edythe, weaving through the spent crowd to join Eleanor.

"I'll go be with Edythe," Aedon said as Basaal arrived. Then Basaal stepped into his place beside Eleanor, and the music began.

Slower than a reel, they turned in close proximity, facing one another, taking simple steps. Eleanor found herself craving the pressure of his hand on her waist, the way her hand brushed against his chest when the dance called for her to circle around him, the feeling of his breath against her cheek when he spoke. By the time the song ended, Eleanor and Basaal had stopped dancing altogether, standing close, her arms around his neck, his chin resting against her temple.

"I still don't understand how to leave for battle," she said.

"You try not to think about it," he answered.

Eleanor's party, her councillors and friends, all found each other before ascending the stairs to Ainsley Rise, speaking occasionally, but mainly content in their own thoughts of the days ahead. Then they separated, embracing, wishing each other a good night, and remembering they would gather again come morning.

Eleanor and Basaal returned to her rooms, sitting before the fire on one of the sofas, wandering in their own thoughts.

"We never danced to my music," Basaal said as he leaned his head back and then smiled.

"That would have been a disaster." Eleanor was sitting beside him, her feet tucked up beneath her. "They wouldn't have forgiven you."

Basaal laugh was slow. Eleanor shifted herself, the music wearing thin in her mind, the anxiety of battle rising.

"Relax." Basaal moved his hand to her knee.

"Is that possible?" Eleanor looked at Basaal's face. The skin there was healing from the burns, and his eye was just slightly clouded.

"No, it isn't possible," he answered.

"Then how are you appearing so at ease?" she asked. Eleanor moved her fingers along the wood grain of the back of the sofa, stopping shy of touching Basaal.

He took a long breath. "Years of practice, I suppose."

He sat up and shifted to face her. "If I am to be honest, I must admit to have never known the terror I'm covering now. The thought of raising my sword to my own men is—I cannot even think it or I—I will watch for my colors in battle and keep as far away as I can. It's—" He did not finish, but Eleanor saw he was now shaking.

She moved her hand towards his face, brushing his cheek with the side of her thumb. Basaal caught her hand, kissing her wrist, holding it gently as he closed his eyes. Eleanor leaned forward, touching her lips to his, trying to ease the pain from his face. Trying to draw out the pain in her own lungs. Basaal responded, moving his hand away from her wrist, placing the heel of his palm on her neck and pulling Eleanor closer as he kissed her in return. Her heart dropped at his touch, and she was losing herself to it when a pounding came at the door of Eleanor's antechamber. There was a noise and then Hastian's voice, stating something firmly.

Basaal pulled away from Eleanor, breathing heavily, resting his forehead on hers stubbornly. "Please tell me no one is wanting to see you just now," he said quietly.

An impatient knock on the door of the audience chamber was Basaal's answer. Reluctantly, Eleanor moved away from him, her fingers hesitant to lose his touch. She smoothed her dress and let one of her feet drop to the floor. Closing his eyes, Basaal sank lower into the couch, reaching for her wrist and pressing it to his lips, before he muttered something softly that Eleanor could not hear.

"Come in," she called.

Crispin burst through the door.

"Eleanor, is Basaal—" Crispin began, but then he saw them sitting together, registering the expression on Eleanor's face. He flushed. "Oh."

"What is it, Crispin?" Eleanor brought her fingers to her temple and closed her eyes.

"Nothing really, I just, well—" Crispin cleared his throat, and Basaal sat up, turning to look back at Crispin. "There are some men back at the encampment who are frightened, determined to leave. I thought that the prince might help persuade them, give them courage before the march tomorrow. But I should have thought—"

"No," Basaal said as he stood, his hands loosely resting on his hips. "I'll be happy to come with you. Just a moment."

Eleanor covered an affectionate smile; he did not sound happy. Basaal disappeared into the corner bedroom, where—as Eleanor had discovered a few days previous—he had been keeping his personal effects after taking up residence on her sofa. He returned with his cloak and his weaponry in place.

Eleanor watched him cross the room, thinking about the first time she had seen him in his princely garb, suited up for war. He had frightened her on that morning in his tent, the day after the pass had come down.

"Will you be gone long?" she asked.

Basaal nodded reluctantly. "I should have thought to go out sooner," he said. "The men need their officers and their leaders with them. And whether I like it or not, that is what I have become. I imagine I will probably sleep at the encampment."

"Oh," Eleanor said, not meaning to sound so disappointed.

"I am sorry." He bent down and kissed Eleanor, moving his thumb across the line on her chin. "If I can, I will come to you in the morning, before we are to march out."

Crispin had disappeared back into the antechamber, or Eleanor would have wished him a good night. As it was, Basaal kissed her again, slowly, his hands holding her face tilted towards his. He stopped just as the kisses became more urgent—too soon for Eleanor—and simply said her name once before leaving, closing the door behind him.

Eleanor could hardly bear him being away.

When morning came, Eleanor reached her hand behind her on the bed to find nothing there. She turned and looked at the bedspread, rumpled by her own restless sleeping and nothing else. The emptiness felt prophetic somehow, and Eleanor shook the thought from her mind as she rose to prepare herself for battle.

Edythe came to help her. It was a quiet morning, and Edythe put Eleanor's hair up ritualistically, placing the battle crown on her head. Eleanor wore a new white gown and the sword she had worn for ornament during the battle run.

"The holes in your ears have grown over," Edythe observed. "Clumsy of me not to have noticed."

"It is all right," Eleanor said. "When I return."

"Yes," Edythe said. "When you return."

Crispin came for Eleanor when it was time to leave. He escorted her down to the courtyard, where Thrift stood, saddled and waiting. Basaal was there, organizing something with a few of the men, and Eleanor saw that a change had taken place: he was a soldier, his mind was in battle, and he was not the same person she had been with the evening before.

Eleanor mounted, as did Hastian, who rode directly behind her. Zanntal was with them as well, having informed Eleanor he would aid in her defense at Colun Tir. With Thrift's reins in her hands, Eleanor turned and looked back up at the towers of Ainsley Castle just as the signal was called.

The company rode out onto the western downs, the banners of Aemogen trailing in the air.

The rumble of the long columns, the pound and jolt of his horse—Basaal was struck by the familiarity of the scene as the small army pressed through Aemogen towards the Maragaide Valley. He conferred with Crispin and Aedon, took time to be among the men, and stepped naturally into his role as leader, soldier, and prince.

Eleanor was there, of course, but Basaal found it difficult to be much in her company. There was always another question for him to answer, another soldier to encourage, or more logistics to review. Then word came from the guards at Colun Tir that Thistle Black and his team had successfully brought all of the powder devices through the mountain. There was no word yet from Thayne and his men, who were going about their work of readying the charges and weapons they would leave along the western lines of the Imirillian camp. But he had to assume all was well with the Marion company.

On the first night, Basaal came to Eleanor's tent late, and she had already fallen asleep. He watched her a moment before grabbing a bedroll and taking it outside, where he lay awake, thinking of the coming days and tracing the patterns in the stars.

Darkness stretched from the mountains down through the valley, unyielding and thick, the only relief being the fires of the Imirillian camp across the plain. Eleanor's officers moved through Colun Tir and its outbuildings with no guide but their own hands on the walls; no light would be lit at the tower.

Basaal took comfort in this blind cover—this absence of vision that gave no confirmation of fear in the eyes of the soldiers, no periphery of the usual images that came—by course—in the preparation for battle: the horses dressed and impatient; weapons sharpened, polished; a young soldier, frozen, emitting youthful terror, looking wide-eyed and fragile. Freedom from these sights delivered a freedom of mind. Basaal wondered why all armies did not prepare for battle in the safety of darkness, where no vulnerability could be revealed.

Basaal, Crispin, Aedon, and Sean knew what they were to do, and they went about it, exchanging whispers and orders frankly: no halting, no hesitation. Basaal had lost track of Eleanor. She was somewhere inside the tower, receiving updates from Crispin. So

Basaal continued with his work. He had been asked to accompany an advanced group of miners, who were ordered to set explosives along the northern lines of the Imirillian encampment as well as the eastern lines among the horses. Aedon's experiences, having grown up in a mining fen, had caused him to be a leader in the group, and he had requested that Basaal join the mission, making use of the prince's knowledge of the camp. Basaal had agreed and followed his acceptance by exerting great efforts to forget that he had.

A messenger from Thistle Black came up the mountain, asking the men to be ready. They would be called down soon. After checking Refigh and leaving his horse in the careful hands of Zanntal, Basaal entered Colun Tir. He must find Eleanor and tell her good-bye.

He found Eleanor in a storeroom, deeply embedded in the center of the fortress, the only place sanctioned to light a candle. She sat at a crate, used for a table, where a map was spread. Her battle crown glittering, the white of her gown looking iridescent, otherworldly. She was surrounded by whatever officers were not busy on Crispin's errands. The young war leader stood beside her, speaking in a hurried voice with Sean. Basaal almost wished he had not come in, for he could now see their faces. The ease of anonymous preparation gave way to tension, and the discomfort of battle settled in his chest.

Eleanor called to him without looking away from the map. "I was wondering if I would see you."

"I've kept him busy in the yard," Crispin said, breaking away from Sean, reaching his hand out to Basaal, who stepped forward and took it with a firm grasp. "The prince has suffered his dignity to help me execute field command." They clapped each other's shoulders, and then Basaal stepped towards Eleanor.

"Thistle's crew leaves down the mountain soon," he said, and as he was speaking, Eleanor looked up into his eyes. "Is there—" He bit off the words, unsure of what to say. The light had revealed no fear or trepidation in her expression, rather a solidity, a grace; she was fixed and resolute, her entire being empowered with a nobility he had never seen in the emperor of Zarbadast. Basaal grappled with his memories, wondering how he could have missed this in her before. He took a step back.

Basaal knew what Eleanor was to him, and he wished fiercely he didn't.

———

It had taken Basaal walking into the room to offset the ordered focus of her mind.

Eleanor had tied her sternest hopes to the work her soldiers would do that night. The focus she gave the attack was only increasing as each hour was spent. All was tightly organized in her mind, and she was fully present in her role. But Basaal's entry had caused the air to swell and ripple, his presence bold enough to challenge her single-mindedness.

"There you are," Eleanor said, her attention still given to the work before her, despite the call of his presence. "I was wondering if I would see you."

Crispin said something from over her shoulder, but Eleanor lost to his words in her focus on the map. It was Basaal's voice who called her back.

He said something, and Eleanor looked up into his eyes. "Is there—" He stopped speaking, and Eleanor watched as a strange expression marked his face. It was the first time since they had left Ainsley that she felt Basaal's tight role of soldier was pulled aside, and all of him—every humor and question and feeling—was showing through. He was incomparable, and mortal. They all were so very mortal. Eleanor felt herself falter, and she stood quickly to cover the thought.

"Might I speak with you privately, before you leave?"

Basaal halted, then swallowed—a soldier once more—and Eleanor almost wished she had not spoken.

"Certainly." His stillness gripped her. "I had come with the hope that we would."

Eleanor stepped around the crate and walked into a side room. The dimness grabbed at whatever light it could, leaving them to see one another, but only just.

Eleanor turned to face Basaal. "There has not been much opportunity to speak since we left Ainsley."

"No."

Eleanor thought she saw Basaal place his hand on his sword.

"The men," she said, "they are greatly relieved you're with us."

No answer came from Basaal. Eleanor sensed perhaps he did not want to speak of it, of the fight. Of his place in it. Self-conscious, she searched for words that might express what she'd wanted to say, . And at the risk of Basaal not feeling the same way, Eleanor heard herself blurt out, "I can't bear you going away without the assurance of return."

Whatever spell or hesitancy had been holding Basaal back, whatever degree of soldierly calm he had carried with him on the march from Ainsley, almost broke—but not quite. Basaal lifted a hesitant hand but stopped short of touching her face.

"Promise me," he said, "that you will retreat into the tunnel if this goes badly. Bar the way, and open it for no man."

Eleanor did not promise, she frowned.

Basaal continued in a whisper. "There can be no promise to be made of return—"

"Promise me anyway," she said.

"One man to every four." Basaal spoke the odds calmly. But the sound of his voice did not match the expression on his face. "You know better than that, Eleanor. I am—" Basaal lifted his hand to her arm but didn't continue.

"I need you to find your way through this," she said so quietly that she could almost not hear the words she spoke.

Basaal kept his mouth in a solemn line as he breathed the air out of his lungs.

Eleanor wanted to speak again but thought better of it. And then, standing on her toes, she kissed his mouth. Basaal closed his eyes but did not respond.

"Basaal," Aedon said, coming into the dark storeroom. Basaal opened his eyes, and Eleanor looked over her shoulder at what she could see of Aedon's outline. Basaal did not take his eyes away from her as Aedon spoke to him.

"The crew is assembled. We go now."

"Yes," Basaal replied, and Aedon left. Eleanor stepped past Basaal, to follow Aedon, when his hand moved down her arm to her hand. His fingers wrapped around hers. And, together, they followed Aedon through the corridor, down the stairs, and out into the courtyard.

The silent crew was ready, with their horses, for Aedon and Basaal to lead them down the mountain. The remainder of the army still waited inside the tunnel. With his hand still holding Eleanor's, Basaal weaved through the men to where his horse stood.

"All is accounted for," Crispin said as he met them. "Are you and Aedon ready?"

"Yes," Basaal replied.

Eleanor felt the brief sensation of his fingers sliding away from hers, and then his warmth was gone. She watched as Basaal adjusted his weaponry from habit, and he did not look back at her. Zanntal, who was standing with Refigh, handed Basaal the reins. It was too dark to truly see, but Eleanor thought that, perhaps, the prince had spoken to Zanntal before mounting.

"If all goes well," Aedon was saying to her, "Basaal and I may be able to return before the attack."

"I'm sorry?" Eleanor said, breaking her gaze away from the shadow that was the prince. "I didn't hear all you said."

Aedon put his arm around Eleanor. "There may be time to say good-bye later is all that I meant."

Turning toward him, Eleanor wrapped her arms around Aedon and took a long breath. "Yes," she said. "I will see you before it begins. Do not lose yourself in the woods."

Aedon nodded, then slipped away to his horse, mounting and taking his place beside Basaal. With the metal on their bridles and saddles wrapped, it was a quiet departure. Basaal exchanged a brief word with Crispin and then moved out. The men streamed past Eleanor, silent and somber as ghosts.

Ghosts. Eleanor lifted her hand to her mouth as she watched the men go. In the darkness, Eleanor thought Basaal saluted her as he passed and looked at her longer than it took to bring his hand back to the reins.

⊷❖⊶

Crispin, Eleanor, and the remaining men of her council convened in the storeroom, around the crate.

"The men will begin their descent to the edge of the woods within the hour," Crispin said, pointing to the torn map. Eleanor watched as his fingers traced the edge of the woodland at the base of the foothills, leading out into the plain before the Imirillian camp. "The ground troops will take their positions farther south, as planned," he continued. "Briant will lead them in. Once Prince Basaal and Aedon send word that the explosives are in position, I, with Sean, will be ready with the cavalry. Only a small company is assigned to Colun Tir," Crispin said, looking up at Eleanor, "consisting of Hastian, Zanntal, a dozen men around the perimeter—"

"Yes," Eleanor asserted. They had argued about this earlier. Crispin had insisted on leaving a stronger guard at Colun Tir. Eleanor refused, arguing they needed every spare man on the field if they were to have any hope of victory. She had won, not because she had convinced Crispin but because she had stated her decision as his sovereign and would not negotiate. Her war leader had acquiesced.

"We better start the men out of the tunnel now," Sean said as he placed his hands on his hips and frowned. "It will take longer than we expect."

"You're probably right." Crispin folded his arms. "I will position myself here, at the tower, until it's time to ride down. Sean, Briant, start directing the soldiers to the edge of the woods, and, for the sake of old Ainsley, keep those horses as quiet as you can."

The remnant of Eleanor's war council was wise enough to stay inside when Eleanor and Crispin went out onto the balcony that overlooked the valley. Across the plain, up on the rise where the

Imirillians held camp, Eleanor saw that there were thousands of fires, blinking and burning, a reflection of the moonless sky.

"Basaal and Aedon should be placing the explosives now," Crispin said through his nervousness. In a quick movement, he snapped the bones in his hands, stretching his fingers out before him.

"That's an awful sound," Eleanor said, pulling her cloak closer around her shoulders as she sat on the edge of the battlement.

"I know you hate it," Crispin replied, his eyes watching the fires ahead. "The explosives along the western lines are in place," he said aloud, his own ears needing to hear it one more time. "Our company of men will cover the east and the north. There will be few, if any, explosives to the south. Thayne's women, two of the women who wash and launder for the Imirillians, should have helped the supply men place the barrels of explosives in the very center, beside the soldiers' tents this evening. Within an hour, maybe two, most of our men will be positioned at the edge of the forest: two thousand five hundred men on horseback, five hundred on foot—" He paused, drumming his fingers on the stone next to Eleanor, and then clenched his fist together in another spackle of snaps. "Sorry, Ele. I'm just so nervous."

"I know."

"I hope the Marions have done their work," Crispin said, drumming his fingers again. "With no word from Thayne, how are we to know if he got through?"

"He got through," Eleanor said. "They placed their powder."

"You're not certain." Crispin looked at Eleanor. "I'm not certain. There is no sense pretending we are."

They did not speak more. Fires began to blink out, though the perimeter remained lit, and the occasional blaze throughout the camp was still watched and tended. The rest fell, one by one, into darkness.

Within the hour, a report came: the first wave of soldiers and their mounts were in position. As the darkest hours of the night crept into the forest, Aemogen's soldiers continued to move cautiously, carefully. The second report, over an hour later, said that the tunnel had been emptied. All the men would be in position soon. Crispin would constantly disappear and then come back to the balcony where Eleanor sat, watching the diminished fires, gripping the hilt of her ceremonial blade.

Thistle Black had been waiting for them in a string of trees halfway across the valley. Each man in what Basaal had nicknamed Thistle's Crew carried a satchel of the explosive devices, wrapped individually in heavy cloth, and Thistle Black reviewed exactly how they were to set their lines.

"There's an unpatrolled dip to the north of the Imirillian encampment," Thistle reminded them, repeating what they had already studied on the map. "We'll take the horses down, and you'll tie them in the little tree cover there. It is there we will set the lines. The Marions have placed most of their devices, even a few bigger ones, at the southern end. Prince Basaal, with Aedon, will be the lead team, planting their devices the farthest west. I will stay behind, in the trees, if any group needs me. Into your groups now, and remember, get those lines as close to camp as you can, but be quiet as a shadow. No sound, no noise."

Basaal nodded and lifted the satchel Thistle handed to him. It was very heavy as he placed it over Refigh's withers. With a silent signal, they headed out.

It was a dark walk across the north end of the valley. As quiet as they managed to be, each noise echoed in Basaal's heartbeat. It wasn't long before they dropped into the ravine on the north side of the encampment.

"We're close to the tents," Basaal whispered to Aedon after they had moved quite a ways. "The night guard walks the perimeter just above us."

Aedon nodded.

They secured their horses in the trees and then hefted the satchels to their shoulders, moving towards the edge of camp. After stopping behind the black form of a tent, Aedon unwrapped his first device. Basaal pulled a wound-up line from the outside pocket of his heavy satchel, and Aedon took a shorter line, already imbedded in the weapon, fusing it with the longer line Basaal had given him.

They moved along the edge of the tents, setting explosives, and gathering the long lines together. Every five explosives, they would twine the lines together and run them back down the hill, towards the ravine where a soldier waited with flint. They had completed three sets of these lines when Basaal froze at the sound of footsteps. He grabbed Aedon's wrist and motioned. A pair of night guards were walking the perimeter of the camp near the edges of the tents.

Basaal motioned for Aedon to lie down and remain still, and then prayed that the darkness would cover them. Basaal was certain they could hear his breathing, labored and loud. His heartbeat almost covered the sound of the patrol's footsteps, and he could feel his pulse in his wrist, beating into the soft earth beneath his arms.

One of the guards stumbled and cursed. Basaal froze. The man must have tripped on a line.

"A branch or something," the guard said in reply to his companion's question. "Cursed place."

Basaal and Aedon looked at each other, and finally, when the patrol had moved farther down the line, they finished setting the explosive and retreated back to the edge of the ravine.

"They tripped on a line," Basaal hissed to Aedon. "In the next hour, there will be hundreds of lines. This is madness."

After counting the remaining explosives in their bags, they moved farther west to set up another group of the devices.

"Let's finish setting these lines and get back to the ravine," Aedon said grimly. "We can't risk being seen."

"There is no hiding the tunnel now," Crispin said once he had rejoined Eleanor. "The forest is trampled down. I've instructed the few guards inside the tunnel door to keep it locked and closed, just as a precaution."

"Yes," Eleanor nodded.

"I wish you would consent to wait inside the mountain," Crispin added as he stood beside her, the sheath of his sword softly sounding off the stone battlement.

Eleanor lifted her fingers to the cold metal of the battle crown, shifting it slightly. Tonight, more than at any other time, it was too heavy. She cleared her throat and straightened her back, looking up at Crispin. "You were a ragtag boy when my father spoke for you, come in off the streets, with adventures and travels. I was in awe. I made you tell me all your stories."

"I didn't mind." She could hear Crispin's carefree smile through his words. "I was flattered you wanted to hear them; the princess royal, the heir apparent, the meticulous copper-headed girl, who insisted on getting a bigger horse because I had one, was interested in me."

"An older brother was quite a novelty," she answered. "I loved you from the first day."

Turning away from the west, Crispin sat down beside Eleanor, pressing his shoulder against hers. They leaned into each other as they had countless times in their youth whenever they had wished to discuss something just between the two of them. "If your father, the king, had not spoken for me, I can't image I would even still be in Aemogen. I would have left, drifted into some port and disappeared. I am so grateful, you know. Ainsley, my room in the travelers' house—it's the home I had always dreamed for. And who ever gets what they dream for?"

"Few, I'd imagine." Eleanor put her hands around his.

"On the heart of Ainorra Breagha, I hope you will," Crispin said quietly. "But I don't think many of us will come away from this, and I've no reassurance for you."

"And I none for you," Eleanor admitted. "Perhaps by tomorrow this time we shall know our fates."

"Well, I'll not badger you about it," Crispin said, and then he ran his tongue over his bottom lip. "I can either be too shaken to be much good, or I can pretend it's a day on the battle run and that there will be drinking and dancing and maybe a pretty girl at the end of it."

It was painful to watch Crispin's face as he imposed the usual canter of his bravado on himself.

"These are my boys, though, my men," he continued. "Clearly, you are our queen, you are our sovereign, but I've a responsibility for their lives now too, and I can't see the end of what that means."

"Don't look yet," Eleanor cautioned. "My father spoke of the times when you have to focus on your decided action—human emotion and feeling be hung—until the thing was done."

"Yes, well—"

"I know."

"Perhaps this will come out better than we've thought," Crispin said, turning his golden smile on Eleanor and bumping her shoulder with his.

Split!

An explosion shattered the darkness into a million pieces. Eleanor jumped up, and Crispin almost knocked her over he spun so fast. Distant yelling began coming from the Imirillian camp.

"Old Ainsley," Crispin breathed out. "Now we're in for it. What happened!" He turned and ran into the fortress, calling for the men who remained. Eleanor followed. "It's off! It's been set off! Accident or devil, we've got to make a go!" Crispin was shouting as Eleanor rushed along behind him. Hastian ran up behind Eleanor as they burst into the courtyard.

"The horses!" Crispin called as they ran through the confusion of men and officers who were mounting. "Aedon and Basaal will be expecting me to send the men out."

They heard another explosion—and then another. The sound made Eleanor wonder if they were ripping the sky from its place. Zanntal brought Crispin's mount just as Crispin turned to Eleanor. Sean was beside him.

"What happened?"

Men were rushing around, horses brought out.

"What have they done?"

"It's on!" Crispin yelled. "Make a go! Make a go!"

"Go!" Eleanor spoke hurriedly as Crispin pulled at the belt of his sword and called for his officers to mount, looking dazed.

"I don't know what happened!" he said.

"Go!" Eleanor said, pushing him towards his horse.

Crispin nodded, pulling her along with him until he turned, kissed her cheek, then her hair, and mounted, calling out to his company as they rode down the moonless trail.

Night was again shattered as explosion after explosion rattled between the sounds of screaming horses and trumpets. Hastian, Zanntal, and the small company of men left behind all gathered around Eleanor as the riders disappeared, chasing their day of battle as fast as they could ride.

"Go! Go! Get the far lines lit!" Aedon yelled towards the miners near him. Basaal came running back to Aedon, hitting the ground beside his friend.

"The east—" Basaal was out of breath. "The lines to the east are being lit."

"What of the central barrels the Marions planted?" Aedon screamed over the sound of a close explosion, dirt raining down over their heads. "Why have they not gone off yet?"

"They should—" The sky sounded as if it would snap and collapse in on itself. With a flash of light, the entire eastern line exploded into turmoil. Horses screamed in pain. Another sound, louder than thunder, rang from the center of camp. Men were shouting in terror. As their cries hit Basaal, his heart sank, and he ducked his head against his arms to protect himself from another explosion, trying not to think of the devastation.

"There went some of the Marion barrels," Aedon shouted, sounding relieved and irritated at the same time, shaking his head for the ringing in his ears.

It had been an accident; the lines were not to be lit for another two hours. But somehow, somewhere, a spark must have grabbed at a line, and the explosions had begun. Basaal and Aedon both knew that if an explosion went off early, they would have to light every line immediately to bring the necessary devastation. So Aedon had sent his men to rush the attack, hoping that Crispin would soon lead the army out of the woods.

Explosion after explosion continued to flash throughout the Imirillian camp. The men were throwing Thistle Black's devilish instruments. There was screaming, yelling. Confusion. As another barrel lit, the earth rumbled against it. Basaal's ears screamed in pain. Several fires were rushing through the Imirillian camp.

There it was. Basaal turned to look back down onto the plain, surprised he could still even hear it. The sound of more than twenty-five hundred horses roaring across the earth. Explosions still rang out, especially on the western lines, where their Marion counterparts continued to follow the Aemogens' lead.

"We must get back to our horses," Basaal yelled, "or we'll be trampled underfoot!" Basaal tried to pull Aedon away as the councillor was searching for any unlit lines.

"There's one more!" Aedon shouted, striking his flint.

"Time is gone!"

Aedon pulled free of Basaal's grasp.

"One more!" Aedon shouted again. He ran forward three steps, and lit the last line.

There was a fizz that almost seemed to sputter out, then the snap of a thousand pieces of metal ringing out with the bright light. Basaal and Aedon dove to the ground.

"Up!" Basaal lifted Aedon, and they began to run out of the

way of their own cavalry.

"The rest of the men?" Aedon shouted, blinking as he ran, his eyes blinded by the flashes. Then several more explosions rang out in the night. Trumpets were sounding, the Imirillian camp was mobilizing.

"The men know to drop back to their mounts." Basaal practically shoved Aedon forward. Basaal could still hear the warhorses' shrill cries.

"It's too early!" Aedon yelled as they dropped down into the ravine, running in the darkness to where their horses were tethered. Above them, the Aemogen army came pounding by them like thunder across the spring plain as they rode up into the edges of the Imirillian encampment. The men were screaming as they rode by.

Refigh was spooked, frightened by the endless explosions. Basaal spoke hastily to the horse as he mounted, urging Refigh to trust him. Responding to the familiar feel of Basaal's touch, Refigh settled into a nervous energy and sprang forward. Basaal pulled out his sword and glanced at Aedon before they galloped upward, into the tumult.

They rode onto the plain, falling in with the Aemogen cavalry. Basaal lost track of Aedon among the shadows of the other riders. He called out to Aedon, but it was of no use. The sounds of the Aemogen cavalry rushed over his shoulders, spilling across the ground below.

He focused on the dark wave before him. And for a moment, Basaal saw every country he had ever ridden into in the name of war and conquest and family, and he felt as if the terror of every soul who had ever cried out in fear was upon him. He screamed, forcing the fear away. Basaal lifted his black sword above his head.

The sounds of clashing metal had begun to lift up through the darkness.

Basaal rode into the tumult of war.

The explosions from Colun Tir had been a spectacular, terrifying sight. The immense wave of each blast rumbled off the mountains, crashing against the stones of Colun Tir itself. Eleanor had watched this with Hastian and Zanntal from the balcony, continuing to cover her ears as she heard the sounds of battle rising.

A trumpet sounded, deep and strong.

"The Imirillian trumpet of advance," Zanntal said in Imirillian. "Shaamil has pulled his armies together."

"What do you think he will do?" Eleanor asked.

"Push the Aemogens away from the camp, down onto the plain," Zanntal replied.

"I wish this day were over," the Queen's Own muttered nervously at her side, not understanding the Imirillian words they had spoken. Eleanor turned to look at Hastian. His eyes met hers, his face grim, and she took his hand before staring back out over the darkness.

Battle, Basaal remembered, was thick work. He brought his sword down on an Imirillian foot soldier, his weapon catching, almost slipping, before he pulled it loose with a cry. Refigh stumbled, and Basaal guided his mount back to the steadiness of the plain below the camp as a wave of Imirillian soldiers forced the Aemogens back.

The air had lightened into the dimness of morning pulling

away from night. From what Basaal could now see above the tumult, the Imirillian cavalry was nearly decimated, their horses had sustained the brunt of Aemogen's attack. But they had thousands upon thousands of men on foot, now organized and pushing the Aemogen forces back from their camp, sweeping them to the south, in the direction of the pass. Basaal was swept with them. His only aim, beyond the struggles of battle, was to stay as far away from his own companies of red-clad Imirillian soldiers as he possibly could.

Basaal was jolted to the side as he pressed into another horseman then swung away. A pain rushed through his leg, and Basaal screamed out, bringing his sword down on the Imirillian assailant who had caused the wound with his own.

The plain was crowded, and fighting turned cumbersome. Basaal swung his sword, forcing his way through the foot soldiers as arrows began to shoot past him. He took down an archer; he did not dare look at his face as light now poured into the valley. He fought, and struggled, and prayed for the day to be over.

⁓⊷⧓⊶⁓

Light had revealed the state of the battle raging below Colun Tir. The Aemogens had devastated the Imirillian camp, and even from the distance, Eleanor thought she could see the bodies of men and horses scattered throughout the destruction. There were two forces discernibly moving against the Aemogens: the deep purple of the emperor's men and the red and black of Basaal's own. As the conflict washed towards the south—a slow and bloody migration—hundreds of bodies were left behind, strewn across the abandoned field.

Eleanor forced herself not to think of it, watching the field like a chessboard. Pacing, arms folded, the sound of battle seemed to be an endless accompaniment to her life. As if she had never lived without the clamor of war in her ears.

That midday ever came was almost inconceivable to Eleanor despite the shadows again beginning to grow long. The battle now lay farther south than she could follow with her eyes. Standing atop the battlement, Zanntal held his spyglass to his eye, poised impossibly still, except for where the slight breeze of the day moved his deep blue robes. Hastian stood back, his face white, his jaw taut. He was no longer even trying to watch the plain below.

Just as Eleanor was about to ask Zanntal what he could see, the Imirillian soldier stiffened and looked back towards Eleanor. He put his hands to his lips and motioned for Eleanor to stand still as he listened. Something in the silence around them confirmed Zanntal's suspicion.

"They've found Colun Tir."

Eleanor spun towards the archway leading back into the tower as the sounds of metal rang up the stairs from the direction of the stable yard. They heard a man scream.

There was a flash of purple, and Basaal pulled his leg from the stirrup instinctively, shying away from the blade of a single Vestan assassin. Basaal heard a sickening sound, and Refigh jerked his head backward in pain. Grasping at the already disappearing reins, Basaal was thrown from his horse into the mass of battle below him as Refigh came crashing down with a shrill cry of pain. Basaal rolled away, escaping the crushing impact as his horse fell to the ground. The Vestan gave Basaal no time to even wonder after his horse, advancing on the fallen prince in three aggressive steps, bringing his scimitar down where Basaal knelt, dazed from the fall.

Basaal heard the sound of conflicting metal and spun away in time to see Crispin materialize next to him, bringing his sword up to fend off the Vestan's scimitar. As Basaal stumbled to his feet and grabbed his own sword, Crispin advanced on the assassin, engaging him as Basaal came from the side, and in one aggressive move, Basaal plunged his sword through the Vestan's purple robes. The assassin stumbled back and sank to the ground. Crispin finished him off.

The sweep and movement of battle did not allow them to speak as they readied themselves for the next onslaught. Basaal's legs were shaky from having spent all morning on his horse.

"Let's fight back toward the closest Aemogen company!" Crispin yelled out across the din.

Basaal called back a word in agreement, swinging towards one of his father's men, cutting him down just as he felt the skin on his own forearm break.

Hearing a scream, Basaal turned to find Crispin beside him, having taken down another Imirillian at Basaal's back. Before any expression of thanks could cross Basaal's face, he saw a knifepoint appear through the front of Crispin's throat—a strange, unnatural image of steel protruding from flesh—and then the blood. Crispin's eyes held onto Basaal's for as long as he could—as though he were asking Basaal for deliverance—before he stumbled forward.

Basaal caught Crispin, laying his body down and letting go of him in the same motion as he lunged towards his friend's assailant. Another soldier was upon him. Before Basaal could even think, his sword came around and caught one man in the neck while the other suffered Basaal's knife between his ribs. A dark rush caught his eye as more purple closed in. And Basaal heard himself say something back to Crispin as he ran.

"I will come back. I will come back for you!"

He may have even screamed it.

———◦◦◦———

Hastian raced to Eleanor's side while Zanntal jumped down from the battlements and swept past her towards the open archway of the balcony.

"We must hide you or get you back to the tunnel!" Zanntal shouted in Imirillian. But sounds rang up the stairs, and from the hollow echo of it all, Eleanor knew they had broken into the tower.

"They're inside," Eleanor said desperately. "It's too late. How did they come to find the tower?"

Zanntal disappeared down the stairs into the fortress, and Hastian backed up towards Eleanor, his sword drawn, breathing fast, watching.

Eleanor drew her ornamental sword just as a sickening sound came from the stone stairway. Eleanor almost dropped her sword, its hilt warm for the sweat of her hands. She gripped it harder, moving her thumb across the metalwork of the handle, as she tried to pace her breathing and waited. Then Zanntal burst out through the door, the blood on his scimitar catching the afternoon sun.

"The Vestan," he said. Eleanor gripped her weapon harder. "It is the Vestan." Zanntal was out of breath. "Three, four of them," he continued. "One is dead on the stairs. They must have picked up the trail and split away from the battle."

Zanntal sheathed his scimitar and pulled his bow from off his shoulder, placing a thick arrow above the grip, pulling back the

BETH BROWER

bowstring. He stepped towards Hastian and Eleanor. "There is no going down," he explained in Imirillian. "Here, we must make our fight."

Eleanor repeated Zanntal's words to Hastian as she watched Zanntal train his arrow on the black archway. Hastian muttered something under his breath.

"We must assume the men in the courtyard are dead," Zanntal continued in Imirillian.

Without any sound, a Vestan swept onto the balcony, his scimitar drawn, his expression grim and satisfied. Zanntal sent his arrow flying. With more finesse than Eleanor would have believed possible, the Vestan swung his scimitar, slicing the arrow in half, sending the pieces flying against the wall behind him. Zanntal had already reloaded his bow and released another arrow, and the scene repeated. But the third arrow hit its mark, catching the assassin beneath the collarbone. He stumbled back as two more Vestan rushed onto the balcony. They swarmed Zanntal as he pulled out his scimitar. Hastian rushed forward, and one of the Vestan turned on him.

"Get back! Back!" Hastian cried to Eleanor as he fended off the Vestan's blows. Eleanor stumbled back, shaking. She could not think. Was she to run forward to help? Was she to stay back? Hastian almost fell towards Eleanor, and she could not see Zanntal save for the flashes of blue and purple on the far side of the balcony.

Someone shouted an Imirillian curse Eleanor had once heard Basaal use.

Rushing forward to aid Hastian, Eleanor tripped on the hem of her dress and fell against the hard stone, her sword clattering on the ground with a terrifying noise. Eleanor reached for the blade,

280

picked it up, and continued forward. She gritted her teeth and yelled as she swung the blade towards the assassin. He blocked it as easily as if he were redirecting a child's blow. The man laughed in the process. But it was enough, for Hastian sank his sword deep into the Vestan's robe, and the assassin's hand shook as his scimitar dropped to the ground.

Zanntal screamed as the scimitar of his opponent found its mark in his arm. He stumbled back and reset himself, sweat running down his face, which was filled with pain. Eleanor stepped behind Hastian, who was now engaging the remaining Vestan. But in a quick movement, filled with sounds and agony, Eleanor felt herself being jerked backwards. Her breath stopped as an arrow was pressed hard against her cheek. The first Vestan, who had fallen from Zanntal's arrow, had pulled himself up to grab her. His breathing echoed the sound of blood siphoning into his lungs—a hellish sluice.

A knife was at her throat, and in his attempts to breathe, the arrow's shaft moved back and forth against her cheek. He pulled harder, and Eleanor dropped her sword. Hastian turned back towards Eleanor, dropping his weapon to the ground, holding his hands up, his face still, his mouth set. He stepped over the fallen Vestan at his feet and bent his knees slightly, pleading with the assassin as the knife began to split open the skin of Eleanor's throat.

Zanntal had stumbled back from his opponent, but the Vestan he was fighting turned and, in a singularly powerful movement, cut through Hastian's back with a sickening sound. Hastian's mouth opened, a spasm rattling through the muscles around his spine, causing his chest to fly forward in an ungraceful contortion as Hastian tried to remain on his feet.

His blue eyes looked for Eleanor's, and she screamed, trying to fling herself towards him. But the Vestan pulled her back. Hastian dropped to a knee as the assassin behind him flung a knife that thudded into his back.

The Queen's Own shuddered and fell forward, catching himself with his arms, scrambling desperately towards his queen. With a sickening cough, Hastian left blood on the stones before him. When the Vestan stepped forward to finish the job, Zanntal, from behind, ran the assassin through with a scimitar.

"No—" Eleanor tried to say, but she could not swallow as her captor pulled her another step backward. She could feel a line of blood running down her throat. Hastian was still trying to come to her, his fingers veined from the pain.

Zanntal retrieved his bow—his face pained from injury—notched an arrow, and sent it flying at Eleanor's face. It sank into the throat of the Vestan behind her with a spray of blood, and Eleanor could taste the metallic zing of it on her lips. As he fell, Eleanor fell with him. Zanntal was upon them, tearing the man's arm from around Eleanor's neck, throwing the knife away.

She did not watch what Zanntal then did to the Vestan, for Eleanor could see only Hastian, her Queen's Own, stretched out before her. She crawled over the blood-covered stones, reaching her hand towards his face. Pushing against his shoulder, Eleanor turned his body to face her. Hastian's head rolled carelessly to the side, his eyes blank, his back still sending spasms through his muscles.

He was dead.

Emperor Shaamil made an impatient noise, and Ammar looked

up from where he was preparing a drink for each of them. They sat alone in the luxurious pavilion of the emperor—a flap rolled up on one side—and watched from comfortable chairs the progress of the battle. Shaamil's tent had been far enough away from the camp's destruction that his private luxury remained intact.

Shaamil sighed. "We are advancing but not as quickly as I would like."

Ammar gave no response as he walked towards his father, handing him a drink while taking his own, and sitting in an adjacent cushioned chair. Shaamil's generals had directed the soldiers to push the fighting down into the plain, away from the Imirillian camp. But the battle had now traveled farther away on its own accord, and it was difficult to see much of the fighting, if any.

The Aemogens, despite their attack of the night before, were still outnumbered by two to one at least. Ammar considered this as he rolled his cup between his fingers and then took a long sip. They would fall in only a few hours' time.

Shaamil sat patiently, watching the waves of death play out in the valley before him. He also took a drink. He set the cup down and folded his fingers together.

"Not much longer now," Ammar said.

The emperor looked towards his son but said nothing.

Ammar finished the contents of his drink in one long movement and set the empty cup aside. "I am sorry it had to be this way," Ammar stated. "But this needed to come to an end at some point."

Shaamil looked at Ammar's empty cup and then at the contents of his own. He stared at Ammar's face. "You've poisoned me."

"Yes," Ammar said, touching one of the two gold bands around his wrist. "I have."

Fury filled Shaamil's eyes, and he tensed as if he would move, call a guard, or take out his own dagger and end Ammar's life. Either of these the physician knew could happen. He sat coolly, watching the many avenues of his fate play out on his father's face. Then a private realization touched the emperor's mind. His body relaxed, and his shaking mouth steadied into the hint of a peaceful expression.

"Well done," Shaamil said, clutching the scrolled ends of his chair's armrests. "Can I expect much pain?"

"I am no barbarian," Ammar replied. "If you go into your sleeping quarters and lie down, you will find it no harder than falling into sleep. I would imagine a quarter hour, no more, is what you have left in this world."

Shaamil grunted and looked out over the plane, his jaw working back and forth as he was thinking. "You have broken your physician's covenant. You have given up the right to practice medicine. Was I worth it?"

"Physician's make two covenants, Father. One is to never take a life. The other is to uphold life and to uphold Imirillia—" Ammar paused and moved his fingers across his chin. "I desecrate the first to consecrate the second."

Shaamil's laugh, when it came, was full of irony. "The only pleasure this gives me is the thought of what your brothers must do with you now. A physician willing to kill—that is far more terrifying than anything I could have become."

Ammar almost smiled. "Pity Emir."

Shaamil's face sobered as he looked down on the plain. "And what is your plan? Get me out of the way and signal the trumpet for retreat?"

"Yes," Ammar answered.

The emperor coughed, and turned his dark eyes on Ammar, victorious. "I did not bring it."

Ammar frowned, fingering the base of his empty cup. "I had anticipated that, which is why I brought it myself."

Shaamil was pale, whether from the surprise or the poison, Ammar could not know. As the emperor laughed, his breathing already sounded labored. "You always were the smartest of my sons, perhaps even the best."

"No," Ammar disagreed. "The best was always Basaal."

Shaamil gave no response, and he began to try to stand.

"Would you like me to help you?" Ammar asked dispassionately.

The emperor stood. "I desire to be left in peace," he said. He studied the face of his son, looked out across the plain at the mountains of Aemogen, and the warm shadows of a spent day, and then disappeared behind a curtain.

Ammar studied his fingernails, pensive and thoughtful, before he stood, retrieved the trumpet from his trunk, and called on the guard outside the tent.

They were losing. The Aemogens were falling under the relentless Imirillian attack. And Basaal, heavy-limbed, tired, could find no thought to describe the horrors transpiring there. The Aemogen right flank was decimated, but not without leaving a trail of Imirillian blood in its wake. The center company, where Basaal found himself, had the advantage of falling farther south, but it was disorganized and desperate. No captains led the field. Basaal could not stop to call out any order. The left flank was isolated towards the west and would soon fall.

Basaal pulled back as another wave of Imirillians came down upon them. He stumbled over a body and did not look down to see if he knew whose it was. Basaal felt as if he were drowning.

Someone called out to him.

Clutching his sword, he twisted. Seeing only a flash of metal, Basaal's movements went before his sight. He swung, only to be fended off and sworn at as somebody grabbed his shoulder and shook him.

Annan. It was Annan. Before Basaal could speak, a man in purple came down upon him. Swinging his sword, Basaal fended off a blow, losing his footing as he did. The Imirillian soldier moved to strike Basaal, but Annan was there, eliminating the man in one motion, just as an officer in the emperor's army swung his scimitar, slicing through Annan's stomach. In the time it took Basaal's world to go silent, a dagger was plunged into Annan's heart.

"Annan!" Basaal screamed, his own voice ringing in his ears.

The motion of the battle around him disappeared.

Basaal threw his weapon to the ground and tried to catch his stumbling friend. Annan's eyes were frozen with inexplicable pain as he slumped from Basaal's grasp, falling, clutching his hand to the death wound.

"Annan! Annan!" Dropping to his knees, Basaal flung an arm beneath Annan's back, pulling his friend up towards him. Annan's eyes locked onto his. "No, no, Annan, I didn't see—Annan!"

The last flow of Annan's blood soaked between Basaal's fingers. Annan's eyes rolled, his chest making a sucking sound of lungs fighting liquid cut short. His eyes were staring at Basaal's face in stunned terror, then their focus was lost completely. Annan went limp.

"No! Annan!" Basaal cried. "Please, please come back. I didn't see! I'm so sorry! No, God, please!" Basaal jerked his face towards the sky, pleading. "No!"

A wail of grief fought its way into Basaal's words, and he gave into it as he clutched Annan's motionless body to his chest. Basaal kissed Annan's cheeks, bent over the body, overwrought, drowning in the blood of the day.

The movements of an approaching figure did not dissuade Basaal from his grief. He paid the man no mind, even as the shadow of a raised scimitar stretched out across the ground before him. Basaal wished for annihilation—he waited for it.

Then, another figure wearing red rushed forward, engaging the soldier of Shaamil, cutting him down with a cry. Too dazed to care, Basaal continued stumbling over words of apology to his friend, hardly even looking as another soldier in red, then another, rushed about him. Men who had sworn to Basaal unto death began to form a loose circle around him, preventing any of Shaamil's soldiers from reaching their prince.

The perimeter grew, a circle of red extending out from him, railing against the purple waves. Basaal bent his face into Annan's still chest, the tunic saturated with blood, disoriented by the ringing across the battlefield where bodies lay, torn, bloodied, discarded.

A sound, a low horn rising across the sacrificial earth, caused Eleanor to turn her head, looking away from where she sat cradling Hastian's limp head. The late afternoon sun, preparing to flee behind the western hills, blinded her eyes.

"The trumpet," Zanntal cried as he motioned towards Eleanor

with his uninjured arm. "It is the sound of retreat. The emperor has called for a retreat."

"Impossible," Eleanor muttered as she stared at Hastian's dead face.

The trumpet sounded again, in three quick successions. "The men are separating out! Running back toward the Imirillian camp. Right on the edge of their victory, Shaamil has called a retreat." Zanntal's voice was incredulous.

Eleanor finally stumbled to her feet, shielding her eyes, her hands stiff with dried blood. There, on the plain, a wave of purple was breaking away in groups, disengaging from the fight. Some pockets and shapes seemed to rush after the retreating Imirillians, but the remaining figures on the field stood still. Eleanor could make out a contingent of Basaal's soldiers, dressed in red, standing near what appeared to be the men of Aemogen. But there was no movement, no shouting, no fighting amongst them.

"We must go down," Eleanor said, but the sight of the Vestan and of Hastian's body seemed impossible to leave. Eleanor reached for the floor as her knees gave way, and she crumbled, numb, looking at the fallen men around her. Suddenly, the battle crown felt very heavy indeed. Lifting a shaking hand, Eleanor clutched the metal crown, now smeared in blood, and pulled it away. It slipped, clanging against the stone, sounding like the strike of a dull sword. It spun to a nervous stop and remained still. Eleanor did not move to pick it back up.

───◦─◦◦◦◦◦─◦───

Someone was clutching Basaal's shoulders, pulling him up, coaxing him to release the still corpse he held in his arms. The sound had been terrible—and merciful—the trumpet calling Imirillia into retreat. Basaal thought it had sounded distant, as if coming from across the world.

Numb, stiff, and covered in death, Basaal felt the blood of his own countryman caked into the garments he wore, stained into his skin. The trumpet sounded again, and someone was determined to set Basaal on his feet, patiently prying him from Annan. His friend's body was already going stiff, Basaal realized, and his eyes were still open.

"Prince Basaal."

It was Sean. Basaal looked up, then around himself, where dozens of soldiers in red were waiting in uncertainty.

"The trumpet," Sean began. "And the men, the emperor's men, they all began to run back towards their camp in retreat." It was an uncertain, untrusting statement.

"Why would my father have sounded the trumpet for retreat?" Basaal muttered in Imirillian.

Ashan, third in command of Basaal's army, knelt on the other side of his prince. "The emperor has called the men back." Then, he added, "At least half of your remaining army banded together to fight for you. They drew their swords against the foes of their prince."

Sean looked confused, and Basaal could not remember what he was supposed to say to either of these men. He moved his fingers to the red Safeeraah on his arm and closed his eyes.

"Basaal?" Sean spoke in his Aemogen tongue.

"The trumpet call," Basaal heard his own voice say, "was of final retreat. The Imirillian army has declared itself defeated. I have never thought, in all my days, I would live to hear such a sound."

Basaal opened his eyes and placed his hands on the ground, steadying himself as he rose to his feet. Ashan and Sean, one on

BETH BROWER

each side of Basaal, did the same. Basaal scanned the plain, awash with fallen soldiers. Here and there, small groups began to gather in confusion. Men cried out from wounds. Bands of red began to gather and make their way towards Basaal's immediate guard. A wave of purple, what was left of it, was on the far field, retreating towards the Imirillian camp. Eleanor's soldiers were calling out, uncertain. They were weaving among Basaal's soldiers, searching for the wounded, finding each other, clasping hands.

"I couldn't leave him," Sean was saying at Basaal's left. "I came upon him screaming and quickly saw there was nothing to be done. So I ended his pain there, for pity."

Dazed, Basaal turned towards Sean. "Crispin?" he asked.

"No," Sean replied, looking struck. "Your horse, Refigh. I believe Crispin is dead."

"Yes," Basaal said as he shook himself awake. "Yes, I know. I saw it happen. He saved me, damn it. Damn it all."

"What do we do now?" Ashan asked, watching Sean with uncertainty.

It was sudden as a lightning strike, and it shot through Basaal with force. His heart felt it again, and agony jolted him wide awake to the destruction of the day. Basaal shook his head, startled, taking a moment before he could look Ashan and Sean in the face.

"We must organize the men," he said in Imirillian. "Search for the living among the fallen. Bring all the wounded Imirillians to the western rise. Count the survivors, both able and injured. But let us be vigilant. Do not let the men believe in this retreat until I can confirm it is so."

He turned to Sean and spoke in Aemogen, giving the same orders. "Take all the Aemogen wounded to the eastern rise, below the trees. Have you seen the other officers? What about Aedon?"

"I cannot say," Sean replied, looking grim. He wiped his mouth with the back of his hand. The man was covered in the burnt color of drying blood.

Basaal reached for Sean's arm and stepped forward. The injury in his leg from earlier in the day had hardened into a stiff, swollen pain. With a sharp breath, Basaal began to limp towards the band of red-clad men who had surrounded him, men who had sworn to uphold Basaal until his death. As they gathered him in—however bittersweet this reunion might be—Basaal was home.

CHAPTER
SIXTEEN

Ammar stood at the door of the tent, waiting for Shaamil's general to return.

"It is done," he told Ammar when he did. "The captains under me are organizing the retreat, pulling all the men back." He looked at the physician prince with skepticism on his face, as he held the trumpet in his hands.

"Once all the men have pulled back," Ammar said. "I want them away from the battlefield, at the far western end of the camp, until we can assess the casualties and discuss the burying of the dead with the Aemogens."

"And the emperor?"

"Has asked I leave him in peace," Ammar said the truthful statement casually.

"The conquest, then, is over?"

"It is over," Ammar said. "Send a messenger to discover the fate of Prince Basaal, seventh son. Notify me as soon as he is found." Then Ammar turned back towards the tent.

Eleanor and Zanntal laid the bodies in the stable yard behind Colun Tir. Even the dead Vestan were carried down to await their burials. The thought of leaving Hastian lying in his blood on the tower any longer was beyond what Eleanor could endure and so Zanntal obliged her quietly when she had insisted he allow her to help carry her dead.

The hole that had begun inside of her upon hearing of Doughlas's death, the grave that had opened there, was larger now, and the weight of Hastian and the other soldiers, found dead outside the tower, worked to enlarge this gap between her ribs and her heart. Eleanor's white dress was soiled with dirt and blood, forever stained. Her heart felt much the same.

Thaniel, her fen rider, arrived as they had just brought out the last body.

"Your Majesty!" he called, out of breath as he reared his horse up and dismounted, a flurry of news and exhaustion. "The Imirillians have ordered the retreat. We have begun counting the dead, seeing to the wounded. Sean asked me to send this report in hopes of finding you safe."

"I will come down soon." Eleanor motioned toward the bodies there as if in explanation. "And Basaal?"

"Prince Basaal has gone to ask for assurances from the Imirillian camp."

Eleanor drew in a breath and pressed her fingers to her eyes. He was alive. It took a deep breath, and then another, before Eleanor could again feel her lungs, not realizing until now how much she had been waiting for this news.

"That is not all," Thaniel said. He had caught his breath, though the sweat from riding fast across the late afternoon still glistened on his face. "The prince received a message from his

brother before leaving for their camp: Emperor Shaamil is dead."
He gave a ghostly grin despite himself. "The emperor is dead, and
the conquest is over."

"Shaamil is dead?" Eleanor cried. "By whose hand?"

Zanntal stiffened, seeming to guess what had been said.

"I know no more than this," Thaniel answered.

It was as strange as it was miraculous, but Eleanor did not feel
the miracle of it yet. She only felt hollow and thin. She reached
a hand out, and Zanntal steadied her. The fen rider, having
delivered his message, finally saw the blood on Eleanor's dress.
Then he studied the bodies lying on the ground, his eyes ending
on Hastian. He walked slowly towards the corpse of the Queen's
Own, crouching down and touching Hastian with the barest edge
of his shaking fingertips.

"Not Hastian," Thaniel said as he bent his tired head. "Not all
the good men."

"Who else? Aedon? Crispin?" These words escaped from
Eleanor faster than she could stop them, for she did not truly wish
to know. It was too endless, this knowing.

The fen rider shook his head. "We have just begun gathering
the dead, but—"

"Speak no more." Eleanor held up her hand. "I will come
down...I will see for myself."

⌘

Basaal refused the horse they had offered him and began to walk
towards the Imirillian encampment, followed silently by his
own, red-clad, battle-weary soldiers. They stepped over endless
bodies, and when Basaal came upon his own horse, its throat
slit compassionately by Sean, he stared at it numbly until Ashan

moved him onward.

They continued across the plain.

Upon arriving at the burned encampment, Basaal saw that Emperor Shaamil's men had been ordered to the far end of the desolated Imirillian camp. Death had come here, with the aid of the devilish powder devices, and men and horses were scattered with abandon across the earth. The emperor's tent still stood, farther up the hill, untouched.

It was there that Basaal carried his tired soul. No guards greeted him, and he motioned for his men to remain in wait. He pulled back the tent flap and let himself in.

Ammar sat in a chair, quiet and contemplative, swirling the contents of a brass cup in his hand. Basaal's entrance caused him to look up.

"Where is he?" Basaal asked. His own words sounded young in his ears.

Ammar nodded towards a drawn flap that led to the emperor's private sleeping quarters inside the pavilion. Basaal crossed the room, passing his brother, moving his fingers along Ammar's shoulder to anchor himself before moving on, pulling the ornate curtain aside. He entered the enclosed bedroom and stood, letting his eyes adjust to the darkness around the lifeless figure on the ornate sofa. Basaal stared, blinking back the oddity, the power vacuum he was now surrounded by. The emperor of Imirillia was dead.

Basaal had always loved the Zarbadast theatrics as a boy, the plays and performances, the grief and triumph of the players. Now, as he took a few steps towards the silent, still man before him, the memory of these plays crossed his mind, and he knelt down, feeling as though he were doing, perhaps, some great thing and should feel more emotion for his father's death. But, whether it was the carnage of the day—growing stale in the late afternoon—or his own exhaustion, or both, Basaal could not access the feelings of his heart, certainly nothing worthy of a son kneeling beside the corpse of his father.

He lifted his hand and touched his father's brow. Shaamil's skin was cold, already stiff, but Basaal moved away as if he had been burned by fire. The gray hairs around his father's temple and in his neatly trimmed beard were accompanied by quiet lines of age around his eyes. His father was dead. Annan was dead. Crispin was dead. Everything was death.

"You were always your mother's son," Ammar said from behind Basaal. The younger prince turned towards his brother. Basaal's mouth twitched. Shaking his head, he looked back down at the lifeless corpse.

"Yes. But I feel as if I have always been my father's shadow."

"Do you believe I did right?" Ammar asked. It was a rare moment of hearing a tone of question in Ammar's voice.

Slumping over, bent and bowed, Basaal shook his head, staring at the ground. "Do not ask me what is right and wrong. I am of the damned. I know nothing of such things."

Ammar did not respond. The sound of the curtain dropping into place was followed by quiet. There was a prayer, Basaal knew, that was to be spoken over the body of a dead Imirillian emperor. But he did not know the words, and his father had stopped allowing holy men to travel with him to war.

The rush of energy that had propelled Basaal to organize the chaos on the battlefield and then stumble up to the Imirillian camp was now gone; he fell into a numb state, so lost he could not remember what it had ever been to be found. For several hours,

Basaal knelt before his dead father. The afternoon ended itself, and the dim light of dusk filled the space around him. Candles were lit and torches set as darkness fell. And still Basaal did not move from his place of numb mourning.

Eleanor and Zanntal had buried Hastian before descending from Colun Tir. The other soldiers would have to wait. The bodies of the Vestan Eleanor would send back across the plain. Aemogens who had survived were walking the battlefield, searching for wounded, and gathering them to a single place just inside the woods. It was there that Eleanor found Sean.

"We've begun to gather in our wounded men," Sean said as he took Eleanor aside after greeting her. "A company was just sent up the road to bring down some large tents that we'd placed inside the storeroom—and food, with whatever blankets can be found. Some of the wounded should not be moved, even to the tower," he explained. "Edythe will bring the women through soon, I suppose, with more supplies."

It was then that Sean brought Eleanor to Crispin's body.

"Briant is dead," Sean said flatly. "And Crispin, as you see. I am about all that's left of your war council." Her councillor of husbandry was looking at Eleanor, but she was not certain he saw her. She did not mind. The air around Eleanor was heavy and stiff, and as she moved she kept thinking to convince herself it was all a dream. Why should it not be the same way for Sean?

"And Aedon?" she managed to say.

Sean shook his head. "He is not yet accounted for."

Eleanor blinked, and swallowed, glancing aside as Sean continued speaking. "We've a messenger back just now from the Imirillian camp, sent by Prince Basaal. The retreat is final, the emperor no more, and the Imirillians will be returning to their country once they have worked out the logistics of burying their dead."

"Did the prince say when he would return?" Eleanor asked as she looked tiredly across the plain toward the rise of the Imirillian camp.

"No," Sean answered.

Tents were brought down, erected on the edge of the woods, a short trail away from the overgrown road that ran north of the pass to Colun Tir. Eleanor asked that Crispin's body be placed in the smallest tent, tucked behind and apart from the others. Once his body had been laid out, Eleanor meant to leave and attend to the wounded, to organize the men and ask for reports on casualties, and to send a message across the plain. But as darkness fell, it was here that Eleanor sat, beside the cold, torn body of Crispin.

Sean did not let her stay any longer. When he guided her away from Crispin, Eleanor concerned herself with the first wave of her wounded soldiers, working into the night, attempting to bring them comfort, to clean their wounds, to call for desperately needed water—and more water. But when the fifth man died as she held his hand, Eleanor—her vision blurry, her head heavy as a stone—gave strict orders to notify her once Aedon was found and disappeared into the small tent to convince Crispin somehow that he could return back to life...that he should return back to life.

Hours passed, but each time she reached for his hand, there was still no response. Eleanor would press the back of her hand against her forehead, supposing perhaps she had gone mad, wondering why she still hoped that Crispin's fingers would respond to hers.

Later, when night was at its deepest, and when Eleanor could no longer sit beside Crispin wishing she could take back the day, she left the tent and asked Sean for a report on the wounded.

There were more men than the tents could hold. Eleanor found herself again weaving through rows of bodies. The groans and cries were insufferable until Eleanor learned she could close her ears, stop the sounds from penetrating, remain apart, even as she mopped their wounds with a rag and a bucket of water. It was the only way to move from one soldier to the next.

"Your Majesty!"

Sean had been asking her a question, or so Eleanor thought.

"Yes?" she asked.

"The dead. What would you have us do with the dead?"

"Have all the wounded been brought up?"

Sean's eyes were rimmed red from exhaustion. "As many as we could find in the darkness. We've begun to bring up the dead now and have found one or two men yet alive amongst them."

Eleanor brought a hand up to brush her hair from her face and paused. It was bloodstained. Bringing it down slowly, Eleanor looked out towards the battlefield. There, men holding torches were wandering the plain in groups of three or four, lifting and carrying corpses until they were piled below the tents of the wounded. Someone had found a wagon and was bringing the dead back a dozen at a time. Some of the torches belonged to the Imirillian soldiers, who moved about in their operations as a mirror image to Aemogen's as they took their own dead back to their camp.

"It's a devilish business," a soldier said to Eleanor and Sean at some point during the night. "We are stumbling around these fellows, none of us speaking a word of the same language, gathering our own dead and ignoring the fact that the man next to us, who is gathering his dead, would have killed countless of our men."

Those words were still stuck in Eleanor's head when she answered Sean's question regarding the place of burial. "We will bury the dead here," she said. "This side of the mountain range is still Aemogen land. We will bury them here, at the edge of the woods, and will make a single marker for each man, using the surviving fen lords—or any man—who can identify the dead. We must also keep a record of where each man has been set to rest—for his family. If King Staven finds cause to complain," she added, "well, let the man fight me for it." Then Eleanor went back to her work, whatever that work was.

There had yet to be news of Aedon.

Eleanor could not remember later when it had happened or how many hours from dawn it might have been, but at some point, arms began to surround her, soft, matronly arms. Eleanor became aware that the Marion women had come with blankets, food, and teas; fires were lit and kettles were put on. The men who still drew breath in agony, facing the horror of their half-hacked limbs, were given gentle treatment, or soothing stories, before they lost a hand, or a leg at the knee.

And then, it was not just the Marions but the women of Aemogen, sober-faced and labor-minded. Edythe had found Eleanor, and Thayne had also come. Eleanor was too tired to fight as they took her into the small tent, which now held not only Crispin's body but every other member of her war council and every fen lord found dead on the field.

Aedon was not yet found? Eleanor remembered asking.

No, Thayne had answered as he shook his head. Aedon was not yet found.

Thayne left the sisters alone, and Edythe stripped Eleanor of the bloodied gown and washed her body with water, cold from the mountain. She carefully placed Eleanor's hands into the bowl of water, scrubbing the blood away. Then Edythe slipped a simple blue dress, which any Aemogen farmwife might have worn, over Eleanor's tired body, wrapped Eleanor in a large blanket, and tucked her down into sleep.

To her own relief, Eleanor did not sleep long after the sun was up. Tired as she was, she did not wish to be away from the operations of the day, and the tent now smelled heavy with death. Outside they had to begun to bury the dead.

"How many?" Eleanor asked Thayne after she had spent a few hours treating the wounded. "Have the dead yet been counted?"

"They are still bringing bodies up from the plain," Thayne replied. He stood with a paper in his hands, marking the dead as they were delivered to their burial sites, his blue eyes surveying the marks before him.

"What do we know so far?" Eleanor asked.

"I estimate we will have lost almost two thousand men." The fen lord cleared his throat and frowned as he watched the next wagon approach, filled with the battle's dead. "That is not including the wounded."

Eleanor stored this number away, unwilling to look at it or to think about it until she was alone. "When there is a final count, find me," Eleanor said as she placed her hand on his arm.

They worked the day long. The Aemogen women and any soldiers left standing went about feeding and washing and digging grave after grave. Someone suggested a mass burial, and Eleanor's glare burned so fiercely into the man that he retreated, his shovel in hand. These soldiers were not to be nameless.

The women prepared the dead for burial with great reverence. There was not time to pay full homage, for the smell of death had risen with the sun, and the work stretched out before them in endless rows. But sometimes extra care was taken: a wife burying her husband, a neighbor, or a child. And the woman would not be moved until his body had been prepared according to the honor she felt he deserved.

Eleanor joined the women in the washing. Moving from corpse to corpse, she worked alongside, wishing that those who recognized her would not, craving oblivion. Late in the day, Eleanor dropped her bucket beside the body of a young man, a boy really. A woman was already preparing his body for burial.

"Let me help you," Eleanor muttered, saying the same words she had said countless times throughout the day.

"No!" The woman flung her arms protectively across the body, the set of her lips defensive, her eyes, beleaguered with sorrow. "No other will prepare my son for his death. He is mine more than he ever was Aemogen's. I will see to his washing. I will see to his rites." She looked up as if she were a wild thing, injured and fierce. There were large black circles beneath her eyes; they were desolate.

Eleanor retreated without words.

She and Edythe prepared Crispin's body for burial and accompanied the wagon that took him to his grave. A soldier, one of Thayne's men who had taken on Eleanor's mandate to identify each corpse, marked the grave and Crispin's name before leaving Eleanor and Edythe to watch Crispin's still form disappear beneath each shovelful of dirt. Then the fieldstone, dug up from the place of Crispin's own grave, was set into place.

"Is Basaal still with the Imirillians?" Edythe asked.

"I believe so," Eleanor said, admitting her ignorance. "He is, I am sure, overseeing the same work there that we are about here."

Not long into the day, Zanntal found Eleanor and let her look through his spyglass to see the long trenches dug by the Imirillians.

"I believe that they wish to leave as soon as they can," he said in Imirillian, "so they will bury the men in mass graves."

"Can I ask a favor of you, Zanntal?" Eleanor asked.

"I will serve you as I can," the soldier said as he adjusted his blue robes, stained with blood. He had been helping gather in the wounded and dead. He had also, Eleanor found out, stood watch outside her tent as she slept.

"Go to the Imirillian camp," Eleanor said, "See if Basaal is well and find out what they mean to do. I should send a formal delegation across, but we have too much work here, and I know that he would be pleased to see you. Stay as long as you need to—stay as long as he needs you."

Zanntal went, and hours passed without a sign of his return. She found that she did not have the space to pay his absence—nor the lack of a message—any mind.

In the late afternoon, Eleanor disappeared into the woods, into the solitude of a tree-filled ravine. There, she sat and forced herself to think of the numbers Thayne had shared with her. Possibly two thousand men. Almost two of every three men of Aemogen, dead. Hundreds more injured. Aedon still missing.

Finding a moss-covered tree trunk, Eleanor sat, her finger rubbing against the rough wood as she tried to elicit an emotion, any emotion, for the events of the last two days. But nothing came. A blank, heavy weight seemed to hang from her collarbones, a pressure against her chest, but there was nothing else—no tears, no relief that it was ending—nothing.

She felt numb. No, not numb. She felt dead. Eleanor sat, her head in her hands, weary and dead. The numbness had begun with Hastian's death, and had continued with Crispin's. It had been beaten into her with all the wounded she had tended, and all the bodies she had prepared—this inability to reckon what had happened to her people.

It was almost belligerent, the way that spring ignored the foolish things men killed for—the flitting of birds from branch to branch and the green growth of living things, felt at once a desecration and a promise of cleansing.

"Please," Eleanor petitioned, not knowing why or to whom she spoke. "*Please*."

"They've found him!" Edythe came running at Eleanor as soon as she could be seen coming down through the trees. "They found Aedon!"

Eleanor forced her shaking legs into a sprint and passed Edythe, grabbing her sister's hand and pulling her around. "Where? Is he alive?"

"For now," Edythe said, pulling Eleanor to a hard stop. "He is in a very bad way, and I do not know if he will last the night. They've taken him up to the tower."

"Colun Tir?" Eleanor said. "Why?"

"Come." Edythe pulled Eleanor towards the line of what few horses remained. Thrift stood there, waiting for the queen. "They found him in the woods below Colun Tir. He lost much blood, his face was slashed, and his body was run through at least once. He has yet to regain consciousness. But a Marion physician is attending to him now. Go!"

A soldier waited to help Eleanor mount her horse.

"Will you come up with me?" Eleanor asked, clutching Edythe's wrist, feeling small and young.

"Later," Edythe answered shaking her head, overwhelmed. "There are so many here who need me. I can't leave them."

Nodding, Eleanor mounted, snapped Thrift's reins, and guided him to the tower road with a cry of urgency.

Edythe's report had not been exaggerated, it had been edited. Aedon looked like death. The cut on his face stretched from his left temple, across the bridge of his nose, and through his cheek. It was split wide and caked with dried blood. His chest was slashed across twice, and a bloody, gaping wound below the line of Aedon's left ribcage was infected and deep.

"I found him one hundred yards down the hill—" a soldier told Eleanor as she watched Aedon's chest move so subtly it seemed impossible he was not dead. "Amazed to find him," the soldier was saying, "still breathing after two days."

"I cleaned Aedon's wound partially," the Marion physician stated. "But let me be very clear with you, Queen Eleanor, any further treatment would be a waste of time. This man will not live."

"Yes, he will," Eleanor contradicted doggedly. "Bring me fresh water and a clean rag if it can be found. I want a drinking flask as well."

When the Marion physician did not move, Eleanor stared at the man, motioning towards her soldier to fulfill her command. The young soldier left immediately, and Eleanor's expression scared the physician from the room as well.

"Aedon," Eleanor whispered, touching his head, moving his hair back from his forehead. The skin on his face was already ashen, his lips blue, and his breathing slight. Upon the soldier's return, Eleanor took the bowl and rag from his hands. He slung a flask from off his shoulder and set it down beside his queen.

"I need you to send a message to the Imirillian camp. Can you bring me paper and ink?"

"An Aemogen messenger rides towards the camp," Ashan told Prince Basaal as soon as he was called into the emperor's pavilion.

"Send him straight here," Basaal said, not bothering to look at his officer but rather at the scribbling on the paper before him. That afternoon, he had ordered his men to prepare to leave. The trenches would be finished tomorrow night, and the dead buried. The wounded that could travel would have to suffer the journey home, for the Imirillian army was leaving in two days' time.

When the door to the tent again swung open, a young Aemogen entered, sweating from his swift ride across the plain. Basaal stood, his fingers stretched out and resting on the tabletop.

"Soldier," he said.

"Prince Basaal," the young man answered as he rushed a bow. "I've an urgent message from the queen." The soldier held out the missive toward Basaal.

Basaal left his table, walking over to the soldier and taking the note from his hand, uncertain. He had just sent Zanntal back to Eleanor with no message. What could he have to say? Zanntal had told Basaal months ago he would not swear unto the prince until death, and Basaal could see the man's allegiance was now to Eleanor. "You serving the queen is better than any message I could send at this point," Basaal had said casually to Zanntal, as if it had still been his right to direct him.

"This is not for me," Basaal said, leaving his thoughts as he now stared down at her familiar handwriting.

"Sir? The queen directed me here—"

"Yes," Prince Basaal interrupted, handing the note back to the soldier. Then he walked over to a chaise, where his sword lay. He belted it on. "It's for my brother. Come."

They left the pavilion, and Basaal frowned as he led the Aemogen soldier through the destroyed camp to a line of tents that had been set up to protect the wounded from flies. The tents did nothing for it. The stench of blood and death was beginning to ease now as the bodies of the dead were carried to the trenches and the wind blew toward the east. For this Basaal was grateful.

"Ammar," Basaal called to a figure leaning over a wounded soldier. "A message for you from Aemogen."

The physician did not look up but continued to sew his patient's wound together. Basaal watched the procedure, knowing he must wait for Ammar to finish. He also knew that Ammar was forbidden under Imirillian law to continue his practice of medicine after having committed a murder. This did not stop Ammar, and he went about his work of healing. The wounded man was a soldier of their father's. Basaal grimaced as Ammar was finishing his procedure, and the one time Basaal met the invalid's eyes he was greeted with an awful contempt.

Basaal smiled in return. It was a default reaction for maintaining power: prove that you are above it all to keep the men in check. It was a disgusting business, but the soldiers of Shaamil must be subdued until they were returned to Zarbadast. A few of the generals had tried to rally the men against the prince and his troops. Basaal, who was unable to afford an uprising, had them put to death. This had silenced any further thoughts of rebellion.

Once Ammar finished, he motioned to his assistant, washed his hands, and then dried them with a towel. Basaal told the Aemogen soldier to give Ammar the message. The crisp sound of paper being unfolded felt out of place when surrounded by so much death.

"She wants me to come across the plain to a place called Colun Tir to see to a patient," Ammar said, folding the paper again and tucking it inside his white robes. "Do you know where this tower stands?"

"Yes," Basaal said, lifting his hand to the hilt of his sword and resting it there. "Why don't her own doctors see to the wounded man?"

"She has been told that it is a hopeless attempt, but Eleanor will not settle for that. She wishes me to see what I can do." Ammar walked from the tent, followed by Basaal and the Aemogen soldier. "There are still wounded here to attend to."

"Yes," Basaal replied again, unsure of why he was speaking at all, wondering whose life Eleanor would be so desperate to save.

"Very well." Ammar began to walk towards the pavilion. "I will gather more supplies if someone can ready my horse."

Basaal ordered a soldier to do so, then he followed his brother to their pavilion. The Aemogen soldier also followed, nervously. Basaal looked to his left, across the small valley and up in the mountain, and saw the glint of sunlight off of something metal. Stopping and scanning the trees, Basaal tried to see the actual fortress. He could not see the tower itself, only where he guessed it would be—only where he guessed she would be.

It was strange to Eleanor that seeing Ammar, of all people, could free the anguish she could not otherwise feel. For as soon as he was led into Aedon's sickroom, Eleanor began to cry. She was so relieved he had come.

Ammar set about his work. If he recognized Aedon, he made no indication. Through the tears she continually brushed away, Eleanor could see the physician's determination to save this man. She blessed him for it, again and again. Edythe arrived soon after, assuming Eleanor's duties as Ammar's assistant. Then Thayne took Eleanor into another room of the fortress that was prepared with a blanket and some weak soup. He tried to help her eat, but Eleanor fell asleep before she could even taste the broth.

Eleanor slept for several hours, waking in the middle of the night. The sliver of a moon had reappeared again in the sky, giving only the slightest layer of blue relief in the dark room. As she came out of sleep, she realized someone's arms were around her. Eleanor began to turn, surprised at the stiff resistance of her muscles. She groaned from their soreness. Then the arms shifted slightly but did not let her go. Eleanor lifted the palm of her hand to the forearm around her, feeling several bands of Safeeraah, filthy and steeped in old blood.

Reaching her fingers around his wrist only a moment, Eleanor turned herself into Basaal's chest, clutching his black war jacket, pressing her face against the fabric. She heard him catch a sob, and Eleanor opened her heavy eyes, shifting her head back to see his face. Basaal's eyes were open. They were rimmed and swollen, with streaks across his face catching the faint moonlight from the tower window. Eleanor's own eyes burned, and she pulled herself tight against him. Despite the stifled emotion, Eleanor could feel his chest shake as he buried his face in her hair. She wept with him.

Basaal was gone when she woke again come morning.

CHAPTER

SEVENTEEN

Aedon had developed a fever.

"Ammar fears that it will rage quite fiercely," Edythe warned, yawning, and pressed her hand to her eyes. "I did not understand everything he said, but he did not know when he left what Aedon's chances might be."

"A fever means he is alive, at the very least," Eleanor said as she sat down beside her sister.

"The last of the dead will be buried today." Edyth sounded worn thin. "I should go down with you."

"Go and sleep," Eleanor pressed. "I will wake you later."

Leaving Aedon in the company of an Ainsley woman she trusted, Eleanor rode back down to the tents of the wounded near the burial grounds. The work there would be finished before the day was out, and then they would be left with the task of bringing their wounded home.

At day's end, Eleanor had not yet returned to the tower, and it was there, amongst the graves of the dead, that Basaal found her. He had come across the plain, first to the tower and then down the old road to the burial grounds. By the time he came to her, he had already visited the wounded.

Sean must have told him where she was.

Walking among the hastily filled graves, Eleanor was checking the careful notes of Thayne's men to be certain no grave had been left nameless. Redundant as the task was, Eleanor had needed to ground herself, needed something to count and order and wrap her mind around.

Eleanor had been crouched beside a grave marker, set for a young man she had known, when Basaal's presence caught her attention. She turned her head in his direction, blocking the last surge of brightness before the sun would disappear below the horizon.

He looked awful, tired, and grave-weary. Basaal had yet to change his clothing. She stood, leaving her report in the dirt beside the makeshift headstone.

"Have you successfully buried all your dead?"

Those were his first words. Eleanor could not process them, and Basaal would not look at her face.

"Nearly," Eleanor said when she finally understood the question through her exhaustion. He did not move, so she did not step towards him. "There is more work to do yet," she said, claiming a deep breath, "as I assume Sean told you. And what of your camp?"

"We lost over seven thousand men." Basaal's voice was graveled, broken. "Almost half of which were casualties during the initial attack. The rest perished on the field. In the end, my own soldiers turned against my father's, inflating the casualties significantly." After looking at the lines of Aemogen graves on the hillside, Basaal continued. "There was not time, you see, to honor each one. We've buried them in mass graves." His mouth twisted in such agony, and it seemed like he hated himself.

"You look—" Eleanor began to say but halted. "Have you even—?"

As if in answer, Basaal kicked the toe of his blood spattered boot into the dirt and shook his head, looking anywhere but at Eleanor. "The Imirillian army will be leaving the encampment to take the emperor's body back to Zarbadast. The conquest is over."

"Can you say that for sure?" Eleanor frowned. "Surely, if the Imirillians—"

Basaal's head snapped up in response. "I am Imirillian," he said, and his eyes connected with hers for the briefest time possible, before he looked away again. "I am a prince of Imirillia," he reiterated. "And nothing will change that."

"Why are you saying this?" Eleanor said defensively.

"I—" Basaal ran his fingers through his hair and breathed out slowly. "When the Imirillian army leaves, I will be with them."

"You will be with them," Eleanor said, repeating his words in a way that made it sound as if she were only confirming something she had already known. But in truth, she was stunned. "I admit I had assumed a formal meeting would occur between myself and, well, you, I suppose, or whoever is leading the camp, to discuss the terms of peace."

"There is nothing to be done at this juncture," Basaal said. "Peace must be negotiated officially. How all this is to be reconciled when we reach Zarbadast is a question I do not yet have the answer to." He put his hands on his hips and began again to kick at the dirt. "Things must be sorted out with Emir now, after the funeral has been arranged. I can all but promise on my own blood he will not pursue any further action against you, especially if trade lines were legalized between our two countries. He is more businessman than soldier. Ammar and I will need silver tongues to save our own necks. But let the truth come out, and so be the results," he added, before glancing at her face once more. "I will speak for Aemogen. I will stand as your voice and see what I can ensure of peace," Basaal said as if he were relating a travel itinerary, with a tone of casual indifference, his hand moving through the evening air.

Eleanor wished to say several things, but her courage faltered. Instead, she said, "Your voice on behalf of Aemogen would be appreciated. I trust you to represent our interests well." Eleanor wiped her hands on her skirt, needing something to do. "That saves me the trouble of sending a diplomat to argue for an end to all this."

Basaal was biting his bottom lip, and he swept his eyes over her, before nodding.

"Trust that you will hear word, then, from Zarbadast," he answered as he took a few steps away from Eleanor. "I must get back." Basaal looked as if he were about to move west across the plain, but his back foot kept him anchored to the ground. "I just need to ask you for the space to decide. Can you not understand that, Eleanor?"

She looked up again.

Basaal took a few steps down the hill and then turned again to face her. It was a severe movement, edged with the look of feeling trapped. "Can I have one year?"

"A year of what?"

"I must—" Basaal shrugged off his discomfort, looking at Eleanor earnestly. "I must decide, you see, what I will do with my life. I cannot stay with you in Aemogen to know this. You see that, Eleanor. Don't you? For me to ever be happy in this life, I must choose it?"

She did understand. She understood why he needed to go.

"Yes," Eleanor said simply.

"Give me a year's time," Basaal said, "before you move on, before you choose another."

The sun disappeared the moment of his asking, leaving only the purple light of sunset between them, and the pale moon over Eleanor's shoulder. His words sounded strange to her, for there was no other.

He stood looking at her, his eyes traveling her face in question, waiting for her response.

"I will wait until the snow falls next year. That would seem fair, for both of us." Ashamed as she was for sounding so distant— even to her own ears—Eleanor could not bring herself to say it differently. There was nothing intact around her heart as it was. She moved her hand against his mark on her skin. "I really should—" Eleanor hesitated, pressing her lips together, bent down and retrieved her report. Everything inside her was beginning to tremble. "I should get back."

The question in his face clouded over, and he took another step away from her. "Yes," he agreed. "So must I if we are to be ready. There is still much to do."

He almost came back to her. But when Eleanor did not—could not—move towards him, Basaal stalled, holding her gaze for only a moment before turning away, head bent, shoulders slumped, as he walked away, limping back toward the Imirillian camp.

Eleanor watched him disappear into the gloaming before taking her eyes away from his solitary figure, adding—with a shaking heart—the memory of Basaal to the open pit of graves already filling her soul. What was one more loss, she asked herself.

Everything.

She feared it was everything.

CHAPTER

EIGHTEEN

*In loss the Illuminating God declares a journey. His
mortals release their loves, just as the desert is stripped
of its beauty, and they, His children, are hollowed and
hallowed. For loss is His sanctifier.*

*And when emptiness upon emptiness has been
consecrated and the work that spins mortality is declared
complete, the Illuminating God will open the hands of
the sanctified, and all He has ordained to His children
will be poured into their palms, to fill the smoothed
places—having been prepared by loss, now to be crowned
with joy and purity.*

*And it pleases the Illuminating God to prepare His
children to receive all, though they be numbered more
than every grain of the desert sands. And all are in His
hand, and all are known.*

—*The First Scroll*

"You do realize before everything"—Aedon made a slight gesture
with his hand and coughed—"you had never actually visited me

in my personal chambers."

"I was thinking about that," Eleanor admitted as she looked curiously around the room of deep blue tapestries and dark woods. "I can't imagine why," she admitted. "We've been one another's confidants since, well, my father's death."

"I've never spent much time in my rooms. And you always sent for me, besides."

"Hmm." Eleanor continued to look around the room. It was neat, clear, clean.

"Now, are you going to let me look at those harvest reports?"

Eleanor looked down at the papers in her hand, reports of the harvests from each fen. "The physician will commit regicide if he knows I have given you any work," she said. They were scant and thin, the harvests. It would be hard for all of them come winter. Yet, the hardness of winter sounded like a welcome relief to Eleanor after the stagnant grief of summer and fall.

Aedon was only just now coming out of a second round of infections. He'd miraculously survived at the tower, not even regaining consciousness before an infection had set in, a ravenous thief that had stolen whatever strength it could. Aedon had weathered it. Now, his lungs were rough and filled with fluid, his cough a testament to the second infection not having yet been dispelled. There was no guarantee he would pass the coming winter. But Aedon planned for it, and so Eleanor gave herself the liberty of believing him.

"I'm still not certain it is a wise idea for you to see the reports myself—but as I know we've stores to shore up the weak harvest and can ensure basic survival, I will trust you to keep your emotions in check about the numbers."

Aedon laughed. The sound itched and rattled around his lungs.

The scar on his face was healing, at the very least, into a long strip of white. Ammar had stitched it together at Colun Tir. And when Eleanor's own physician had removed whatever string Ammar had used, several weeks later, he had marveled at the Imirillian practice, asking Eleanor if she might request a scroll from the physician prince upon her next convoy of Aemogen goods and signed diplomatic treatises to Zarbadast. Eleanor did not even know if Ammar was still alive, let alone in a position to send a scroll.

"Eleanor?" Aedon asked, pulling her from her thoughts.

Eleanor handed Aedon the reports.

Looking about her, towards the window near Aedon's small desk—the quills, ink, reports, and scrolls meticulously in place—Eleanor remembered she had been surprised by the arrival of autumn, not because it had come but rather because when it did come, the decayed emotions—numb and stiff inside her chest—gave way to the weight of raw feeling.

The dead had long been buried now, and the people of Aemogen had returned to the usual tasks of their lives—but with no pretense towards normalcy. The country would be forever changed, generations must come and go to claim any recovery.

Eleanor had spent little effort in her studies, attending rather to the losses of her people, although her interactions with them were now more quiet, observational, and subdued. In part because Eleanor could find nothing in her soul to grab hold of, in part because the loss of her country had been so tremendously deep, so filled with sorrow.

A message had come from Zarbadast. Emir, emperor of Imirillia, sent his greetings, along with a formal extension of an alliance with Imirillia. He offered terms and asked questions in regards to future trading. The sea-lane from Aemogen to eastern Imirillia would thrive. The port out of Krayklan would be expanded. Emir expressed his grand plans for intercontinental exchange and vowed that Aemogen interests would be accommodated. He also sent a token gift—of Imirillian gold, spices, fabrics, and perfumes—with the treaties, along with an invitation for Eleanor to visit Zarbadast in honor of their new alliance.

She declined, sending her reply to Zarbadast by ship through the Krayklan port with a token of Aemogen goods to show her own good faith: silver, wood, and herbs, with other small gifts that might amuse the princes and their families. Although Eleanor dreamed of the seven palaces and their astounding beauty, she did not wish to go there again. Of how Basaal fared, she heard nothing.

Aedon's voice coaxed her again from her thoughts, and she saw that he was watching her.

"You're different, Eleanor, from who you were just a few years ago."

"A common occurrence, I believe," she replied, smoothing her skirt. "The war caught me on the last edge of my girlhood, as it was." Eleanor studied Aedon in return. "You've not changed, though. Here you are, same as ever before—save the injuries."

Aedon set down the reports and considered what she had said. "No, I suppose I haven't," he said. "Be it virtue or folly, I am who I am."

"Uncommonly good," Eleanor added.

"Uncommonly stubborn, perhaps," Aedon countered.

As ambitious as Aedon had been earlier to read the reports and to give Eleanor his thoughts regarding Aemogen's position, it was clear he was tired.

"If you don't mind too much," she said, "we will have to continue later." She took the papers from his hands. "I have some other commitments."

"I don't mind," Aedon replied with grace, knowing full well she was sparing him the strain rather than keeping to some demanding schedule.

"Thank you," Eleanor said. "I didn't think you would mind."

The Illuminating God has called forth fidelity;
The Illuminating God has called forth patience;
The Illuminating God has called forth brotherhood;

And man, in his foolish vanity, calls forth blindness.

—*The Second Scroll*

As Aemogen tipped over the edge of fall, Aedon was able to join Eleanor and the council in their meetings, discussing their new position as an ally of Imirillia, how to maintain their strength in that position, and what points should be negotiated in the final treaty. Aedon also drew up plans to enlarge the harbor at Calafort, but Eleanor asked him to put them away until spring. She had not yet decided if any foreign ships would be allowed to enter the port.

Edythe had not lost her newfound assertiveness or her desire to understand better the tasks of Eleanor's position. This caused more than one heated discussion between them regarding Aemogen politics, but Eleanor was relieved, for Edythe was steady, capable, and determined. She was a welcome voice when Eleanor could not speak.

On late nights, when the harvest winds rattled through the fields and woods and set Ainsley Rise all a clatter, Eleanor would think about Crispin and his eternal absence. There had been no laughter and far less movement. They had become stiff without him. They had become older.

And then there was Hastian. More than once, Eleanor left her bed at night with the hope she might find a specter of him standing outside her bedroom door. She never did.

Death, she felt, was endless.

⤙⧓⤚

Just as the bluster of winter blew into Ainsley, when the white flakes crowded and clung to the windows of Eleanor's apartments, creating frozen pictures on the glass, Edythe entered with excitement in her eyes.

"Eleanor! Just come up from Calafort is the latest shipment from Imirillia, and you will never guess who has come with it!"

Eleanor's heart jolted so thoroughly, she snapped the quill in her hand. A familiar figure walked into the room.

"Ammar!" Eleanor stood quickly, knocking her chair to the floor.

"Your Majesty." Ammar bowed as he spoke this carefully in Eleanor's language. He then raised his eyebrows in surprise when she greeted him with an embrace.

"And what has Emir sent down from Zarbadast so precious to warrant your accompaniment?" Eleanor asked and smiled fully. Then her mouth shifted towards a more serious expression. "I hadn't thought we would work out the final treaty before spring. Are you here to witness the signing?"

"No," Ammar said, reverting back to Imirillian. "This is embarrassing." His mouth twisted in a way that reminded her of Basaal. "I so seldom feel discomfited by anything that I've no doubt it has physiological or spiritual benefit." He paused before speaking again. "I have come—I have actually come to seek sanctuary."

"Sanctuary?"

"Emperor Emir has chosen to not offer me a pardon. He did, however, permit me the choice of exile. And so, I ask, will you accept me into your country?"

Overcome, Eleanor was shaking her head from surprise even as she said, "I would have you here one thousand times over. Yes!"

Ammar offered a thankful nod and looked towards the darkening snowstorm, rushing against Eleanor's windows.

"Although," Ammar added, "upon seeing the infernal nature of your winters, I may have changed my mind, ready to face the oblivion of the executioner's axe rather than this devilry." He waved towards the window.

Eleanor laughed out loud.

As Ainsley Rise grew accustomed to the physician's company, Ammar's presence did a great deal for them. Beneath the careful eye of two physicians, Aedon improved. Zanntal was relieved to have Imirillian conversation, especially when the foreign nature of Eleanor's country became too much. Edythe took to Ammar easily, and they developed a respectful friendship as she shared her knowledge of the records hall and convivially encouraged him to study there. Eleanor, when she could forget Basaal, simply slept better.

Not many days after his arrival, Ammar carefully approached the subject of his youngest brother when they were sitting privately in her rooms.

"Far be it for me to intrude," he began, "but if you have not heard from Basaal, I want you to know the reason."

Eleanor felt herself retreat into the frozen tucks of her internal scars, where she kept all thoughts of Basaal, but she nodded, listening.

"Upon returning to Zarbadast," Ammar said, "Basaal was brought before Emir and given judgment. The truth of his betrayal was bad enough, but the rumors in Zarbadast were pure specimens of fictional genius," Ammar continued calmly. "I know that Emir gave much thought to Basaal's fate. Would he go to his death? Would he be stripped of his army? What about his wealth? Should he also be sent into exile? Emir's wife, Laaeitha, pled on Basaal's behalf, or so I have heard. In the end—"

"Yes?" The word came out almost as a whisper.

"Nothing," Ammar said with a wave of his hand. "Emir offered Basaal a full pardon; he maintains his place in the royal house of Imirillia."

"Nothing?" Eleanor repeated. She took a breath, not realizing until that moment she had been holding it. "I admit I'm shocked," she replied when the words came. "I have been expecting to hear the worst."

"Blood runs deep," Ammar said as he shrugged.

"But not deep enough for a physician?"

"My profession declares it so," Ammar answered, with as serious a tone as she had ever heard him use. "I have killed, so great mercy was shown to me in allowing me exile." Ammar paused, then continued. "Basaal did not choose to remain in Zarbadast, though."

"He didn't," Eleanor said, preparing herself.

"There is an old sanctuary, a monastery of sorts, in the northern mountains, the Deeatnaah monastery—Zanntal knows the place. Few who are not training to join the order of holy men ever go there."

Eleanor waited for an explanation, wondering why, then, Basaal would have gone.

"I believe Basaal went to Deeatnaah," Ammar continued, "in order to fulfill the steps of deep purification: prayer, meditation, the reading of the Seven Scrolls, and—hopefully—a redemption. During the little time he did spend in Zarbadast, Basaal kept muttering to himself about how he was damned, how he had broken his covenants—his eyes were haunted; his dreams, horrific. I was worried he might lose his mind," Ammar explained. "Then, after one especially difficult night, Basaal woke up, insisting on going to the monastery. I could not stop him, no matter how I tried."

"Is it so bad," Eleanor asked, "going through these steps of purification? Is there no chance it will bring him peace?"

Ammar shifted. "The truly devout attempt to strip themselves of everything—the paths of their thoughts, their assumptions, the history of their actions—it is a painful examination at best. At worst? Well, this is accompanied by a physical manifestation of the spiritual journey; seekers fast for days, sometimes weeks, until just before the point of death, when they are given the smallest modicum of food, added to slowly as their learning and study increases. This process serves as a symbol of their inner reconstruction.

"I will not pretend that many have not died from this process," Ammar said honestly. "Others have been forever altered, changed beyond recognition from who they once were. Some have even gone mad. That is why few choose this path. And also why I felt the need to tell you, so you would understand when he chooses not to return—not to Aemogen, and not to Zarbadast."

"Not to Zarbadast?" Eleanor could not help showing the emotion she had so carefully hemmed inside of herself. She moved to the edge of the settee, clutching the cushion on either side of her. "Basaal loves Zarbadast more than anything! Could he not find solace among you there? I know, I know. The battle and all the death is—" she began, but hesitated. "I understand the feeling of going mad inside one's own head. But—"

"There will be no solace found in Zarbadast for Basaal any longer," Ammar stated.

"Is it the death of Shaamil?" Eleanor did not hesitate to mention it.

"No." Ammar was not ruffled. "Certainly, all the death took its toll, all the men killed, and Basaal's part in it. The grief of Aemogen and Imirillia. Giving his allegiance to too many opposites and being unable to reconcile his actions—" Ammar waved his hand. "But what broke Basaal, what I am certain keeps him away and walking through his hell, day after day, is the death of Annan."

"Annan didn't live?" Eleanor choked out. She had not thought, even once, to question whether he had survived. Annan had always been there—so kind, so loyal.

"You hadn't heard?"

"No," Eleanor managed to say.

For the first time, Ammar looked hesitant to speak. "Basaal feels he killed him, that he ought to have saved Annan somehow, but did not."

"Do not fear, small child," the Holy Man said to the boy. "Is your master so unkind?"
The boy answered, "My master is a great merchant, and he has entrusted me with one storeroom. But the lute

*players in the street beckoned me come, and I went. All
in the storeroom was stolen out."*

*"Have you petitioned your master for mercy?" the Holy
Man asked.*

*"I am afraid. I dare not go unto him for fear of banish-
ment."*

—*The Third Scroll*

She had never known how the cold wind wound through the
streets of Ainsley, for Eleanor's winters had always been inside the
comforts of Ainsley Rise. She was bound up, unrecognizable, and
already wishing the wind did not persist so. Her bones felt iced
over, the cold overlapping the grief that permeated everything else
inside of her.

When Eleanor reached the familiar door, she knocked, an impatient sound in the cold wind.

Aurrey opened the door, saw Eleanor, and then pulled her inside with a mother's scolding. "It's too cold to be out, Your Majesty!" she said as she brought Eleanor in beside the fire and deftly
began to remove her outer layers of cloak, gloves, scarf, and hood.
"What possessed you?" Aurrey asked. "And on such a day?"

"I needed to get away from my work for a few hours where no
one would find me," Eleanor confessed.

"Hmmm," Aurrey said, inspecting the stitching on Eleanor's
cloak before setting it down. "You and Haide both. The man
sounds like a demon in his workshop today. He's not taking to
his work, and I can hardly convince him to man up about it. The
children are all in there," she added, "playing among the scraps.
Shall I call them in?"

Eleanor had found Haide and Aurrey, not two months after the battle. Her unexpected arrival had all but frightened Aurrey to death. But Haide took it in stride and seemed humiliated, rather, that Eleanor would pay them special mind when there was so much struggle everywhere. She had not stayed long on her first visit, but had returned often.

Haide had no desire to speak of the war. Neither did Eleanor. Aurrey spoke out according to the conscience of her own tongue, crossing lines that neither of them were willing to even touch. She seemed to feel no compunction about discussing the prince, though Eleanor and Haide just looked on in silence. It wasn't a bad thing to discuss, Eleanor had decided, when she could bear it.

On her third visit, Eleanor had collected her courage enough to ask them for the favor she had been wanting: A home for Sharin.

"The one who cannot speak?" Aurrey had responded.

"Yes, that is right," Eleanor had said. "I've wanted to find a family that could take her in as their own, to be raised alongside their own children. The crown would compensate for any expenses and beyond," she explained, and then paused before continuing. "Would you consider doing this? Sharin is just older than your eldest, and the companionship may be desirable too."

"Your Majesty." Aurrey had run the palms of her hands along her skirt. "Taking in an Imirillian child could be—I cannot know how to say it—but I worry for my own children among their friends. Might they be shunned—?"

"We'll take the girl," Haide had interrupted from his brooding corner by the fireplace, rubbing the stump of his wrist unconsciously.

"Haide, what if—" Aurrey began, but Haide interrupted her again.

"An innocent child, in need of a home, will have a place with us," Haide insisted. "And we'll take no money from the crown," he added. "A man has his pride and his way of supporting his own." Aurrey flushed and looked as though she would have rounded on Haide had Eleanor not been present.

"The two of you may discuss this first," Eleanor said. "And if you like, I can bring Sharin tomorrow to get to know you and your children. I ask that you take time to decide. What is best for all is what is best."

When Eleanor returned the next afternoon with Sharin in hand, Aurrey had looked at the child—eyes black as night, mouth sober, cheeks soft—and taken Sharin into her heart before Eleanor could even introduce them properly. It was settled.

When Haide came in later from his workshop, looking angry, for he could do almost nothing, he had nodded towards his wife and Sharin, and then had shrugged. "I knew it," he'd said. "I talk all compassion, and Aurrey holds against it. But as soon as a kitten comes begging for scraps, she's the first to set down the cured ham that's been saved for an occasion. How did she ever think she could resist a child?"

"I will only agree to leave Sharin with your family if you accept a stipend from the crown for her support," Eleanor had stipulated. "And I will send a tutor—for the benefit of all your children. I promised to give Sharin the best life I could, and a family is crucial in that, but so is education and opportunity," she added. "You will not move me on this point."

"You aim for a tutor to teach my children reading and numbers, philosophy and all that?" Haide had asked, frowning as he eyed Eleanor with suspicion.

"Yes," she'd replied. "And language and music and anything

else."

Then Haide's unshaven face had broken into the first sincere smile Eleanor had ever seen him give. Seemingly forgetting himself, he held out his remaining hand and said, "You've a bargain."

Eleanor had taken his hand and shaken it firmly.

Now, as Eleanor warmed herself before the fire, Aurrey called the children in. Haide followed them in, as he often did, to sit and speak with Eleanor.

"Have you heard anything of your prince?" Haide asked uncharacteristically. "Rumors say he is not coming back."

"Prince Basaal is away, at a monastery of sorts." Eleanor did not expound.

"Cleansing himself from all the bloodshed?" Haide asked with an edge in his voice.

"I believe he is trying to."

"Would that we all could," was all Haide replied.

Eleanor looked down at her hands. "Perhaps the spring will help."

Later, Eleanor kissed the children on their cheeks, marked the happiness in Sharin's eyes, and disappeared back out into the snowbound wind, returning to Ainsley Rise.

And there was sorrowing throughout all the lands, much weeping and heaviness of heart. And the prophets went before the Illuminating God. And when they had lifted up their voices, He said unto them: Give unto them my law that they might be redeemed.

—The Fourth Scroll

Eleanor continued to manage her losses in a private way, rarely acknowledging the painful process to Edythe or Aedon or anyone. After months of hollow existence, her numbness was fully working itself out, her heart tingling like an arm whose blood flow had been stopped and was once again pulsing through its veins. Eleanor knew it would be a painful resurrection. As feeling returned, it came with waves of anger—searing, white anger—followed by a gripping guilt that twisted like a weed inside her heart. Under the burning suffocation of such internal sorrow, she couldn't have spoken of it to anyone, even had she desired to do so.

She kept moving each morning. Stifled and bound as she was, she did not shy away from her work or her people. As strange as it seemed, for Eleanor had never truly had a marriage, her people considered her a widow of the war. This made Eleanor feel, at one moment, wildly relieved that Basaal had chosen to leave and that she had not kept what so many had lost. But in the next moment, her knowledge—of him being gone from every familiar thing, slowly eating away at himself in hopes of purification—would break her, and it would take days for her to again feel steady on her own feet, days to shore up and mend the break.

One late-winter day, as the icicles melted in the golden sun of the afternoon, Eleanor began to believe that it might be possible for healing to come, someday. That the horror might be able to fade. And it would come independent of whether Basaal chose to come back or never returned. Eleanor admitted to herself it would be its own relief, to let him lay buried with the dead, and not have to question the consequences if he were to return and again change his mind, only to leave her once more.

It felt like a horrible thing: this relief-ridden confusion. Of course Eleanor wished he would return, that they would find their way to each other again, didn't she? Yes, beneath all the stains of war, she loved him still. But Eleanor knew she must be ready for it, and he must be ready for it too. If he would ever be, she did not know. Eleanor had, on occasion, awoken with his screams in her ears. Every time this happened, Eleanor had fallen back onto her bed, gripping the fabric of her nightclothes over her heart, forcing herself to breathe slowly.

Basaal's cries began to melt away with the snow, and she welcomed the peace of their absence. She no longer took out the pendants he had gifted her from her desk drawer, but rather left them untouched.

"What is it that man seeks when he kills another?" the warrior asked the Illuminating God.
No response came down from the heavens.

"What must I do to consecrate myself to thee?"
No response came down from the heavens.

"Am I among the damned of this world?" the warrior asked.

Then Seraagh came and placed her hand on his forehead, on his lips, and then over his heart.

"Do you wish cleansing and understanding from the Illuminating God?" Seraagh asked, and the warrior knelt.

"Yes."

"Then put down that which binds you to death, and come," Seraagh said, taking both his hands.

Basaal looked away from the ancient scroll and wept.

Spring came to Aemogen with all its rituals. The festival was subdued; the ceremony, reverent and somber; the evening's festivities, filled with more conversation and silence than dancing. Still, there was a strength found. It felt good, a relief, to gather together—talking of the rain and forecasting when the crops could be sown—the women as much as the few men, for many were now husbandless and worried over their farms.

Eleanor continued as she had before, working the sorrows and ghost stories of winter into the spring earth, and into the business of ruling Aemogen. Aedon, as he had been every year before the invasion, was close at hand for the organization of the coming growing season. His body continued to heal.

Eleanor also chose a new leader of the fen riders. He was not as fast as Doughlas, neither did he smirk nor laugh with the same puckish delight. Eleanor had not yet appointed another Queen's Own, and she took the suggestion she should as a violent intrusion. Those closest to her soon learned never to mention it.

Spring fled into the heat of summer. And though there was much work, there was little peace found by Eleanor at Ainsley Rise. Edythe suggested they visit the old fortress of Anoir by the eastern sea. Eleanor asked to be excused from the journey. Edythe did not go.

"Do you wish you had never chosen to fight?" Edythe challenged, after a string of days where Eleanor had been particularly silent.

"Excuse me." Eleanor looked up from her work. "What did you say?"

Edythe lifted her eyebrows in frustration. Her hair was bound back in a mature twist, paired with a gown of deep purple, and when she spoke, her tone reflected the adult manner of her bearing.

"I understand this fog that's about you Eleanor, you know I do. But Aedon and I feel—we wonder whether you could reconcile the decision to fight, if you were willing to accept the reality of it and move past what has happened. Bury the dense clouds that surround you. You can't keep second-guessing a decision made over a year ago. Could you even say you would have done differently now, knowing the outcome? Would you rather have us carrying the weight of the Imirillian taxes, unable to feed our children, starving our bodies of food and our souls of identity and independence? Would you trade our freedom now for the lives that were lost?"

"I can't say what I would do!" Eleanor rested her elbows before her, pressing her face into her hands. "Some days, I feel with *such* surety that I did right, that my duty was to see Aemogen preserved. Other days, I think, 'What is a land worth preserving for if so many lives are lost for it?' I'm happy that Shaamil is dead, that the Continent is rid of him. I am glad we have come off victorious. Yet I can't look at the people of each fen but see the fatherless, and all the fields lying fallow. Is that really a victory?"

"Eleanor," Edythe said firmly. "You chose to fight. The people of Aemogen chose to fight. Shaamil could have died years ago. Shaamil could have died as a boy. All of these things would have altered what happened, but we can change none of them. Now, it is up to you to stop pretending you could still alter that decision if you paid enough personal penance."

"I'm not trying to feel sorry for myself," Eleanor answered.

"No, you're not. You're trying to carry all the sorrow in Aemogen on your own shoulders," Edythe said, "thinking that, somehow, it will diminish the pain of those around you. But you can't, and it won't."

Eleanor lifted her head and stared at Edythe.

"Grieve with us, Eleanor, not for us."

"And what of joy?" Seraagh asked the Illuminating God.
"Joy is to be found in the fulfillment of all promises; it comes of purity and understanding."
"Is it not to be in this life?" Seraagh asked.
"Joy will come, and so, be joyous. Peace will come, and so, live in peace. Eternity will come, and therein is joy everlasting."

—*The Fifth Scroll*

Thayne came. He arrived on a cool morning of mid-summer, just as the flowers born of the seeds Basaal had given Eleanor were bursting into full bloom. The red flowers, bearing the wanderer's mark, now filled her garden. Eleanor embraced Thayne eagerly, relieved not only by his company but also for the reminder that life still existed beyond Ainsley Rise.

"May first marked one year since the battle," Thayne said as they walked near the river a few days after his arrival. His statement came with the force of having thought it for days.

"Yes," Eleanor said.

"Edythe says she believes you are doing better," Thayne hedged.

"She's made me step outside of myself," Eleanor replied. "It has helped."

"No news of whether he will yet come?"

Eleanor looked down at the vermillion bloom of the wanderer's mark between her fingers.

"No," she answered. "I've heard nothing, and neither has Ammar. I am almost glad of it. I—" She paused and grimaced. "You can understand, can't you, Thayne? I wish for him to come, I have dreams that he comes, or attempts it…never quite arriving. But I could not have survived this year had I not buried him with all the rest. So, I've left him for dead. Basaal is a casualty. And that is how I must reconcile it."

"Do you define your marriage as a casualty of war, then?" Thayne asked, turning towards the blue river, his arms crossed over his chest, the silver of his bound hair glinting in the summer sun.

"Was it ever anything else?"

Eleanor tossed the red flower into the river's steady current, watching it catch in the swirl of an eddy before it dipped and disappeared.

"None are lost from before Him. He reaches after all who are scattered."

—*The Sixth Scroll*

"It is incorrect," Ammar insisted to Eleanor and Aedon who had joined him in the records hall. Edythe worked quietly nearby. "I've been studying the ancient documents of Aemogen, and the grammatical structure of your language clearly delineates the differences between the uses of such an article. Thus, the opening phrase of your oldest historical document is an absolute atrocity."

Eleanor began to laugh and was joined by Aedon, who had just returned that morning from a late-summer tour of the fens. Even Edythe looked up from her work, enjoying the debate.

"You're insufferable, even in exile, Ammar," Eleanor said once she'd stopped laughing, brushing the back of her hand against her wet cheek, wiping away the eager tears. Everyone was smiling, and even Ammar stooped so low as to look pleasantly amused.

"Your lawless language," he said as he shook his head in disapproval, "causes me endless pain."

Eleanor's cheeks hurt from smiling, and she was glad of it, for Eleanor could not remember the last time she had laughed. Aedon was watching her, pleased, and when she stood to leave the records hall, so did he.

"I would like to meet this afternoon to discuss your tour."

"Yes," Aedon replied.

"And the people?" she asked as they turned north, walking along the east side of Ainsley Castle towards the northern gardens. The scar that crossed Aedon's face gave him the appearance of additional sobriety, if that were possible. And he frowned just long enough for Eleanor to look away, worried.

"They go forward, as do we," Aedon finally said. "They send their love for you. All the fens send their love."

Swallowing hard, Eleanor said, "I don't know if it's their love that I need."

Aedon waited a moment before pressing his question. "What then do you need?"

"Their forgiveness," Eleanor replied.

"All of Aemogen has been asking forgiveness of someone, be they dead or living."

"Is obtaining it worth holding a hope for?" Eleanor asked, for herself, and she also asked for Basaal, whose existence was so silent, so separate from her own. He was still isolated from everyone he had ever known. No word had been heard from him in Zarbadast. Sometimes Eleanor envied his self-imposed oblivion. Mostly she worried he would never be able to find his way out of it again.

Settling his weight on one leg, Aedon stood with his hands behind his back, answering her question as he looked out across the late summer gardens. "Have you seen a winter that was not followed by spring?"

"No."

"I trust myself to that," he said.

"Has trusting eased the pain?"

Aedon studied Eleanor's face for a long moment before answering. "I believe it undergirds the process."

*When the last trumpets declare the work of the Illuminating God, the wanderer will be brought home;
Peace shall be his inheritance, and love shall be his joy.*

—*The Final Mark of the Seventh Scroll*

Basaal looked up. His desk sat before the open window, which framed the endless maze of peaks and valleys below. He read the final line again before binding up the scroll and setting it beside the others. Pushing his nondescript gray sleeve away from his forearm, Basaal moved his palm along his empty skin, remembering. He looked again towards the open window.

⸺◈◈◈◈⸺

The ground sounded thin and tired in the late fall. It had spent what it had. And as Eleanor worked in the soil, dividing plants and loosening stones, she could not help but feel that she was as tired and fatigued as the earth from the work of harvest. This had been the most taxing autumn of her reign, but Aemogen had managed, and the food stores were secured. Now, Eleanor longed for the quiet of winter despite knowing the loneliness it would bring.

Sitting back, Eleanor lifted her eyes to the gray sky; it was heavy, the air warmer than it should have been.

"Snow," she said aloud as if the clouds were prophets and she could hear their whisperings. Another long winter at Ainsley, everything swathed in white for months and Eleanor continuing with the precarious work of healing oneself. She pressed her bare fingers against the cold ground, staring at nothing as the first light hint of white fell around her.

Snow was falling.

A sound—neither loud nor unusual—brought Eleanor's thoughts back to the garden. She stood, brushing the dirt from her skirts, and turned to look towards the western gate.

There was a figure, blurred through the falling white, standing, watching her; his face thin, gaunt, pale. Eleanor opened her mouth, then closed it again.

It was Basaal.

He lifted his hand, hesitant now that she had seen him, running his fingers through his hair in that familiar nervous habit, while his face battled with uncertainty. There was a mark, a wanderer's mark on the top of his hand. One on the top of each hand.

He saw her take note of them, and what he saw on her face assuaged him, for he smiled, and his face shifted into a singular expression. It was not the look of a traveler returned home, neither one of duty, nor of penitence. It was something Eleanor had never seen—that of a husband coming home to his wife, having been long away.

A few steps towards him carried her into a run. Basaal's smile faded into an expression of unparalleled relief as he caught Eleanor in his arms, wrapping one arm around her waist as the other hand held her head gently against his shoulder. She pressed her face into his chest, a desperate, exhausted sound coming from her lungs, and Eleanor was aware that something inside her was easing, a palliative force she'd not known for years.

Basaal's words were soft as he dropped his head, pressing his cheek against hers, bringing her even closer to him. "When the last trumpets declare the work of the Illuminating God, the wanderer will be brought home; peace shall be his inheritance, and love shall be his joy."

The confident sound of his voice permeated Eleanor, and she pulled away to see his face, lifting her hands to touch him. He was thin and worn, but in his Marion blue eyes, Eleanor saw something she had never seen before: peace.

Her hands moved down his arms towards his hands, and she paused, surprised by what her fingers could not find. Eleanor pushed his sleeves back, revealing only two Safeeraah: a golden band, marked with the symbols of the sun, on his left wrist and a matching silver band, delicately carved to carry the faces of the moon, on his right. Then Eleanor noticed that the symbol of her own house was marked in the skin of Basaal's right forearm, opposite his own symbol on his left.

She brought her chin up, and he nodded, sincere affirmation evident in his eyes. And Eleanor knew he was anchored to her—and anchored to Aemogen—and she could trust herself to be anchored to him. Her eyes dropped again to the beautiful bands on his wrists.

"The gold, marked with the sun," Basaal quietly explained, "is my new covenant with the Illuminating God. And the silver is my covenant to you."

Eleanor passed her fingers across the deep green mark in his skin, then touched both the gold and the silver Safeeraah in reverence.

"Are the symbols of the moon for me or for Seraagh?" Eleanor asked as she looked back up into his clear eyes.

So quietly she could almost not hear his pleased laugh, Basaal answered Eleanor with an affectionate twist in his smile. "Yes."

ACKNOWLEDGEMENTS

My detailed and heartfelt acknowledgements from The Queen's Gambit and The Ruby Prince still stand, and to those words I want to add a few fresh lines to reflect my appreciation for the last several months.

Thank you to my generous beta readers. Thank you to the friends who have gathered round me in myriad ways. Thank you to my siblings for holding me up. Thank you to mom and dad for the hours of seeing me through. Thank you to Kip for reading on the train.

Thank you to my team: Phillip Jackson for inking the maps, Kevin Cantrell for my beautiful covers, Julie Ogborn for copy editing, Allysha Unguren for substantive editing, & Stephanie Winzeler for the layout. Also, Ben Unguren, for being a magician.

Thank you to the characters of these books, who could have chosen to be less, but fought forward, determined to become more. Spring will always come.

And, now that we've begun to find each other, thank you to my beloved readers. All your words of encouragement have made me smile, and grin, and want to laugh for the joy. It has been the deepest pleasure to cross paths with you in the fens of Aemogen, or the deserts of Imirillia. I am just delighted to have found you, and I hope you're up for many more journeys ahead. I write them, after all, for you.

photo by Aaron Thompson

ABOUT THE AUTHOR

Like many of my siblings, I would sneak out of bed, slip into the hallway, and pull my favorite books from the book closet. I read my way through the bottom shelf, then the next shelf up, and the shelf above that, until I could climb to the very top shelf—stacked two layers deep and two layers high—and read the titles of the classics. My desire to create stories grew as I was learning to read them.

Subsequently, I spent my time scribbling in notebooks rather than listening to math lectures at school.

I graduated with a degree in literary studies, and have spent several years working on the novels that keep pounding on the doors of my mind, as none of my characters are very patient to wait their turn. I currently live in Orem, Utah, with my wonderful chemist husband, and books in every room of the house.